Holy Mayhem

Pat G'Orge-Walker

Kensington Publishing Corp.
http://www.kensingtonbooks.com

DAFINA BOOKS are published by

Kensington Publishing Corp.
119 West 40th Street
New York, NY 10018

All Kensington Titles, Imprints, and Distributed Lines are available at special quantity discounts for bulk purchases for sales promotions, premiums, fund-raising, and educational or institutional use. Special book excerpts or cus-tomized printings can also be created to fit specific needs. For details, write or phone the office of the Kensington special sales manager: Kensington Publishing Corp., 119 West 40th Street, New York, NY 10018, attn: Special Sales Department, Phone: 1-800-221-2647.

Dafina and the Dafina logo Reg. U.S. Pat. & TM Off.

First trade paperback printing: November 2012

ISBN-13: 978-0-7582-5968-4
ISBN-10: 0-7582-5968-9

10 9 8 7 6 5 4 3 2 1

Printed in the United States of America

ACKNOWLEDGMENTS

And Moses said unto the people, Fear ye not, stand still, and see the salvation of the Lord, which he will shew to you today: for the Egyptians whom ye have seen today, ye shall see them again no more forever.

Exodus 14:13 (KJV)

On Christ the solid rock I stand, all other ground is sinking sand. I give all praises to my Lord and Savior Jesus Christ.

I offer boundless love to my best friend, my husband, Rob, a steady rock for half of my life. To my beautiful daughters: Gizel Dan-Yette, Ingrid, Marisa, along with my grandchildren, great-grandchildren, and my latest great-grandson, Emmanuel Garrard Brewer, I love and thank you all.

As always I remain sustained by prayers and support from those too numerous to name. I thank them all.

I am eternally grateful to my entire St. Paul's Tabernacle City of Lights Ministry congregation led by my beloved Bishop John L. and Lady Laura L. Smith, Pastor James D. Tucker, and Co-Pastor Phyllis Johnson. My unconditional appreciation goes out to numerous and supportive churches and organizations.

Deep gratitude and appreciation to: my editor, Selena James, and the Dafina/Kensington Publishing family, and long-time friend and attorney Christopher R. Whent, Esq.

Without a doubt, I thank my online and offline readers, my supporters, family, friends, numerous book clubs, and many fellow authors who share prayers, encouragement, and offer wonderful virtual hugs. Of course, I must thank the woman who makes my phenomenal promotional items, Debra "Simply Said" Owsley.

Finally, gone from this earth in 2011 but never forgotten: Aunt Ovella, Cousin Vera, Cousin Linda, and my precious baby sister, Arlene.

Holy Mayhem

Prologue

Saying, touch not my anointed and do my prophets no harm.

Psalms 105:15

"Jesus, Lord help me! I can't believe it!"

Forty-two-year-old single woman and church missionary Joy Karry sucked her teeth then took a deep breath to keep from cussing. The curly red wig she'd worn to work as maintenance supervisor at the Pelzer, South Carolina, police precinct flopped about her chubby dark brown cheeks.

As she hustled down the empty second-floor hallway, Joy's two hundred pounds of dark flesh jiggled on her five-foot-one frame. She took up from where she'd begun moments ago, spewing loud angry words, not caring who heard them.

"Ten years of cleaning toilets and these demons gonna lay me off. Homicide and robbery done already lay off my cousin Patience and now today, me! Enough of this crap!"

Five minutes later, Joy barreled through the back door and exited to the precinct's employee parking lot. Eyes blazing, head down like a raging bull, she rushed toward two of the precinct's detectives, Blake and Johnson. By the way they quickly dropped their heads and moved to the side, she knew they'd already heard her bad news.

"Don't do it, Miss Joy!" said a voice.

Before Joy could spin around to see who'd called out, she heard it add, "Your godson ain't on duty today, so you might wanna check that temper."

Both Blake and Johnson turned quickly and headed back inside. The mention of her second cousin and godson's name, Detective Percy LaPierre, one of Pelzer's most admired and respected detectives, had stopped her in her tracks.

"Thank you, Jesus." She'd forgotten her hands weren't empty. She'd already pulled the cap off a bottle of bleach and was holding onto a sharp gum scraper. There was only about a yard between her and the car belonging to the head of human resources. "Jesus, if You don't continue to help me, I'm going back inside in handcuffs. Now I ain't got a job and no bail money."

Joy quickly discarded the bottle and the gum scraper. Climbing into her 2008 Toyota RAV4, she began praying. "Father God, I ain't looking for no turning-water-into-wine miracles. I need you to help me squeeze twenty-five cents out of a nickel. Patience laid off yesterday and now me, Lord. Neither me nor Patience got husbands—our choice of course, but now the Devil done barged into our lives uninvited."

Joy drove home slowly, going out of her way to allow her time to think. "Lord, I guess me and Patience gonna do what we always do. We just gonna praise You. At least we ain't gotta pay to do that."

Just as Joy pulled into her driveway, she noticed a flyer stuck to her mailbox with a large headline that read: A PROPHETIC RETURN TO WEALTH. GOD'S GRACE IS SUFFICIENT AND SALVATION IS FREE . . .

She stuffed the flyer into her pocketbook. *Free is a good thing*, she thought. *Most of the time free costs too much.* It would have to wait until she delivered the bad news to Patience.

Chapter 1

"How long have you been out of work, Mrs. Karry?"

Joy squirmed in her seat as she answered the unemployment benefits interviewer. "It's been about three weeks now."

She'd prayed a lot in the three weeks since her lay-off. Despite the warm weather that day, she'd worn a heavy blue cotton dress and a long-sleeve jacket. With her Christian upbringing, she'd never appear in public with her flesh exposed, no matter how hot it got. Hell was hotter, she'd always say.

She didn't quite feel comfortable with her interviewer. He was as slow as a turtle with arthritis; he even spoke slowly. He was also pasty-colored and wore a ridiculous cheap blond toupee, slicked down to appear more costly. What was worse was that human turtle had made a ludicrous assumption about her. After all, she'd spent time and effort to fill out the mountain of forms using flawless penmanship, and he had yet to take a peep at it.

"It's *Miss* Karry," Joy said slowly, fighting to keep from chewing on her bottom lip that poked out. "It says it right there on the first page that I'm a single woman."

"Of course you are," the interviewer replied after scanning her slowly up and down, side to side, like an MRI machine. He pushed his glasses further down upon his small yet freckled hooked nose, as though to get an even better look. "Forgive me," he replied, frowning. "I don't see how I could've made such an assumption that you'd be married."

"Excuse me?" Joy's hand remained in her lap, but she could feel the blood pulsating through it as it struggled to morph into a fist. She wanted to knock him out, then maybe pray him back.

The interviewer, obviously used to threats real and imagined, didn't respond further. Instead, the man finally began thumbing through Joy's paperwork. Silently, like the wolf in the Three Little Pigs fairytale, he huffed, puffed, and appeared ready to blow away Joy's peace of mind.

Joy's dark moon-shaped face began sparkling with perspiration at the same time, dampening her curly raspberry wig du jour. While the interviewer contorted his face, she'd slid both hands under the weight of her heavy pocketbook, using it much like a paperweight, hummed her hymns, and whispered her prayers. She also thought about Patience and wondered how she might be faring two cubicles over, also applying for the unemployment benefits.

Though they shared the same home, the two hadn't been the same since the afternoon Joy came through the door to say she, too, had been laid off. The sudden shopping sprees, restaurant-hopping several times a week, and their beloved QVC shopping network were things of the past.

Two cubicles over, Joy's cousin Patience Kash sat as still and stiff as a statue. Being thin as a rail made her appear that way no matter how she sat. She swept aside her long brown hair she normally kept hidden under a scarf; today the tresses peeked out as though they wanted to be a part of whatever was going on. She'd also worn a long pink skirt and matching top with sleeves stopping at the elbow. Her shoes, pocketbook, and even her cell-phone case were pink. She loved being coordinated and could care less if folks thought she overdid it at times.

Patience squirmed in her seat, making just enough noise to gain attention. She placed one hand under the chin of her elongated mocha-colored face while her thick glasses perched precariously on the tip of her pointy nose. She peered over her glasses at the young black man going over her paperwork slowly with a pen. He pointed the tip of his pen line by line, and seemingly word by word, as though he were reading a novel.

Waiting for the man to finish his methodical read, she looked at the paneled frosted-glass cubicle, toward where Joy had gone. She said nothing but began to remember, as she'd done almost daily since her lay-off, how things were when she worked.

"I'm almost finished," the young interviewer finally told Patience. "I'm just trying to find one more item."

"No rush," Patience replied with just a hint of cynicism, and then she smiled. She understood how looking for things was a tedious task. After all, there were always two things she could never find during her time in Robbery and Homicide: her spare glasses and a typo.

For the next thirty minutes the cousins sat inside separate cubicles. Each gave their interviewers an earful of what happened when they worked at the precinct and their hopes for any future employment.

In the beginning, they revealed, they'd taken whatever tests came their way in their efforts to obtain their ultimate dream job. Both wanted to become detectives. "If our godson Percy LaPierre can become a superstar detective, so can we. After all, snooping is in our blood," they'd each told their interviewers.

They also conceded that their dream had never happened.

Five of their ten years at the precinct they'd spent taking and passing written police tests, scoring higher than most.

Unfortunately for them, their dismal failures at the physicals brought the test scores down to almost zero.

Joy's problem: too short, too overweight, and too knock-kneed. Co-workers talked about Joy behind her back, calling her "Joy the neat-freak, who can't run fast enough to clean up crime."

Patience also suffered physical setbacks. Skinny Minnie weighed more, and Patience couldn't see two inches without her glasses, let alone see a crime.

Finally, the head of the Pelzer Police Department's Human Resources told the cousins to throw in the towel. "Y'all might as well stop taking and failing these physicals. Y'all need to stick to cleaning toilets and typing reports. Leave the crime-solving to the professionals."

The interiewers each told Joy and Patience they'd hear from unemployment within two weeks and wished them good luck.

"I don't need luck," Joy replied. "I ain't worried. God's got this all under control."

Patience told her interviewer the same.

"We know that faith without work is dead," Joy later told Patience. "No matter what we told those interviewers, we need jobs."

Chapter 2

While Joy and Patience waited to hear from the unemployment interviewers, they continued worshiping, racing off to prophecy services, telling any who'd listen that God would see them through. Yet, in reality, dreams die hard. So while they waited on the Lord, the cousins relived their real-life failed detective dreams from the comfort of their living room sofa. While thumbing through their Bibles for clarity and gorging on handfuls of popcorn and donuts and drinking coffee, they watched television.

With their imaginations in free fall, they set about solving crimes by watching their favorite *Law & Order* episodes, the *NCIS* television series, and *Murder, She Wrote*, as well as any movie of the week with a mystery theme.

The cousins weren't alone in their love of anything crime-related. They had their beloved, neurotic dog, Felony, constantly wagging his stumpy tail. He'd lay spread between them on the sofa.

Around Pelzer, and anywhere the dog went, Felony's appearance caused jaws to drop or tongues to wag. He had the features and temperament of so many breeds: long floppy ears like a beagle, pot belly like a bull dog, and short stumpy legs like a dachshund. With a stubby tail like a boxer's added to the mixture, he looked like a Doctor Frankenstein–type experiment gone wrong.

Doggy heaven for Felony was watching an old television episode of *The Thin Man*. Felony wagged both his stubby tail and tongue, excited each time the phobic dog, Asta, was in a scene. As long as Felony's favorite china bowl overflowed with warm, buttered popcorn (though it sometimes caused him to release a loud and foul-smelling mutt-gas when Joy massaged his fat belly) he was good. Woe to anyone trying to interfere with that mutt-pup's personal space.

At their home church, Mount Kneel Down Non-Denominational Center, Joy carried on her missionary work. "You know, I'm beginning to see things the Lord's way," she told Patience over breakfast one morning. "I can use this spare time while I find another job to continue to do God's work and see if there's anything needing investigating along the way."

"How you gonna do that?"

"Well, let me see. I can read folks' mail that ain't up to snuff to do it themselves. I can straighten out closets for them that can't do that, either."

"Joy, what if you come across something you shouldn't?"

"I'll investigate. What's the point of finding dirt if ya can't dig into it?"

Patience then decided she'd do her thing, too. She'd come to the same conclusion as Joy: perhaps God had changed her assignment. Part of Joy's acceptance of her early retirement situation was to try to become president of the missionary board. The only thing standing in her way was the possible reelection of Mount Kneel Down's current missionary president, Sister Boodrow.

Later that evening, Joy continued sharing her thoughts. "You know what, Patience?"

Patience stopped peeling the potatoes she intended on fixing for their meal and wiped her hands on her apron before joining Joy at the kitchen table. She would've continued her chore but Joy's excitement of God's new direction had already spilled over from breakfast right on through lunchtime, and now it didn't appear she had any plans of waiting for supper to continue.

"That Sister Boodrow still is a big problem with my wanting to become missionary board president."

"That's a shame, too, Joy. I know you're much more of a Christian than that supposedly turned-around stripper."

"I most certainly am. That's why I don't trust the woman's instincts about morality. She ain't fit to lead the missionary board, and I don't care how long she been leading it."

"So what are you gonna tell the folks the next time that you ain't already told them the last three times you tried to uproot the heffa?"

Each time Joy had pled her case before the church board, she'd only said she had a better vision for the missionary board, but without giving details. It wasn't easy, because she also needed to convince someone on the church board making the final decision to give her a chance. Preferably someone Sister Boodrow hadn't bedded. In order to do that, Joy needed to step up her missionary game.

Joy's opportunity came one Friday afternoon. Out of the blue, the telephone rang, and Patience answered it before Joy could.

"Praise the Lord, may I speak with Sister Karry? This is Deacon Campbell Whistle."

Patience mouthed the words *Deacon Campbell Whistle.*

Joy sucked her teeth at the mention of the man's name. Almost two years ago, from the moment she'd first laid eyes upon him, Joy's third-eye—what she called her Spirit of Discernment—had begun twitching. It hadn't taken her long to understand why that third eye went on alert. In her opinion, Deacon Whistle was a pasty-looking, self-righteous, middle-aged skeezer. He'd claimed he was a retired investment banker with a lot of cash. To Joy, money didn't equal class.

Most of her mistrust came about when he began coming to church service only twice a month. She'd seen him on several occasions lurking around the pastor's study and inside his private office. Of course, he'd only dallied around the pastor's study whenever Rev. Stepson was too ill and couldn't make it to service.

"That man just wants to see that all his money is working and doing the will of the Lord," Patience would always tell her when Joy complained. "After all, he is the church's largest investor and tithe payer. And whether we or the pastor like it or not, the church board did make Whistle a temporary head of the finances—although they done gone ahead and made him permanent now. You might need to make nice with him 'cause he does okay the auxiliary positions, too."

She took a deep breath to keep a measure of Christianity in her voice as she answered his call.

"Hello." Joy's single word was as stiff as she'd hoped it would be. Her greeting of "Praise the Lord" was reserved for her fellow Christians.

"I'm sorry to learn of your lay-off"—he suddenly began wheezing into the telephone like a hairball was stuck in his throat—"and that it's taken me so long to acknowledge your situation. It is not how I connect with the saints of God in the pastor's absence. However, I understand from our First Lady Stepson that you are planning on campaigning for missionary board president again. Is that right?"

"Yes, I am." Joy took pains to keep from laughing at his struggle to sound extra relevant as he wheezed and snorted.

She quickly decided she'd need to adopt a more Saved-Christian tone. "I believe I can bring another Christian view; especially the one God keeps giving me in His and mine constant conversations."

"Do you converse with our Lord often?"

"I most certainly do," Joy replied. She wanted to brag about her prayer and fasting habits, but now wasn't the time.

"That's good to hear, Sister Karry. Another reason for this phone call is to have you come by the church this afternoon so we can discuss your *Christian view*."

She didn't know what to make of the added little extra something when he imitated the way she'd said *Christian view*. Was he snorting, choking, or being sarcastic? Whichever, she'd soon find out when they spoke in person.

The appointment to meet at the Mount Kneel Down Outreach Center, right next door to the main church building, was set for three o'clock that afternoon. Joy had no intention of being late, but she also had to decide what she'd wear. She planned on walking through the door already looking the part of a missionary president. But she'd still carry her Bible and a can of mace in case he wanted her in another sort of missionary position.

After showering, she dusted her body with lilac talcum powder. Lying across her queen-size bed, lifting her sagging breasts up to where they rested upon her collarbone, she grabbed a large feather duster. After dipping it, she dusted extra powder under her breasts. Once the dusting was complete, she shimmied, pushed, stuffed, and prayed her way into an expensive body-shaper corset. The material felt like something a NASA scientist would design; supposedly it was her size and guaranteed to redistribute her fat.

The weather wasn't too hot, but the humidity was high. Joy chose a bright yellow muumuu with brown circles dotting its bodice and long sleeves. Since Patience had gone to run a few errands, she wasn't there to tell Joy the dress made her look like the sun with planets orbiting about it.

Normally, Felony would've curled up at the foot of the

bed, staring as she put on each piece. He'd have jumped around, barked his approval, or growled his displeasure. At that moment, though, she supposed he was outside terrorizing the neighborhood—or he may have passed out from growling.

It didn't matter. In Joy's mind, she looked good.

Chapter 3

Before rushing off to the church's outreach center, Joy left a note for Patience explaining where she'd gone. She drove with the A/C blasting, imagining how a soldier driving through a desert felt, braving the hot sun in bumper-to-bumper camel traffic.

Joy arrived and the reception area was empty. She was certain she had the time right. Perhaps he was running a little late.

Fifteen minutes passed, and she grew anxious for Deacon Whistle to show up. As much as she wanted the missionary president position, she wasn't happy waiting around for him.

Joy was in the middle of reciting scripture, trying to keep calm, when she happened to look down the hallway from where she'd sat. Suddenly two doors away, she spotted the shadow of Deacon Whistle's potbelly looking like a mountain lying on its side. It was so big it protruded over the pastor's study's doorsill.

"Ahem!" Joy almost shouted the warning as she pretended to clear her throat. She didn't care what tone her voice had; she was way past annoyed.

She stood up this time, with her hands on her wide hips, a huge pocketbook dangling from one wrist. Tossing aside her good manners and caution, she called out louder. "Listen, Deacon Whistle, time is passing. You called and set up this appointment for three o'clock. It's almost three-thirty!"

Deacon Whistle stuck his head all the way out of the doorway. The deer-in-headlights stare told Joy she'd surprised him. Two seconds later, when Sister Boodrow stuck out her head, too, hair tussled, with several of her top blouse buttons unbuttoned, it was Joy's turn to be surprised, sorta.

Fornicating right next door to God's House, she thought. She then quickly dismissed the thought, hoping she was wrong. She felt set up; particularly since she hadn't expected to see Sister Boodrow, her competitor, at this meeting, offering show-and-tell for extra credit.

Instead of speaking, Deacon Whistle shook out his pants leg that appeared crooked and quickly regained his composure. He stood fully in the doorway to the pastor's business office. Sister Boodrow stood about a couple of inches behind him, yet she still looked as though she were at his side. Another few seconds passed before he nodded Joy's way and Sister Boodrow stepped forward, closing the study door behind them.

Stopping briefly to turn, he placed a peck on Sister Boodrow's cheek saying, "Thank you so much, Sister Boodrow. Your assistance and offerings in our church matters are well appreciated."

Sister Boodrow didn't reply. She hurried toward the stairs, disappearing so fast she looked almost like a blur.

Joy plopped back onto the chair. She balled her fists, turning in her seat and fixing her large brown eyes upon Deacon Whistle's stubby T.rex dinosaur arms as he walked towards her. She leaned forward, anxious to hear his weak excuse for an obvious sham of a meeting.

"Please come with me, Sister Karry, into the pastor's office."

Joy followed Deacon Whistle inside the pastor's private

office. She didn't like it before, when he and Sister Boodrow were inside there, and she wasn't feeling comfortable meeting inside it, either. The entire church knew that if the pastor wasn't in his private business office, then no one should be in there. *There's no excuse for this,* Joy thought. *There's other rooms available.*

"Have a seat, Sister Karry."

Joy didn't sit right away. She watched him; he didn't even look embarrassed but was acting as though everything was just fine. She quickly looked him up and down, further showing her disapproval. And when he returned her stare with a questioning one of his own, he appeared to look old.

She'd thought he was in his late forties or early fifties, but now she wasn't certain. At that moment, there was something odd about him that she hadn't noticed over the past few months. It was probably because she'd never fully trusted him or looked at him eye-to-eye when he often appeared inside the church kitchen offering his unwanted help and advice.

What white man brags about how good he cooks collards and makes fresh deep-dish peach cobblers, talking the King's English one minute, slapping high fives with the deacons the next? she thought.

No sooner had she thought those things than she realized what it was about him that she couldn't cotton to. This white man often acted a little too "black." He didn't seem to do it on purpose, and that bothered her. She didn't know enough about him to figure out where he'd gotten his "hang-out" card. She didn't know much about him at all. That bothered her, too.

Joy was just about to rebuke herself from thinking such a thing when Sister Boodrow rushed back through the door.

She still didn't say a word to Joy. She began looking toward the floor instead. "I couldn't find my car keys—"

Joy thought she'd seen a set of keys lying on the floor a moment ago. She reached down, picked up the keys, and held them in the air. "Are these the keys? You must've dropped them when y'all was in here *blessing* them and calling on the Lord."

Sister Boodrow snatched the keys from Joy's hand without saying so much as a thank you. And just that quick, she turned and raced out the door.

I can't believe these heathens were bouncing around in both these offices.

He appeared to be reading her thoughts, but not wanting to explain anything because he couldn't. Suddenly one of Deacon Whistle's blue eyes began wandering, as though looking for something over his shoulder.

"Just give me another moment, please."

Deacon Whistle, ignoring that she hadn't sat yet, adjusted a brown and tan striped tie that appeared crooked. With no discernible emotion other than a shaky hand, he pushed aside strands of sparse, dark brown hair.

Suddenly his hands became a blur, quickly gathering a few papers scattered on the pastor's cluttered desk. The papers looked as though they'd been swept aside for something more urgent. Finally, he took a seat behind the small gray wooden desk as though he owned it.

"Thank you, Deacon Whistle." Slowly laying her huge pocketbook on her lap by its strap with its wide metal clasp toward him like a shotgun, she added, "I'm sorry; I didn't mean to get here on time." She stopped, allowing her words to settle before she continued. "I certainly didn't intend to bust up your meeting with my competition, Sister Boodrow." She turned her head aside, not caring if he knew she'd been sarcastic.

Lines drawn, Deacon Whistle and Joy went on with their meeting, which lasted less than thirty minutes. During that time, Joy calmed down enough to lay out her vision. She wanted to bring the church and the community closer by interaction rather than just preaching. There was a need for further outreach, she explained.

A half hour later, it was obvious to both that the meeting needed to end, each well aware their minds wandered trying to figure out each other's real thoughts—such as, about what had or hadn't happened in the pastor's private business office.

Joy had also brought with her a few quickly typed bullet-point suggestions. He asked her to leave them with him, and he promised to get right back to her.

With the meeting over, Joy returned to the parking lot. No sooner had she used the remote to unlock her car's door than she heard her name.

"Sister Karry, Sister Karry!"

Joy turned around, a wide smile replacing the look of concern she'd carried from the meeting. "Hi baby," Joy stretched out her arms, pulling in the young woman and almost smothering her. "How are you? I haven't seen you in so long."

The young woman, twenty-eight-year-old Reign Stepson, was the only daughter of Rev. Lock and First Lady Deborah Stepson. A real beauty, with a sassy short haircut and Barbie-doll shape—unlike the fake troll, as Joy always called Sister Boodrow.

"I'm doing well," Reign replied, struggling to extricate her small, redbone frame from Joy's grasp. The light green above-the-knee skirt she wore had begun climbing towards a place she didn't want shown to the world. "I'm back in town for a few days and thought I'd surprise Daddy. He's still not looking that well to me lately; I think he's working too hard. Is he upstairs in his office?"

Joy took her time responding. If she told Reign that the deacon had been up there showing Sister Boodrow why some of the abominations in the book of Deuteronomy weren't all that bad, there'd be trouble. If she didn't say something and it got out she knew about it, there'd be trouble. So Joy simply replied, "No baby. He's not up there." She let it go as that and began questioning Reign.

"So, are you and Lil P stopping by the house? You know my godson don't come around as much when you ain't in town. When are you two gonna come out of just being engaged and tie the knot? Y'all need to give me some grand-god babies and third cousins! Has the television station WPAK made you their lead investigative reporter yet?"

Joy knew exactly what she was doing. The only way to avoid one problem was to create an even greater one. Like an automatic machine gun, Joy's verbal-questioning technique pelted Reign, soon causing the young woman to speed up her good-byes, sending her and Joy speeding off in separate directions.

Chapter 4

Several hours after Joy's meeting with Deacon Whistle, she'd just begun fixing dinner when Patience arrived home.

"Chile, sit down!"

"What's wrong?" Patience's skinny bottom had barely sat before Joy raced over with one hand on her hip and a hot food mitt on her other hand.

"I'm about to quote you chapter and verse from what thus sayeth that lying demon Whistle!"

For the next several moments, Joy gave a detailed account of her encounter with Deacon Whistle and Sister Boodrow.

The only interruption came from Felony's growls for attention that went unanswered as the cousins chatted nonstop. The dog, unaccustomed to being ignored, began lifting one of his hind legs. It was a warning that he was only one piss squirt away from dousing the carpet, or some other dirty deed.

"Felony, don't you do it!" Patience warned once she'd spotted his lifted leg.

Patience raced to the door to let him out. Instead of putting Felony on his leash or at least securing the gate so he couldn't go further than the yard, she just slammed the door behind him.

It was a miracle Felony made it outside with urine still inside his bladder. She'd slammed the door so hard it'd nearly decapitated Felony's tail stump.

Once she realized what she'd almost done, Patience reopened the door and called out to Felony. "Sorry about that."

Her apology was a bit insincere, but for now Joy was about to get to what she'd said was "the good part" about what'd happened earlier with Deacon Whistle. Patience wasn't about to miss one piece of the story.

"You got to be kidding." Patience followed Joy out of the kitchen and down the hallway and into their living room. She was clawing at her invisible chest, begging for more sordid details. "That shameless liar didn't even try to lie his way out?"

"He couldn't," Joy hissed. "That reptilian demon turned almost as neon red as Sister Boodrow's cheap wig when she came back. She burst through the door yapping about she'd left her car keys in there. I don't know why some folks won't believe that every good-bye ain't gone?"

"Mercy, Father." Patience jumped up off the sofa, grabbing a handful of tissues to wipe away tears from laughing so hard. "So what did she say when she saw you sitting there?"

"That scandalous heffa didn't say nothing to me. What could she say, after ignoring me before?"

"So what did you do?" Patience had gone through the tissues in one pack and was opening another, laughing, wiggling, still crying so hard her skinny body looked like a letter S.

"I did the Christian thing," Joy said as she snatched the pack of tissues from Patience's hands. "As I handed her the car keys I told her, 'I guess these must be the keys y'all must've blessed earlier when you was in here calling on the Lord.'"

"*Bwaaa-ha-ha*, Lord, please help me." Patience wanted to join Felony outside; she was about to tinkle on herself from laughing.

Joy then mentioned she'd seen Reign, but didn't want to

start trouble when Reign had asked if her father was in his office. "I had to think fast on my feet," Joy bragged. "But I got her and Lil P's number when I wanna get rid of them quick. I mentioned babies and Reign folded like a cheap made-in-Japan fan. She couldn't get away from me fast enough!"

The laughter went on for a little while longer before Joy finally asked Patience how her day had gone.

"My day went just fine. When I came back and found your note, I went next door to chat and pray with Sister Betty."

"Oh my goodness, Patience," Joy said, no longer laughing but now shaking her head. "Why do you continue to encourage that old lady's fantasies?"

Joy felt she had reason to question her next-door neighbor's grip on reality. Almost two years ago, the cousins moved into their wealthy Pelzer neighborhood on the outside of town. They'd sacrificed, saving for the day they could escape the asphalt jungle of downtown West Pelzer. The moving van had barely pulled away when Sister Betty appeared from nowhere, offering the first of several neighborhood welcomes.

She came bearing all sorts of information to navigate their new neighborhood. She also carried a jug of cayenne pepper sweet tea, a tin of saltine crackers, and offered an unbelievable testimony of how God had called her on the telephone for spiritual duty. By the time she finished running her mouth about the way God communicated using her arthritic knees instead of healing them, she'd only stopped blabbing one time; it'd been to secure her false teeth. Once she'd left, it was more than a fence dividing their homes. She'd presented a divide between Joy and Patience, too.

Since that time, Patience always acted a bit friendlier and Christian-like toward the quirky old Sister Betty. Joy was different. After two conversations, she'd concluded the woman, wealthy or not, had mental issues beyond her grasp.

"Who communicates with God through hot flashes and

arthritic knee pains?" Joy argued. "And don't get me started on God calling on a telephone."

Now Patience began to protest Joy's opinion of Sister Betty. She stopped when they heard Felony growl.

"I wonder what's wrong." Joy turned away from Patience and raced to the side door, where she heard Felony scratching on it.

"Joy," Patience warned, "be careful. Felony only sounds like that when there's trouble lurking about."

Patience might've saved her breath, because Joy had already grabbed a broom, ready to sweep away whatever was troubling her beloved Felony.

Setting her own warning aside, Patience moved swiftly to catch up with Joy. She stopped in time; any closer and Joy would've popped her in the head with the broom.

Once Joy opened the door, it wasn't Patience in danger of a broom beating. Felony was no longer growling but circling in and out between Sister Betty's legs and wagging his tail. Joy slowly lowered the broom but she could've sworn she saw Felony smiling at his little joke.

Perhaps it was payback because she'd almost caused the dog to pee on himself.

"How are you, Sister Joy?" Sister Betty asked sweetly as she began to march in step while petting Felony. "I'm returning Felony. I happened to come outside and found he'd left your yard and was over in mine. He was head down, munching on a half-empty bag of popcorn I tossed into the garbage earlier. I've already cleaned up after him."

Sister Betty's words interrupted Joy's rather unkind thoughts about her.

Rather than answer right away about her dog's quirky habits and the mess he'd caused by knocking over her garbage can, she stood back a little. Laying a finger to the side of her face, she slowly eyed Sister Betty's short, nutty brown skeleton layered in everything white from head to toe. Despite being neighbors for the past two years, Joy could never get over how Sister Betty's neck didn't snap from the weight of her extra-large cross dangling from her wrinkled neck. That cross and the oversized Bible she always carried were the only accessories Joy had ever seen on her.

Without asking her inside, in part because Sister Betty continued marching in place like she were smashing grapes, Joy gently pulled Felony inside. Then she finally asked, "Can I help you with something else, Sister Betty?"

As soon as Sister Betty spied Patience standing quietly behind Joy, she stopped pacing, pointed toward Patience, and replied, "Well, Sister Joy, besides bringing Felony home—for which I don't expect any thanks—I'm on a mission from the Lord."

"Say what?"

Sister Betty fingered her huge cross as though she were prepared to use it as a weapon against Joy, should the need arise. She continued, "Miss Patience stopped by earlier today, asking me to pray and agree with her—"

Joy cut her off before she could go further. "Yeah, it sounds like something Patience would do." Joy folded her arms, searching for a sign from heaven to proceed or slam the door. Instead, she grabbed Felony by the scuff of his neck, leaving Patience and Sister Betty to chat in the doorway.

"Sister Patience," Sister Betty said as she unfolded a flyer she'd held in her hand, "I been praying and asking God for guidance about your financial situation and other matters you discussed with me earlier."

"Oh thank you, Sister Betty. I knew I could count on you."

"I want you to take a look at this flyer and then make sure you go there this evening no later than seven o'clock, like it says on that paper. You don't have much time, but I believe this is the start you need to begin serving your purpose for the Lord. I had a few misgivings when the Lord first brought this mission to my attention, 'cause I done heard something pertaining to some illegalities on the part of this here Prophet Monee Coffers. He was supposedly selling blessed snatches of red cloths and such, but God knows best. Besides, we all know Salvation is free but y'all gonna need some cash to buy things that ain't Salvation-related."

No sooner had Sister Betty left than Patience raced down the hallway calling out to Joy. "Joy, hurry up and get dressed. Sister Betty was good enough to come over and tell me what thus sayeth the Lord. . . ."

Joy wished she'd stayed at the door. If she'd done that, she could've snatched Patience inside the house before Sister Betty's goofball influence won out. Now they were nearly dressed, on their way to a sure-to-be disaster.

"Are you still set on going to that meeting this evening?" Joy asked softly as she entered Patience's bedroom. It was all she could do not to laugh when she saw Patience standing as though she were a queen with one hand on her non-existent hip. She stood admiring a star-patterned, multi-colored, African-style head wrap covering her long brown hair.

"I've just had a thought," Joy began, as she sat on the edge of Patience's bed. "There's a *CSI: Miami* marathon coming on tonight. Why don't we just pop some popcorn, grab some soda, and see if we can figure out the plot and the perp without reading the synopsis?"

"Now, Joy," Patience replied slowly, "I know what you trying to do."

"You do?"

"Yes, I do. You are trying to let the Devil use you to stop us from going out tonight so we can begin our purpose-filled duty for the Lord. You know we ain't laid-off to just lay around."

"But, Patience." Joy couldn't get the words out in time. Patience had already picked up her pocketbook and a Bible.

"Listen, Joy." Patience stopped, letting out a deep sigh. "I already explained things, but if I must I'll explain it to you again. Sister Betty said to me, 'Patience, God's got somewhere He needs you and Sister Joy to be tonight. You and Sister Joy need to attend a Rev. Monee Coffers 'Prophecy in a Hurry' commercial taping tonight." Patience put a finger against her cheek, then added, "Sister Betty admitted that she really didn't know much about the man; but she'd heard rumors about a false advertising, some illegalities or something like that. She told me that nobody proved it, but supposedly he had sold red prophecy and miracle handkerchiefs that'd left a lot of folks with their financial bottom lines showing the same color."

"Folks lost money, and she referring him to us?"

"He's coming on God's referral. It don't mean he don't know a little sumpthin' about the Lord. None of us are perfect."

Patience began fishing through her pocketbook until she found the keys to the van. "Anyhow, he's shooting what they call in television talk a commercial. They'll open the doors for taping around six. They need our names, church positions, where we worship, and so on. It's a first-come, may-be-first-picked, so we'll need to hurry."

Chapter 5

Twenty minutes had passed since Joy and Patience arrived. As instructed, they'd filled out the audience forms. Five minutes later, they got a tap on the shoulder and then were escorted inside Channel BLAB's small cable television studio.

BLAB was an acronym for Braggarts, Liars, and Busybodies, the cable station where "No truth told but everything interesting featured" was their slogan.

Joy and Patience, along with two hundred eager souls all in declining stages of Christianity, were herded inside the small studio. They sat packed, shoulder to shoulder, hypnotized sardines in a hot tin can. All had something in common: itchy ears, little money, and a willingness to pay someone for something God gave for free.

A few minutes later, the show's theme music sounded. It sounded a lot like James Brown's recording of "Get Up Off that Thang," and time for Monee Coffer's Prophet for Profit fake commercial taping.

"Do ya feel it?" Rev. Monee Coffers' question burst through the sound system. A spotlight, circling like a halo, lit up the forty-five-year-old reverend. Beneath a pair of large thick glasses, which did nothing to hide the fact his eyes looked like an owl's, he'd begun smiling. He threw his head back and screamed, "Say hallelujah! God's Word is alive!"

He was his show's director, producer, creator, and charlatan-host. As soon as he sprang onto the stage, he began prancing, repeating his mantra, insisting with hand signals that his audience echo, "God, hurry! Bring me money, and lots of it."

Time was money. The bad economy had taken a swing at his wallet, too, and he rushed to get things over and done. He'd only bought thirty minutes of studio time for this one-time taping, plus there were camera crew and other production costs to consider.

Once he got the footage edited, he planned to run a fifty- or sixty-second spot on BLAB cable television and the more legitimate WPAK television station. Repeated airings needed financing.

Of course, he had needs, too; the kind one acquired as a former guest of Seattle, Washington's, prison system, where he hobnobbed with a few other pharisees of the caught-cloth. Anyone eyeballing him now wouldn't recognize Coffers. He'd had a complete transformation.

He'd done his two-year sentence, five-year parole stint and stayed out of the public's eye for those last five years. During those years, after watching television, seeing how the game had dramatically changed, he'd turned to an online divinity school to give scamming a second try. To set aside any suspicions, he made a public apology, swearing he'd left his 1980s damaged reputation behind.

It'd taken time to gain public trust, but less than a year ago the shyster had popped back on the evangelical television scene, this time as a teacher of spiritual laws and finances. He again announced that he was the new-and-improved version of the old Rev. Monee Coffers.

There were some things, however, he wasn't willing to sacrifice. He remained somewhat of a fashion horse, who wore tailor-made robes and expensive Nieman Marcus suits. He wasn't satisfied with just a pinky ring; he wore diamonds on all ten fingers, a visual advertisement for the *I got it and if you got enough money to give me, you can have it too* effect.

He wasn't physically appealing, but it never stopped him. That grifter preacher set aside all decorum and Christian manners, sprinted down the money lines, snatching rent and grocery finances from folks' hands along the way.

"Y'all will live and not die," he repeated, at the same time tapping foreheads. Immediately, the gullible started falling down like dominoes from his supposed power.

It made Joy cringe. She leaned back in an uncomfortable metal folding chair. She began sucking air through her teeth, refusing to participate, lest she look as ridiculous as the others.

She finally exhaled loudly, giving a side-glance at Patience seated next to her, squirming in her chair. She'd focused on everything else and almost missed it. Sitting next to Patience was a man who seemed to be looking straight at Rev. Monee Coffers while at the same time moving closer to Patience.

Finally, the stranger leaned over to Patience, tapped her wrist in a much too familiar manner, and whispered, "Have you seen his performance before? You seem to be truly enjoying it."

Patience turned and looked at the stranger. She wanted to give the man a *how dare you* glare by narrowing her eyes and leaning away like he had cooties, but something about the sharply dressed, lemony-complexioned man wearing a pair of expensive shades stopped her. In an instant, he almost mesmerized her without adding another word to his question.

Looking up toward one of the few working air vents, Joy prayed, *Lord, please help your child, Patience, and unclog her common-sense.*

Shaking her head, Joy turned her attention back to the reverend. With a Bible in one hand, he adjusted his binocular-looking glasses. He bent his knees, began duck-walking like a fake Chuck Berry. He also began flipping the pages of his Bible like strumming frets on a guitar. "Y'all ain't believing like ya should. Ya were holding back on Gawd!"

"I'm waiting on ya word," Joy heard Patience cry out.

The stranger moved even closer to Patience, joining in with a few words as well. "Obedience is better than sacrifice, and we're willing."

Joy, embarrassed by them, slumped in her seat. *Lord, why did I even bother to come here? Folks have truly lost their ever-loving minds. That old faith-killer ain't real. If I get a word, I'll need a real one.*

Aside from one person working the camera, Rev. Monee Coffers had two ushers. The male ushers, shameless and obviously rehearsed, dressed head-to-toe in bright money-green colors, looked into the camera. Together they urged the audience, "Line up again, for a special word from the Lord."

By the time Rev. Coffers walked to his spot in front of the camera, his ushers had completed their task. They'd shepherded the foolish faithful with the exception of Joy, Patience, and several others into lines of ten-, twenty-, fifty-, and one-hundred-dollar suckers.

Joy shook her head in wonder again. *Why didn't I just let Felony bite Sister Betty? That would've kept the old sanctified busybody off my property and out of our lives.*

"Joy, quick, hand me that fan next to you, I need to get the reverend's attention," Patience demanded. "Lord, have mercy, Jesus! I should've gotten on one of those lines."

Patience, ever the eternal optimist, wouldn't wait for Joy to politely hand over the fan. She turned and snatched the fan, with a picture of Martin Luther King on the front, from the stranger's hand, leaving him stunned.

Her two skinny fingers now held a fifty-dollar bill. Seconds before, she'd retrieved the money from a secret place inside her wallet. Now the bill covered Martin Luther King's face on the fan. She waved it back and forth like a lantern.

"Come on and move Holy Spirit; move all up in this place right now!" Her scream and the waving of her money fan was a signal to any usher with good eyesight and fluent in bribes.

"Praise Him, sister! Praise Him!" The loud and eager encouragement came directly from Rev. Monee Coffers.

From the corner of his eye, he'd already seen and heard Patience. Of course, after years of practice in jailhouse survival maneuvers and churches, he knew a willing giver when one shouted, especially when the fifty-dollar bill erased all doubt.

Rev. Coffers rushed over and snatched Patience by one of her reed thin arms. The man's eyes looked wilder than before. He pushed Patience into the aisle.

Joy couldn't tell when it'd happened, but he'd already yanked the fan from Patience's hand. In one swift blurry movement, he'd thrown it to the floor, but not before he'd ripped the money from it. Turning away from the camera, he'd quickly scanned the fifty-dollar bill, making certain it wasn't counterfeit before pocketing it.

Now the skinny woman had his full attention.

Patience's five-foot-nine-inch frame, with its one hundred and fifteen pounds of mocha-colored flesh, looked like a discarded and stained barbershop pole. The long red and white skirt she wore had whipped up, exposing skinny legs and knobby knees. Once Rev. Coffers tossed Patience into the aisle, she had to spread her legs apart to keep from turning like she was on a barbeque spit.

From that point on, Joy couldn't keep up because the fake Rev. Coffers had already started circling Patience.

The thick-lensed, wing-tipped eyeglasses Patience wore magically disappeared from her face. In an instant, Rev. Coffers held them in his hands. It was as though he didn't want her nearsightedness corrected while he did the dirty deed again.

He then started moving so fast Joy thought Patience would turn into a puddle of syrup like the tiger in the old African fairy tale, *Sambo*. He was mumbling and pointing, pointing and mumbling. All the time Patience kept repeating two words, "Yes, Lord."

Joy didn't remember standing, but she had. She also didn't remember moving away from the uncomfortable chair and into the aisle, but she did. She'd had enough and was about to grab Patience out of the unholy séance when the stranger stepped forward. He gently yet somehow forcibly pushed her aside.

Out of his chair, standing under the glaring lights of the camera, he appeared taller. Immediately, Joy's eyes swept over the stranger.

His complexion seemed brighter than when he'd sat next to Patience under the hot lights. His face seemed pleasant enough but his eyes, the windows to his soul, remained hidden beneath sunglasses that seemed to cover the middle of his face from ear-to-ear. He also had a cleft in his chin, sexy like a young Kirk Douglas. She wasn't much of a boutique shopper, but she knew good tailoring. The dark blue suit he wore fit him like he'd been born to wear it. Shined shoes and a subtle white tie with thin stripes somehow gave him more substance.

But why had he stepped up and interrupted the charade Rev. Coffers had going? Were they in cahoots, she wondered.

The stranger adjusted his sunglasses but not enough so that anyone could see his eyes. But from the shock on Rev. Coffers' face, there was no doubt he knew the stranger, even if the others didn't. Quickly, he turned away from Coffers, his other hand pointing directly at Patience as though to accuse her of something, and he spoke.

With no direction from the still frozen-in-time Rev. Coffers, the camera moved in, just in time to hear the stranger ask of Patience in a voice dripping with sarcasm, "Why would you sit on your gift God's given you? Why would you ignore that gift? God has shown you in part, and it's up to you to discover and investigate—"

There were probably a good fifty more words that flew out of the stranger's mouth at Patience, yet all Joy heard was one. "Investigate."

At that moment, unfortunately for the town of Pelzer, Patience heard the same word, too.

Rev. Coffers and the cameras moved away from the cousins, finishing up the show. Within a few minutes the studio was nearly empty with the exception of a few stragglers looking for more chaos for their money. The lemon-colored stranger approached Joy and Patience.

That time he smiled and shook the hands of both cousins. With a softer voice he apologized for his earlier intrusion.

"Unlike Rev. Coffers," he said, "I do the work of goodness. My name is Prophet Long Jevity, or just Prophet by some. Up until three hours ago, I was in Anderson, South Carolina, alone and was led to come here. As we can now see, obedience has won and is victorious."

As soon as the word *investigate* leapt off his tongue again, the cousins hugged, cried, and started shouting. Even though the police department didn't want them, all their years of watching detective shows were indeed a part of God's plan.

Prophet Long Jevity, despite the circus-like atmosphere, had validated God's plan for their lives. They didn't need a government-issued license to investigate crime. They could snoop because God had sent them an impromptu prophecy. The cousins had spent almost a lifetime yearning to be detectives because that's what God wanted.

It took Joy and Patience a minute to realize that Prophet Long Jevity hadn't left the studio yet. He'd stood a few feet away with his arms folded, watching them and smiling.

Joy glanced at Patience, not quite liking what she saw. Joy

knew Patience well, and it didn't take her a minute to see a change come over her.

Patience, despite Joy's look of concern, had already begun sizing up the man who'd given her permission to call him Prophet. *What a handsome, godly man.*

As though he'd read Patience's thoughts, Prophet Long Jevity spoke. "Excuse me ladies, I'm sorry to interrupt. This evening has been quite extraordinary."

"Oh yes," Patience blurted.

"She needs more prayer," Joy quickly added.

Prophet Long Jevity smiled but didn't comment on what they'd said, instead adding, "By the way, please help me out. I've a terrible memory. I'm trying to recall during our praise-fest if y'all told me what church you attended."

"We attend Mount Kneel Down Non-Denominational," Joy replied before mentally clamping her hand over her mouth. She suddenly didn't want to give more information than that.

However, Patience didn't see it that way. Her mouth went into rapid-speed mode. "It's located over in West Pelzer. Reverend Stepson is the pastor. We've got more than two thousand members . . ."

Before Joy shot her an angry glance, she'd blurted out everything except how many pews were on the first level of the church building.

He snapped his fingers, again breaking out in a grin. "Many years ago when I used to follow a little politics and was a year into studying criminal law, I had a professor who'd been a superior court judge. Folks called him Give' Em Time and Hell Crazy Lock Stepson."

"Well, suh!" Patience squealed. This man Prophet knew about her church and pastor. Patience was beside herself. If she'd worn a bra larger than a current AAA, he'd have seen her chest poke out. "Our godson, Detective Percy LaPierre—we call him Lil P—is the big cheese around these parts when it comes to fighting crime. He had our pastor as a professor a while back, too."

"Crazy Lock Stepson, that's him!" Joy interjected. She wanted the questioning over, and for Patience to stop giving out so much information about the family. She also needed to go home and get her praise on without the confines of her girdle. "We thank ya for the chitchat, but we gotta go!"

Again, a smile slowly crept across his lemony face as beads of perspiration raced down his cheeks. He was ready to go, too; he didn't want nor need the women watching a change come over him.

"Please. Hold on a moment." He tried to sound surprised as he asked, "You're telling me that he's gone from a judge to a pastor?"

"Oh yes," Patience replied as her mouth went into over-drive again. "He's no longer down at the courthouse, but he's still judging folks. You'd best believe that ain't ever gonna stop."

"I don't know if we still talking about the same man of God and gavel, but folks that truly know my pastor will tell you something different. Folks I know will tell you he earned the nickname *Crazy* because he's always been as crazy about his Jesus as he is about his judging."

"That's right," Joy chimed in. "You ain't been judged or preached to until you've stood in the presence of our beloved Rev. Crazy Lock Stepson. Of course, I should tell you that nobody at Mount Kneel Down calls him crazy unless he asks them to."

Feeling she'd made her point, Patience quickly tag-teamed Joy, not giving Prophet a chance to respond. "You should come by our service sometime and see for yourself. In fact, next week is the missionary anniversary. Joy's campaigning on behalf of the missionary board. I'm certain Reverend Stepson would love to reconnect if he's the one you think he is."

"Yes, indeed, I might do that sometime." Prophet quickly added, "Although, I doubt if he'll remember me. There were so many—"

Prophet never finished his words; instead, he reached out with both hands, tapping Joy and Patience lightly on their foreheads. "Give God the praise. You know I, too, see a presidency in both your futures."

Without another word, he quickly turned and walked away.

"Do you think he'll really come to Mount Kneel Down?" Patience was beside herself with excitement.

"Well, he did tell us that God wanted us to investigate," Joy blurted. "And that's our lifelong dream."

"That's right," Patience laughed, "and he couldn't have known anything about the open presidency office at the church, 'cause all I said was you was running on behalf of the missionaries."

"Well, obedience is better than sacrifice. Maybe whenever he comes back to Pelzer, he'll want to see if we've been obedient and followed through. I'm sure he follows up with all his prophecies so he can keep score."

The cousins weren't the only ones amazed at the turn of events that evening. Patience came with a plan to increase her finances. Joy came because she'd felt forced to do so. And now the Prophet Long Jevity, a stranger, had given them what they'd not hoped to discover there. In their minds, he'd prophesied God's purpose for their lives. They couldn't wait to get started snooping and solving misdeeds wherever they found them.

Back in his studio dressing room, Rev. Monee Coffers couldn't stop shaking. Tonight wasn't the first time he'd felt like a modern day Jonas. He'd only fished inside the pockets of those who should've known better. He'd checked all of the maps of the United States, knew there wasn't a town or village called Nineveh such as where Jonas had fled; why did God harass him?

With every question that came to mind, the answer remained the same: Prophet. Having that man around meant there'd be two too many prophets in Pelzer.

Rev. Monee Coffers packed his bags. He'd already determined not to look back despite that he'd lose money from investing with several others in his commercial. *They can do what they want with it. I'm outta here,* he thought.

The whale in the Bible had swallowed Jonas; the darkness of the South Carolina night did the same with Rev. Monee Coffers as he fled onto Highway 85 going anywhere but there.

Outside the studio, hands gripping the steering wheel of his 2009 Toyota Corolla, Prophet Long Jevity couldn't move. *What in the world had just happened?*

"Are You really anointing me again, Lord? I've heard from You five times since—" He couldn't finish the question; he was perplexed, conflicted. Had God actually interfered, taking him off his prepared script and his federal investigation involving the Reverend Monee Coffers?

He'd think about it later, after filing his report to his FBI team supervisor. *In the meantime, I need to come up with a good explanation as to why I went against protocol. Why couldn't I just observe Coffers? Of all the people I could've sat next to, it had to end up being someone from Mount Kneel Down and my partner's kinfolk. If God don't give me the right excuse, I certainly won't be able to come up with one. If someone blamed a mistake on God, aside from Adam, I know I certainly wouldn't believe that God somehow interfered with plans of His own.*

All he could do was whisper a prayer. "Lord, help me. Somehow I know these women haven't seen the last of me."

Prophet released his cell phone from its pouch and began dialing. "Hey, Percy, it's Prophet here. I'd hoped you'd be able to chat a moment. It appears I've gone off script," he paused and inhaled, "and not in a good way. Your return is necessary. Call me."

Chapter 6

It was Sunday morning and a week had passed since Joy and Patience received the prophecy from Prophet Long Jevity.

Not once had Joy and Patience let their feet touch the ground. Instead, they'd chatted like wind-up toys, rushing around Pelzer, trading heavenly praises, testifying of all they'd gone through preparing for God to change their earthly assignment without revealing the nature of their assignment.

And just as Prophet Long Jevity prophesied to Joy, her blessing didn't take long to start happening. A few days later, they saw a snippet of themselves on television in Rev. Monee Coffers' "Prophet for Profit" commercial. They almost knocked the sixty-inch flat-screen TV off the wall while they were high-fiving and praising God. Even Felony happily ran around chasing his tail stump.

And then an avalanche of blessings began. Two days later, Joy nearly fell off the scale after a doctor's visit. She had lost almost three pounds just from shouting and racing about town. "Father, if I keep at it and use more faith, I believe I can lose enough to almost reach my birth weight!"

"You got that much faith?"

"Yes, Patience, I've got just that much faith."

And if that blessing weren't enough, Joy also received an unexpected telephone call from Deacon Campbell Whistle. He mentioned that he, too, had seen them in the television spot.

"I didn't know you were close with that Rev. Monee Coffers fella. I wished I'd known. I heard he walks in some pretty high cotton and with deep pockets, too."

He continued, congratulating Joy, excitedly tossing around multisyllable words as though he were reading from a dictionary. Then he said, "Sister Joy, it's happened. The church board, based upon my enthusiastic recommendation, has approved your petition. From Sunday on, folks can call you President Joy Karry—president of the missionary board. And you tell Deaconess Patience there's a bonus in it for her, too. I know how close y'all are and that she's coming off the finance board. By my authority, the mantle of vice president will hang around her neck and she'll work with you on the missionary board."

"You don't say . . ."

"Oh, but I do say, and I'm not finished saying either," he continued. "Sister Boodrow and I have decided to change the way we do devotion. We will only call out the Lord's name in a church service." Pausing, because he'd suddenly begun wheezing, he added quickly as though speaking in Morse code, "Are we clear?"

I ain't letting that worm off the hook that easy, she thought. He'd probably screamed "Jesus" during his sexual romp with Sister Boodrow. Without saying another word, she hung up the phone.

"Good Lord, Patience, where are you?" she called out as she raced through the house shouting out the good news along the way. They'd both hopped out of bed before God's sun had a chance to stretch and rise. "Can you believe this?" Joy called out to Patience, who was in the next bedroom. She would've continued talking loud, but she needed to conserve air while she shimmied her wide hips into a neon red two-piece dress suit.

"I most certainly can believe it," Patience shouted back. "Prophet Jevity told you there was a presidency in your future. God is so good; he even threw in a vice presidency blessing for me. I got to admit God's timing was impeccable. I wasn't happy with too much of what I seen going on—" She hesitated a moment, thinking. "Oh, never mind. I could never talk about any of my misgivings about the churches financial matters with anyone who wasn't on the board. Like I said, it don't matter. God don't half-do His work. He'll straighten out whatever needs straightening. And, if I'm wrong in my thinking that some of the church monies ain't adding up like they should, then I'll ask the Lord to forgive me."

"You're right. We gonna let them sleeping dogs lie." Joy winked at her reflection in the bedroom mirror. She'd tuned out the last part of whatever Patience had said; the gorgeous outfit reflected in the mirror demanded that she stay positive. She called out, "You know, Patience, I truly believe that it's an added blessing just knowing that we're anointed presidential-type crime solvers, too! Pelzer detectives better watch their backs once we get up and running."

Bathing in perspiration from rushing around her room, Joy pushed Felony aside with her foot. As soon as he began whimpering, she tossed him his old chew shoe so he wouldn't gnaw on one of her good ones.

Grimacing, she pulled a trunk from her walk-in closet into the middle of her bedroom. She retrieved an oversized, three-tier, red peacock–feathered hat affectionately named a pulpit blocker.

"This is just the first step in our pathetic walk and crime-solving for the Lord," Patience called out. Like Joy, she'd begun dressing from head to toe in a bright red ensemble.

"You mean prophetic, don't you?" Joy wasn't sure if she'd misunderstood or not, but words had power so they needed to be careful.

"Oh yeah, that's what I meant!" Patience replied while using two large safety pins to hold up a size 0 slip. She also donned an outrageous two-tiered feathered hat, wide and wild enough to hide a flock of small birds.

"I wish our godson Lil P could be there. Having him at the service would've made this day completely perfect."

"I feel the same way," Joy replied. "I betcha he's probably off somewhere moping, especially 'cause I heard Reign's out of town again. Then again, he may even be working under-cover someplace, locking up somebody and spoiling their day." She began giggling. "But we won't let nothing spoil ours."

"Amen and ah-men."

Satisfied they could still shout without any clothing rip-ping or falling off, they rushed to their vehicle, prepared to throw down at the Mount Kneel Down.

An hour after Joy and Patience arrived at Mount Kneel Down, the church's missionary anniversary service began in earnest. The choir sang until exhausted and their robes soaked with sweat. The Prayer Posse prayed until they thought God had heard enough. Of course, the deacons still begged for money until the collection plate creaked.

And then it was time for Mount Kneel Down to sho' nuff get down for the Lord.

It truly began in earnest when Joy and Patience's teary eyes fell upon their beloved Rev. C. L. Stepson.

The pastor's aide posse ushered Rev. Crazy Lock Stepson into the sanctuary. In his late sixties, the stout man of average height, with a peanut-buttered complexion, sat in his wheel-chair with a Bible lying in his lap. A posse surrounded him made up of several old church mothers, four old gals dressed top to bottom in gold and black tunics. They were the church's A-Team.

Although only two of those old gals used steel walkers to get around, all were certifiably menopausal. Rev. Stepson had handpicked the women years ago. Because of their loyalty and tenacity, he knew they'd stomp a mud hole in Satan's behind to protect him.

A young male adjutant carried the reverend's robe, his handkerchief, and a glass of water.

Until Rev. Stepson's health began failing five years ago, he'd tried unsuccessfully to keep his condition from his church.

For years, he'd also dealt out stiff prison sentences, in his no-nonsense manner. He'd been Columbia, South Carolina's, longest-sitting Superior Court judge before his failing health forced him to retire.

However, all during that time, and for more than thirty years, he pastored Mount Kneel Down. It never mattered whether it was from behind a judge's bench or a pulpit, he'd uphold God's law without adding to it or taking away. "What God says, I say," he always said.

Joy leaned over a bit and nudged Patience's shoulder with her own. "Oh my, look at Rev. Stepson. He's so clean this morning, I betcha if he could walk, he'd squeak."

Patience said nothing. In her mind she agreed with Joy about his dress. However, there was something a little off about the way he'd begun to slump in his chair.

His head had begun to fall forward. The movement was more exaggerated than she'd seen before. She remembered Reign mentioning that her father hadn't looked that well and attributed what she'd just seen to his bad health.

Maybe the pastor has a cramp in his neck, she thought. She quickly dismissed the thought and returned to concentrating on her big day.

The adjutant quickly placed Rev. Stepson's gold and purple preacher's robe around his shoulders. The young man then helped the reverend place his arms through the sleeves. As he'd done many times before he smoothed the robe about the reverend, making it appear it was completely on him. One of the A-Team elderly women adjusted the robe's diamond crusted belt, causing its jewels to shimmer from sunrays pouring through multicolored stained-glass windows.

Now that he was dressed, it was time for Rev. Stepson to lead his flock as best he could until he tired and one of the associate ministers took over. Rev. Stepson began rocking side to side.

He stopped for a second, catching his breath while pushing back his dyed blonde tresses from his forehead.

The hair was a gift. Several months ago, the mothers board made a promise to take him out for his birthday. Those ole gals had kept their word, surprising him with a prepaid wheelchair visit to the Bald-Be-Gone Hair Club of America.

Within four hours, a Bald-Be-Gone specialist had removed extremely long, curly gray hairs from his chest and his hind parts. The hairs were then surgically implanted on his scalp and dyed blonde. He'd walked out with a headache but he'd become a new man.

The downside: he needed to wash his new hair often to keep it smelling good. Transplanted butt hairs were still butt hairs.

Smiling broadly, he leaned forward over his Bible, greeting the congregation with a sweep of his hand. "Give God some praise!" He struggled to raise his tired hands, but he soon began clapping, his palms barely touching. If it'd been any other installation service, one of the other ministers would've presided. This morning, Rev. Stepson insisted he'd do it.

Making a small circle with his hand, he leaned over and spoke into a microphone now held by the pastor's aide. His voice sounded stronger than he actually felt as he spoke to the six missionary representatives. "Come here, daughters of the most high King."

The missionaries raced toward their pastor. Six self-declared prophetesses followed close behind. In the meantime, Joy and Patience sat several feet away. They looked almost angelic, smiling broadly while surrounded by several young and energetic female ushers holding fans and modesty cloths.

"Point your fingers toward your new president and your former finance trustee, now vice president," Rev. Stepson began in a halting voice. "Open your hearts and minds. Let the power of the Lord work through you. Concentrate, thou women of God. Let God use you to bless Patience Kash and Joy Karry."

Then, true to form, because he'd never surrender to bad health or mankind, Rev. Stepson led off the ceremony with a few mumbled words meant as prayers. "Empower them, Lord. Give them wisdom, Father."

All was going according to their rehearsal, but then God decided to show up and show out.

The spiritual shift began with the six prophetesses. Suddenly the oldest woman, First Lady Deborah, known for her gift of prophecy, stepped away from her group. First Lady Deborah, a tall, middle-aged, ebony-complexioned woman, had worn a blonde wig, designed to match her husband's transplanted hair, over her short dark hair. The matching wig showed solidarity. For this occasion, she'd stuffed most of the wig under a tall white fez that made her look like a rickety old smokestack.

"Now hear a word from the Lord," First Lady Deborah declared. Her eyes danced about while she lay a hand against her ear to show she'd already started hearing from heaven.

No sooner had she hijacked crazy, the other prophetesses threw their heads back and joined in. Their lips started fluttering, tongues began stuttering, and they began laying hands on Joy and Patience.

The cousins had attended all three pre-ceremony rehearsals. They knew everyone's part and could've gone through the ritual, flawlessly, in their sleep. Now they sat stunned, trying hard to hide their surprise.

Joy recovered first. She leaned over, whispered to Patience, saying the opposite of what she'd wanted to say. "Well, suh. Shut the front door."

"Better do it quick," Patience mumbled. "Ain't nobody sticking to the script?"

Joy and Patience turned, smiling and nodding towards their pastor. He appeared as shocked as they, but could do nothing from his wheelchair. They would've kept smiling, going along with the revised program, but then those prophetesses became a bit too excited.

One of them snatched the bottle of blessed oil from the reverend's hand. One by one the bottle passed between prophetesses, each anointing the cousins with slaps upside their heads. In no time, they'd knocked Joy and Patience's expensive hats onto the floor.

And then prophetesses began squirting blessed oil all over the cousins' expensive red dresses. Grease stains appeared as prophetesses' spittle, like sharp wet darts, hit Joy and Patience in the face.

Joy jumped up first, and then Patience, shooing away prophetesses.

In the meantime, the congregation started a separate service. Some began calling on God to help them feel whatever spirit Joy, Patience, and the others felt. Others began calling on God to get rid of whatever spirit the others felt.

Ain't this about a mess? I know heaven must be confused, too, Joy thought as she peeked at Patience. By the glazed look on Patience's face, she knew the feeling was mutual.

It seemed an eternity, but it'd taken him less than a moment to recover. Rev. Stepson ran a tight church like he ran a tight courtroom. Sick or not, and though he didn't have a gavel, he still had the microphone. With renewed strength, he almost smashed through the wooden back of the nearest pew with it. "Come to order right now! When I want order, y'all know I mean it."

However, the reverend wasn't the only one feeling power—someone else was, although hers was more on a heavenly plain. Before he could speak further, First Lady Deborah set it off again.

Sensing her husband might interrupt what she had begun, she ignored him and his leadership. She'd already decided she'd use her own craziness like a weapon.

She began prophesying, solo that time.

"Oh hear what thus saith the Lord, I say." First Lady Deborah began swaying side to side, whispering and purring to her team of prophetesses. "Sway with me, dahlings; pray with me."

The other prophetesses, while swaying, propped her up between them lest she fall. She'd done it in the past, and they didn't want her hitting her head, misinterpreting God's surprise visit, as well as the unrehearsed message.

Looking at Joy and Patience, her eyes narrowed, finger pointing toward them. She didn't want another sound uttered or a movement made. "Hush! Hear the word of the Lord!"

First Lady Deborah had the full attention of the cousins, the church, and especially her husband. She began setting things in order.

She began speaking slowly. "My God has opened the heavens. He has shown me and told me of His Will concerning the two of you."

Patience immediately began calming down. She always loved a good prophecy, especially where it concerned her. *Oh my. Lately, I feel like heaven has me on speed dial. God is really keeping me in the loop.*

Joy, on the other hand, kept looking at her expensive hat that now lay perilously close to the feet of the first lady, who'd begun to move. *Help me Jesus. If she steps on my hat, my presidency will be the shortest one in history. I ain't playing up in here.*

First Lady Deborah began shaking as though she'd been tasered. "Judges, chapter four, verse 6—And . . . Deborah . . . sent . . . and . . . called . . . Barak . . ."

"The Lord empowers Deborah, in Judges, to deliver the Israelites from oppression by any Canaanites." Rev. Stepson hadn't meant to butt in, but he did.

He took a deep breath. While he still held the microphone, he immediately began interpreting his wife's prophesies. He believed it had something to do with what was currently happening as it related to Joy and Patience.

"God is revealing to you," he said in a voice that soon began to falter, "that like the Israelites, you two are His, and He has favor upon you. It was His will that you were no longer held back by working a regular nine to five. You've now other means and ways to pay your tithes and offerings."

Rev. Stepson peeked over at the only person ever able to keep him in check, his wife. When she didn't give him an evil eye, he smiled, thinking he'd done good.

First Lady Deborah continued swaying and jerking to a rhythm heard only in her head. The other prophetesses continued propping her between them.

Patience, now captured by it all, including her pastor's odd reference to monies, continued listening.

In the meantime, Joy's eyes remained glued on First Lady Deborah's feet, which were moving a little too close to her expensive hat. She moved her feet slightly apart, ready to spring into action if needed.

"The book of Judges holds your promise," First Lady Deborah continued. "God has shown me in the spirit that He will have your help in high places."

On cue, the reverend began interpreting. "The Bible tells us that this Deborah"—he pointed to his wife before continuing—"as well as the Old Testament Deborah needed to enlist the help of Barak to lead the army of Israel against the Canaanites. But Barak wouldn't go if she didn't . . ."

As soon as he spoke, somehow he began feeling that he might've misspoken. He couldn't put the horse back in the barn. By the looks on Joy and Patience's faces, it'd already galloped away.

And that's all it took for Joy, Patience, and the entire church to lose their minds, again. The praises went up so loud, a jet engine would've sounded like a whisper.

"Wait a moment," the reverend began pleading, taking short breaths, trying to continue his interpretation. "Lest we forget all that the Word tells us." He then started stuttering, trying to explain until his voice began cracking. "Remember, church, that First Corinthians, chapter thirteen verse nine instructs us as thus." He yelled as loud as he could, which by then was barely above a whisper.

"For we know in part and we—" He stopped speaking and, almost near collapse, pointed a finger toward his wife as though aiming a pistol. It was too late. She'd already joined in the shoutfest. Shaking his head, he continued speaking, his voice fading fast. "First Lady Deborah prophesied in part. She ain't privy to everything—" The reverend's head dropped almost onto his chest.

The mothers board almost collapsed in tears; their pastor amazed them. The same man, who over the past two years had begun displaying signs of memory loss, remembered so much scripture.

Yet because everyone else was lost in the revelry, none

heard nor cared about the reverend's warning. All his members cared about was that a prophecy came forth; and no matter what he'd said, they'd heard him mention *Barak*. Of course, it had to be President Barack Obama.

First Lady Deborah shouted because her hotline between the church and heaven was still active. It meant that—despite a lot of sinning and other foolishness (some almost criminal) going on inside Mount Kneel Down from members who weren't fully toeing the Christian line—somehow the gifts of the spirit had survived.

"Oh Jesus," Patience cried out. "President Barack!"

"My Lord," Joy added, with her arms stretched toward heaven, "we can't get no higher help other than from the Lord."

It hadn't taken but a few seconds for Joy and Patience to get off on the wrong track. God Almighty could've come down from heaven and personally told the church what He'd actually meant and they wouldn't have cared.

When it was all over, only two things mattered to Joy and Patience: God had taken them off their day jobs to make them His personal snoops, and President Barack Obama would see to it that nothing and no one would interfere.

A little later the pandemonium finally died down. Joy and Patience had shaken a few hands and gathered their belongings when they spied Prophet Long Jevity. It took them a moment to recognize him behind his extra-large sunglasses.

They also noticed he wasn't still dressed like a movie star. But he wasn't on television, either. They couldn't tell how long he'd sat almost hidden behind one of the stanchions, as though he'd not wanted anyone to see him smiling.

Those same hats Joy and Patience cared so much about suddenly became flying saucers. They tossed the hats, their shoes, and church service decorum to the side. Within minutes, they double-dipped into the praise pool, for a double portion of blessings, and begun shouting again.

Prophet Long Jevity hadn't looked their way or given them a nod that he'd seen them. It didn't matter. They took his second appearance as God sending a second confirmation for the first confirmation.

Chapter 7

Before the week was out, instead of Joy and Patience changing for the better, now that they were licensed heads of the missionary board, they worsened. They became spiritual terrorists.

"Snooping for the Lord is serious business, and amateurs need not apply," Joy would say while going over her "Who in Pelzer to Terrorize" wish list.

"Yep, it's definitely gonna take some holy boldness," Patience agreed.

One of the first places the women began investigating, and where their snooping went awry, was at the mall in East Pelzer.

Joy overheard one of the young men on the junior choir talking about buying some movies from a kid selling bootleg DVDs out of a trash bag by the Nip and Tuck girdle shop. "I'm going down there Wednesday, see if I can get a horror flick," he'd said.

Joy immediately told Patience they should get right on it, instead of reporting it to the precinct. "I don't think we should bother superstar detective godson's department with this small job. Although I wouldn't be a bit surprised if that kid gets his movies from some mafia or something."

"You could be right. Let's watch that episode of *Monk* where he busted a drug ring. It can't be much different than what we about to do."

"You're right. We need to start small and work our way up."

Armed with information from a scripted television show, the cousins showed up at the Nip and Tuck around five-thirty that Wednesday afternoon. No sooner had they arrived than they saw a short, young scraggily brown-skinned kid with huge dreadlocks hanging down his back. He struggled to pull a large dark garbage bag from a shopping cart to the front of the store.

"That's gotta be him," Joy urged. "Let's get ' em."

"Don't you think we oughta wait right here until he takes the movies out, and somebody buys one? We need to get a better look at him."

"That's just crazy, Patience. The next thing you'll wanna do is wait around for a commercial break. It's up to you. You can take root in this one spot if you want. We already know he's guilty 'cause he's got the garbage bag, and he's waiting near the front of the Nip and Tuck."

Without waiting for a reply or Patience to become more aggressive, Joy lumbered over and flashed her missionary license card in the face of the young man. She quickly closed the small case letting him get only a glance at the conveniently placed silver star, which was pinned next to the small card. She'd received the silver star from selling the most sweet potato pies during last year's Mount Kneel Down bake-off.

"No, Joy, stop!" Patience sprinted towards Joy and the young man. "He's not the one we want."

It took almost fifteen minutes of Patience pleading with her former supervisor from Robbery & Homicide not to arrest her and Joy for impersonating police officers.

"But I never said I was a cop," Joy explained sheepishly. "We just wanted to put an end to some illegal activities going on."

"It wasn't no *we* in it," Patience complained. She didn't like the idea of a crowd gathering, or the fact that she'd been too late in recognizing one of the undercover cops who'd apparently already arrested the guy selling the bootleg movies. "We didn't know he was moving the evidence out of the way so folks could walk around . . ." She stopped and, with her lips pouting like a child caught with her hands in a cookie jar, she used another tactic. "Sergeant Bentley, you ain't gonna tell our godson about this little accident, are you? After all, you've had accidents too. How many times did I cover for you when your wife called?"

The women were let go with a rebuke after they'd apologized and promised to leave police work up to those who were actual law enforcement.

Undeterred by their near-arrest, the cousins decided that they needed to find another way of breaking into the investigation business. That afternoon's interrogation had taken a serious turn. They could've been arrested and would've been had they arrived a little earlier and interfered with the undercover officer's bust.

Sensing a bit of excitement between the women as they chatted entering the front door, Felony began feeling left out. He hadn't liked being tied up while they'd been gone. Not one bit.

A few days after the mayhem at the mall, Felony confronted Joy as she was about to leave the house. He raised his big head and allowed one ear to dangle before lifting one hind leg with a growl, threatening what would happen if they left him behind again.

Minutes later, Felony joined the missionary posse, riding shotgun in the backseat. They'd made sure Felony had his favorite bowl of popcorn, hoping to keep him from lifting that hind leg in the car.

Within a few hours, they'd swept through and over every inch of possible wrongdoing all over Pelzer, Belton, and nearby Williamston and Piedmont. It didn't matter who or where—while pumping gas, paying at a checkout counter, or waiting for a traffic light to change, everywhere and everyone became a part-time missionary-turned-prophet-snoop-and-fact-finding show for Joy and Patience.

Their methods may have been unorthodox, but they'd stopped a pocketbook snatcher, with Joy sitting on him, Felony growling, and Patience calling 911 while kicking the perp's behind with her pointy-toed shoe. They also managed to stop one of their church members from selling food from the food pantry. She'd been embarrassed and apologetic. She even insisted on paying extra in her tithes offering, to make amends and confess to God for forgiveness. "You know I still have access to the finance records," Patience warned. "Don't let me see that you ain't paying fifteen percent. I know what you been paying and there'd better be an extra five percent added to it."

They took their snooping even further after that. If anyone challenged their authority, neither woman backed off. They flashed their missionary licenses, reading the back of it as though giving a Miranda warning:

Bearer is authorized to visit the sick in their homes and hospitals, to visit the imprisoned, and to render services wherever duty may call, despite time of day or night. May God bless her every effort and crown her labor with abundant success.

★ ★ ★

Those words became their mantra.

After a couple of weeks, anxious townsfolk began resenting Joy and Patience's inquiry tactics.

But everything didn't always work out for the cousins. For every good work, there were triple the amount of near-misses and downright failures. They'd even come close to causing a rift between a husband and wife when Joy thought the man was cheating. "How was I supposed to know they were playing some kinda freaky, nasty sex game by dressing up as strangers?"

By the third week, a pushback began. Lawyers saw a rise in clients. The 911 service couldn't keep up with the emergency calls. A good thing they'd worked for the police a long time because most of the times, they got off with a warning.

"We need to rethink our methods again," Joy announced one evening, after slamming down the phone. She'd heard yet another complaint, one of about a dozen. "Perhaps, we need to just go undercover, stay out of sight for a while."

"Was that another lawsuit threat?" Patience asked. She had warned Joy several times that they were being rather pushy. Perhaps now Joy would listen to reason, especially since their efforts produced not one miraculous unsolved case or even contact from their beloved President Barack.

"Yeah it was, and a beat-down, too," Joy replied sucking her teeth. "It only means that we've hit a nerve somewhere." She still didn't care what the police or the lawyers said; she refused to believe folks complaining could be innocent and fed up.

In the meantime, they tried finding different ways of reaching out to Prophet Long Jevity. "That Prophet started us off, and perhaps he can give us further advice on what we need to do," Patience insisted.

"Are you certain? Perhaps we should just wait until Lil P returns from wherever he's gone to fight crime."

"Reign said she hadn't heard from him, and we ain't either. Time is wasting, and God's expecting good results for giving us this opportunity. I say we at least ask the man. If he hadn't wanted us to bother him, then he wouldn't have approached us with what thus saith the Lord."

After days of hoping to find him at one of their church services and not being able to find a telephone number in the Anderson phonebook, the Prophet showed up at their home. It was the first time they'd seen him since their installation service.

Patience had just parked the car, having been shopping most of the afternoon. She'd left Joy piddling about the kitchen, trying out some new recipe she'd seen on television's Food Network.

"Can I help you?" Patience stuck her head out the car window. She left the engine running, in case this stranger was someone up to no good. As soon as he turned to face her, she almost broke the ignition key, trying to yank it from the steering column.

"My Lord, Prophet Long Jevity. We've been looking for you!"

"I know."

Like Patience, Joy was just as excited. She still had reservations, but they weren't enough to keep her from peppering him with all sorts of questions pertaining to what he'd told them earlier.

"Now, you said when you tapped my forehead that God wants us to investigate. Do I have that much correct?" Joy slid a plate of mushrooms stuffed with crabmeat surrounded by folded lettuce leaves overflowing with lobster salad in front of him.

"I just say what God tells me to say." He paused, allowing

the scrumptious taste of the lobster to kiss his palate. "Oh my goodness. I haven't had anything this tasty in ages."

"So you're not married or have anyone cooking for you?" The not-too-subtle question flowed with invisible honey off Patience's tongue. There was something intriguing about this man. He hadn't removed his sunglasses, not then and not before. She couldn't see into the windows to his soul, yet felt compelled to accept him as is. "Let me refill your glass with this freshly squeezed lemonade. It's just what you probably need, especially since it's so hot in here—*err*, I mean outside."

Joy eyeballed Patience, sucked her teeth, and did everything but hit her upside her head for her overzealous approach to the man. She'd already prayed, fed, and begun her questioning. Patience's overt, inexperienced attempt at being sexy could've derailed everything.

Yet the cousins hadn't quite gotten the answers they were looking for from him and it seemed the Prophet did just as much questioning as they. Their questions were about how and where God might've wanted them to dig into folks' business, and when should they involve police. His questions seemed all about Mount Kneel Down and its eclectic congregation.

It wasn't too long after that first visit before he began ingratiating himself slowly into their lives. It got to the point where the house seemed too quiet when he didn't come around, stirring things up. He also managed to disappear whenever they really needed him for further advice. Reluctantly, without his heavenly direction, they agreed to change course in their investigation methods.

They also needed to put a stop to those threats from several church board members. They'd been calling nonstop, claiming to speak on Rev. Stepson's behalf. Everything was on the table, from revocation of their missionary licenses to the church personally suing them.

One of the elder board members, eighty-year-old Deacon Push, threatened to punch them in their mouths. He'd become upset after finding warning notes taped to the windshield wipers of his thirty-year-old wife's Bentley. No matter how many times Patience tried to explain that the notes probably came from one of her boyfriends, Deacon Push wouldn't hear it. He even yanked out his hearing aid to prove his point.

As usual, Patience tried to put a positive spin on their situation. "Well, I guess we'll just remain mindful that we do have God's authority. Even Daniel had to face a liar."

"You mean lion." Joy sensed she'd need to pay closer attention to whatever Patience said when she was in her upbeat mode. Words had consequences.

"That's what I meant. Anyway, we might as well get back to case hunting."

They then decided that if they couldn't snoop face-to-face, they'd do it from the comfort of their sofa. They bought several newspapers, including some they'd never read before. They poured through the police crime-log sections word by word, hoping that something would pique their interest. However, often Felony got to the newspapers first, and they couldn't read the faded ink or stand the smell.

They watched the daily news, particularly on local channel WPAK. They hoped to catch their future goddaughter-in-law Reign reporting, or perhaps another reporter giving up-to-date reports, while also secretly hoping the law might've missed something. That didn't work either; they couldn't catch a case, a cold, or a clue.

One day, Patience poured through her Bibles and reference books. "We ain't dressed properly to snoop for the Lord," Patience announced. "I read where the Bible says, in Ephesians six, verse eleven, to put on the whole armor of God.

"*Hmmm.*" Joy's interest came alive at the mention of the word armor. "We don't have a gun nor have a license to carry a weapon. Here we are going about, possibly running into dangerous criminals, flashing our missionary licenses."

It wasn't exactly what Patience meant, but Joy had a point.

They decided that perhaps chasing murderers and armed robbers would present a challenge without weapons or licenses to own one, so they decided to regroup. They needed to snoop in the one place that was a snooper's paradise.

They held to their belief that if there was a sign of a scandal brewing, God would lead them to the bottom of it. If nothing more, it'd be safer than street snooping.

With renewed energy but no plan, Joy and Patience began snooping inside God's house. They knew church folks were chatty. What possible trouble could they get in if they combined actual missionary ministry and detective work? They just had to be careful about not upsetting Rev. Stepson or the church board.

They began by visiting noonday prayer meetings, church anniversary celebrations, and revivals. They waited around after the services ended, flashing their missionary licenses, saying, "Ain't God good, and ain't the Devil busy?" However, a lot of the information they received in response was routine. They'd hear, "Yes, he is, and that's the Devil's job."

If they could've gotten away with it, they'd have put truth serum in the soup they delivered to the church's soup kitchen, too. People were holding back and needed prodding.

All they got for the hours of slaving over a hot stove making the soup were rumors of deacons cheating the church out of money or on their wives. None of it was news or newsworthy.

Rumors weren't clues, and Joy and Patience became ever more restless. They wanted a case so bad they'd have looked for a missing pet roach for free.

Since the president was an unwitting but strong part of

their prophesied plan, but hadn't made contact, they decided to make the first move.

To get the president's attention, Joy suggested they use overnight Federal Express, the kind that required a signature upon acceptance. "We need proof the president receives our personal letters. It'd also be nice to have his personal signature, too."

Patience liked Joy's suggestion. She came up with the idea that they write letters informing President Barack Obama of their intentions without fully divulging the entire prophecy. "We will visit you shortly to personally thank you for your assistance in helping us," the letter read. She also thought it was cute when she signed it, "With much respect and admiration, your partners in crime."

Drawing on all their years of experience cleaning and typing for the police department, they also decided that a bit more sensitivity and respect should be shown to the president's Secret Service department. To put the Secret Service at ease, they put a separate sealed envelope in the Fed Ex. A part of the second letter read,

> *Dear Men in Black with dark sunglasses and walkie-talkie earplugs, we want you to remain vigilant against any real or imagined threats. After all, we're on a mission for the Lord, and we require an unnerved and vigilant POTUS's participation. Also, if there is any doubt about our intentions or sanity, we have a godson who once worked in law enforcement for Washington, you can ask Lil P if we're crazy or not. We're also hoping to be on television, preferably with our future goddaughter-in-law, Reign Stepson.*

The cousins decided to make the trip to the FedEx office in the appropriate attire befitting missionaries. After all, they were on a mission for God. So they dressed in one of their best missionary outfits, consisting of white floppy hats, two-

piece white buttoned-down long-sleeve blouses, rolled up
since temperature was in the low nineties, white pleated cotton skirts, and white orthopedic shoes.

"Well, we've done our part," Joy announced after flashing
her missionary license to the clerk at the FedEx office, hoping for a ten percent or senior discount. She didn't get the
discount, so she sucked her teeth to show her displeasure
while handing over the envelope.

"I see you don't understand who we think we are," Joy
said accusingly, pointing her finger at a sign that read WEL-
COME TO FEDEX: WE AIN'T BROWN OR SCARED. "Right now,
we ain't feeling too welcomed. I wanna see your manager."

Joy winked at Patience before turning back to face the
clerk, who hadn't budged. "Why are you still standing here? I
wanna see the manager and regardless of what that sign says,
you need to be scared, and moving."

With that said, the clerk pushed the unpaid package back
toward Joy. He took his time, but he did head toward a cubicle in the back. Moments later he returned with another man
wearing a white shirt and tie with a name tag that read *Manager*.

The manager took a double look at Joy and Patience. He
quickly turned his head, catching a glimpse of the clerk who'd
already begun walking away. Before the manager could speak,
Joy spoke up.

"I've seen you somewhere," Joy said after scanning the
man up and down. "Why do you look familiar?"

The manager looked a bit sheepish, his paper-bag-brown
face turning a nauseating shade of almost pink. "How y'all
doing?" he asked. "Miss Joy, Miss Patience, I haven't seen
y'all in years since me and Percy graduated high school. Are
y'all still working over at the Pelzer police department?"

"No, we quit," Patience lied. "But I knew you looked familiar. Ain't you Dexter, Sister Laura Smith's boy from over at
Tabernacle of Peace and Prosperity in Piedmont?"

"Yes ma'am," he replied then adding, "but I ain't been a *boy* in quite some time. I'm married with three kids now."

"Well suh," Joy chimed, sensing an opportunity to use familiarity as a way to get that discount she wanted. "That's a blessing. Here you are a married man with three kids working as a manager for FedEx. I wish Lil P had done something similar. He ain't married yet, and it don't seem like he's thinking about starting a family. He can't seem to find time for either, with him becoming a famous detective and such!"

If either Joy or Patience saw the pained look appear on the man's face they didn't show it.

Joy pushed the package towards the man, asking, "How much does it cost to mail this package to Washington, DC?"

Patience added her two cents, though she hadn't planned on putting any actual monies towards the cost of mailing. "Since you a church boy and Sister Laura's your mama, we can tell you about something you'd understand."

"I ain't a boy, Miss Patience."

Again, she ignored his growing aggravation. She began smiling as she continued. "We got a prophecy that said President Barack Obama gonna help us become investigators for the Lord. We sending him word about it, so we gonna need a receipt proving he got the message."

"Oh," Joy blurted, "and there's another letter in there for the Secret Service agents protecting our first part-black and part-other American president. We don't really need a receipt that they got their letter. They'll probably be nosing about, anyhow. It's what they do."

Again, if they saw the now-incredulous look upon Dexter's face, they didn't show it. They kept on grinning at him like he was fresh meat, especially when he replied, "You know what, Miss Joy? This ain't gonna cost y'all nothing. Y'all just leave everything to me, and I'll see that it gets to the proper folks."

He then winked, and Patience almost cracked one of the lenses in her glasses, trying to wink back.

"Thank you, Mr. Dexter. We gonna leave our precious FedEx envelope in your professional and capable hands. I always did think you was patriotic. I'm glad to see FedEx ain't squashed none of that."

Patience turned to Joy and accepted Joy's offer of a fist bump while boasting and adjusting the glasses that'd slid down on her nose. "Can't nothing go wrong now. We've put Washington on alert, and Dexter done helped us."

If they'd bothered to turn around before going out the door, they'd have seen Dexter shaking with laughter. He'd begun trying to press several keys on the telephone keypad.

Chapter 8

Two days after they'd FedExed their letters to Washington, things began changing again for Joy and Patience. In addition, they'd suddenly lost a church member.

Like several other missionaries from Mount Kneel Down, and some smaller churches who fellowshipped with them, they got the news about Sister Boodrow before dawn on a Thursday morning.

Oddly enough, the call came initially from Sister Laura Smith, the same woman whose son they'd run into at the FedEx office. She'd been at Anderson General hospital through the night praying with one of her members when the EMTs had wheeled Sister Boodrow into the emergency room. She'd already called the Stepsons and now wanted Joy to gather her missionary team.

"Joy," Sister Laura ordered, "y'all need to get whoever you can find and get down here. That Boodrow hussy's soul is in bad need of prayer. I overheard one of the doctors say she wasn't gonna make it, but we know God can turn things around. I'm gonna petition heaven on her behalf until y'all get here, but I was in the midst of praying for one of my own members, too. But I'll do my best."

First Lady Deborah arrived at Sister Boodrow's bedside before the others. By the time Joy, Patience, and three other missionaries made it to Anderson General, they learned that Sister Boodrow hadn't.

It wasn't until after her quick funeral, where no one claiming to be a family member showed, that they learned she'd had a heart attack.

The only one at her funeral who'd cried, or at least asked for a tissue to wipe his eyes, was Deacon Whistle. From where Joy stood, he hadn't started tearing up until he lay down Sister Boodrow's obituary.

Well ain't this about nothing, Joy thought after glancing over the obituary. *She came to the church talking about beauty contestants and such. Here it is, she was nothing but a judge at a couple of them contests and she wasn't thirty-five either. That gal was strangling forty-seven.*

Joy had to admit, Sister Boodrow did look pretty and in her thirties, wearing the soft lavender silk dress borrowed from First Lady Deborah. It wasn't until later, when she and Patience discussed how the service had gone, did they both wonder aloud not what, but who, gave Sister Boodrow a heart attack.

From that moment on, they looked at Deacon Whistle with his short T.rex arms a little different. They wondered if he and Sister Boodrow hadn't gone at it just one time too many. To be safe, they wouldn't so much as shake his hand.

Joy and Patience had just changed their clothes and were about to enjoy a light snack and a glass of lemonade when the conversation awkwardly turned to Prophet Long Jevity. They couldn't seem to shake their now common feelings about his questionable comings and goings.

They discussed how twice in between the times he'd visited their home that they'd already seen him from a distance lurking around the back pews of Mount Kneel Down. They didn't doubt it was him, because he was still wearing his giant sunglasses that seemed permanently attached to his face.

Patience began poking a slice of lemon with her straw, like she was trying to tenderize it. "You know, I couldn't give a description of the shape of that man's eyes or their color if someone offered me a gazillion bucks. He moves well, but that still don't tell me how old he is."

Joy nodded in agreement. In between nibbling on a tuna sandwich, she reminded Patience of the last conversation she'd had with Prophet when he'd visited the church. She'd used the opportunity to tell him, in a nice Christian way, how dumb he looked wearing sunglasses inside the church and, in fact, indoors period.

" 'Prophet Jevity,' I told him, 'I know you got to have your privacy. We respect that, but you can remove your shades inside church, even if I've never asked you to remove them inside my home. We here at Mount Kneel Down don't bother folks if they don't wanna be, whether they think they're celebrities or not.' "

Joy threw down the last piece of crust from her sandwich, folded her arms across her bosom, leaned back in her seat, and added, "And do you know what that man told me?"

"What did he say? I can't seem to recall it from the last five times you've told this story."

Joy just sucked her teeth and turned sideways in her seat before continuing.

" 'I'm sorry, Missionary Joy,' he told me. 'I guess I'm just so used to wearing them, I don't think of them being a hindrance to others needing to get all up in my business. Since it's obviously a bother, between me and you, I am quite sensitive to all sorts of lights, which has plagued me for quite some time, whether I'm indoors or outside. But if you still have doubts, I can assure you that I'm not a vampire.' "

"Are we certain about that?" Patience asked, laughing and

tapping the side of her face, trying to realign her newly purchased honey-brown contact lens.

Joy joined in the laughter as she again reminded Patience that, even with his explanation for never removing his sunglasses, she hadn't quite made up her mind.

"I'm still wavering between whether or not he'd been or was a blood sucking vampire, or just thought others were the suckers. And after all, we ain't never seen him say a hello or a good-bye to no one but us at the church. Seems to me, if he thought our pastor was the same Crazy Stepson he knew back when—whether wheelchair bound or not—he'd have said something to the reverend, or at least have said that it wasn't him."

"Well, I don't have an answer for that," Patience replied, then added, "but let's remember that he'd at least not dressed flashy those times. He'd sat there blending in with everyone, seeming to enjoy the service. Besides, oddball or not, haven't we still been searching for the man? And for the life of me, I still don't know why. I guess I'd be even more suspicious or have lots of other questions about why he's always asking about folks at our church, if he hadn't started us off on this journey."

"You're right about that," Joy laughed. "That don't say a whole lot about us. But then again, he was once a student of Rev. Stepson. I guess our pastor must've left a lasting impression. When I think about it, I still ain't never seen him go up and shake the pastor's hand after service."

Joy rose and reached for a shopping bag she'd set off to the side. "By the way, I've got to take this punchbowl next door to Sister Betty. I promised I'd return it when I was done and that should've been yesterday. I wouldn't have done any borrowing if Felony hadn't broken my good bowl."

Immediately, Patience's body flinched. Her being so skinny made it look as though a strong wave had come up from behind and pushed her around. She tried not to sound suspicious or slightly jealous when she asked, "Since when did you and Sister Betty become so chummy?"

"We ain't all that chummy, but we have chatted a bit when you and I weren't always in the same space or place. She's not quite as crazy as I thought, but I'll tell you one thing . . ."

"What's that?"

"She's one serious praying woman. She prayed so long and hard one afternoon the gravy on the biscuit she served me turned back into flour."

That observation was enough to make both women chuckle. So Joy gathered the punchbowl and her pocketbook, leaving Patience still sitting in the kitchen and at least smiling.

Once she heard the side door close, Patience didn't rise immediately. She was a little tired so she laid her head on the table, planning for it to be just for a second or two.

Normally, she'd have gotten her Bible and a few reference books, spread them on the table, and relaxed reading God's word. Instead, relaxation fled with more thoughts of Prophet taking its place.

She thought about the Prophet. From the very beginning when he'd begun his unannounced visits, she felt she'd see a lot more of him, and she'd been right. However, she'd never imagined he'd come over at his convenience.

These thoughts became uncomfortable for Patience. So she took her reading glasses from their case, rose, and went into the living room. She wanted to retrieve her Bible and one of her favorite audio tapes. It didn't make sense to fast and to pray without consulting God's Word, and relistening to President Barack Obama's *Audacity of Hope*.

Months ago, she'd decided that whenever she and her President Barack finally met, she'd want to discuss her favorite parts of what she thought was more like a sermon than just dialogue.

She smiled as she placed the huge headset on her head with the earpieces completely covering her ears. "I guess I got some audacity happening, too."

Yet, as hard as she'd tried, Patience couldn't keep her eyes open. She wasn't just physically tired; her mind couldn't hold two thoughts if they came glued together.

With her reading glasses dangling off the perch of her nose, her head fell forward. The soft whirring sound of snoring accompanied the peace and rest her body needed.

Alone in her home, there was no one to rescue her from the truth. But Patience needed saving, so although held tight in the grips of sleep, her fingers began a tapping sound on the table. Unconsciously, they became like ten thin drumsticks beating a war rhythm, a rhythm meant to protect her from self-incrimination, a questioning of existence and failing at it miserably.

Patience couldn't deny a change had indeed come over her. She'd done nothing to prevent it or stop it in its tracks. She didn't want to.

It'd begun almost from the day Prophet began showing up when Joy wasn't home. Patience never asked him why or how he knew she'd been home alone. They'd become close, sharing tidbits of their lives in confidence, often unintentionally. She'd learned he'd been an only child, too, and didn't have any close relatives.

He'd always end the visit after revealing his secrets, which never included anything she felt was damaging. "This is between you and me," he'd always say. "You can't tell anyone, not even Joy or your church members."

Smitten and keeping to her word, she'd not told Joy or anyone a single thing they'd shared.

Oddly, until then, outside of the church's financial business, Patience had never kept anything from Joy in her entire life. She was in over her head, never questioning why she didn't feel guilty in being so.

It also became apparent to her that he planned on staying in Pelzer for a while.

He'd gone on to ask if she knew of any "out of the way" rooms or apartments for rent. He didn't need an expensive one because, as he rested, he was also saving for the future. One time, whether on purpose or not, he'd slipped up and said, "for our future," and then quickly apologized for being too forward.

But Patience had already done the math in her head. One plus one meant the two of them, and she soon began putting her math skills into practice.

She secretly visited her and Joy's only other first cousin, Porky, Lil P's father. He owned the Soul Food Shanty on Ptomaine Avenue where she'd taken Prophet to eat, hoping he had an iron stomach. She didn't have time to tell Porky who she'd wanted the apartment for before he'd flat out said he no longer rented the upstairs. He needed to finish what he called "renovations."

Patience figured that probably meant the Health Department had cited him for something disgusting again. She'd thought he'd stopped letting the place go without repairs. If she'd known Porky's place was on the Centers for Disease Control's hot list, she'd have never brought Prophet there.

Of course, she never worried Porky would say anything to Joy about the visit. He and Joy didn't get along and never had because their Grandmamma Truth always favored Porky. For a long time, he was her only male heir.

But Patience didn't give up. She'd help Prophet find an apartment one way or another. It so happened that on the same day she learned Porky wasn't renting, she'd stopped next door to the Shanty to get her hair shampooed by her childhood friend, Shaqueeda.

Shaqueeda was the owner of Shaqueeda's Curl, Wrap, and Daycare Center, and she also owned the apartment building next door to Porky.

Patience mentioned the man was a prophet and, more importantly, traveled about wearing expensive jewelry and clothes.

"Well if you say he's okay, then I'll take that as a good reference," Shaqueeda told her. "All of this reminds me that you and I need to get together when you ain't in such a hurry and my hands ain't deep in hair relaxer."

"Is anything wrong?" Patience asked.

"I'm not quite sure how much longer I want to rent to your church deacon, Mr. Campbell Whistle."

Shaqueeda didn't elaborate beyond that. Neither had the women questioned why anyone would want to live in a place void of clean streets and fresh air.

As far as Patience was concerned, despite Joy's constant reminders of finding a case, everything in her little world was fine.

Patience sat down at her kitchen table. Nodding approvingly as if it were the first time she'd been in there, she noticed everything in the kitchen lined up. From the bisque-colored refrigerator to the matching double oven, everything was spotless and just the way she and Joy always kept it. However, tidy kitchen or not, she soon began feeling a bit guilty that she'd wavered, not holding up her end. She truly wanted to help Joy in fulfilling their two-time prophecy. She also wanted to play feminine games, hoping to fix Prophet's unmarried status, especially since he wasn't a fella she had to chase or pretend she wasn't interested in. In the end, she'd concluded that investigations couldn't give her compliments, kisses, or hugs.

And then, about a month later, just as he'd started becoming her full-time job and distraction, he disappeared again, that time for almost three weeks. He never said good-bye or how long he'd be gone.

She thought she'd embarrassed or angered him. If she had, it was purely accidental, so he didn't need to avoid her. She waited a few days and visited his apartment. The key he'd given her in case of emergency didn't work. She'd never had a reason to use it before, so she wasn't certain it ever had.

She immediately sought out Shaqueeda. She learned he paid his rent in advance. "Chile, I minds my own business when cash tells me to," Shaqueeda told her. "But if you got a minute I still need to chat about that Deacon Whistle. You know as much as I still love Mister Almighty Dollar Bill, I still have to go with my gut about some things."

Patience once more begged off. She didn't want to engage in idle gossip while seeking the Lord for a helpmate. Shaqueeda's hair salon was a one-story wooden gossip mill. For more than twenty years, lies and half-truths, aided and disguised by shampoo, cheap hair relaxer, and conditioner, thrived. Patience later marveled her old friend told that lie about minding her own business, especially knowing she knew better. Yet Shaqueeda said it without lightning striking her or turning into a pillar of salt.

Later, after giving her relationship with Prophet Jevity more thought while trying to save face, sanity, and find forgiveness, she decided perhaps she'd read more into their friendship than she should have. She also needed to apologize to Joy. It was time she stepped up and took her share of the burden to find cases to solve.

Nearly falling off the edge of the chair was enough to break the self-inflicted truth spell. Patience bolted upright, just in time to keep her head, the headphones, and her skinny bottom from embracing the kitchen floor.

"Jesus!" That was her foundation word. Jesus was her rock. Her Jesus was supposed to be enough.

From somewhere in the house Felony raced inside the kitchen. The dog took one look at Patience and, with a confused look, the dog fled as though he'd never seen her before and was afraid.

She couldn't blame him. Now standing in the middle of the kitchen, surveying her Bible and headphones lying one atop of the other upon the table, she didn't know herself.

In truth, she'd bounced between self-rebuke and feeble attempts at self-analysis quite often these days. She really hadn't decided why she wanted Prophet's friendship so bad.

Was it because she believed she'd have more access to God's mind? If that were true, then she'd truly lost hers. Deep down, she knew the truth. She'd set aside the notion of being set aside for God for a man she hardly knew. And worse, because he was bound to show up again with flowers and an excuse, and she'd accept them as though it were for the first time.

Just as Joy entered Sister Betty's yard she ran into First Lady Deborah. The first lady was dressed in one of her usual garbs of expensive designer wear from her favorite clothing magazine. It was an online magazine favored by most women in the megachurches, called *Be a First Lady for More Than a Second*.

She looked like the old Southern saying for gorgeous: new money. She held her head high, nearly strutting, wearing a below-the-knee champagne pink and white two-piece dress and jacket, matching shoes, and her favorite I'm-a-first-lady wide-brimmed hat with mesh netting covering her face.

She'd already started down the steps from the patio, as though she knew Joy was coming over.

With both hands still clutching the punchbowl, Joy could only lean over and offer a quick peck on her First Lady's cheek. She moved fast. Avoiding getting hit in the eye from a hat's brim required experience, and being a wide brim-wearing woman, she knew the moves. At the same time, she was more than a little surprised, not having ever seen the first lady in the neighborhood except to visit her and Patience.

Immediately after sharing the holy kiss on the cheeks, the two women then offered the required *Praise the Lord* verbal greeting. They'd barely gotten into the reasons for their visits to Sister Betty's home when Sister Betty came outside.

"Y'all come on inside," Sister Betty told them. "Nosy, unsaved folks will be peeping through windows, trying to figure out why y'all standing here kissing cheeks and trying to hug."

They followed Sister Betty back inside. Of course, Joy under different circumstances would've had many questions to put to Sister Betty. However, once she sat down inside the living room there remained but one.

"So what's going on here?"

And that's when Reign entered the room from Sister Betty's kitchen. She was wearing the same WPAK blue blazer, gray pants, and blouse she'd worn earlier, when she'd given the news, supposedly from a location in Greenville.

Joy almost leaped off the sofa. "Reign's here too? It ain't nobody's birthday that I know of; are y'all having a prayer meeting or something?"

"No, it's not anyone's birthday." First Lady Deborah embedded her answer in a nervous chuckle that she certainly knew Joy saw through.

"Well then, somebody better tell me something! And y'all better tell it quick!" Joy then narrowed her eyes and, with precision, shot each a look like she was at target practice.

Yet neither Sister Betty nor the others even winced.

Instead, Sister Betty pulled her ever-ready canister of blessed oil from her apron pocket. She rose and began spraying her own holy ammunition about the living room, all the while praying for God's presence and the absence of evil. When she finished, no one not on their way to heaven could've survived.

"I'm sorry, Sister, err I mean Missionary Joy. I didn't know you were coming over, and I certainly didn't mean to surprise you like that." Reign's apology did little to nothing to take away the look of impending anger on Joy's face.

Ignoring whatever was going on between Reign and Joy, Sister Betty glanced at her wall clock. Suddenly she raced out of and then returned to the living room. Her small hands carried a platter of cookies and a pitcher of Kool-Aid, dropping them onto the coffee table with a thud.

Flinging napkins like they were Frisbees at her guests, and pointing to the platter and the pitcher, she announced with finality, "I've got some errands to run in a short while, so why don't we just get right down to it."

"Get down to what?" Joy directed her question directly to First Lady Deborah as well as Reign, who now sat at her side.

The First Lady simply nodded toward Sister Betty, giving the woman her due respect, since they were her guests, before reclining further into her chair.

Sister Betty caught the hint. She smiled, a gesture meant as a thank you to First Lady Deborah. Then she clucked her false teeth, ensuring they were a snug fit, before she cut straight to the heart of Joy's concern with her discernment scalpel.

"So how are things with Patience?"

"Excuse me?" Joy had just placed a cookie in her mouth. Now cookie crumbs had begun forming a blanket on Joy's lower lips. She hadn't expected that type of question from Sister Betty at all.

"She's speaking about how we see Patience up and about around town with a man." Sister Betty leaned forward and said conspiratorially, "I've known y'all for a couple of years, and I ain't never seen Patience so happy in the presence of a fella other than your godson Percy."

First Lady Deborah chimed in. "Don't fret, Missionary Joy. There are no surprises with God. However, there are many surprises for us. I imagine you must be very shocked to see the deep changes in your cousin's life. Whether you know it or not, I know it's coming from Prophet Long Jevity's involvement. I might add that I, too, know of Prophet Long Jevity."

Joy could only mumble a reply. The cookie crumbs had finally tumbled back inside her mouth and given her lockjaw.

Reign immediately added her observation. "I know my socks almost blew off when I first started noticing, since he's been coming around, the change in Patience."

"Reign honey, please. I'm not finished."

First Lady Deborah turned again to face Joy. "Setting aside our suspicions that Patience may have become enamored with the Prophet Long Jevity, we have other fish to fry. With the reverend getting sicker by the day, there's been big problems at our church, and they're about to become bigger. Making matters worse is that it looks like Patience may be caught up in it, hopefully unknowingly."

Joy felt her blood pressure rising. She felt as though she'd stepped into a television reality show. Her eyes scanned the room looking for hidden cameras. "Do you know the Prophet because he used to be a student of the reverend? Why would Patience be caught up in anything?" Their only replies were a barrage of hems and haws with blank stares.

Finally, First Lady Deborah spoke. "Why don't you just finish saying what's on your mind, and then I'll speak."

It was then that Joy came to realize that every angst she'd felt all along was beyond real. For the next twenty minutes or so, she began informing First Lady Deborah, Reign, and Sister Betty about how she'd begun noticing a change in his visiting patterns. She'd also realized Patience had taken a particular interest in holding long chats with Prophet Long Jevity, but he seemed more interested in the goings on of their church.

"I should've known better; Patience had begun dressing and acting different. I knew she'd lost her mind when she came home one day wearing honey-brown-colored contact lenses. Her eyes reminded me of baby poop. And then, she got rid of those old thick binoculars for some store-bought reading ones."

For the first time, Reign spoke up, interrupting with a laugh. "I saw her several weeks ago wearing them lenses and some long fabulous eyelashes. She was looking hot!"

"Reign," First Lady Deborah scolded, "why don't you just report the news like you gets paid to do and save the commentary on folks' hotness."

Catching her mother's not-too-subtle hint to shut up, Reign dialed it back. "I'm sorry, Missionary Joy. I didn't mean any harm."

Joy acted as though the remarks hadn't happened. "I'm telling y'all it got downright scary. We supposed to be visiting the sick and doing God's business and other stuff I can't mention, but Patience was looking like she needed more help than ever. We were some poor saleswomen for the Lord."

Joy then went on to clear up any unspoken suggestion that she'd not tried to rescue Patience from her demons.

"So you're saying that there was no reasoning with her?" Sister Betty asked sadly.

"Sister Betty, I did try. I tried using all the common sense and pretty words I could. Other than me finally commenting one time when I said, 'Patience, you need to sue your skinny legs for nonsupport,' I never offered another word of criticism."

Reign got up and went to Joy. Although she and Percy were only engaged, she'd known Joy and Patience practically her entire life. The women were her extended family.

Setting caution aside, she spoke up. "Listen, Missionary Joy, there's a lot you don't know, and once you find out, we're depending on you to keep a level head."

"How can you expect me to do that when y'all told me that my precious cousin Patience in all her stupidity might be

headed in a wrong direction? I'm telling you, do what you
wanna with whomever or whatever trash you trying to sweep
up, but if I find out that man is on the down and dirty and
leading my dumb cousin astray, when I get my hands on that
Long Jevity, I'm shortening his life!"

Suddenly Reign looked about the room for more direction from either her mother or Sister Betty. Her mother said
nothing, her hands folded in her lap. Sister Betty kept pointing to the clock on the wall.

"Missionary Joy, it's not that clear cut. If you say anything
about what we discuss here, then we may never be able to
help Miss Patience if she gets too involved with this man. We
need his mind steadfast on investigating what's going on at
church."

"Now what are you taking about? Reign, why would he
be investigating something? He's the one who told me and
Patience that God said we should investigate! Lord, Jesus, I'm
getting a headache from all this."

Before Reign could continue, First Lady Deborah finally
spoke up. She began unfolding her hands as well as a revelation.

"Listen, Joy, all I'm asking is that you remember the
prophecy from your installation service about seeking a higher
power and such. You decide what you wanna do. However, do
you really think going to a higher power like President Barack
Obama with some mess that may be in y'all's closet is gonna
allow him to help you?"

Reminding Joy of the prophecy that'd set things in motion was a touchdown for the first lady. All in the room saw
Joy's body suddenly relax.

With all of Joy's concerns now placed out in the open,
First Lady Deborah spoke up again. "Joy, I am not going to
beat around the bush. You need to know what's going on
with our church and how it may affect Patience."

I think I'd better add more prayer to what Sister Betty's already prayed. Joy opened her mouth to speak. She hadn't gotten the first words out when Felony's anxious barking came through the window.

The women raced over to the side window to look out, and a collective hush spread. They were shocked into silence.

It was Deacon Campbell Whistle. He stood on Joy's doorstep with his hand stretched out from his short arm, obviously ringing the doorbell. He also had what looked like a large envelope under his other arm.

Joy stepped away from the others. "I don't know how long that demon's been standing on my doorstep, but I'm about to do an exorcism right now." She'd not let go of the punchbowl since she'd arrived, but she was about to.

She'd barely opened Sister Betty's door to confront the Deacon when she heard a whispered chorus: "Don't leave!"

Reign quickly leaned over Joy, closing the door before leading her back inside the living room where the others now sat. Gently pushing Joy back onto the sofa, she said, "Missionary Joy. With everything that's going on I'd wanted to wait until Percy returned before I went any further in discussing this without him."

"What's Lil P got to do with this?"

Reign folded her arms. She began marching back and forth in front of Joy, stopping only to gather her thoughts.

"I can't wait for Percy. I must ask you something now. How often do you and Missionary Patience get together with Deacon Whistle? I mean, despite the fact that you obviously don't like him. What happens when the three of you get together?"

"What do you mean, get together? If I wasn't looking to go to heaven, you know I'd put in some full-time work just hating that man." They'd moved away from dissing Prophet Long Jevity's attention to Patience. Joy welcomed that.

"What about Patience? She did work with him for quite some time on the finance committee before she became vice president of the missionary board."

First Lady Deborah didn't come right out and accuse Patience, but she might as well have. In Joy's mind, the question she'd just asked revealed why she wanted Joy to keep quiet.

"Neither me nor Patience like reptiles. We ain't got nothing to do with that dinosaur T.rex–looking, barking snake."

"A barking snake?" Although Reign was a grown woman, the impatient look that appeared upon her mother's face was like a hand over Reign's mouth. She quickly withdrew any further questions.

No one noticed Sister Betty had gotten up again until she announced, after peeping through her window, "He's done turned around and already walking down the block. I wonder if he took the bus here, because I didn't see him walking to no car nearby."

She returned to where she'd sat and added, "I guess Sister Patience didn't want to be bothered, because ain't no way the rest of the neighborhood heard Felony and she didn't."

"I've had enough." Joy nearly pushed Reign's small body aside like a piece of lint as she rose. "I'm heading home unless y'all stop dilly dallying and tell me what the hell is going on!"

As that little bit of profanity left Joy's lips, decorum and church niceties went with it.

The revelation started off slowly, with First Lady Deborah telling Joy what she knew and when she knew it.

She revealed that some months ago, when her husband's health had declined to the point where she had to become his chief caretaker, she'd left a lot of church business unattended. "But then, before Sister Boodrow had that heart attack," First Lady Deborah said, "she'd begun coming to me for counseling. She had a lot of problems, and most of them carnal in nature."

Joy didn't respond to that revelation. Neither did the other women, who thought Sister Boodrow a common floozy, anyway.

Much of what First Lady Deborah revealed had to do with discovering from Sister Boodrow that funds apparently were embezzled from the church.

"She wouldn't tell me who'd done it, but she kept insisting that I have the financial records secretly audited. I didn't believe her at first, but it kept nagging at my spirit to do so, and I did."

First Lady Deborah told Joy what she'd discovered and how hard it'd been keeping it hidden from her husband. She believed Deacon Campbell Whistle had stolen from the church.

She'd soon gone to the authorities and she insisted they place Percy on the case. She made them promise to keep it undercover as long as possible.

"Why didn't y'all just have that mangy deacon arrested?" Joy thought it was cut-and-dry. The late and lying Sister Boodrow hadn't named the still-living and lying Deacon Whistle, but the funds were missing. In her mind, it all added up and pointed directly at him. She didn't see why they had a problem with putting the cuffs on him.

"It's a matter of proof," Reign offered. "Mama visited Sister Boodrow just before she died. She was so out of it from the pain and anesthesia, confessing so much, Mama couldn't be sure what or who she'd accused."

Putting aside her prejudice towards Deacon Whistle, and still not telling the others about finding him and Sister Boodrow in the reverend's private office, Joy allowed the first lady to continue her story. Seated in Sister Betty's living room sandwiched between Reign and First Lady Deborah, Joy couldn't manage to suck her teeth during the entire revelation.

Most of the information came from First Lady Deborah. She told Joy that Long Jevity, sometimes called Prophet, had indeed once studied under Rev. Stepson when her husband was working as a professor and a superior court judge. At that time it'd been in Columbia, South Carolina.

When recently contacted, Prophet had come out of an early retirement for two reasons. The first reason was that the reverend, as a professor back then, had never given him an ounce of slack. Judge Stepson pushed Long Jevity almost to the brink of tears every time he'd stepped into his classroom.

The second reason was that he needed to find a way to thank and repay the judge. It'd become obvious the judge had seen something in him and had made it his mission to shape and hone his skills so that he'd become the best law enforcement had. And he'd done so.

It was even more ironic that years later, Long Jevity had also gone on to instruct Percy, when Percy was a student at Columbia Law School in New York.

The women had hoped Joy would find comfort in knowing that at least First Lady Deborah had gone to the feds when she'd finally suspected Whistle of possibly embezzling church funds. If it wasn't him, then she needed to know who—and she needed to know quickly. She'd done what was necessary, although behind her sick husband's back.

Rev. Stepson's reputation went far and wide. Over the years, his position as a former, formidable superior court judge garnered respect from several Supreme Court judges. Notwithstanding, he was also a longtime community activist, and Mount Kneel Down's philanthropic reputation reached beyond Pelzer. Those reasons were a part of what'd caused the feds to keep the investigation tighter than normal, working closely with the local authorities as well.

However, the first lady still hadn't involved Patience. She doubted Patience would know about any scam. Until she learned different, First Lady Deborah kept Patience out of the official investigation. If Patience were guilty, Prophet would find out using his own methods.

Halfway through listening, finally able to find her voice, Joy wouldn't let Sister Betty off the hook either. She asked her about her part in bringing Long Jevity into her and Patience's lives. "You said God sent you that message through your knee-phone."

Joy watched Sister Betty respond. To her credit, she thought Sister Betty seemed truly puzzled. She listened as Sister Betty explained that she hadn't known about everything at first. She found out later on the same day she'd prayed with First Lady Deborah, and then later told them about Prophet Monee Coffers' commercial taping; Prophet Jevity was more with the law, and less with the Lord. "I don't think the way he's acting is the way a man of God should."

Slowly it sunk into Joy's mind that her church's reputation was at risk. If true about the deacon, it hadn't helped when the First Lady added detailed information about Prophet Long Jevity. The whole thing made Joy feel betrayed, a total fool.

"And so now that Prophet Long Jevity is involved, as a retired federal agent, I believe we can rest somewhat better," the first lady said, "and despite his obvious attraction to Patience, of course. I'm still going to straighten that out before it goes any further. I can't tell you any more than that right now."

"Hold up!" Joy snapped. "That man offering heavenly advice, prophesying, and eating up my food is more than just some regular law enforcement? He's a federal agent?"

"He's retired," said Sister Betty, and added, "and to my way of thinking, this is a part of God's plan to straighten him out. I know a Jonas runner when I see one. That man's been running from his gifts!"

First Lady Deborah said nothing. She smiled at Sister Betty

instead. She appreciated and believed God had given her, and Sister Betty, the same revelation regarding Prophet.

She also knew Sister Betty's urgent errand had more to do with her need to meditate with the Lord than her leaving her home. It was all right with her. She often felt the need to do the same.

Before it was over, Joy also learned the reasons for Prophet's sudden disappearances. They'd had more to do with the church investigation than avoiding her and Patience. First Lady Deborah also put more emphasis, again, on the need for a thorough investigation. Although he was their chief suspect, they needed more proof against Deacon Whistle. Perhaps there'd been something in his past that'd make him go after their church.

"I'm truly glad you did come by Sister Betty's, Joy." First Lady Deborah laid a hand on Joy's shoulders. "We haven't announced it yet, and I can't until I have a final meeting with the church board."

"What now?"

"I've got to take the reverend away to a rehab center. I'm not certain how long it will take us to get settled." She stopped and looked up. "I yet believe that God will turn his health around."

"You mean that y'all won't be in church either? I don't care what you discuss with the board; I want to know now who's going to lead the church?" Joy began feeling like God had set her up. How much change was she supposed to endure?

By the time the information bomb had fully exploded and its implications felt, it'd shaken every fiber in her body. Joy had become speechless, and now sat holding her wig in her hand.

All she'd wanted was to drop off the punchbowl she'd borrowed, and to snoop for the Lord like He'd promised.

Now she wouldn't know who or what to trust. Was her church family and the prophecy real or a hoax?

By the time Joy was ready to leave, her spirit and her heart were broken. And they weren't the only things. Now she'd have to break her word to Patience to never hide anything from her again.

Chapter 9

Warm sun rays poured through Joy's bedroom window, their warmth kissing her face this morning as if to apologize for the past two days of bad weather and karma that had turned her prayer life upside down and made her feel as though she were life's punching bag. Despite the sun's warmth, she still awoke thinking, *Lord, thank You for letting me hold that punchbowl in my lap. It was the only thing that kept my jaw from hitting Sister Betty's living room floor.*

There had been one consolation. She'd learned after she'd gone next door that Patience had fallen asleep with her headphones blasting in her ears. Patience never heard Felony barking, which is why she hadn't seen nor heard Deacon Whistle at the door.

Since then, over the past two days all Joy had wanted was to just take a walk alone, work in her garden alone, or visit the sick and the shut-in, alone. Yet a steady downpour of rain had flooded most of Pelzer as well as kept her inside with Patience, where she'd kept her chatter to a minimum. "Just trying to stay one step ahead of the Devil by less talk and more prayer," she'd told Patience.

Barefooted, she walked over to her dresser, looking into

the mirror and frowning at her reflection. No longer able to stand what she saw, she returned to sit on the edge of her bed, allowing it to take her full body weight and burden.

Joy looked toward her bedroom wall. Her eyes fell upon the picture taken several months ago when they'd received their missionary licenses. She and Patience, smiling as though they'd captured the heart of the world and their God, dressed royally in their red.

She quickly turned away. "How could something so beautiful turn so ugly?" she murmured.

She knew too much now, and it'd become difficult to see her and Patience as the same people she knew two days ago.

Even as she rose to gather her clothes to wear, she couldn't push aside what she'd learned. Discovering FBI Agent Prophet Long Jevity secretly worked for the church knocked her off her sanctified feet. If guilt were money, she would be carrying a burden now that made her a millionaire.

Apparently, Federal Agent Long Jevity, alias Prophet Long Jevity, was not only a man she'd mistrusted. And he wasn't just a reprobate who'd ignited Patience's carnal urging. He was also a retired law professor reprobate. He was the worst kind of reprobate, an educated one.

Even then, putting everything she'd learned aside, he still failed them by his unprofessionalism. He was supposed to make certain Patience wasn't involved. *Why ain't he pushing Patience away instead of making her think she's so sexy he can't help himself? How can he push and pull at the same time? He can't be that much of a lawman if he's making a mess of finding the real culprit! Why in the world did I promise Reign I wouldn't discuss it with Patience or Lil P?*

Joy didn't care for how they'd responded when she finally asked angrily, "Can I at least discuss it with the Lord?"

"Of course you can pray about it," the first lady had said. "We've already done that. We've also decided on how to handle Prophet. We truly don't believe Sister Patience had a hand in this mess, and you can rest assured we won't let him get any closer to Patience and break her heart."

Joy had clasped her hands together and begun praying. "Lord, I know You got the *real* handle on this mess but if You need me to do something in the natural please send me a sign—a real clear one, please."

Joy crept down the hallway and peeped inside Patience's bedroom. It was almost seven-thirty. Sunbeams cascaded through her window, making her seem almost angelic as she slept with a wide smile upon her face.

"Thank goodness for blissful ignorance," Joy murmured as she closed the bedroom door behind her. She couldn't depend on Patience being naïve for too long with them sharing the same space. So she hurriedly dressed to leave and fed Felony so she wouldn't have to lie or make up a plan on the spot if Patience woke.

Despite the bad weather over the past two days, Joy didn't have a lot of errands to run. However, she managed to stretch the time by window-shopping and idle chit-chat with some folks she hadn't spoken with in ages.

Looking at her watch, Joy noticed it was almost noon. She had one last stop to make before returning home.

She'd just turned into the parking lot of a local Costco wholesale store when of all the people she expected to see, there stood Deacon Whistle.

While most shoppers used the provided boxes from the wholesale outlet, he hadn't. Instead, Deacon Whistle, with a yellow baseball cap covering his dome, dressed in a two-piece purple jogging suit and a yellow T-shirt, had brought cloth tote bags. She imagined he wanted to look as though he cared about the planet. Instead, he looked like a purple Barney the Dinosaur with those tote bags dangling from his short arms.

As often as she'd shopped there for Felony's doggie treats to add to his favorite popcorn, and other bulk items, she'd never run into him before. He'd already given her the creeps showing up uninvited the other day. If she didn't know better, she'd have thought he was following her.

Before she could put the car in gear and leave, he was standing next to her sideview mirror. After quickly stifling a scream she looked around. Others had also started arriving, so as much as she'd wanted to she couldn't run him over and get away with it.

"Give Him praise, Missionary Joy!" Deacon Whistle greeted her while at the same time raising his T. rex arm to doff the baseball cap he'd worn. "What a surprise seeing you here. I came by the other day to see how things were going with your tithes and outreach ministry, but no one answered the door."

Joy looked at him as though he were a brand-new fool. *I know this demon didn't just open his lying mouth and speak to me.*

"Oh, I'm sorry about that. I was out, and Patience must've known it was you at the door and didn't answer it."

She sucked her teeth, narrowing her eyes as they swept him up and down, all the while massaging her steering wheel cover as he glared at her. She then began fidgeting in her seat, looking over to the passenger side as though seeking a weapon. With the car's club, a metal anti-theft device lying out of reach, all she could do was think, *Lord, thank You for salvation. Heavenly Father, please don't let me find something else and kill this man in front of witnesses!*

Gritting her teeth, she added, "As to your first question, I'm doing just fine."

He rambled on as though she hadn't insulted his intelligence.

Joy answered with one or two words before he finally turned and walked away.

Once inside the store, she was surprised to meet him again while standing on the checkout line. *My goodness, one of the reasons I hadn't mentioned to Patience he'd stopped by was because I didn't wanna even say his name.* Besides, she'd already acted as nice-nasty as she could back in the parking lot when she hadn't verbally rained hell and damnation upon him. It appeared he was gearing up to say more. *Is there nothing to stop him from parting his lying lips other than a brick in the mouth?*

"I'd also meant to ask when we were outside if you'd heard about our pastor and his most recent heart attack. Ain't it sad to know that the Lord could just swoop in and take our beloved Rev. Stepson out of that wheelchair at any minute?"

Joy almost missed his question as her eyes for the past few seconds were fixed upon the huge plastic bag of collards. Somehow, he'd managed to hold the giant clear plastic bag close to his chest with those short arms. Despite him looking ridiculous, she'd never known a white man, single or not, to eat as much soul food as he. The cooks at Mount Kneel Down jokingly teased that they had a special NAACP card for wannabes such as he.

"I don't worry about if it's sad or not," Joy finally replied, pushing her shopping cart back and forth close enough to run over his feet. "If you live right, then you shouldn't fear death."

She stopped, looked around to make certain others wouldn't doubt her pastor's godly relationship before she added a bit louder, "Our beloved Rev. Crazy Lock Stepson gonna give you devils hell before he leaves for heaven."

"Excuse me?" Deacon Whistle's thin lips almost disappeared as he began snarling. "What do you mean by *you devils?*"

"Did I say *you?*" Joy replied, grinning. "I hadn't meant to say that so loud."

As the two stood together on the checkout line, she watched him hand over his Platinum American Express credit card and the church-issued tax-exempt form to the cashier. *Why would he need a tax-exempt form?* she wondered. *He ain't shopping for the church.*

She placed her weight upon the handlebar of her cart. She could feel annoyance creeping into her spirit, becoming angry at his obvious abuse of authority. He lived alone in Shaqueeda's apartment building; he didn't need that form. She certainly didn't have one for her missionary work when she shopped, buying necessities for some of the elderly church members, so why should he?

Joy looked down at the sales flyer in her hand because if she kept getting angry, her prayer credits from fasting would dwindle quickly.

Yet she couldn't help recalling how, out of the blue, more than a year ago, one cold March evening at one of the meetings, he testified that God had visited his spirit. He'd told the members how God wanted him to go to Africa. He'd sow good seed using a financial gift in that barren land on Mount Kneel Down's behalf. His financial hoeing in Africa's Eden hadn't taken but a couple of months before he'd returned. Not one word said on whether he'd planted a good or a bad seed. It hadn't mattered. They still hadn't seen a financial harvest.

It'd been shortly after his return to Pelzer that the church board elected him chairman of the finance committee. The board had welded its veto power and done so, despite Rev. Stepson's unexplained concerns.

Whatever apprehension the reverend had voiced soon gave way, once he'd begun feeling poorly. Since it wasn't an illness that'd initially kept him from preaching and attending most services, no one really paid attention to Deacon Whistle's financial skills. Most thought the reverend, the church board, or at least the First Lady still had a hand on the money wheel.

"Excuse me, Miss. Are you gonna shop with your eyes or put your items on the conveyor belt?"

Joy was so deep in thought she hadn't realized Deacon Whistle had paid for his things and moved on. She didn't give the cashier a nasty reply; instead, she exhaled.

Chapter 10

By midmorning the day after the First Lady's revelation shattered Joy's simple errand of returning a punch bowl to Sister Betty, she and Patience lay sprawled around their living room. They were both worn out from disbelief although, for the most part, for different reasons.

"God is not the author of confusion," Patience said after thumbing through one of her Bibles lying nearby. "And if this ain't a confusing time, then I don't know when one is."

"Lord, please forgive my unbelief." Joy wrung her hands. It didn't make sense to rehash where they were in their lives at that moment, but she did.

"I have to admit, I'm struggling with my faith and with the revelation; my patience has grown thin. If someone had come to me after they'd been laid off, talking about how God told them they would solve crimes using a couple of missionary licenses, with at least twenty years of crime solving from sofa and television university, with or without President Barack's help, I'd have wrestled them to the ground and strapped them into a straitjacket."

"We're a sad pair . . ." Patience couldn't go on. Her words became lost.

"Yeah, but if we get to meet the president of these here United States, we'll be a happy pair!"

"Amen. Remind the Devil where we stand!" Although Patience had not voiced her concerns about moments of lacking faith as Joy had just done, it didn't mean she didn't have them. After all she'd kept things hidden from someone who was not only her loving cousin but her best friend. Moreover, she'd done it for a man she barely knew—worse, she really couldn't explain it.

Patience's strong words came from a weak voice as she rose and stood by the living room window. "I want us to be real crime solvers for the Lord and the public. I want us to be the ones the cops come running to when they can't find the bad guys."

"Say that!" Joy snapped.

Patience was on a roll so she continued, "And the ones to put out Hell's fire when we do it. I want the Secret Service to respect us!"

Joy was just about to add another amen, but had to put it on hold.

"Whoa, wait a minute Patience. We don't want the Secret Service anywhere near us."

Joy's pleading went unanswered because Patience's commonsense had fled the room.

Suddenly, Patience stood quickly. Standing before a red velvet-backed picture of Jesus, she raised her hands, that time adding not in defeat, but in prayer, "Lord God, You said You'd give us the desires of our hearts. You said all we need to do is to ask."

Joy, watching Patience praying before the picture of Jesus, quickly clasped her hands in prayer, too. She began praying, thinking her cousin might have just regained her sanity, tapping into something spiritual she hadn't felt yet.

Chiming in, Joy added, "After all, Patience dealt in twos. And Lord," Joy pleaded, "please don't forget You said if there were two or more gathered together You would be in the middle. Patience and me is as about as together as we can be."

Snatching back the prayer lead from Joy, Patience began again, praying softer that time. "Heavenly Father, we don't wanna leave no stones unturned. While we wait on President Barack, we want to be in Thy will. Can You, Father, please just give us another sign?

"We don't completely believe Prophet Jevity. We're starting to waver about First Lady Deborah. I'm starting to question that You're even speaking through Sister Betty's bad knees. We're suddenly feeling a bit concerned that we might take steps out of order."

Patience slowly opened one eye, peeping at Joy, who still had both eyes shut. So Patience continued praying. "Can we truly be Your Christian crime solvers even though we only got missionary licenses? We need a strong right-now sign, Heavenly Father."

Encouraged by Patience's prayer, Joy finally opened her eyes, nodding in agreement. "Please Father, like Patience says, just a sign. We'll accept the next sign, Father. We won't question it, no matter what shape it comes in or how crazy it is. We'll know that it confirms Your will."

Joy and Patience would've continued with their badgering of heaven's throne, but a loud knocking at their door put an end to it.

The knocking began sounding like ricocheting bullets. Except for an errant salesperson and Sister Betty, they rarely had company, and with as crazy as things were at that moment, they didn't want to see Prophet Long Jevity so soon. Nevertheless, someone was knocking like they'd lost their mind.

Despite what they'd just prayed and asked God for, they'd never received an answer that quick before. They then figured no one or nothing with good news would pound on a door like that.

Joy and Patience, expecting the worst, cautiously crept across the carpet, choosing to look out the front window instead of opening the door. They saw the shadow of a man, which meant the worst probably stood on the front porch.

Again, forgetting they'd just prayed, asking God for a sign, each looked about the room for a weapon. Joy grabbed a fireplace poker. Patience settled for a flower vase. It was small but as scared as she was, it'd do the job.

Both now armed, Joy tapped Patience's bony shoulder. Nodding toward the window, Joy signaled that Patience should lead the way, and she'd have her back.

Feeling a bit emboldened by the vase she held, Patience tiptoed across the carpet. Joy held on tight to the poker, following close enough to appear like a hump on Patience's back.

They stood still for a moment. Each took a deep breath. Joy decided to take a few steps back, which allowed Patience enough space to peep through the side window.

Tiptoeing backward across the carpet, Patience, whispering as she set down the vase, said, "It's Lil P."

Joy rolled her eyes and gave a sigh of relief while loosening her grip on the poker.

Instead of opening the door, they laid their weapons aside.

Patience put her hands on her nonexistent hips and hissed. "He's got some nerve suddenly showing up like this. Reign mentioned he was supposed to be going away with Porky for the last few weeks. But he couldn't call anybody often?" She switched her hips with each word, thinking the moves added weight to her complaint. "You'd think he'd been more concerned about our well-being since we raised his sorry butt."

Never one to let a fake outrage go to waste, Joy did her usual: she sucked her teeth. She did it this time to make a snarky remark more effective. "Probably too busy pretending he didn't take his father fishing in some Washington lake. He ain't fooling nobody, ain't no fishing in Washington; everything just smells fishy there."

Patience quickly corrected Joy. "You mean, with the exception of our spiritual son and soon-to-be advisor, President Barack."

Remembering they hadn't yet opened the door, not wishing to give away their presence, Patience adjusted her glasses, put a finger to her lips and whispered, "What could he want now? I hope he is not coming by to tell us he's leaving Pelzer again on some case."

"How would I know what he wants to tell us?" Joy snapped, still careful not to speak loudly. "Whatever he wants, it can't be nothing good, or he would've called first to see if we were home."

That time it was Joy's turn to signal silence. She quickly put a finger to her mouth and then waved her hand across her throat, several times, signaling they cut off movement and chatter.

It was too late for precaution. Any other questions the women had didn't matter. When they looked towards the open window again, there Percy stood glaring through the open Venetian blinds, right at them.

"Y'all open the door, please!" Percy hissed through perfect ultra-white teeth. "I can see you two! Stop playing games."

Puzzled and still annoyed by Percy's sudden appearance, Joy took her time moving; yet she reached the front door ahead of Patience. She threw it open, narrowing her eyes, giving him the once over before saying anything. "Come on in, young man."

"That's right!" Patience stuck her head out from behind Joy, snapping, "Bring your narrow behind inside."

Chapter 11

Percy LaPierre, single, thirty-two years old, often mistaken for a male model or El DeBarge, owed everything he'd accomplished in his law enforcement career to two women. None of the adoration he received on the job and its gold plaques or other compensations compared with what he got from his second cousins and godmothers, Joy and Patience.

Percy was the only child of Joy and Patience's first cousin, Porky LaPierre. Since he had what Joy and Patience always wanted, a successful law enforcement career, they'd made certain he never forgot their youthful sacrifices, showing up at every award ceremony or news interview, exclaiming their Christian influence and choice of television shows.

From the moment he entered the Washington, DC, police department six years ago, his career took off. Solving cases seemed to come naturally to him. Within a short time, he'd become the go-to detective within the robbery and homicide division.

Joy and Patience had come to his rescue in his infancy, when his mother, Maurette, diagnosed with postpartum depression, walked away one afternoon. She left Percy, a three-month-old infant, alone with nothing but a bottle, which he could neither reach nor hold.

Although they were young, with much finagling and help from their church, the cousins stepped in. Joy and Patience had barely gotten into their mid-teens when they took over the complete care of little Percy. If they hadn't, child welfare would have. And when Porky lapsed into a nervous breakdown, the cousins put off dating and attending college altogether.

By that time, both sets of the infant's grandparents were deceased, and Grandmamma Truth's Alzheimer disease had long stolen her mind. Taking care of their infant second cousin became their life.

When the baby became six months old, Joy and Patience had their second cousin christened. They also became his godmothers and nicknamed him Lil P.

When he could barely walk or talk, the cousins, just graduating high school, brought Percy into their imaginary world of crime fighting. Often they'd sit Percy between them and watch their favorite detective series. The one they swooned over at that time was *Miami Vice*.

"Look at Little P," one cousin would point at him, giggling. "I don't believe Philip Michael Thomas, as handsome as he is now playing Detective Tubbs, was as cute as our baby when he was this age."

"Wouldn't it be something," Patience would often remark, "if our Little P one day became a handsome, fashion-model-type detective?"

She said it so much, it was as though she were prophesying—or spent too much time in the hot sun on *Fantasy Island*.

The years passed quickly, and by the time Percy turned eighteen, he'd graduated from high school with a 4.0 GPA. He had indeed become very handsome, almost pretty by some standards. Football came easy, and he received a full ride scholarship to nearby Clemson University. Under the watchful eye of his godmothers, who seemed to block about every female looking his way, he graduated with honors.

Yet the ambitious Percy wanted more. He received financial aid from his father, Porky, who by then had come to his senses. Percy also received several scholarship grants, and he went on to earn his master's in criminology from New York's Columbia University.

Joy and Patience had taught him well. With a killer smile, good manners, and focused ambitions, he learned the value of networking. No sooner had he a degree from Columbia, he was on the fast track. Unlike some who'd graduated along with him, Percy had made a few political connections along the way. In less than six months, he was in Washington, DC.

A year and a half after graduating from the police academy, instead of joining the DC Police Department, he joined the Department of Justice.

Although he'd not attended church as much as he had as a young man in Pelzer, by earthly and heavenly standards, he seemed highly favored. By the time he turned twenty-seven, his innate skills at crime solving made him the go-to guy when a case needed a little extra something. His undercover skills were never fully revealed to those wearing uniforms, and only the suits knew and appreciated his talents.

Of course, being easy on the eyes served him well, too. Percy's six feet three height, broad shoulders, slender waistline supporting a six-pack, and ultra-handsome cinnamon complexioned face stood out. From head to toe, those good looks and chiseled body told the world Mother Nature had been in a real good mood the day she sent him to earth.

However, two years ago, without explanation, he left the Justice Department. Percy returned to Pelzer and in no time he'd become a superstar detective.

Chapter 12

Other than a low humming sound coming from the wall air conditioner in Joy and Patience's living room, there was silence.

They looked him up and down, watching their Lil P as he finally made a move toward them. Of course, he wasn't little anymore and hadn't been for quite some time, but this was still their house.

Joy and Patience leaned against the wall, shuffling their feet, glaring and anxious. Each wanted to hug him and, at the same time, break his neck. It was how they'd felt each time he'd pull his disappearing act, making them worry.

Percy's muscular six-foot-three frame seemed to grow taller with each step as he moved slowly down their hall foyer. He stopped when he came face-to-face with Patience. "Who did you think was knocking on your door?"

Patience almost broke her glasses in half as she snapped. "Well, we certainly didn't expect you."

"Godmother Patience," Percy began, lifting the hand off the holster belt. He figured if he used both hands to try and plead his case, she'd weaken.

"Don't you *Godmother Patience* me. Just because Joy and I

live alone in a fancy neighborhood, where you think a phone
call is okay but you hardly ever come to visit—"

Patience didn't bother finishing the sentence. She looked
to Joy with a raised eyebrow, giving a signal that Joy should
get a piece of his butt while she had him wilting.

Joy said nothing; silently tag teaming Patience with a
raised eyebrow too, she stepped forward.

Wagging a chubby finger in his face, Joy let him have it. "I
guess it doesn't matter that we're more than just your second
cousins. We're also the godmothers who babysat, fed, and
changed nasty designer diapers on your pissy, raggedy, narrow
behind."

Stepping in front of Joy, Patience decided she'd better interrupt Joy before she took the rebuke train off the rails.
"That's right," Patience blurted. "Where we live don't mean
we can't be too careful about safety. But it sure wasn't no reason for you to stand in a flower bed spying—"

"I stood on the porch—"

"Whatever!" Ignoring his correction, Patience continued.
"You pounded on the door like someone had a gun to you.
You could've given us heart attacks."

Percy's cinnamon-colored complexion turned red, annoyed they hadn't accepted his apology. He decided to try
again.

"I know the two of you are a bit upset that you live alone.
I'm sorry I haven't been around to visit too often, especially
since you're my beloved godmothers and still probably upset
that you got those layoff notices a while back while I was
away."

"You just oughta be sorry," Joy snapped. "You and Patience could've still worked together even after they let her
go. She could've done a lot for you from right here inside this
house. Who knows what clues she could've come across that
you might've missed whenever she typed up those reports for
you!"

Ignoring her outburst and all its implications—especially the part where he wanted to ask who'd pay Patience's salary—he continued trying to explain his side.

"I don't know why y'all acting like you don't know after I came back I had a ton of paper work, then got a notice I'd soon have another case and I needed a break. So I helped around the Soul Food Shanty and then took Dad away on a fishing vacation. Reign already told me she'd spoken to you. Besides, Dad and I both needed to take a break from the Shanty. We've only been back a few days."

He suddenly held his chin with its two-day stubble in his hand. Percy cracked his knuckles then laid a finger against his nose and stared. It was now his turn to act indignant. "In fact, had you two gone by the Shanty to visit Dad like a family oughta, you'd known it was closed."

Joy responded in her usual way. She sucked her teeth, thinking, *I spent almost twenty years cleaning that pigsty of a police station, why would I wanna go to Porky's slop house if I don't hafta?*

Patience and Percy ignored Joy's annoying teeth-sucking habit again. Both did it for different reasons. Patience was used to it; Percy remembered, *Aw hell, she's about to go off.*

"Anyway," Percy's tone suddenly became more respectful, "Dad got hurt while we were fishing. He sprained his wrist trying to untangle a line. It's in a sling, which means he can't even put together a sandwich or cook. The Shanty's supposed to reopen soon, but I can't take more time off."

Percy stopped to catch his breath, waiting to see if he'd catch a hint of sympathy from his godmothers. So far, they looked disinterested. He needed to find a way to appeal to their sense of family, something he'd rarely ever seen when it came to his dad.

"It wasn't easy for me, trying to hold things down before we went fishing. It's a twenty-four-hour-a-day job just to keep one foot ahead of the department of health."

I've cracked cases easier than trying to break through their stub-

bornness. Percy smiled, hoping what he said next would whittle them down a peg. "I'm not supposed to say anything, so y'all keep this between us."

He wasn't certain, but he thought he saw their bodies relax a little, so he might as well go for it. "Hell, all I've done is work my behind off. Come on, Godmothers, I need your help with a small matter. I can't say exactly what it is at this very moment, but I'm gonna need y'all to trust me just a little longer, because I've got a lead in a big case I'm working on. You know how it is. You raised me watching *CSI* and all those other crime shows; you've worked with detectives before."

"Spill the rest of it." Patience demanded while suddenly thinking, *Did he just say he had a big case? That's what we're trying to get, and he's complaining about that old nasty restaurant and his crabby daddy.*

Patience folded her arms, tapping her foot as she continued. Her eyes narrowed like an X-ray machine looking right through him. "I know you inside and out. Stop with all the flimsy excuses for turning away in our hour of possible need. What's really wrong?"

"Yeah, what's the matter?" Joy had heard the same thing as Patience. She just needed to act as though she didn't care about his big case; although she figured it was the one she was supposed to keep quiet about concerning their church.

Patience decided she'd flip the script, suddenly playing a routine of good cop versus Joy's bad cop. "Aw, Joy, give him a break." Her voice took on the same soothing tone she'd used when he was a child, or when she wanted him to do something he didn't want to. She looked him straight in the eye while she talked about him—to him.

"Pelzer ain't Washington or New York. We know he's spent long hours solving those big Capitol Hill, Big Apple crime cases before he came back home to Pelzer. I'm certain without me working with our Little P, inside homicide and robbery, typing reports, having his back, he's had a hard time getting readjusted. Lord knows Reign ain't no help. She stays gone as much as Lil P."

"Godmother Patience, please, Reign is a popular news reporter. She goes wherever the news—" One glance at Patience twitching her nose like a bunny let Percy know he needed to shut up and take it. "I'm sorry. Go on."

"Joy, like I was saying before I mentioned his little female weather reporter, Hurricane Reign, I've been holding his hand during just about every case he's worked, typing all hours of the day and night."

At that moment, they remembered his Washington, big city connections. They decided trying another tactic. Criticism took a back seat because Percy had connections that could become good for the two things they needed: President Barack's help and information about his big case. Their godson had just returned from vacation, so he wasn't going anywhere anytime soon. Whether he knew it or not, in their minds, their Lil P needed them. They'd think of another way to show disapproval later.

"By the way," Joy said, trying to follow Patience's lead yet keeping her voice edgy, "where is that sweet-and-sour-pork daddy of yours?"

Percy opened his mouth to answer but not fast enough.

A stuttering, whimpering sound rang out, like a bear with a lisp had gotten a paw caught in a steel trap. It couldn't have come at a worse time, barreling through the front door.

He looked deranged.

Chapter 13

"I'll kill them trifling, nasty dogs! Lowdown scallywags! Thieving-azz pig kissers!"

Joy, Patience, and Percy's heads popped up. They were too far down the foyer to have heard the front door when it'd first opened, but they recognized the intruder's voice.

Percy pounded his fists on a nearby wall. He began breathing hard, sputtering like air leaving a balloon. "Damn! I told him to wait in the car!"

Porky, with his fatty stomach wobbling side-to-side like Jell-O on steroids, sailed down the foyer. He had his lips twisted, still cussing, waving his one good hand about with his other hand held captive in a sling. "My place got hit last night! They tore it apart!"

His mouth quickly shifted into overdrive, making less sense every time it opened. "Did Percy tell ya?" The rubber from the flip-flops on his feet squealed to a halt. He began rocking side to side. "Somebody got me!" His dark brown face turned from ashy to shiny, and he looked like someone had polished his fat cheeks with Vaseline.

"How does this happen? I can't even go away to do a little fishing with my one and only son without somebody violating me." Pointing his good hand at Percy, his voice rose. "Everybody knows I'm in good with the police."

"He never listens!" Percy could hardly believe his bad luck. He'd told his father to wait in the car; although they were cousins, neither godmother especially liked Porky, though Patience did treat him better than most of the family members.

Percy had hoped to put them in a good mood before he asked a favor of them. But Porky hadn't stuck to the agreed plan, so Percy hastily jumped to plan two. He grinned like a Cheshire cat, hoping his 100-watt smile would charm his godmothers as it'd always done.

Percy turned to Patience and Joy, still smiling, hunching his shoulders, which meant he'd nothing more to add to what stood before them. "I've delivered Dad to you ladies so you can handle your family business."

"What family business?" Joy snapped. Percy had snatched away her rapidly prepared lecture with that remark, so she added, "All I see is him standing there looking like he's been to a Build a Fool factory and wearing a stupid look."

Plan two wasn't working like he thought it would, so Percy made up plan three on the spot. His finger shot out, pointing toward his father, who just stood there looking like he'd rather be somewhere else, which he would. "That's family business standing over there. He's your cousin."

Patience had had enough. Since keeping quiet was no longer an option, she met Percy's finger pointing with one of her own. "So what—that's your father."

Porky looked all around the room before finally asking, "What am I, invisible?"

He might as well have been invisible because they didn't bother to answer him.

"No matter whose father he is, Godmother, he's your problem now. I did my part earlier when I took him down to the precinct, filled out the report, and brought him back here like he insisted. Although, Lord knows why he'd wanna come here; it's not like you're close like most family or Christians would be."

What Percy said was true. Joy wasn't particularly fond of her only male first cousin, Porky. Twice, he'd gotten what she'd wanted—a child and, when their Grandmamma Truth passed away, he'd gotten the family Bible, too.

Time after time, she'd placed those angry and jealous feelings on the altar for God to fix. Time after time she'd snatch them back whenever she saw Porky.

Joy wanted to pluck Percy up by his collar and pin him against the wall for bringing his father to her house, willingly or not. She sucked her teeth again, cracked her knuckles instead of Porky's head, then silently prayed to keep her anger in check. She already knew she wouldn't do anything to mess up the investigation with her church.

All she needed was to get the information without babysitting his whale of a daddy. But how?

She was just about to give a half-hearted apology, but then Percy's cell phone rang. By the time she'd fixed her mouth to speak, he'd already taken the call.

Percy, knowing he'd get no privacy where he stood, made a move further down the foyer. When he thought he'd put enough distance between them, he spoke into the phone.

"When did the call come in? So why are they just telling me? You could've told me thirty minutes ago, before I made plane reservations!"

Percy began pacing, then turned around suddenly, retracing his steps back down the foyer. Eyes bulging, he barked into his cell phone. "You've got to be kidding me! They wrote letters to who—saying what? Tell him I'll holla at him later!"

Percy slammed the cover to his cell phone and, nodding toward Porky, now cowering in the corner covering his face with the sling, he announced, "I've got something to do. And when I get back we're gonna talk."

He then walked a little closer to Joy and Patience without trying to hide the threat. "And don't neither of you two so-called workers for the Lord even think about going near a FedEx office, a mailbox, or licking a stamp that even has a picture of the White House on it!"

Whatever Joy and Patience wanted to say, they knew better than to say it. They'd have to be two times past stupid not to know he'd found out about the letter to President Obama and the Secret Service.

Why he was mad at Porky, too, didn't matter. Their precious Lil P was upset with them, and that they didn't want. It could interfere with them finding out about the *big* case.

Satisfied they knew he'd meant business, Percy pivoted. He pointed directly at his father and his godmothers. "I'll check back on him later."

Porky turned his head side to side. One look at Joy's and Patience's angry faces, he saw nothing but trouble. He'd never heard of a sprained butt, yet it was a strong possibility that his could wind up in a sling, just like his wrist.

Porky began pleading. "Son, I've changed my mind. I don't wanna stay here. You can't just leave me. Somebody robbed me, son. Where are you going?"

Still fixated on getting into Percy's good graces, even if it meant putting up with Porky, Patience finally found her voice and gently shoved Porky to the side. She then smiled hard enough to get a face spasm. "Lil P, it sounds important, so you go on."

Peering from behind Patience, Porky hollered, "I'm your dad, Percy!"

Percy left, saying nothing, as Joy, Patience and Porky remained rooted.

Patience was the first to react. She didn't bother to double-check to see whether Percy had locked the front door on his way out. She had other things that needed her immediate attention.

Patience grabbed hold of Porky by his good elbow, dragging him toward the living room with him kicking and screaming.

"Porky, man up! Stop that twisting and whining," she ordered.

With Patience now pulling him like a sack of flour across the floor, whining and resisting was useless.

"You're hurting me, Patience."

Quickly turning towards Joy, who'd stood by watching the spectacle, shaking her head, he continued pleading. "Joy, make her quit it!"

Joy's eyes grew larger, and her jaw dropped as she watched, thinking, *Lord, have mercy. Patience pulling his big behind is just likes an ant pulling a truck, and now she's talking like she's got a badge. I'm proud of her.*

Patience's legs began to buckle. She stumbled slightly on her heels, her cheeks puffing in and out, gasping for air, while she fussed at the same time. "Man up, Porky. Stop being such a crybaby, and think. I'm trying to help you."

"You ain't helping; you doing nothing but hurting me."

"How am I hurting you when I've got you by your good arm, Porky? It's your other that's in a sling."

"My good arm's got sympathy pain. You just need to stop pulling on me."

Once inside the living room, Patience began feeling Porky's resistance weaken. He'd come to the point where she could manage him, so she released him and started in.

"Now back to your robbery." She folded her arms, pacing like a windup toy in front of Porky. "I'm sure if we put our heads together we can come up with something that will help solve this thing real fast, even if Lil P has to help." She stopped moving and quickly added, "That is, if he's not too busy with another case. Of course, any help he can offer will only make you look good, too."

Joy still refused to speak or interrupt. Instead, she began praying.

Lord, help Patience get that blabbermouth to blab. I know our Lil P saying he's got a big case is a sign from You, Lord; he's working on finding out if that skeezer Whistle embezzled money from our church. And he's worked in Washington, so I know he's probably friendly with President Barack. And Lord, if Lil P can make things right in case the president or the Secret Service got annoyed about the letter, it'd be appreciated. We were just trying to do Your will like the first lady prophesied.

Joy continued clasping her hands in prayer, asking God for help. Somehow, she'd also ended up blaming the Lord, too. She kept reminding God that they were where they were because they'd tried being obedient.

She also prayed to maintain some restraint, so she wouldn't just snatch Porky like Patience had done and punch him in the throat to get the information out of him.

Meanwhile, as Joy stewed and prayed, Patience probed.

"Porky, think hard, there's always some riffraff hanging around your neighborhood. I know most folks will turn a blind eye to crime, but somebody must've seen something, especially with all those nosy folks that frequent your dive—"

Patience quickly corrected what she'd said with a well-meaning fib. "I meant 'fine restaurant.' You'll just be a little inconvenienced until the police look over the film from your surveillance camera."

It took all the strength Porky had, which by that time was a quart low from all his struggling and whimpering. He finally snatched one fat wrist from Patience's unusually strong grip before replying, "Got no camera."

That's when Joy threw her hands up in surrender, slapping

away serenity like a pesky mosquito. "Heavenly Father, please tell me I heard wrong. Dear Lord, why my family so crazy? Why Lord? Why?"

"Of course you have a surveillance camera." Patience ignored Joy's outburst. She poured a glass of water for Porky, making certain she placed the glass upon a coaster to keep Joy from stroking should a water stain appear on the table.

Patience pursed her lips; this time it was she who sucked her teeth as a familiar warning for Joy to curb her remarks. Satisfied she'd made her point, she then turned her attention back to Porky.

"You're just too upset to remember what you have or don't have. I know about the camera, because I've seen it mounted over the door to your back storeroom. It's got wires and everything sticking out."

Porky gulped the water and wiped his wet hand on his grimy apron while stammering, "Ain't real—it's useless." Still frustrated, he then began waving about his good arm. His words became garbled again. "I only—the camera—to give place class, some pizazz. I wanted—"

Now it was Patience's turn. She reared back on her feet, placing her hands on her tiny hips. She looked to Joy, who responded with a *harrumph* and then looked away.

Patience couldn't get as mad as she'd wanted with Porky if Joy shunned her. So she turned away from Joy and began shaking her head, lowering it to keep from showing more disbelief, thinking, *Lord, if he'd spoken the King's English, he still would've sounded stupid.*

As far as Joy was concerned, she had seen and heard enough. She didn't think Porky had anything of value someone would want to steal from inside that pigsty posing as an eatery. Yet it was what it was, and it didn't matter whether she understood or believed it. One thing was for certain; she wasn't about to turn away a potential case that the Lord had obviously dropped in their laps along with this nut that'd fallen from her family tree.

"Okay, Porky," Joy remarked, crossing her fingers behind her back, praying for forgiveness. "I'm sorry you got robbed. I'm even sorrier for whoever was dumb enough to think you had something worth taking, including your signature recipe for pigeon pot pie and lukewarm pizza with ain't chovies. But right now, we've got to be about God's business."

"Joy!" Patience's interruption was abrupt. "If you're talking about visiting the hospital and shelters today, we have other missionaries on call to do that."

Patience knew they hadn't let another missionary lift a finger since they'd decided to fulfill their duties in earnest. But she couldn't let that little detail hinder things. She continued from where Joy left off.

"Porky is our only cousin here in Pelzer. We can't count our second cousin Little P, transplanted from Washington and New York. Besides, he's also our detective godson who's busy working on a big case." She'd emphasized the last part about Percy's police work, hoping Joy would catch her hint.

Patience summoned a little more false pity. "Porky's hurting, and you won't even extend a kindness in word or in deed. Right now, he's our business. I'm sure the Lord won't mind if we hold off on missionary work until later, when he's calmed down. And, I'm certain he's just as much concerned about Lil P's big case as he is about his place getting hit."

Joy had witnessed the faux-sexy performance Patience gave when Prophet Jevity dropped by. She'd never again place doubt on Patience's dubious capabilities.

Oscar worthy performance or not, it didn't matter. At that moment, Joy still wanted to put the match to Porky and light him up. She didn't have a book of matches, but she still had a fiery tongue.

"No kind word or deed?" Joy snapped. "Wasn't I kind

enough not to slap that ridiculous nasty cap off that bald dome and have it condemned? And if that wasn't a good deed for Pelzer, us, and the world, then I don't know what is!"

Porky's eyes pleaded with Joy. "I don't know how long you gonna hold it against me because of what Grandmamma Truth left in her will. I never asked her for that Bible, and you know it. I ain't a churchgoer and never have been, unless you counting Bedside Baptist where I can lay and pray."

"You old heathen, you didn't turn that Bible down either," Joy said sharply. She couldn't be around him without jealousy riding her. That jealousy would've cost her dearly if Jesus called her at that moment. She'd have gone to hell.

Porky ignored the obvious as he continued trying to get on Joy's good side, if he could ever find it. "I truly need something from you, and I'm appealing to your Christian side, which I don't see no evidence of today."

"What you want that I got?" Joy snarled. His truthful remark about her current non-Christian display stung even if it was true. "If it's what I think, then I done told you a hundred times, I ain't sharing Grandmamma Truth's recipes with you. You already shaming the family with that fake shanty home-cooking. So what else are you talking about?"

Porky took a deep breath. With as much courage as an old punk could muster on such short notice, he pushed his chest out and said loudly, "That Felony you got, Cousin Joy. I need one, too. I want folks to take me serious, fear me, like they do you."

No sooner had the word *Felony* left Porky's mouth than a sound like large marbles hitting the hall floor echoed, each loud tapping sound coming closer.

A wheezing sound followed the tapping, and as if he'd heard his cue to appear, Felony raced inside the living room. His four legs were tripping over each other, knocking over whatever was in their way as he lunged straight at Porky.

"No, Felony!" Because of her weight, Joy miscalculated

her moves when she leaped to catch her dog by its collar. The meat of her fat thighs slapped together, sounding like two leather straps held together by molasses. "Lord, please have mercy. Father God"—Joy's large hip hit the edge of the coffee table—"Jesus!" She landed on the carpet with her arms flapping like a fish out of water.

And then Patience decided she'd help. Her kerfuffle was no better. She jumped so fast to grab the dog, her glasses nipped the tip of her pointy nose.

"Dangnabit!" She added more words, none of which would ever pass for anything close to Christian talk.

None of that mattered, because Felony was in full attack mode. Only a mouthful of human flesh would calm him. Felony, with his untreatable Pet Attention Deficit Disorder, raced about the room. Wisps of gold-, brown-, and white-speckled fur befitting Felony's psycho mindset flew about the living room. Seconds later, pandemonium happened all over again. Felony knocked Porky down, and a taste-test followed. It was a mess, with Felony barking and nipping at Porky, and then sometimes Porky barking and nipping back.

Joy didn't move, allowing the display to play out while she laughed inside. She finally rose and came to Porky's rescue. "Felony, you heel. Let him go before you catch something."

No matter how hard Joy pulled at her dog, nothing worked. Each time Felony slipped from her grasp he went back to chomping on Porky.

Seconds later, Patience joined in again. Together they finally managed to pull the overweight Felony off Porky. However, not before Felony had nipped Porky's big toe along with a piece of Porky's ugly slippers.

Finally leashed, Joy led the still growling and resistant dog from the living room. "You know better, Felony. I ain't got money to take you to the vet if you've caught something from that mangy man."

"I'm suing," Porky called out as he tried to get his balance.

Again, Patience's blocking skills went into action because Porky obviously didn't feel chewed up enough. She kept jumping side to side, blocking Porky while he was trying to limp after Joy with his empty threats. In the meantime, Felony continued growling, waiting to nibble on a second course of Porky meat.

No sooner had Joy returned to the living room than she found Porky still complaining. She'd returned just in time to hear him say to Patience, "How many times I got to get bit by that mangy mutt before y'all put a muzzle on him?"

"How many times do you wanna get bit?" Joy sashayed to where Porky sat and pointed her finger. "How many times I gotta tell you my dog don't like you? To him, you look like a fat, nasty chew toy."

Joy started wagging her finger faster, that time like a pendulum in Porky's face. "And—don't even think about taking my Felony out of his home. 'Cause next time, I'll put him betwixt your knees and let him hunt for that little furry rabbit you keep tucked in those Fruit of the Loonies."

Chapter 14

From the time Percy answered his cell phone at his god-mothers' home, he knew his day would only get worse. He pretended he had not a clue about the robbery at his father's diner last night, while at the same time he felt relieved Prophet had already shared what Porky had bragged about telling Deacon Whistle. And then the call from Washington, followed shortly by the one from New York City.

He didn't smoke, never had, but at that moment, baking like a potato from the hot sun, he could've used a cigarette, a shot of liquor, or something. Where was a distraction when he needed one? Nervousness was a foreign feeling, but lately it'd visited a lot.

Percy hadn't seen the car when it first arrived, but he sensed it. Perhaps it was a shift in his spirit, a gut punch honed by his experience as a detective who'd sometimes worked secretly for the Justice Department. Or it could've been the purring of an engine in a very expensive car, instead of the rattling sound from his 1998 rebuilt Honda Civic he knew so well.

In the daylight, on this quiet block, he hoped he wouldn't stand out. If he'd known there'd be work involved on his day off, he'd have dressed in a suit and tie. He could've carried a few pamphlets in his hand, disguised himself as a salesman or someone handing out Bible tracts.

But he hadn't. Instead, he looked and dressed more like a cover model in a neat pair of tan khaki pants, a white short-sleeved shirt unbuttoned midway to expose his hairless, muscular chest. At least he hadn't worn sneakers and looked even more out of place as he stood between two hedges with a giant oak tree towering over the brush. He stuck his head out. He looked around just in time to see her a few yards away, slowly inching her way out of the driver's side of a 2010 black Jaguar X358.

Percy's heart started beating fast. She'd always had that effect upon him. First Lady Deborah, his future mother-in-law, looked striking while at the same time taking no prisoners.

Her pale blue designer dress was a perfect fit. Her short hair looked a bit darker than the last time he'd seen it, no doubt a dye job. He hadn't meant to smile, but he did find it appealing that most women her age liked to keep the white and silver to a minimum.

Somehow she looked out of place, almost regal on a street where the wealthy seniors lounged on patios, or walked their small dogs while chatting about arthritis, stock markets, and other senior matters.

Then, as he'd suspected when he'd first seen the car, First Lady Deborah wasn't alone. From its angle and the way she'd parked he couldn't tell who it was.

Percy slunk back into the cover of the bushes as he watched First Lady Deborah start his way. If she'd noticed him, she didn't give it away. Instead, she stopped in front of the house next door to his godmothers' and quickly began chatting with the neighbor, Sister Betty.

While he hid and waited, Percy thought about his godmothers and one of their latest ventures into the absurd.

Knowing how fond of and close they were to First Lady Deborah had made it very easy for him to add this case to his load. Percy didn't need the first lady learning he'd messed up the investigation. He certainly didn't want or need his godmothers getting caught up in what could ultimately be an ugly church situation. *No doubt my godmothers are gonna nail my hide to a wall when they figure out all I needed was their help to keep an eye on Dad for a short time.* But since his godmothers were already in enough mess, having written crazy letters to the president, he'd decided at that moment he probably shouldn't feel too afraid.

They'd better be glad Michelle Obama didn't come after them. Thoughts of the FLOTUS coming after Joy and Patience almost as hard as she campaigned against obesity made Percy shake his head.

It's a good thing Reign and I know low folks in high places and FedEx. I'm glad we got ahead of this fiasco, he thought. Was there anything his two comical godmothers wouldn't do that didn't border on Christian crazy?

He saw that First Lady Deborah was still chatting with Sister Betty, but now it'd begun to drizzle. The women hurried inside Sister Betty's house.

He could wait in the rain, get soaked, or he could return to his godmothers and hope for another opportunity to see First Lady Deborah. There was still a possibility that the first lady would visit his godmothers, since she was in the neighborhood.

One thing for certain, he didn't want his godmother Patience, who'd served on the finance board as one of its trustees, involved in anything illegal in or out of the church.

Percy remembered when he'd been approached about the church's dilemma. First Lady Deborah told him, "Percy, I don't know what to do. Me and the Lord chat a lot. This time He's gone silent on me. So I've come to you." She'd gone on to tell him about Sister Boodrow and suspicions about the church's finances.

And what the first lady had discovered was devastating. Someone had forged her husband's name on papers, funneling monies from the church. They'd also gone on to cash in insurance policies of several members who'd died and willed money to the church.

Because of her husband's reputation, First Lady Deborah knew she'd be taken seriously if she went discreetly to the authorities. Once the authorities promised they would begin the investigation immediately, out of respect for her husband and her church, they'd agreed to her demand that Percy be assigned to lead the investigation.

As the rain continued to fall around Percy, he recalled Reign's response to the whole sordid situation. About a month into the investigation, Reign had rushed over to Percy's apartment. She'd barely entered before she began apologizing, telling him that her mother called her earlier in the week. The call had begun calmly enough but then her mother confided, which she often did to Reign, saying she'd received one of her *grand* prophesies.

Percy tried helping her out of her jacket and into his arms, yet Reign ranted on. He did everything but tape her mouth to change the subject. That *grand* prophesy wasn't what he'd wanted to talk about, especially since they didn't get together as often as he'd like. Besides, he'd already begun investigating her mother's real problem. He just couldn't tell her that. *Those Stepson women sure put me in a bind*, thought Percy.

But Reign wouldn't shut up, and that's when he was glad she'd been insistent. It wasn't what he'd thought.

Reign went on to say her mother had confided that something was amiss, and it involved his godmothers. That got his attention.

A puff of wind blew through the leaves where Percy hid. He slid his hand under the side of his shirt, pulling the Velcro straps holding his bulletproof vest. It was a reminder to get one that fitted better. He almost snapped one of the straps when he felt a whizzing sensation on his hip.

He sighed, realizing he had forgotten he'd set his cellphone to vibrate. The envelope icon on the screen signaled a text message from Reign.

I C you standin by hedges. U can't hide for squat. I'm in mom's car but won't try 2 wave 2 u. Wanted me 2 ride wth her, left dad at the nursing hm. I've more news, C U 2nite. Mk sure U discuss FedEx wth Ur godmothers. Ha! As if POTUS would :-)

Percy suppressed the urge to smile. He began running his fingers over the cellphone's keypad, texting his reply. *I'll C U later afta talking to them. BTW, Ur mom looks amazing, unflustered. Can't wait to bite the young, smart, beautiful apple fr her tree. LOL*

No sooner had he pressed the send button a reply came back. *And mk sure U clean the pork. Disappointed! U kno better. U can't fake it & mk it.*

That was quick, he thought. *We went from flirting back to business without taking a breath. Damn. That's what I get for loving a smart gal.*

He could only deal with one problem at a time.

No matter how he looked at it, Reign had been right about having to set up last night's robbery. How could he have been so stupid, so careless, as to put what he'd learned hidden in his Great Grandmamma Truth's Bible? Moreover, how could he have been so naïve?

If he'd been limber enough at that moment, he would've kicked his own behind. In a moment of bonding with his father, he'd shared some of what he'd been working on; nothing detailed, but he'd confided that he'd placed his evidence and notes inside Grandmamma Truth's Bible.

At the time, he hadn't much to go on. Porky seemed so interested in his cases, and he'd never seen him read that Bible. He'd known that his father thought of the Bible as a keepsake with bragging rights. He only mentioned it when he wanted to taunt Joy, who'd truly wanted it. "Who robs a place and steals a Bible?" Porky had repeatedly asked Percy last night. "Nobody other than family cares who was born when and who married who."

At the moment, his father's actions had tied Percy's hands.

His clueless father's shameless reputation for freely running his big mouth was no secret. From the night he'd stopped by and watched Deacon Whistle leave the Shanty close to closing time, he'd become more suspicious. As long as the man had lived next door to the Shanty, he'd never seen him stop there more than twice.

He'd listened to Porky admire how Deacon Whistle carried the *Wall Street Journal* under his arm. He'd seen him with at least two finance papers the last time he'd come by for some last-minute takeout.

"You know that Deacon thinks he's a pretty smart fella," Porky told him, "but I let him know I've got some smart genes I done passed along, too."

Percy couldn't prove it yet, but his gut warned him since he had the only smart gene his father had ever produced, Porky's bragging to Deacon Whistle placed his career, but hopefully not their lives, in jeopardy.

So now, even if he'd wanted, he couldn't take away his father's fear and anger about the missing Bible. Porky brought it on himself. Only he and Reign, an unwitting partner by virtue of her being a Stepson and a more-than-capable reporter despite teasingly being called the weather girl because of her first name, knew the truth.

Yet Percy harbored self-recrimination. He could've just removed the Bible. After all, solving problems, whether something criminal or just plain life, had always came natural.

What he was feeling at that moment was as close to unnatural as a pig wanting a bubble bath.

Chapter 15

While Percy remained hidden among the bushes, Deacon Whistle stayed out of sight. He parked his rented midsize black Neon near the end of Joy and Patience's block.

Ever since Joy's odd reference to calling him out as a devil at the wholesale store, Deacon Whistle had been troubled. Her outburst and obvious annoyance had taken him off his plan. He didn't like it. Unable to catch her at home, he'd begun spying on Joy, parking and watching like some repo man.

In fact, it was the fourth time he'd done it from that very spot while she toiled in her garden or fed her dog. He'd wanted to grab her and ask, "What do you know and when did you know it?"

He should've known better. Getting First Lady Stepson and the board to bypass Sister Boodrow—bless her cold, thieving heart—to give Joy that missionary president position was the easy part.

Getting Joy Karry to forget what she'd seen, and treat him in a Christian manner, would be a miracle. She'd double downed on her snobbery after she'd almost busted him and Sister Boodrow performing their lewd acts. It hadn't been the only time he and the good Sister Boodrow committed a few "no-nos" from the Book of Leviticus.

As much as he'd disliked Joy's uppity ways, even before that day, he'd still always found her intriguing. She was like a Sudoku puzzle; something he'd never been able to solve yet every so often he felt the need to try.

Also, she wasn't mousy like her shy, underweight, and ever prayerful, Bible-researching cousin, Patience.

Patience never questioned or read one single transaction he had her sign off on. He'd simply grab her right after a service, when she was high on the Lord and gullible.

He'd had a simple plan. He'd be the first to count the money, writing the total with an erasable ink pen, and she'd sign off on it. By the time the report went to the finance committee members, he'd used his money scalpel, shaving off a little here and there. He'd also made certain to give Sister Boodrow a little here and there for her pocket and libido. Hopefully, she'd either spent it all or at least hidden it so no one could connect it to him.

Deacon Whistle pulled a small black leather-bound spiral pad from his shirt pocket. He began writing, capturing bits and pieces of his thoughts and observations, a recent habit he'd developed. With so much to plan for his final haul from the church's assets, now with the added task of keeping an eye on Joy, he might forget something.

He scribbled a few words—none of which would make sense to others. He thought about how easy it was to spy on Joy. He'd sometimes spy on the Stepsons too.

On the occasions when Whistle parked in that particular spot, he'd often worn a Fedora, an expensive suit, and a tie. He dressed and looked like any generic white man in an expensive car carrying out business in a wealthy neighborhood.

He'd learned the worth of keeping up appearances at the foot of his older cousin, Chester. Chester, the Big Willy of

Fraud back in the seventies and eighties, was snatched off the Fed's Most Wanted list when he was caught hiding out in Europe. Now Chester, elderly and overtaken by a host of illnesses, lay hidden in a place attended to by nurses who did everything for him. Except Chester could still make phone calls—for that, Whistle was glad.

However, like his cousin Chester had been, he was ever the careful planner. If anyone had recognized him, he had a legitimate excuse ready. After all, on occasion, he'd had reasons to visit several of the church members in a particular neighborhood and nearby.

All the members on the finance committee had a duty to collect monies when a member requested a visit to do so or couldn't get to church or a mailbox.

However, on this day, he was glad he'd rented a car. He actually owned another car he kept hidden from his pastor and the other church members. It was a bright red 2010 BMW with the license plate *Spoiled$* that he never drove around Pelzer too much.

When he wasn't fleecing the sheep, he kept his BMW stored securely in a parking lot fifteen miles away in Piedmont. He also paid the garage a ton of pilfered church money for the anonymity.

Deacon Whistle tugged at his shirt collar, pulling it forward while he reclined the car seat a little. He'd already seen First Lady Deborah's car. He couldn't have planned it better. With the arrival of the first lady he could watch both women.

He fished around in the bag he carried, pulling from it a pair of binoculars. He had to be careful. There'd be no explanation if caught with them. Adjusting the sights, it still wasn't clear but he thought he saw a man who he thought might've been the cousins' detective godson. He couldn't be too certain, because for whatever reason, the man had disappeared behind a bush. He wondered who was watching who, and if they were all after the same thing?

Deacon Whistle rested his head on the steering wheel, watching the young man's head drop as though he were looking down at what could've been a cellphone in his hands. He couldn't take a chance that somehow he'd been right and that this was the young detective.

He began to wonder about other things. He wondered if, perhaps, he should take the monies he and Chester had pilfered over the past five years and go to New York. He quickly rejected the notion. They didn't have enough yet; besides, he wanted more than just money. He wanted what his cousin Chester had long sought—the golden Stepson name and reputation tainted and destroyed.

Whistle pushed aside the distracting thoughts. "Back to the business at hand," he thought.

Another question came to mind. What if the man's talkative daddy, Porky, had repeated any of their private conversations? He could've confided in his son everything he'd shared with him. Anything was possible.

One moment, he'd been deep in thought; the next, there was a clawing on the driver's side door. He looked up just in time to see Joy's mutt, Felony. The dog stood on his hind legs with his enormous head peering into the window, growling.

Deacon Whistle met the dog's growl with an angry stare. He didn't dare yell at it, fearing that'd bring attention. Felony's barking became louder, and that's when he knew he had to leave.

Surprised the dog didn't try to follow, he pulled away from the curb quickly, and then slowed down as he drove past the spot where he'd seen the man beside the bushes. This time, although he still couldn't see more than a profile, the physique confirmed his suspicions. It was indeed the detective Percy LaPierre.

A frown crept across Deacon Whistle's face as he looked into the rearview mirror. The dog now stood in the middle of the street barking in his direction. *Mangy mutt!* He began gripping the steering wheel until the blue veins in his hands started pulsating.

Whistle drove a few blocks away in the direction of the highway. He shook from anger and pulled into the parking lot of a fast-food restaurant. He needed to regain his focus before he did something stupid that'd bring unwanted attention, or the cops.

As soon as Whistle turned off the car, its engine made a *whoop* sound, as if it too had a maintenance problem. *He* certainly did. Over the years, he'd had anger management issues. He knew that. Sometimes he'd become angry and couldn't cool off if he lay in a freezer.

Two days ago, he'd been visiting Chester and had done a little Internet snooping. For fun, he'd hacked into First Lady Deborah's e-mails; she often sent out e-mail blasts about things he felt were ridiculous yet fun to read about. What he read that day gave him an opening for what Chester wanted him to do next. Her e-mail had been a gift.

According to the first e-mail he'd read, it appeared the first lady had concerns because she hadn't heard from Joy. It was about the color scheme for an event happening in the fall at a big church in Anderson County. Things were too hectic in church, and as soon as she could get away and the pastor felt better, she'd stop by if Joy didn't respond to the e-mail. He remembered wondering who has a meeting about a damn color scheme that's happening months later?

He'd decided he'd better not go too far. Answering the e-mail on Joy's behalf, even for fun, when he didn't know what the event or color scheme was about, wasn't a good move. It hadn't mattered; he preferred lurking and, in his mind, he'd gotten rather good at it, too.

He'd gone on to dismiss what he considered nothing but female chatter. He'd continued online for another hour or so, while Chester slept nearby with tubes running out of him, making him look like he had a garden hose stuck in every crevice. Chester, in one of his rare moments of clarity, had already asked him to research into their latest Wall Street scheme, although he'd never call it that. But then, surprisingly, the good Rev. Judge Lock Stepson's name appeared in one of the search results.

On that day, why the judge's name appeared when it had nothing to do with what he sought, he'd never know. He couldn't resist, and hacked into the judge's medical records.

He'd done it several times over the last several years, when information had begun flowing over the Internet. There'd been nothing useful or threatening to the embezzling he'd done.

That day, Whistle had become almost delirious with joy. He'd almost flipped his laptop off his lap. He remembered smiling until his face ached, because after all the time spent planning revenge on the old judgmental judge and reverend, everything was falling into place. He'd hit pay dirt.

"Vengeance is ours before God's," he remembered thinking while his eyes swept across the computer monitor, gobbling each word like Pac Man. He couldn't believe his good fortune.

In a confidential report, he discovered a link to make their plan succeed beyond what they'd wanted. He'd quickly written down what he'd found.

It looked like the old wheelchair-bound fool had had a change in his health status. A diagnosis of early dementia was added to his history of high blood pressure, diabetes, and congestive heart failure. Any one of these health problems would make the judge's stay on earth unpredictable. Under the right circumstances, an immediate departure could be arranged.

It'd become almost too easy for Whistle to harbor his resentment. He'd hid it under false fellowship with the church members while slowly undermining Mount Kneel Down's advancement.

And, in his mind, he had good reason. He blamed its pastor for the state Chester now lay in; Chester blamed him even more.

It started when Whistle had begun attending Mount Kneel Down every now and then. Whistle's need for religion came from Wall Street, where religion came into play if someone got caught doing what Wall Street was good at. He hadn't intended on that happening.

He attended Mount Kneel Down Non-Denominational because Chester wanted him to. Some years ago, Chester served time in prison. Prison life had aged him; he'd developed all sorts of disabling illnesses and was released on parole; but he still couldn't get around. Even if Chester could, he still had better sense than to go anywhere near Rev. Stepson, whether the man was in the courthouse or a church. Moreover, Whistle and Chester had an agreement; when one couldn't do the dirty deed, the other would.

Whistle went on to attend church regularly. He shared his knowledge of financial investing—secretly comingled with that of Chester's—with a few of the more influential members. Like most Ponzi schemes, he made certain that first came were first paid. Those members had done so well it'd taken no time to convince the financial board and Rev. Stepson to follow his advice on more financial matters.

A few months later, when Rev. Stepson arrived at his apartment one evening along with Patience and two other men offering him the position on the finance board, Whistle could've shouted right there on the spot. He'd had the old man right where he'd wanted him, appeasing and available. It'd taken time to move up to the head position, but as his cousin Chester always reminded him, "Revenge sometimes needs to age, like a fine wine."

He'd already decided when it was over he'd get the money. Chester? He'd be happy that the old judge would take the fall.

★   ★   ★

Campbell didn't know how long he'd been distracted. It didn't matter. By accident he'd turned into a cul de sac. He placed the distraction square upon the shoulders of the Stepsons. *They're always in the way or in my head. I hate them.*

"Enough!" Deacon Whistle suddenly turned on his radio, not caring which particular station came on. He just needed other sounds in the car outside of his own thoughts. His memories were a threat to stay focused and not become caught up in anything or anyone taking him off course.

Chester will have my hide if I mess up.

Chapter 16

A little past noon, on an afternoon of fasting, events changed again. Joy and Patience sat in the kitchen, still avoiding any mention of Prophet or Porky's inconvenient but thankfully short visit from the other day, yet still trying to figure out Percy's big case—although Joy was still certain she knew what it was. It was all she could do to keep from telling Lil P what she already knew when he'd taken Porky back to his small apartment.

Then the telephone rang. Patience answered it, since she sat the closest.

As far as Patience answering the telephone, that was no big deal to Joy. But Patience giggling all of a sudden, twisting the hem of her dress as she chatted, was worthy of further investigation. Joy abruptly pushed Felony from her lap and rushed over to where middle-aged Patience stood, still grinning like a schoolgirl in heat.

"Of course, I'm fine. Why wouldn't I be? . . . I'll have to break my fast. . . . It will take me some time to get ready. . . ." Then Joy overheard Patience whisper, "Let's say about two o'clock?"

Patience ignored Joy hovering over her. After a few more minutes of giggles, sounding like a code for a rendezvous or a midlife crisis in progress, she gently replaced the cordless phone in its cradle.

"Well?" Joy stood with her hands on her hips, her eyes following Patience who, ignoring the question, floated past her and down the hallway with a wide clownish smile plastered on her face.

Joy pressured her. "I know you heard me ask—who was that? I'm sure it wasn't somebody trying to sue us or sell overpriced insurance. I haven't seen a look on your face that crazy since we were teenagers, and you thought you'd become Mrs. Marvin Gaye when he tossed his skinny hips and his skull cap your way."

Turning around quickly with one hand on her hips and her new reading glasses twirling in her other, Patience replied playfully, "That was Marvin's loss."

Despite her cheerful reply, a smile rapidly replaced an obvious hurt the Marvin Gaye reminder brought on as she continued. "That was Prophet Long Jevity. He's back in town and he's finally gotten our messages. He'll be stopping by to visit us around two o'clock."

"As far as I knew, we'd stopped trying to reach him. Why are you smiling like a lovesick puppy? That man disappearing and reappearing like that can't be the reason for that look."

Joy put her hands on her hips and pointed her finger at Patience. The only thing she could do was keep up the pretense of not stomaching the man. It wouldn't take much acting on her part. "It'd better not be something crazy going on inside that head of yours. We can't be thrown off our fasting, praying, and figuring out what's going on with Lil P."

"Get a grip. I'm fine and happy to learn Prophet's okay. Besides, I got a feeling this visit may be a little different than the others."

"I got a feeling you gonna get your feelings hurt again."

Joy tried hard to hold onto her fasting mode, but Patience

was digging away at it. She hadn't fully worked out a plan to keep Patience and Prophet apart so he could concentrate on church business. *You'd think that man would be more professional, being a federal agent,* she thought.

But what she said was, "All I'm saying is, don't let no man piss on you and have you believing it's rain. That's nasty. Every time that middle-aged playa for the Lord has been here before, it's either because he's in the neighborhood or he's wanted you to type or do something for him. I just can't see the excitement in another visit from him because he's crept back in town."

"I've been thinking," Patience looked up as though her thoughts were circling in the air and she could pull from them. She was also determined to ignore everything Joy had just said. "When was the last time since Prophet visited that we've had a man over to cook for that wasn't family or from the church?"

Patience mentioning the church suddenly reminded Joy that she hadn't heard hide nor hair from Deacon Whistle since he'd come by days ago, or when she'd run into him at the wholesale store, and she didn't want to.

If Patience felt Joy had tuned her out, she didn't show it. She kept on talking. "Aside from a phone call every blue moon, or dumping his daddy on our doorstep, our godson hasn't been by in quite some time, so it'll be nice to smell a little Old Spice."

Old Spice—yep, that's just what's been missing around here. Things can't get no worse unless that other heathen, Deacon Whistle, drops by again.

Joy kept her thoughts to herself, shaking her head in amazement because Deacon Whistle had entered her thoughts. It was the second time in the last few minutes he'd come to her mind. She wanted to shake her head as though by doing so she could bounce him from her thoughts.

Instead, she threw up her hands. "I give up!" She returned to the kitchen and grabbed an apron from a cabinet drawer and straightened her wig. "If we're eating before sundown, breaking the fast for the Prodigal Prophet, I guess God won't mind. I'll make a pitcher of lemonade and a little something to snack on." *If I didn't think that rat would know d-Con when he tasted it, I'd feed that to him.*

Her last evil thought was for Deacon Whistle. At the rate her thoughts had turned to violence, she'd have to forgo any spiritual benefits from her recent fast and begin again.

It didn't take long for them to learn Prophet Long Jevity wasn't on God's schedule but his own. He'd already called several times earlier to say he was running late. It was almost five o'clock before he finally arrived.

Patience started to rush to the door but stopped before entering the hallway. *I ain't giving Joy the benefit of being the only one who can be strong.* She walked towards the door, counting her steps along the way, making sure she didn't hurry and was satisfied she'd made him wait outside, pushing the doorbell several times, long enough.

Prophet stood in the doorway grinning, looking over his shoulder as though he'd been followed. He rushed inside, slamming the door behind him as soon as Patience opened it. "I know I called a couple of times and said I was running late. But I'd like to apologize, again, for my tardiness."

Tardiness is ten to twenty minutes late, Patience thought. However, she kept a smile and purred, "That's quite okay. We weren't doing anything so important this afternoon that we couldn't wait until evening to get a visit from the carrier of God's word."

Already deciding she'd play along from the moment he'd called earlier, Patience escorted Prophet inside the living room. Smiling like a good hostess, she offered him a seat on the two-seater reclining love sofa, thinking that as long as she didn't actually kill him, her fasting would still count. Once he sat, she joined him.

Her eyes grew wide as she pretended not to give his beige trousers, chocolate brown short-sleeved shirt, and polished shoes of the same color the once over. Pursing her lips, she took another look at the copper-colored toupee. She thought, for someone who seemed to put a lot of time, thought, and money into what he wore on his body, he'd dropped the ball that time. She didn't find the false reddish-orange–colored hair appealing at all on his lemony-colored scalp.

When she added it all together, she realized the makeover wasn't her imagination but intentional. But why, she wondered, and for what purpose?

Moving a little closer to him, Patience swept her long hair to the side, letting it lay on her shoulder. With her tiny eyelashes fluttering, threatening to pop out a contact lens or knock the reading glasses off her face, she asked, "Prophet Jevity, your cologne smells fabulous. Do you mind my asking what is that fragrance you're wearing?"

Prophet's face lit up a little more than usual, showing he believed she'd truly forgiven him. More important, he still had it going on. Pushing aside a few stray hairs from his toupee he leaned forward. "My dear Missionary Patience, this is the smell of success. It's otherwise known as Giorgio Armani."

Patience didn't push him away or make him feel he'd invaded her personal space. She couldn't move and wasn't sure where her sudden dizzy sensation came from. She felt light in the head. Was it from sniffing too much of his cologne? Was it from sitting next to a man who seemed to overtake all she'd kept tempered? Or did she need to eat after fasting most of the day?

Patience and Prophet suddenly burst out in laughter. It was a silly move on both their parts, but it certainly lightened the mood. Neither had acted with the least amount of Christian decorum, both playing games and claiming mistaken victory.

In the kitchen, Joy had been bustling around when she heard the front doorbell ring. Even though Patience hadn't bothered to let her know Prophet had finally arrived, she knew he had.

Too busy to leave what she was doing to greet him properly, she'd hollered, "Welcome, Prophet Long Jevity. You a few hours late, but we glad you could finally make it. Excuse me, I'm back here in the kitchen, but I'll be out directly."

She didn't get a response, so she was not certain whether or not Patience and Prophet had heard her. She cocked her head, pointing it towards the kitchen door. Squeezing her eyes tight, as though that would help her hear better, she picked up sounds of too much snickering followed by too long a period of silence.

Joy didn't know what was happening, but knowing Prophet and Patience were alone in another part of the house didn't sit well. She was supposed to stop any further carnal desires. A short time later, Joy walked out of the kitchen carrying the huge tray of food into the dining room. After setting the tray on the dining room table, she then decided to slow things down a bit. She wanted to give Patience more time to put the screws to Prophet, if indeed that was her plan. She turned, catching a glimpse of her reflection in the mirror.

Turning side to side, Joy smiled at the mauve-colored caftan she'd chosen, with patches of pink roses spread about the hemline. She didn't seem to notice or care that the patterns on her wide hips made her look like a floating rose garden.

Then she blew a kiss at the mirror. She felt more feminine at that moment wearing her latest cinnamon-colored curly wig than she had in quite some time. She actually felt good for the few seconds she hadn't had thoughts about hurting anyone.

With everything now in place inside the dining room, she arrived at the entry to the living room. Her mouth gaped, as though she'd sniffed too much cookie dough or tasted too much macaroni.

There was Patience, waving a piece of paper around while at the same time sniffing Prophet's neck. Joy almost passed out. She'd never seen Felony sniff another dog or even his own butt as aggressively as Patience did Prophet.

It was obvious they hadn't seen Joy, because they didn't stop.

What is wrong with her? I already know what's wrong with him. A child of God and a federal spawn of Satan shouldn't be fooling around like that. She shook her head out of shame for Patience and near-disgust for the unprofessional Prophet.

Joy didn't want to risk embarrassing either of them and create a situation where she couldn't find out what was going on. It didn't matter now that he'd prophesied or stopped by her church. This man in a few moments, just as before, had brought a conflicting spirit into her home, and she didn't like it one bit.

From the hallway, Joy called out, "Patience, please escort our guest into the dining room."

Patience not only escorted Prophet into the dining room, hanging onto his arm like they were Siamese twins, she practically spoon-fed him. The only thing Joy noticed she hadn't done was wipe a little macaroni and cheese from the corner of his mouth. Joy wanted to slap them both silly.

The three chatted almost an hour about this and that, but mostly about nothing. In between murmured belches, Prophet (who was not certain who'd cooked what) continuously praised the women's cooking. He testified that the bounty spread before him was further proof of their many gifts.

He refused an offer of a toothpick. He didn't realize he had a collard leaf stuck between his teeth. He remarked, laughing, "Lord, if I didn't know you two were set aside for the Lord, I'd have to propose to one of you."

"Perhaps, you just need to check my expiration date," Patience said, halfway kidding. "After a while, some things just need to come off the shelf."

The remark brought about high-fiving and more laughter between Prophet and Patience. In the meantime, Joy sat and watched. The more she watched, the more concerned she became. Joy knew a fake laugh when she heard it, and Patience had faked hers. Her cousin wasn't the brightest bulb in the pack, but she'd never act this dimwitted within one day of Prophet returning. Now Joy was certain Patience was up to something.

When it got close to six-thirty, Joy decided it was time for the inquisition to begin. While Patience escorted Prophet back into the living room, still arm in arm, Joy cleared the table. It gave Joy time to set about determining her next course of action.

Walking into the living room, she was surprised to see them thumbing through one of Patience's reference Bibles. Prophet had a pen in hand, scribbling something onto a pad.

"So what's going on?" Joy asked, craning her neck to read the pad while she sat opposite them. "Are y'all studying the Word?"

Prophet turned from Patience and fixed his eyes upon Joy. He appeared to stare right through her.

"I was telling Missionary Patience that my kingdom number is a two. I dabble a bit in numerology," he replied with authority. "It's another gift God has filled me with."

"You certainly full of it," Joy said, her Cheshire grin saying what she really meant.

If Prophet hadn't caught Joy's implication, Patience sure did. She quickly blurted, "Joy, guess what? Prophet Long Jevity and I have the same number."

"I've got both y'all numbers!" Joy sucked her teeth and wouldn't say more.

"Joy Karry," Patience blurted. Joy had embarrassed Patience with the childish mocking of what she'd wanted Prophet to think she'd taken seriously. "The Devil is a liar! Now, you were born a child of sevens, came into this cold world on the seventh hour of the seventh day of the seventh month."

"So now you're saying I'm a number seven kingdom child? That would make me complete, since seven is the number for completion. But what does me being a number seven kingdom child and you being a number, or a size, two have anything to do with anything?"

Patience shuddered slightly. Her weight was a sensitive matter, and Joy knew better than to tease her about it.

Trying to laugh away the slight, Patience gave a nervous snicker. "Joy, you know I wear a size 5. I am only talking about me being a number two kingdom child, not somebody's dress size. Being born on the second day of the second month at two o'clock at night has a special meaning. My number two means unity, truth. That was why Jesus sent His disciples out in pairs to do kingdom work."

"That's right, Missionary Patience," Prophet chimed in. "We're a pair of twos doing the Lord's work."

Again, Joy sucked her teeth in exasperation. *This smells more like number two,* she thought, but said aloud, "Get to the point, Patience."

"One of us is to pray while the other speaks of the Lord's goodness. I'm also just saying that seven and two make nine. Anyone who knows anything about the Lord's way of figuring knows it's the number for judgment and finality."

"Say what?" Joy's head spun toward Patience so fast she almost caught whiplash.

"Joy, keep up. Our total number is nine."

Without giving Joy a chance to respond, Patience instead

gave Prophet a teasing poke with her bony elbow. "Ain't that right, Prophet Long Jevity?"

"Please, Missionary Patience," Prophet said sweetly. "Just call me Prophet Jevity. You can call me Long after you get to know me better."

Patience's blush was undeniable, but she kept it under control by acting as though she hadn't caught any sexual innuendo.

Turning to Joy, a half-smile crossed Patience's face and then quickly disappeared. She said, "Prophet Jevity has revealed that, while you were in the kitchen, God has led him to ask us for our help with a certain delicate matter."

"A—and, pray tell, what could that matter be?" Joy sang the words, again her way of being snarky.

Not waiting for Patience to explain what he'd meant, Prophet took over. "Well, it just so happens, as Missionary Patience was trying to explain to you—" He stopped speaking and, leaning his head to the side, looked directly into Joy's eyes, as though willing her to believe whatever he said. "I hope I'm not being too forward, but I feel so comfortable around you God-fearing women."

"Go on," Joy said. Her eyes darted around to show she wasn't buying it, yet.

Prophet smiled, continuing where he'd left off. "I need to take care of a few personal matters out of town. I would like for you two to go with me as my guests. I never see you two going anywhere. I'm sure you'll enjoy getting away from Pelzer."

"Why?" Joy asked as she shifted her weight, turning a little to relax one hip while meeting his stare.

"While I'm there, I have the use of a time-share. You ladies appear to need a vacation, so I thought you could relax while I handle my business."

"You didn't tell me that," Patience blurted, with a hint of false disappointment in her voice.

"Aww, that's so nice. But you really need to quit—"

Prophet didn't let Joy finish. "I never quit on anything or anybody."

"Well, I don't know if we can," Patience replied while trying to act indifferent and not too eager. In her head, she'd already packed her bags. "It sounds like your personal business and time-share offer will be about the same time we plan on giving our godson an early surprise birthday party."

"That's right," Joy chimed in. "Our godson is very important to us and, in fact, to this community, too."

"Well, I certainly don't want to interfere with any plans you have for your second cousin and godson Percy."

Joy shot forward in her seat. She'd forgotten that she knew he already knew Percy. "How do you know all that about Lil P?"

She suddenly realized it wasn't a bad move on her part. If he'd suspected she knew anything, then what she'd just done should've dismissed his suspicions. However, her suspicion toward Patience hadn't moved an inch. Joy's accusing eyes pierced holes right through her.

Patience shrugged, then dismissed Joy's accusation with a wave of her hand. "Why are you so surprised that I'd mention Lil P? I'm very proud of our godson. Besides, Prophet already knows cousin Porky 'cause he lives right next door to the Shanty. He would've met Percy sooner or later."

Joy gave Patience a look that read *We'll come back to this later*. She then turned her attention back to Prophet. "We'll decide what and when we want to involve our godson."

"Well, I didn't know you'd already made plans. It's too bad. Perhaps another time would be better." He stopped and exhaled. "Come to think of it, I probably wouldn't have had too much time to spend with you ladies after my business. I've also been invited to a political event, a fundraiser, where I'm told President Obama might be in attendance, though for only a short while."

That's when Joy's mouth dropped so hard her bottom lip almost banged against her chin. *Can we take the risk of disappointing Lil P about a party he knows nothing about? And who is Lil P to tell us not to do anything pertaining to the White House?*

Patience could feel more forgiveness for the man creeping into her spirit as her heart began racing. She quickly sucked in her top lip to keep from screaming *hallelujah*. However, her skinny knees were already knocking, one against the other, making a clicking sound like crickets chirping, a dead giveaway.

Now looking directly at Patience, Joy communicated silently with her eyes. Then came a sucking of the teeth, which this time meant *Lil P will have other birthdays.*

Turning away from Patience and Prophet, Joy laid her chin in her hand trying to remember where she had laid her coffee mug. She had a sudden urge for caffeine with a thimble full of blessed Hennessy Cognac. She'd need strong spirits just to keep up with the way her world had begun to spin. She'd also forgotten to ask Prophet what state or city he'd wanted to take them to.

Chapter 17

The exit Prophet needed was coming up—bumper-to-bumper traffic had turned the highway into a parking lot.

All he could do was turn off the engine and save gas. He was surprised at how tired he felt at that moment, yet energetic at the same time. He looked at the lane next to him, and it appeared whatever was happening had caused the other cars to do the same as he.

While the traffic stalled Prophet folded his hands and thought about how unpredictable the case was turning. Several days ago, he'd tailed Whistle and lost him for a short time. It'd been his fault for not alerting the backup team that he would need assistance. Today, he'd decided it wouldn't happen again. It'd taken some ingenuity and a few deductions of where he'd go but he'd found him. He'd tailed him to the block where Joy and Patience lived.

It wasn't long after he'd arrived before he'd gotten a signal from Reign. She'd parked at the opposite end of the street and rolled her window down. Pretending to adjust the side-view mirror meant Whistle was on the move. "I wasn't too keen on having Reign involved; she's too close to the situation. But this just might work out after all," he'd mentioned to Percy during one of their quick radio exchanges.

He'd already seen Felony up to his shenanigans with his paws clawing at the driver's side of Whistle's rental. He'd have to get the mutt extra butter on his popcorn the next time he stopped by.

He hadn't wanted to chance anyone seeing him using his cell while he drove. "Gotta obey the law," he'd thought before he'd signaled to Percy with a quick toot from the car's horn as he approached. It'd been prearranged he'd do it, to let Percy know that they needed to bust out. To anyone looking, it should've looked innocent enough. He'd noticed Percy had lowered his head for a moment. It appeared both of them had become a little sloppy. That wasn't good at any time and particularly when dealing with the level of criminals they tracked.

Within seconds, the squeal from Prophet's car tires had sent birds flying as it'd skidded to a stop a few feet shy of Percy. With the agility only someone in great shape had, he'd come barreling into the car.

Squirming around in the passenger seat, nearly blocking Prophet's view, Percy hadn't time to do much more that day than pull a jacket from the back of Prophet's car. The shirt he'd worn was soaked from the rain. A closer look could've exposed his bulletproof vest and hip holster.

In the meantime, after careening from the curb, slowing down just before entering onto the highway, Prophet had stayed within the speed limits and contacted the rental agency where another team awaited. In case Whistle got too far ahead, they didn't want to lose him. Within minutes they'd activated Whistle's car's GPS by remote.

On that same day Prophet and Percy had tried to trail him Whistle left the car rental office. He didn't need to be a genius. He was certain he knew what'd happened on his way there a short time ago. If he hadn't activated the GPS system in his rental, someone had. Could the GPS system have turned on accidentally? He doubted it. He certainly wouldn't rely on the noncommittal answer he'd received from the agent when he asked about it. A natural born liar such as he could usually tell another liar. That clerk had lied.

But why?

Whistle wanted to clear his head as well as detect anyone that followed, so he chose to walk the ten blocks to the apartment he kept on Ptomaine Avenue rather than take a bus. It wasn't easy for a man with a cumbersome gait, but it was necessary. He could feel it in his soul. Something was amiss. He quickly dismissed both Joy and Patience. In his mind, they were too stupid and too churchified.

At least now he didn't have to worry about whether some woman, like Boodrow, was 100 percent in his corner and down with the plan.

Since he'd returned from his latest trip to Wall Street in Manhattan, he hadn't quite decided whether to let romance reenter his world. He didn't need another Boodrow becoming jealous, accusing him of cheating.

Of course, he cheated. After all, he was a man in his late fifties; but from what he'd read in her obituary, she'd lied about her age and had already passed his usual expiration date of thirty-five. A man with his appetite needed to drink from the fountain of feminine youth from time to time, but it didn't mean from the same fountain all the time.

But before he could move ahead, leaving ordinary folk and religious zealots behind, with their pockets emptied, he needed to move or remove a few people and things that stood in his way.

He hadn't always stuck to Chester's plan, and as much as he loved his older cousin, he'd never want to be on the old man's bad side. He held a grudge longer than most Middle Eastern tribes.

As usual, standing in his way was the church. It was always about the church. It had always been about the church.

Chester wouldn't move on until he'd brought down that particular church.

Whistle quickly checked his watch. He had a tight schedule to keep, and he'd need to light a match under things. Right now the only thing hot was him.

Chapter 18

"Patience, what are you thinking about?" Joy snapped. "I'm sorry; didn't mean to be abrupt. I guess too much is happening."

"Joy, I'm not upset with you, personally. Perhaps, it must be something in the weather or the water. It's raining cats, dogs, and Porky, and I'm about fed up with all of it."

Joy sighed and smoothed invisible wrinkles on her housecoat. "I can't quite figure out God's message about what's going on around here. And having Lil P push Porky inside the door a while ago and driving off without a word, ain't helping my loving disposition at all. I do know that Porky needs to stay out of my way until I do know!"

Several hours later it began growing dark and the rain had completely stopped. Patience and Joy were content that Porky kept out of their way sequestered safely in the spare bedroom. Joy was in the kitchen and about to pick up a tray of snacks to bring into the living room where she and Patience had been playing a game of Scrabble when the kitchen phone rang. It was First Lady Deborah.

"Something has come up, but I wanted to check and see how you were doing. I'd e-mailed but you never replied," the first lady said.

"Patience and I are fasting and playing Scrabble for the most part." She said Patience's name in such a way to let the first lady know she wasn't alone. "I haven't been online."

They chatted another moment about nothing before Joy hung up, thinking perhaps First Lady Deborah had really called just to see if she'd spilled to Patience. How the woman could tell whether she had or not, Joy wasn't certain, but she was a First Lady with prophecy skills and a notorious gift of discernment.

Although many times she'd accused Sister Betty of being crazy when the old woman said God had called her on the telephone, Joy hadn't quite put down the phone when she, too, spoke into it, with its dial tone humming, and began talking to God. "Now, Lord, You said in Your word that we should seek wisdom. Father, I'm looking. Where is it? I'm more confused now than I was on the day when You laid me off from my good-paying job. First me and Patience is supposed to meet with the president, and then we ain't?"

Joy stopped when she realized she should've been looking up toward heaven instead of into the mouthpiece of the telephone. She quickly placed it where it belonged, like it was hot, but added, "And I don't know why You using Prophet Jevity to help my church and the government, Heavenly Father, 'cause there's something about that man still don't set right with me. But Your Will be done . . ."

She'd barely picked up the tray when seconds later Joy heard Patience and Porky going at it. Slamming down the tray, she raced off to the living room.

The sniping stopped as soon as she stuck her head inside. She barged fully into the living room. "What'd I miss? When did he come out of hiding? What's going on?" She could feel the change in the atmosphere.

"I heard the phone ring a few minutes ago. Who was it?" Patience's question was quick and to the point, minimizing

Joy's intrusion. "Please just tell me it wasn't the last person I wanna hear from."

"I'm not certain who that could be from your short list, but it was First Lady Deborah."

"You know she's not on my short list just as well as you know who is."

Porky's head swung between the two as though he were watching tennis. At that moment, he didn't mind being ignored.

"She wanted to know why I hadn't answered an e-mail she sent. I told her we were on a fast." Joy's half-truth bothered her but only for a second. She quickly folded her arms, which meant Patience hadn't thrown her off track at all. "Spill it! Why are you two arguing now and what has he done in the few minutes I've been out of the room?"

While Patience paced back and forth, pulling at her hair and twirling her reading glasses by the arm of its frame, she tried explaining to Joy what Porky had just revealed. "I can't believe this crazy man would be so stupid."

"Why not?" Joy said. "It ain't like he just met stupid. They've been on a first-name basis for a while."

"You're a nasty something, Joy Karry." Porky's chest began heaving from anger.

Joy began losing more fasting credits as soon as she opened her mouth again. "Nobody's nastier than you, Porky LaPierre! Why don't you introduce yourself and that pigsty you feed folks from to some soap and water?"

"Better yet, Joy Karry, why don't you introduce yourself to the Jesus you always claiming to know?"

"Will you two please stop it?" Patience looked around the room as though for Jesus, or a weapon.

"I don't see why I should," Porky snapped before returning his attention back to Joy. "Why you always talking like you the only one that knows Jesus? I know Jesus, too."

"Then act like it, Porky."

"I don't wanna act. I wanna be for real about it. You do enough acting for the two of us."

Joy spun around and faced Patience. "You see, Patience. This is just what I mean. This heathen got the nerve to act like he's kingdom-bound. God wouldn't even let someone like him anywhere near heaven!"

"Joy, stop it. You gonna be judged by the same yardstick you judge with. That's the word."

"It ain't judging if you telling the truth."

Of course, Joy was right and Patience knew it. She'd hoped that she, herself, would calm down, especially after what Porky had just revealed.

It wasn't working at all. She wanted to take that yardstick she rebuked Joy about and beat Porky with it.

While his cousins whittled down his character, again, Porky made a decision. Before he'd try explaining anything further to Joy or to Patience, he first needed to explain his side of the mess to God.

He closed his eyes. He held his head in his hand as though doing so would immediately put him in touch with heaven, and that God would read his thoughts and hear his silent prayer.

Lord, I know You already know I've been practicing lying since I first learned to speak. Folks say practice makes perfect, so I know You already know I've gotten quite good at it. That's my only excuse for why I didn't tell Patience everything and told that Deacon Whistle almost everything. But Lord, that man looked money-smart and knew scripture. He had me at—Our Father which art.

Porky opened one eye, peeping to see if his cousins noticed him. They hadn't looked his way yet.

Meanwhile Patience paced back and forth struggling through her anger, trying to tell Joy what Porky had finally told her. "This fool bragged about the work Lil P's doing on a big embezzling case to Deacon Whistle."

Patience stopped pacing and, with her pointy chin now in

her hand, she asked, "Joy, I know Lil P didn't tell me nothing about what his big case was about. Did he mention anything to you about it, or something to do with embezzling?"

"Of course, he didn't!" Joy let her answer suffice. She hadn't lied. It wasn't Lil P that'd told her.

"I didn't think so." Patience eyeballed Porky again and continued from where she'd left off as she whittled his status down to amoeba-size.

"Still can't believe he'd allow Deacon Whistle entry into someone's personal affairs just because he was a man carrying on and talking about finances as if he were a billionaire. For heaven's sake, the man lived right next door to this knuckle-head in Shaqueeda's tenement building. If Whistle was all that smart about money, why wasn't he living somewhere else? You'd think Porky would've realized that before he tried to impress that man."

Joy hissed, "He must've had his best friend, Mister Stupid, by his side when he came to that conclusion."

Patience nodded at Joy before adding, "And he even went so far as to show the man the place where Percy had placed his notes about the embezzling case for safekeeping—and wait until you hear this!"

Patience stepped quickly in front of Joy, who'd already made a move toward Porky. "Hold up, Joy. Don't maim him yet. Let me finish telling you the rest."

Joy loomed over Porky, sucking her teeth, and if looks really did kill, then she'd go up for murder.

"Just to show that he had money, too, he even told Whis-tle that it was hidden in Grandmamma Truth's Bible."

"Oh Lord, he didn't," Joy could almost feel the breath leave her body. "Not Grandmamma Truth's Bible?"

"Yes, and that Bible was an expensive heirloom worth in the thousands of dollars."

Patience's voice had already begun rising, and by the time she finished she was fussing in the key of high C.

All through Patience's rant, Joy's eyes remained narrowed. She didn't even part her lips when she hissed, "Does Lil P know?"

They were now looking at him like road kill that needed running over again. Porky's eyes went back and forth between the women, looking for some sympathy. It looked as though none was coming from them or heaven, and he heard Felony scratching at the door, no doubt to bite him again. Porky figured he'd better be completely honest.

"No, I haven't told Percy. He did ask me right after we found the place torn apart if I'd said anything to anyone, but I was too ashamed to tell him the truth."

Porky stopped. His dark complexion somehow reddened with anger. "My son finally trusts me enough to let me in on something important, and I messed it up. I could just take that deacon's financial newspaper and advice and shove them so far up his arse he'd see sunshine and a headline every time he opened his lying mouth."

Joy and Patience's eyes bulged with more disbelief. Neither could believe their lying cousin wouldn't know another liar on his level when he saw one.

Joy's mouth was the first to become unglued, allowing what she'd held in to fly out. "So why are you telling it now?" Joy barked. "We wanna know and you'd better not lie."

Porky raised his arm, sling and all, while looking and pointing to Patience. "I also wanted him to know that I, too, had more assets other than the Shanty. Just like he knew about money and lived on Ptomaine, I knew about money living there, too. Plus, when he told me that he and Patience were on the finance committee, he seemed to light up just mentioning her name. I never saw him smile like that whenever I saw him around the neighborhood with that booty woman before she passed away."

"Booty woman? What booty woman?" Patience asked.

"I think he means the very late Sister Boodrow," Joy said

dryly. "I'm sure before she said hello to the Devil they called out the Lord's name at his place, too. Go on, Porky," Joy insisted.

"I sorta got the feeling that he liked Patience. I was trying to impress him so she could finally get a man, but now I'm not too sure."

One look at Patience snatching off her glasses again told Porky she might not have agreed with how he'd summed things up.

He looked at Joy and that time he spoke more truth than he knew she'd want to hear. "It's never been a secret that I don't particularly like you; but you know I've always been close to Patience. I don't wanna see her get hurt by no man. She's not as ferocious and grizzly bear–like as you."

Joy's reaction wasn't a surprise to either Patience or Porky. Yet neither cousin realized how mad Joy was until she began smashing some of her beloved ceramic figurines.

Patience moved quickly. "The power of life and death lies in the tongue," Patience quoted. Calming Joy down to where she stopped hissing, smashing, and near cussing took a lot. She'd had to haul Joy's big butt with the little strength she had left over from hauling Porky's a few days ago.

Patience stood shaking and exhausted after Joy's outburst. She began apologizing repeatedly on Porky's behalf for that bear reference. When she couldn't stand on her skinny legs any longer, she plopped down in a chair saying, "I'm sure Porky's so embarrassed at his own stupidity that he'll never withhold anything from family again. Ain't that right, Porky?"

Joy ignored Patience's pleas. Wagging her finger in Porky's face, she blasted him again. "I oughta bring Felony back inside and let him just gnaw on your butt until your cowardly black veins turn to mush."

"Why don't you just stop with the threats, go ahead and serve my arse to that deranged mutt on a plate of Kibbles 'n Bits!" Porky snapped.

"Stop giving Joy ideas," Patience interrupted. "You know she ain't above trying it."

Joy plopped down onto the sofa, too. She hung her head. She couldn't tell either of them what she'd learned from First Lady Deborah. "I can't believe you let that cretin deacon just walk in there and steal Grandmamma Truth's beloved Bible. You didn't have the courage to tell anyone, especially Lil P, what you did."

"I don't know for certain that the man stole the Bible, Joy. I'm just laying almost everything out there. Believe it or not, I'm sorry."

"You just oughta be sorry. If you'd let me have it then it would've been safe and sound," Joy shot back before realizing he'd qualified his admission. "What do you mean by *almost?*"

Porky went on to explain, mostly to his shame, the missing part of why he'd bragged. The deacon's race had a lot to do with him revealing Percy's skills. "After all," he told them, "we have a black president; black is the new smart. I knew better, and I'd felt a little guilty after I'd mentioned Percy's case to the deacon."

"And?" Patience asked although she wasn't certain she could stand any more piece-by-piece revelations.

"I happened to mention what I'd told and showed the deacon, and why I'd done it, to that Prophet Long Jevity." Porky began talking fast, as though his life depended upon it. "If Patience had arrived on time that day and hadn't kept him waiting, I probably wouldn't have said anything."

"I knew it!" Joy narrowed her eyes toward Patience, showing her disapproval at her actions, again. But she wasn't about to let Porky off the hook, especially with him mentioning Prophet's name.

"He and I started off talking about the neighborhood," said Porky, "and how so many different kinds of folks had moved into it. When I told Deacon Whistle about Percy investigating a church being embezzled I forgot that Prophet had moved into the same building. Since I'd already told the deacon, I didn't think twice about telling Prophet. After all, it didn't take a genius to figure out that he and Patience had more of a chance of getting together than Patience and that Deacon Whistle."

After repeating one dumb excuse after another, only that time mentioning that what he'd told the deacon had to do with a church being embezzled, it'd all come down to Porky just running his mouth. He'd bragged to Prophet as he'd done to the deacon.

Patience had heard enough. She suddenly looked older. She grabbed a rubber band lying on the table, threading her long hair through it so it hung down her back as a ponytail. Right before Joy and Porky's eyes, it was as though she'd begun transforming back into her old drab self.

"I don't care about Deacon Whistle and what he may or may not feel," Patience said. "Once we tell Lil P what happened, he can add that information to his robbery report. I just hope it won't make our church look bad if Deacon Whistle is somehow involved in robbery, innocent or not."

Joy had already begun tuning out Patience. She didn't need to hear much more to know that Deacon Whistle had probably put it together. Once Porky told him that his son was investigating a church embezzlement and where his notes were hidden, the Bible was just a bonus.

In the meanwhile, Porky's stomach churned with anger. He'd been called stupid on more than one occasion but hadn't felt the full impact until now. He remained silent and, like Joy, he had already tuned out Patience.

However, Patience hadn't stopped venting. "I just don't understand folks stealing what don't belong to them. It's terrible some other church is dealing with their money being taken. I'm just happy that as long as I'm on the finance committee no money will be stolen from Mount Kneel Down."

Of course, when she'd said it aloud, she remembered she was no longer on the finance committee and, worse, she still wasn't sure why the church monies hadn't added up.

Joy finally started listening to Patience. Again, she'd taken on another unnecessary burden.

"It looks like guilty church folks not only come to church, but they remain in church, too." She'd merely murmured her words but quickly covered her mouth with one of her fingers. It was the only way she could keep her mouth shut and not reveal Prophet's part in the investigation.

Right now, Joy felt the only revelation spurring her to action had come from Porky. Leave it to him to tip off Percy's main suspect about the embezzlement investigation.

Of course, as sad as Patience was, she still couldn't let it go. "But I'm just plain ole conflicted. We've let this man Prophet Long Jevity into our home, our lives, and he's even visited our church. We're all just as guilty as Porky." *And I can't wait to give Sister Betty a piece of my mind for sending me to that prophecy taping in the first place,* she thought.

Sitting among the shattered pieces of ceramic, the three cousins tried to come to terms with their situation. One thing they finally agreed upon: Percy needed to know immediately.

Joy started rocking in her seat, wringing her hands one minute, pointing to pictures of Percy the next.

"He's my godson, and I'll search all four corners of hell and beat the crap outta you," Joy threatened, pointing at Porky, "and whoever the perpetrator is, if my baby Lil P gets hurt!"

Later, things quieted down somewhat, and Porky was allowed to spend the night. Percy had finally called to check up on them after dumping Porky off earlier and driving off. Patience thought he'd seemed distant even when he asked to speak with Joy. Once he'd learned she'd already gone to bed, he'd spoken to Porky. The entire time Porky held the phone to his ear he'd turned darker, repeating apologies but without details.

And it was the one time since the cousins had him that Felony wouldn't sleep inside. He remained vigilant on the patio, lying on his purple blanket, his floppy ears spread wide, like antennas.

Chapter 19

Days ago their surveillance of Deacon Whistle had failed. Percy and Prophet had missed Deacon Whistle at the car rental by almost ten minutes.

Today, the two men agreed to meet at a Comfort Inn off Route 85 near Piedmont this morning around eight o'clock.

Prophet had already rented a room there the night before. He and Percy agreed that it made no sense in going back to his apartment in Shaqueeda's building. They were certain the deacon's routine or plan had changed as well.

Porky's intentions didn't matter when he bragged about Percy's case. Every detail he revealed had changed the game plans of everyone involved.

Sitting in Prophet's motel room, Percy spread his surveillance log across the table alongside his family's supposedly stolen heirloom Bible. He took a moment, as he'd done since he arranged his father's place to be robbed, to appreciate the workmanship. His father might not have been a churchgoer, but he certainly took good care of this Bible. It was one of the reasons Percy chose to hide his notes in it. It'd stayed in such good condition because no one had constantly handled it.

"Here's my notepad." Prophet wasn't comfortable with

the young detective hiding his case notes inside a Bible. Although he'd decided years ago, like Jonas, that he didn't want to prophesy, using the gift God gave him in the way God wanted, he still revered a Bible—any Bible.

But that was then.

Prophet laid his notepad next to Percy's. "So I hear you've gotten some interesting info as to why that Whistle blows so hot and heavy in whatever's illegal."

"Percy, I gotta tell you, I've been digging up every source and buried info I could find. It appears our man Whistle comes from a real nasty and mean bunch of human DNA–depraved folks."

Within minutes Prophet had laid out to Percy what he'd discovered. Years of sowing dollars and favors in thug street gardens had paid off.

"You're telling me that Whistle and the infamous Chester Lauder are real cousins? And since old Chester is diseased and messed up, literally crapping in an adult diaper, his cousin is doing the dirty deeds in his place?"

"Exactly."

"Damn, I didn't see that coming."

"It seems that ole Whistle attended Mount Kneel Down on Chester's behalf. Whatever financial investing tips and expertise those two came up with Whistle used as fishing bait to hook some of the more influential church board members."

"A spiritual Ponzi scheme?"

"You'd better believe, Percy. Whistle made certain that first came was first paid. Of course, those members did so well it took no time to convince the financial board and the Reverend Stepson to follow his advice on more financial matters. It appears the only one not to make out was Patience. She never had the extra money to invest."

"I could've told y'all that. But an investigation needs to be thorough, and let the chips fall where they may."

"I'm still glad she wasn't involved in that aspect; it's just our hunch but, like you said, we need to keep our investigation top-notch, with no stones left unturned."

"Well, I'm sure Whistle, being the old bloodsucker he is, like any reputable vampire, couldn't get in there unless they invited him."

"Exactly, so you know I'm betting dollars to doughnuts that when the reverend, Patience, and a few other financial board members showed up offering him a position on the finance board, Whistle probably could've shouted right there on the spot."

"I wouldn't have been surprised if old Chester got up and changed his own diaper that day. They had Rev. Stepson right where they'd wanted him, appeasing and available."

The two men carefully continued comparing routines, corroborating Sister Boodrow's information with their recent findings. So far, she'd been honest about what she'd revealed as well as with the little evidence she'd given First Lady Deborah.

"Hell hath none of the fury of a scorned woman," Percy bristled, shaking his head as he opened his log to a new page. "They can burn you from the grave!"

"You got that right." Prophet let out a long toot as he rose and sipped from the coffee cup in his hand. "I don't ever want a woman to turn on me like that."

Percy didn't want to veer off into another direction, but the opening had fallen into his lap. "So what are you gonna do when my godmother finds out about you? You can't say that you haven't added a little something extra to your investigating methods. In fact, I can't say that I like it at all."

Prophet quickly put down his cup, using both hands to cup his chin instead. He appeared thoughtful, almost to the point of crafting each word of his response to get the least amount of pushback.

"Well, if you don't like it at all," he began, "then what I'm about to say won't change your feelings."

It was Percy's turn to lean back in his seat. "Say what you mean."

"Only on one other occasion have I ever allowed my feelings to interfere with an investigation. You know that, don't you?"

"And so?"

"And I certainly never wanted anyone who hadn't experienced the world and most of its sins, if you get my meaning."

"I do."

"I felt from the first time I saw Patience at that phony Rev. Coffers' prophecy commercial taping, she had nothing to do with her church's missing monies."

"How did you come to that conclusion?"

Prophet Long Jevity went on to explain how he'd observed Patience's eagerness to receive a prophecy and to what lengths she'd gone to do so. "She is a woman who relies on God," Prophet said. "She is no thief."

"Yet, it seems like my godmother has stolen your heart."

Chapter 20

During the time Percy and Prophet pored over their plans for Deacon Whistle, both First Lady Deborah and Reign called Percy. First Lady Deborah wanted an update. With her husband becoming sicker by the day, she wanted and needed something positive to hold onto. Percy assured the first lady that everything was on track and that she should focus on her husband.

Before he could relate the first lady's call to Prophet, Reign called him. She'd been on assignment again in Anderson and was on her way to Spartanburg for a special report. There was a Democratic fundraiser and town hall meeting coming up in a few days at which the president would make an appearance.

He'd completely forgotten about it.

Reign wanted assurance that she wouldn't end up reporting on something crazy his godparents had done.

"They don't have thirty-five hundred dollars apiece to attend a fundraiser," he told her.

"We're talking about Joy and Patience, who believe Barack Obama is a part of God's plans for them. Do you think they'd let money deter them?"

Percy didn't mention too much of Reign's phone call to Prophet. He still hadn't fully heard the man's explanation for going after his godmother, they needed to stick to trailing Deacon Whistle.

Percy and Prophet spent the entire day going over plans, calling in favors, updating their superiors. Since they weren't certain if Whistle was onto them, they had another detail trail him and report back to them.

Twelve hours passed before Percy left the Comfort Inn. He'd received a report that Whistle hadn't moved all day.

Prophet decided to use the time to carry out his part of the next step, which assured Percy that Prophet couldn't go near his godmother's home that night.

Driving along the highway, Percy wavered between picking up his cellphone and calling his wayward family or stopping by unannounced. By the time he reached the exit to go to his godmother's home, he'd already decided to forgo any telephone checkups. Whatever he had to say would need a personal touch.

All he had to do was figure out exactly what he'd say.

Percy arrived at his godmothers' home with two plans. First, to convince them beyond a doubt how crazy it'd been, and would be, to keep trying to contact the United States president. And, secondly, to beg, even threaten, if they didn't let his father spend another night.

Ten minutes ago, he'd walked through the door with his shoulders high and his jaw set. Yet he'd barely gotten the requests out of his mouth before they'd said yes.

Even though Percy hadn't discussed with Porky the plan to spend another night, Porky didn't protest. He never said a word beyond *okay*.

The docile behavior from that trio of nearly mid-life protesters was Percy's first clue something had changed. But it wasn't change he believed in.

It gnawed away at Percy, the way they'd all sat around the living room quickly agreeing to everything he'd said or asked.

It'd been almost as though they wanted him to hurry and leave. He'd especially felt that way when Joy had asked him, "Don't you have somewhere to go?"

He'd been reluctant, but since it was late and none of them were what he'd call old night crawlers, he'd left somewhat hopeful.

During the drive back to his apartment, an eerie feeling surged in his gut. He couldn't shake it. Every time he'd thought about exceeding the speed limit so he could get home quickly, knowing Reign would soon be there, he'd think about what'd happened at his godmothers'.

Something else is going on, he thought. *Whatever that something else is, the three of them are in on it. It's gotta be something crazy or dangerous; only two of them even like one another.*

By the time Reign arrived at his home, Percy had just showered and begun heating up bits and pieces of his bachelor culinary specialty—takeout Boston Market meatloaf and canned string beans. He could tell she'd had a hard night from the way she nearly collapsed into the closest chair to his door.

He had let her catch her breath while he unfolded her hands around the bag she'd brought with her. Opening the bag, he'd smiled, thinking, *At least she thought to bring two bottles of Evian water.* If she hadn't, they would've been left with city gin from the sink's faucet.

While Reign had sat sprawled across the chair, he told her what'd happened at his godmothers' house. "Normally, before they'd have let me leave their home, they would've forced a bag of food into my hands."

He had to coax Reign into eating. She told him her mouth was so tired she couldn't chew.

Fortunately, he knew how to revive her. "I don't see why your mouth is tired, but not your hands," he told Reign. "The way you blasted me with that text message, it's those fingers that should be sore."

She mouthed *whatever.*

Percy smiled before he lowered his bait. "I'd have replied more, but I figured you'd wanna hear what I learned today when you got here instead."

He'd not had to say another word. Reign's journalistic need-to-know switch powered on.

A short time after they'd shared information, and food, Reign told Percy she felt too tired to drive to her apartment across town. Percy fell asleep before she completed the sentence.

Despite her being there when he'd dozed off, the next morning when Percy woke, Reign was gone.

He'd already begun feeling a kick to his manhood, wondering if she'd left the night before. *I know she was pissed. I must've been more tired than I thought—nothing I can do about it now.*

His romantic problem with Reign last night wasn't the only problem he had, as he discovered when he turned on his cellphone.

Things were already hot across town.

Chapter 21

An hour later, Percy had no time to sulk over whatever problem he and Reign might've had. Instead he stood wanting to hold his nose to block the stench of smoke, lye hair relaxer, homemade concoctions passing for hair conditioner, and bits of burnt weave hair clinging to his jacket. A mess of greasy gunk and other mysterious solutions, clung to the bottoms of his shoes. He could hardly take one step without walking like a zombie.

Percy found one of the detectives from his robbery and homicide unit off to the side of a building barking orders to his team; yet he spoke with respect to the arson investigator.

Percy had one thing going for him. Pelzer was a small town. Everyone knew just about everyone.

Because the investigators knew Percy from robbery and homicide, once he walked over and joined them they shared more information than normal. They also accepted Percy's explanation that he'd arrived on the scene quickly because of his father's recent robbery.

According to the lead detective, Shaqueeda's Curl, Wrap, and Daycare Center was probably a robbery, with fire as a cover up. Fortunately, no one was on the premises; it'd all gone down before sunrise.

Percy could've added his own observations; he didn't want to. He knew it was easier to get information when you kept quiet and listened. His attention to the detectives' details cut short when he heard his name and felt a tap on his shoulder.

"LaPierre, step this way for a moment, please."

Percy nodded to the other men, who'd already returned to the business at hand.

With a half-smile yet appearing serious, the man said, "I see you've already begun your homework."

The observation came from a short, squatty, freckle-faced man with the name Brannigan on his name tag. The fire inspector's dark-colored helmet and olive complexion, each scarred by years of poring through soot and inhaling smoke and burning flesh, did little to hide his age. At that moment, the man looked about fifty, and Percy began looking the same.

"I know you've probably spoken with your father this morning, but I may need to speak with him, too. I need to question some of the other business owners around here."

Percy hadn't informed his family yet, but wouldn't say so. "Okay, but you wanna fill me in?"

"No problem; look it ain't been a week, and this is the third suspected robbery, including your dad's place, and the second suspicion of arson since last night."

"What other fire happened last night? I didn't hear anything about another fire."

"Son," Brannigan said slowly, "did you sleep under a rock or something? One of the offices at Mount Kneel Down's Outreach Center sustained major fire damage during the night—"

Percy couldn't have asked another question if his life depended upon it. All the professionalism he'd shown over the years while chasing criminals, even shooting a few, solving hard, often cold cases, he now placed on pause.

swer. She began pacing back and forth, her eyes ablaze, saying things her mouth couldn't. "Of course, I wouldn't do some crazy mess like that."

She stopped for a breath. Pointing a finger in Percy's face, she exhaled and continued. "To my way of thinking, and since I know all six of my tenants, there's only two that come to my mind that been acting suspicious."

"Two?"

"You heard me, Percy. I said two. Now, number one; I ain't had nothin' but a bad feeling ever since Patience brought that Prophet fella to me for someplace to stay."

"You suspect Prophet Long Jevity?"

"Yeah, that's the same one." Shaqueeda looked around again. She'd no doubt suddenly noticed that a couple of the investigators could probably overhear their conversation. Percy put a hand on her shoulder again, bringing her closer, signaling she should lower her voice.

"Percy," Shaqueeda whispered, "I'm telling you if that fella hadn't paid me in advance and with a ton of cash, I'd've told him no. But Patience looked like she was truly interested in a future with him; and I don't mean the kind that he says God talks to him about."

If Shaqueeda didn't have his full attention before, she had it now. Percy listened intently and after a few moments began walking her back toward her car. On the way, she told him how she was tired of folks always coming to her just because she was the landlady, looking for Prophet Jevity, whenever he'd disappear for a few days or weeks at a time.

"At first, I really thought he was a big-time celebrity preacher man 'cause of his name. He was dressed in tailored suits, clean shaven, and fine as he wanted to be. I'm tellin' you, from the moment Patience brought him to me, I never saw him not wearing them big sunglasses. I don't know why celebrities won't even take a crap without sunglasses; they probably sleep in them, too."

Unable to say what he'd wanted, he covered his silence by looking around as though inspecting the area.

From a few yards away, Percy saw another investigator rushing toward them. The man wore a similar uniform as Brannigan, and he carried a burlap sack. A familiar smell quickly made its way to where they stood.

The man was Asian and short; he wore his hat cocked to the side, and looked to be in his early thirties. He didn't acknowledge Percy. He spoke directly to Brannigan, loud enough for Percy and others to overhear.

"Inspector Brannigan, sir, can't say for certain until we test it," he offered, "but I'm willing to bet that it came from the apartment building next door. It's got a lot of water and smoke damage from putting out that salon fire. It couldn't be helped. Red Cross can help those who need shelter until the owner gets the building back to living conditions."

The young investigator stopped speaking; holding the bag, he then pointed toward Shaqueeda's Curl, Wrap, and Daycare Center. "This is probably a mixture of human and synthetic hair along with some old perm chemicals, other hair products, and an unknown accelerant. It looks like it was tossed in a hurry. I discovered it in a common trash receptacle. Another thirty minutes and Sanitation would've had it."

Percy's mind fought to regain its control. He didn't like what he was thinking, but it couldn't have been an accident at both Shaqueeda's and Mount Kneel Down in the same night. What if they'd spooked Deacon Whistle when they'd followed him?

"I know my father's place used that trash bin, too. None of what's in that bag would've been on his menu. I guess that's a good thing."

Fortunately for Percy, Inspector Brannigan had chosen to ignore his gibberish and amateur attempt at humor. Inspector Brannigan called out to another man while quickly walking away.

Percy treaded carefully. He wasn't a part of the robbery investigation team on the scene. Moreover, no one knew if the fire was arson or accidental. He quickly regrouped, kept his mouth shut, observing from a distance.

Every now and then he'd catch a snatch of a question or response. They said they would get around to questioning everyone, including Porky, a questionable character; but could his father be trusted not to run his mouth? He doubted it.

He'd already been there an hour; during that time, some of the neighbors had stopped by to gawk.

Percy took a moment to check his voice mail. There'd been three messages left. One frantic call was from Reign. He could tell from the timbre of her voice, she wanted to cry. He didn't need to listen to the entire message to know she'd learned of the fire at the church's business office. Yet Reign, being ever the professional reporter, said she was going into the field to file a report. He could also hear First Lady Deborah wailing, praying in the background.

The second message was just as frantic. It was his father. From the way Porky stuttered and cussed, he'd learned of the fires, too.

The last call was from Prophet. Whistle was on the move; so was he. He'd also decided to relocate. He'd found an out-of-the-way hotel that would keep him better concealed. Prophet left the name and address. Percy had never heard of either in all the years he'd lived in Pelzer.

Percy decided he'd leave to check up on his family. He was thinking that he didn't think he'd learn anything new, when he heard his name. He turned around in time to see the queen of gossip, Shaqueeda, her talkative mouth rivaled only by Porky's.

Others in the neighborhood gawked, yammered, and left. However, when Shaqueeda learned her business had burned and that the apartment building was water-damaged, she refused to leave.

There was no mistaking her anger. She was hopscotching on the sidewalk, throwing shadow punches, obviously not caring if one landed on someone. Every time she opened her mouth, her head swung from side to side, revealing tracks from her multicolor weave that looked like they'd derailed.

She could've spoken to one of the other fire investigators, but being an old-school gossip, now possibly out of business, she wouldn't. She headed straight for Percy.

Shaqueeda, half-bawling and cussing, started broadcasting just how angry she was. "Damn cockroaches, all of 'em. Skunks think they're gonna rob and burn me out. They don't know who they messing with. I'll do the damn crime and the time."

Percy reached out gently, bringing her closer, whispering, "Miss Shaqueeda, I'm so sorry. I know you've worked hard, but the police will get to the bottom of this. I promise you."

Another female would've melted, had they Percy's huge, muscular arms folded around them. Shaqueeda didn't fit into that *any female* category. Steel-minded Shaqueeda gave natural birth to her now fifteen-year-old twins, Camry and Corolla, on her cold linoleum shop floor.

She'd pushed and birthed those two six-pound girls not five minutes after pulling the trigger on her ex-husband, former record producer Shank. If she hadn't been bothered, seconds before, by an excruciating labor pain, she wouldn't have missed.

"You know, I should've spoken up sooner, but I minds my own beeswax," Shaqueeda barked, moving away from Percy. Suddenly, as though she'd changed her mind, she returned, this time closer and her mouth louder. "I can rebuild, but I shouldn't have to and it's my fault!"

Percy wanted to put one of his large hands over her big mouth. Instead, murmuring, he asked, "You set your place on fire, Miss Shaqueeda?"

"Negro, are you crazy!?" Shaqueeda didn't wait for an an-

He needed to pull her back on track before she derailed. "What changed your mind about him?"

"I changed my mind when I heard he'd started asking around about that gal that won some of them so-called beauty contests a few years ago."

"Beauty contests?"

"Yeah, just like I said—so-called beauty contests."

Shaqueeda suddenly stopped speaking. Old habits die hard with undercover informants—Percy thought she was about to ask him for a few dollars for the information, but then her brow wrinkled and the side of her mouth turned, showing her anger had returned. His gut told him Prophet might've done something else to make her angry, but she wasn't saying. At that moment, it didn't matter, because he just wanted her talking.

He began coaxing her. "Why would him asking about her change your opinion? I don't understand."

"Look Percy, I know you all educated, and if you ain't got to do it you won't hang with low class. But I do hair; so low class and high class sit their butts in my chairs."

"Yes, ma'am, I'm certain they do."

"I knew that gal Boodrow before she passed away. I don't care how much church-going she did. She was a cheap heffa, both with her tipping and her slipping. And everybody at my shop knows she was giving more than just tithes and offerings to that white man, Deacon Whistle."

"Deacon Whistle from Mount Kneel Down?"

"Yep, that's the one—from over there at Mount Kneel Down. He's also been one of my tenants for the past three years, too. Anyway, she thought it was cute to get a pedicure, say *praise the Lord*, then brag about a Menogy Twa."

"Do you mean a ménage a trois?"

"I meant exactly what I said. I ain't no fool; I got two good eyes. I know that Prophet and that Deacon must've found another hussy to do their bidding. They was always disappearing, each around the same time and for the same amount of time. It's disgusting just thinking about those trifling men playing with God like that."

"What do you mean, they *disappeared* about the same time every time?"

"You really need to start hanging with more trashy folk instead of just locking them away." Shaqueeda rolled her eyes, took a deep breath, and began schooling Percy. "Listen, Percy. This is how they done it. First that ole white dude, Deacon Whistle, would head off the block. Less than five minutes later I'd see light-bright—"

"Light-bright?"

"Keep up, Percy, I ain't got all day."

"Yes ma'am."

"Light-bright—Prophet Jevity. He'd head out right behind that Whistle. I'm smart enough to know they can't do the nasty on Ptomaine, so they had to go further downtown or out of town to get some chicken head to hunt and peck with them. And then, just like clockwork, Deacon Whistle would come back followed by that Prophet."

"Wow," Percy muttered, "did you ever see the two of them together?"

"Of course, they wasn't together, Percy. They was smarter than that. Some church folks take staying in the closet for real; besides, I didn't have to see them together to know what they was doing. I knew what Sister Boodrow was doing outta her own mouth, and that was enough for me to figure out they'd need to replace her."

"Did you ever tell my godmother about any of this?" Percy crossed his fingers, his eyes piercing hers for any signs of deception, still praying she hadn't told anyone her theory, but him.

"I had wanted to tell Patience the last time she came around looking for that absentee Prophet. I felt she needed to know that I wasn't too keen on the man and the kind of women he must've liked. Plus, I didn't like how your god-mother had started dressing, a little more hip hoppy and a lot less church."

"But—"

"But nothing; she's a grown woman. And just keeping real, he'd always paid in cash, so where he was or wasn't wasn't none of my business. Plus, everybody knows that Shaqueeda minds her own business when money crosses her palms!"

Percy had heard enough to put urgency to what he needed to do. Obviously, if Shaqueeda figured out there was a connection between Prophet and Whistle, or at least what she thought there was, then he needed to retool the plan. He'd need to do it quick!

Percy needed, at that moment, his godmothers to keep their promise to leave the president alone, and his father to shut his big mouth. It was just as important that he check out something he remembered reading from Sister Boodrow's notes. He'd put Prophet on it immediately.

Percy's mind had momentarily slipped away from Shaqueeda's chatter once it'd became apparent she'd given him what he'd needed. But Shaqueeda hadn't run out of gossip steam yet.

She pushed a weave back into its track and leaned forward, tapping Percy on his elbow. "You tell your scandalous daddy, I said to call me. He'll know why and don't you be asking him about it. This is personal between me, the Playa's Cabin, and him."

Without as much as a good-bye, Ptomaine Avenue's premiere female gossipmonger raced away toward her car, no doubt to file a lawsuit. He was certain she'd make someone pay. She just hadn't figured out whom.

At that moment Percy had too many circumstantial bits and pieces but no glue. He knew Prophet hadn't consorted with Whistle or the late Sister Boodrow.

Things hadn't gone the way he'd wanted since the night

he'd orchestrated the robbery of his father's restaurant. He'd done so under a cloud of secrecy, now he didn't need to trip over new investigations.

Percy needed to find out who'd been assigned to the new cases. He also would speak to Reign. He'd tell her what Shaqueeda said, or as much as he could. Telling her the highlights of the conversation should keep her from revealing something by accident.

He was so busy recalling Shaqueeda's unsolicited but useful gossip, planning his next move, he didn't see the news van arrive.

"When did she get here?" He couldn't interrupt her, so he waited, admiring his fiancée while she stared into the camera, preparing to give a live television report.

Chapter 22

Percy hadn't been the only one searching in the dark for answers about the salon and apartment fires. Across town the situation was pretty dark for Joy, Patience, and Porky, too.

"Have mercy, sweet Jesus!" Joy couldn't say another word as she, Patience, and Porky sat stunned before the television in her living room.

"What has happened to Ptomaine Avenue," Porky bellowed. "Ain't nothing but thieving and burning going on twenty-four seven. Don't them scoundrels ever take a break no more?"

"Poor Shaqueeda," Patience added. "Her Curl, Wrap, and Daycare Center all burnt crispy, and it looks like the fire did some damage to her apartment building. I certainly hope the prophet—" She stopped to correct her truthful error. "I mean, I hope no one got hurt."

"Forget all of that. I need to see a shot of my Shanty. I know I didn't just get robbed and burned down all in the same week!"

The WPAK news van parked nearby blocked a complete view of the Soul Food Shanty; the cousins continued sitting gape-mouthed at the news coverage.

A while ago, Percy had finally responded to Porky's frantic voice message. He promised he'd drop by to see about him as soon as possible. Percy would also bring some fresh clothes so Porky wouldn't stink up his godmothers' home more than he'd already done.

It hadn't taken Percy long to find out when one of the detectives would begin routine questioning of some of the Ptomaine Avenue business owners. He'd sought and received a favor from his robbery and homicide department. They'd allow Percy to tag along with one of the fellow detectives.

It was almost noon before Percy arrived at his godmothers' home. He arrived with another detective, an old-timer, a tall, skinny, brown-skinned man close to retiring. He resembled a black Detective Columbo, but without the trademark half-closed eye and slouched shoulders.

Without emotion, Percy informed his godmothers and father that they were there on official business. They weren't to worry, but they needed to answer a few questions to shed light on what had happened.

Of course, there'd be separate questions for Joy and Patience regarding anything they had to offer about the fire at the church. The detective didn't bother asking Porky about Mount Kneel Down because all of Pelzer knew he didn't go to church. If something developed that challenged Porky's church-going habits, then he'd come back to it.

It was only after Porky had cussed, fussed, screamed, and thrown things that he became sane enough to answer any questions. The threat to lock him up if he didn't calm down played a huge part, too.

The detective asked Porky a few questions. He wanted to know Porky's whereabouts the night before; did he know who robbed him two nights ago?

The questions weren't in any particular order. As an afterthought, the detective asked Porky how much insurance he had on his business, and whether it was in hock to anyone.

There was the lingering question of why Shaqueeda's properties were robbed and torched while Porky's was only robbed. Just like Porky's church-going habits, all of Pelzer also knew questionable people and items moved between the Shanty and Shaqueeda's. Had they pissed someone off?

There were other questions as well, and Porky's answers were surprisingly limited to short replies.

"My arse stayed right here last night," he informed the detective, adding, "I hope the heathen reads my Grand-mamma Truth's Bible."

The reference to the robbery caused Percy to flinch from guilt; he remained calm, and prayed his father didn't slip up.

"And make sure you write this down, too," Porky told the detective. "My insurance deductible's more than what that place is worth. And everybody that knows me does like me."

Of course, it was that last lie Porky told that almost tripped him up. Even the detective who questioned him had never liked him.

All the while, Joy and Patience stood by listening and watching. Under other circumstances they might've critiqued the detective's questioning skills, thinking the man went too soft on Porky, but that wasn't the time. They were genuinely concerned for Porky and their godson. Something wasn't right; they could feel it in their spirit. They wanted more answers about the fire at the church's business office.

Joy had already spoken to First Lady Deborah, but she'd been too upset to answer questions. Joy couldn't share what she knew with Patience, so she kept quiet.

Once the detective said he had no further official questions at that time, it became Percy's turn. He unofficially stepped in.

With the detective then out of earshot but not out of

sight, Percy gathered them together and warned them, saying, "I don't want either of you calling anyone, taking phone calls, or going outside. I don't want you answering a door or peeping through a peephole or the window until I get back. And I need my dad to stay in your spare bedroom because he can't go back to Ptomaine Avenue yet or my apartment. Am I clear?"

Joy and Patience gritted their teeth to the point of almost needing a root canal. The thought of having Porky remain under their roof for another night or even longer hadn't occurred to them. Yet they and Porky nodded in agreement. Felony, who'd not barked or dog-farted since the questioning began, lowered his massive skull showing he'd understood as well.

Percy had left some time ago, yet they still sat, looking stone-faced, in the living room. No one had touched the iced tea Joy had poured moments before Percy and the other detective had arrived with their questions.

Finally, Patience unfolded her arms and stood up. Nodding toward Joy—a signal that she was about to do something probably stupid in nature—she sat next to Porky and immediately pinched her nose, letting him know that he'd need to meet up with soap and water real soon.

"Porky," Patience began, "before Lil P left after giving us all those 'to do' and 'not do' orders, had he made you promise to follow them?"

Porky took a moment to reply. He knew he stunk, but didn't think the reminder would come from Patience. Finally, he answered. "No, he didn't." Porky then lifted his head and that time he looked at Joy. "What about you, Joy? Did you promise?"

"No, I didn't. Why should I? I'm a grown woman who knows how not to smell up somebody's house!"

"I got the doggone message already, Joy. I have a sprained wrist, so get the hell off my back!"

"Get in the shower!" Joy snapped. "I'll get some soap, towels, and a scrub brush. Since you still crippled, I'll even send Felony in with you so he can wash and claw that back!"

"Will y'all please stop?" Patience ordered. "We've got real problems here. And just to make it clear, I didn't promise Lil P either."

"We're sorry," Joy and Porky chorused.

"Good," Patience replied. "The way I see it," she continued as she put on her glasses, "I don't know why we should do what he ordered if we didn't promise."

Once they'd decided to forgo the warnings Percy had left, the three cousins began to plot. Each secretly had a different motive, but a common goal.

Porky's motive was simple. He had as many snitches as he had enemies. Somebody was gonna tell him something. He'd already made up his mind; Percy could follow the police code while he used his street smarts.

Joy had her intentions as well. She was already angry about Grandmamma Truth's stolen Bible and decided that when she found out who'd stolen it, she'd issue punishments that'd make the Old Testament ones seem like forgiveness.

But then there was also her church. No one messed with her church and got away with it. And the last time she'd been inside the church business office so had Deacon Whistle. Even if she'd never watched a detective show in her life, she had enough commonsense. She combined all she knew and the glove fit.

As for Patience, she too had her reasons. She loved her cousin Porky, she loved her church, but she'd also come to have strong feelings for Prophet.

He'd doused her hopes. He'd put out her burning desire

for a relationship without giving one kiss. Somehow she knew that his secrets, his sudden disappearances, and other gut-check feelings she'd ignored up to that moment, now made him her prime suspect. She also decided she owed it to Shaqueeda if Prophet was involved. After all, she'd brought him to her.

Without being told, Felony lay outside the bathroom door while Porky showered. Every so often he'd bark as though he were trying to let Porky know he'd missed a spot and that he'd better come out smelling more human and less dog.

Shortly after Porky was dressed and ready—with a promise Felony wouldn't bite him again—Joy coaxed Porky into their SUV.

None of the three exposed their true reasons or way of getting to the bottom of things; the only thing promised was chaos.

Joy and Patience also needed to find a way to do their deeds without erasing their chances with President Barack. The last thing they wanted was to embarrass him with anything amateurish.

Once the detective said he'd probably not go back and question Porky anytime soon, Percy returned home. He immediately showered. The smell of smoke, soot, and other unidentifiable odors had caused him to gag. He'd also need to deodorize his car before driving it again.

For the past hour or more, he'd walked shirtless around his expensively decorated three-room apartment. Putting on a shirt never entered his already thought-juggling mind, so he wore nothing but a pair of brown boxer shorts.

Seated at his kitchen table, he pored over the notes written on his investigation pad. He'd repeatedly gone over the craziness Shaqueeda told him while trying to push away the feeling that his family was up to something. *I warned them and they'd better listen,* he thought.

Twenty minutes ago, Percy had heard from Reign, saying she was on her way there. Neither said much else; they preferred to discuss things face-to-face.

One thing was certain, if not said over the telephone: she wasn't happy. Her father's church business office had been set afire and she'd no doubt it'd been done as a cover-up. Her mother had had to leave immediately without her help to get her father settled into another hospital; all the while, she had to smile for the television cameras.

Percy felt bad for her; too much was happening that she thought she knew, but didn't. He could've set aside some of her concerns, but he wouldn't.

What he'd kept from Reign was necessary. She'd been instrumental in providing whatever information she'd discovered about the missing funds from her father's church and about Deacon Whistle; he couldn't tell her that he'd set up the robbery at the Shanty and that there'd been no loss of the documents. He still had the Bible. Keeping everything on a need-to-know basis had been the only way he could've gotten permission from the department. The less people who knew, the more successful the investigation would be and, the sooner it would end.

Of course she'd been pissed off; he hadn't been up-front with her about his godmothers pestering the Obama administration beyond craziness when they included a letter to the CIA. And yet, she didn't mention the fire at Shaqueeda's salon and apartment building beyond what she'd reported on the news.

Pushing aside his notes, he placed his hands behind his head. *I know we won't be discussing wedding plans anytime soon.* Percy didn't have a chance to think further, hearing Reign's key turning the lock.

He pushed the pad aside, rose to meet her at the door. He wanted to hug her, calm her. One look at a sooty skirt and the same unmistakable smoky smell he'd had earlier meant she probably wasn't in a huggable mood.

"I need a shower!" Reign gave the announcement in her no nonsense, matter-of-fact tone, much like she'd report the news, all the while tossing some files, a newspaper, and a fast-food bag onto the cocktail table.

The bag looked almost empty, so Percy knew she'd not brought him anything to eat. Since she didn't live with him, she really didn't have to. However, he didn't feel a need to respond or mention it, since neither had yet to say hello.

He watched her disrobe. By the time she reached the bathroom door, she was already free of everything except her bra and slip, before quickly closing the bathroom door.

As much trouble as Percy knew he was in at that moment, he couldn't help but pray that she'd be more understanding when the rest hit the fan. They'd been together long enough for him to know Reign Stepson was as unpredictable as her parents, the original storms.

Percy took the near-empty bag with packets of ketchup, salt, and pepper back into the kitchen, tossing it into the waste can before he sat down again. With his pen he began going over his notes, word by word, line by line, until he'd formed a rhythm with the pen. He began tapping the melody and humming the words to one of his and Reign's favorite songs, "Strangers in the Night."

"Wow," he murmured as he suddenly stopped humming, "where did that come from?"

Chapter 23

He knew where it'd come from. The music, the melody, the words flooded his mind almost automatically whenever he thought of her. In fact, at that moment he also remembered the first time he'd laid eyes upon her. She never knew it, but she'd instantly snatched him off the market. He hadn't thought about being with anyone, physically or mentally, since that day.

He rose, suddenly thinking he'd heard the water stop running in the shower. It hadn't, so he returned to the table and sat, remembering how on the day he'd first met Reign, the choir had marched in wearing dark blue robes with neon orange edging. It was Mount Kneel Down's youth choir, and those young folks sang their hearts out. The music was hot.

That night, just when he'd clapped his hands and tapped his feet until they hurt, it got hotter. Reign Stepson walked out and onto the pulpit.

If feeling the spirit was anything like the way he'd felt, then he'd been filled that night.

She'd been then, and still was, a young beauty with large, brown, almond-shaped eyes and a deep black, short, sassy haircut. Back then, it'd taken him a moment to realize she'd begun moving from side to side, holding the microphone like a seasoned pro, captivating her audience. Who knew she'd one day use it to report the news to millions?

Percy shook his head and looked toward the bathroom. He heard her singing. It meant she'd calmed down and probably would be in there a little longer.

His mind went back to the thoughts he'd had a moment ago.

He should've known that night, by the way she'd held that microphone, that she'd had it in her all the time to be a news reporter or anything having to do with an audience or the stage.

He remembered exactly what she'd worn. It was an ankle-length fuchsia-colored dress with a slender belt exaggerating a tiny waistline that only made him want to see more. She was a caramel-kissed beauty who'd already stolen his heart before she'd sung her first note.

"Wow!" he'd leaned over and whispered to Joy. "God-mother, I'm glad you made me come with you tonight. She's beautiful!"

Mumbling from behind the fan she'd held to her face, Joy had nodded and began giving him the necessary and unnecessary information.

"She's twenty-two now. She's called Reign Stepson, instead of Le Reign as you once knew her before she turned from a weed into a beautiful flower. You might've remembered if you'd attend church more often. She's your former law professor, the Reverend Lock Stepson and First Lady Deborah's only daughter.

"Reign's not only gorgeous, but real intelligent, too. She don't look like her daddy at all, which is a blessing in disguise." Joy stopped and looked up toward the church ceiling, repenting, "Lord, please forgive me for saying that bit of truth out loud."

She'd then continued whispering from behind her fan.

"She's graduated from that Howard University up north, somewhere near Washington and already got a job as a television gal giving social updates or something like that. Rev. Stepson had her primed since birth to get a court career like he'd done, but she went her own way. I think she'd been a distraction in any court 'cause she's too pretty. She did the right thing by choosing television."

Joy mumbled softly yet firmly as she continued fanning. "Unlike you, she's made use of her college degree." She hadn't waited for him to protest, instead she quickly added, "However, she could be yours. All you'd need is a serious prenuptial agreement and favor from the Lord."

"Why haven't you gotten dressed yet?" Reign's question startled Percy. He hadn't heard her come out of the bathroom or go into his room to change clothes. She sometimes kept something extra to wear, just in case. Sadly for him, those just-in-case times were too few and probably designed to keep him honest. She'd been adamant about not taking things further than a little kissing and petting.

She changed into a pair of dark-colored jeans that fit without showing belly skin or butt lines. The white sleeveless buttoned-down blouse exposed bare shoulders. They were what he'd come to refer to as her Michelle Obama guns.

Rather than discuss it, Percy quickly dressed. He returned to the kitchen in time to see her looking over his notes. Fortunately, they were only a few preliminary ones from that morning's off-the-record investigation of the fires.

"I see you spoke with Shaqueeda this morning." Reign didn't wait for an answer as she continued reading his log paper, seemingly line for line. "I suppose whatever information your nosy godmothers and your father gleaned from her you can add to this." She slammed the logbook back onto the table. "I thought you were keeping them off this investigation?"

"I stopped by this morning along with another detective. He questioned Porky, and I gave him extra clothes, since he was going to stay with my godmothers."

"Oh really—?"

"That's right. I also warned them not to make a move toward the door or the telephone until I told them to."

"Well, I guess you set them straight and all, especially with them promising to do exactly as you ordered."

"You know it!" The brag had barely left his lips before he realized they hadn't promised anything. They'd only nodded. "What makes you think they didn't listen?"

"I don't think they didn't listen. I know they didn't. Earlier, on my way here, I saw Felony with his big head looking out the rear of the RAV. It was parked in front of Shaqueeda's other salon. I'd just started to back up when I caught sight of Patience sitting behind the wheel and your dad in the backseat with Felony's butt in his face."

Percy felt his blood pressure rise. He'd been right. The three were up to something and had played him, just as he'd tried to play them.

"By the way," Reign added, "have you heard from Prophet? He called, said you weren't picking up your cellphone. He needed you quick."

Percy didn't answer, reaching instinctively to his belt for his cellphone. He suddenly realized he hadn't seen it when he dressed because he'd left it in his car, still connected to its charger.

Chapter 24

Earlier that midday, Joy, Patience, and Porky, along with Felony still riding shot-hound, discussed their courses of action. Of course, all their actions were based upon the false information they traded among themselves.

They'd finally decided, based upon Joy's need to squash some of her anger, that they'd hit Shaqueeda's other salon first. It wasn't that far away from the salon destroyed over on Ptomaine Avenue.

Once they arrived, Porky started protesting. He didn't like the idea of remaining inside the vehicle. That's when Joy turned around in her seat, reached over, and attempted to snatch him by a strap on his sling. She barked out a few orders. "I ain't gonna keep repeating this. Like I told you before we got here, you keep your big mouth shut and stay in the car."

"You don't tell me what I can or cannot do, Joy Karry!" Porky wanted to add more, but he suddenly felt the hot warning breath from Felony's panting creeping across his face. "You could've asked me nicely."

"I don't do nice when it comes to you. By the way, if I do need you to come inside, limit your lying mouth to a *yes* or a *no*," Joy added.

With Joy and Porky going at it in such a stupid manner, Patience decided not to tell them that she thought she'd seen Reign's car pass by.

Saturday afternoons brought out all sorts of folks to Shaqueeda's second salon, called The Busy Body.

With folks' mouths running under hair dryers, and cash overrunning the cash register, Joy wasn't surprised to find Shaqueeda handling business. She was going about as though she hadn't lost her other shop to a fire and had her apartment building damaged. If the woman was nothing else, she was a businesswoman as well as a snoop.

The more mouths running, the more likely I'm bound to find out something, Joy thought.

The Busy Body beauty salon was no different than most of the male barber shops around town. Pelzer women of all ages scrimped and saved to spend a few hours receiving and trading gossip. The Busy Body gave a new meaning to the old adage, *Bring a bone and take a bone.*

"Well, look who finally realized that not all miracles take place in the church." Shaqueeda snickered as the olive green and orange material of her Japanese kimono clung to pear-shaped hips. She pushed a wad of bills into her bra and wiggled and quick-stepped toward Joy, wearing oriental Gekkos on her big feet.

Stopping within a few inches, Shaqueeda gave Joy a quick air peck and a home girl greeting. "Gurl, what brings you to my exclusive establishment? How are you doin'?" She barely stopped for air before blurting, "I guess you've heard about what happened at my Curl, Wrap, and Daycare Center earlier?"

"Yes, I did," Joy replied. "I'm sorry about your apartment building getting messed up, too."

Joy could feel some of the customers honing in on their conversation, put on alert by Shaqueeda's loud greeting.

To let them know she was onto them, Joy mouthed a

hello toward several of the women. Lowering her voice, she told Shaqueeda, "I'm here looking for a blessing." Joy let her words linger and sink in before she continued. "That is, if you still in the *blessing* business."

"Ach-shoo and excuse me!" Shaqueeda followed her fake sneeze with a quick wink.

Both women knew the game, especially since they were playing their version of the tattletale game, bringing a bone and taking a bone since they were kids. If information needed telling or selling, Shaqueeda told it and sold it.

Joy quickly shot back with a *bless you*. She had almost forgotten Shaqueeda's clue.

She lowered her head for a second. It was enough time to suppress a sly grin while following Shaqueeda, who had already turned and begun walking away toward her supply room in the rear.

Joy tried focusing on the Asian-Afrocentric style of the Busy Body hair salon. Its décor was vastly different from its counterpart on Ptomaine. The one on Ptomaine had been covered from the front door to the back with gold and platinum album covers of every recording artist from Bessie Smith to James Smith, aka LL Cool J. Shaqueeda kept them up, reminding folks that she'd received a ton of money from Shank's record-producing successes.

However, the Busy Body boasted something different. This salon was Shaqueeda's brainchild, and she wanted everyone to know her roots. She'd decorated it with red, black, green, and yellow bamboo lanterns and animal skins, the same colors as Shaqueeda's dyed hair. Joy quickly raised one hand to her forehead. *Lord, please let me find out what I need to know before this Josephine-woman, with the head and shop of many colors like Joseph's coat, gives me a migraine.*

Once in the back of the salon, Joy started her interrogation. "Shaqueeda, I know that you know. I just need you to tell me. C'mon, old friend. Bless me!"

Shaqueeda always bartered in cash. However, they were old friends, so she believed Joy's check would clear the bank. Without once mentioning Patience, she told all she knew about Deacon Whistle and his exploits.

Unfortunately, Shaqueeda really hadn't added much value to what Joy had already learned from First Lady Deborah and her own observations. But she knew she'd better let that check clear. Friends or not, Shaqueeda had tried to shoot her ex-husband moments before she'd given birth. That bit of legend alone made folks stay straight with the woman.

It hadn't taken too long for Joy to confirm without adding anything new. By the time she returned to the RAV, Patience had on her headphones, listening to her iPod while drowning out Porky's complaints of Felony's unwarranted guarding. "If this doggone mutt ain't got his arse in my face, he's got his face in my face. I'm sick of it!"

To keep Porky's griping to a minimum, they gave into his need to return to Ptomaine Avenue. Joy had already told them that she hadn't found out anything from Shaqueeda, so they let Porky have his way.

An hour later, still fuming from the way he'd been played by his family, Percy had dropped Reign off at the WPAK television station. She needed to gather some papers she'd need later when she went to Mount Kneel Down's business office. She had an appointment with the insurance adjuster in her parents' stead.

Fortunately, the reverend when in his right mind had added Reign's name to the church board. He'd placed her in a position to handle business if her mother wasn't available, and as a counter measure if the board got out of hand. However, like her mother, Reign had a life and a career and she'd not participated as she should have. Now, she was trying to catch up and find the culprit stealing the church monies.

Percy sat at a traffic light, fingering the cellphone on his belt. He'd been off his game, again, when he'd left it earlier in his car. He used the few seconds before the light changed to decide whether to go after his crazy family or try again to reach Prophet.

No sooner had the light turned green than he found himself headed towards the Busy Body hair salon. If Shaqueeda told Patience half of what she'd shared with him, then there weren't too many places Prophet could hide to escape her wrath.

"You must be looking for your godmother, Percy. You just missed her by about ten minutes," Shaqueeda told him after he'd rushed inside the salon and she'd taken him into the back.

"You didn't tell her what you told me this morning, did you?"

"I don't see why I would."

"Well, you didn't have a problem telling it this morning so I thought with y'all being old friends and all—"

"Watch out with that *old* talk," Shaqueeda warned. "Besides, if I was to tell anyone, it would be Patience."

Percy's hand flew to his head. His family was gonna kill him before anything connected with his job would. "So you told Joy?"

"Joy paid and asked; I told and will cash the check on Monday."

As soon as he hit the pavement in front of the beauty salon, Percy felt his cellphone vibrate. He yanked it from its case. Prophet Long Jevity's code name popped up. The connection was terrible and whatever Prophet said came across static and garbled. The only clear sound Percy heard seemed like an airplane. It made no sense to hang on, and he knew Prophet wouldn't take a chance on using the walkie-talkie feature nor would he text his whereabouts. Percy tried to redial, and it went straight to voice mail.

The airplane sound in the background made sense to

Percy. It wasn't the first time Prophet had to suddenly hop onto a plane to follow Deacon Whistle. Yet it wasn't the first time Prophet hopped on a plane to handle other business that he'd refused to divulge, either. The man was as secretive now as he'd been back when he taught Percy at Columbia Law School.

He'd long ago believed it was more than irony that connected him, Prophet, and Rev. Stepson; he wished he knew the real reason.

The more Percy thought about it, the more uncertain he became about missing pieces. He also became more unsure that he'd heard an airplane sound at all.

In the meantime, across town, Porky was hell-bent on finding answers. He didn't care if his wrist was in a sling. In his ghetto poor man's mind, he was Shaft.

Chapter 25

It'd just begun to drizzle again and the sun was about to set, but none of that deterred Porky. He'd made up his mind that he'd start with the most likely place to get an answer, the Playa's Cabin.

The Playa's Cabin was an after-hours spot that stayed open twenty-four hours a day, but only if the owner knew you wanted to gamble and do other sleazy activities.

The Shanty and Shaqueeda's places were on one end of Ptomaine Avenue. Providing those in power with free meals or information kept them off the police radar.

Meanwhile, the Playa's Cabin, a stucco and brick one-story building with one window in the front and the back remained on the cops' most-raided list. The police kept re-arresting so many of the patrons, it'd been hard to establish a payback account with the owner, known as the Tower.

By the time they got to their destination, the rain had stopped again. When the RAV pulled up a few doors down from the Playa's Cabin, Porky was the first to notice the undercover car. If he hadn't been so mad he'd have laughed. A trash dumpster on the other side of the street had barely hidden the unmarked car.

Porky looked at his watch. "Some things won't ever change," Porky hissed. "Look at those plainclothes detectives. Everybody in Pelzer except the idiot that owns that joint and whoever stupid enough to go inside knows the routine." He looked at his watch again, saying quickly, "It ain't but fifteen minutes away from them raiding the place. I ain't got much time."

"What are you babbling about?" Joy leaned over him, peering through the SUV's window, to see what held his interest. Once they'd left Shaqueeda's, she'd stayed in the backseat with Porky. She'd grown tired of his complaining. He'd groaned about Felony's gas and doggy breath as if his musk wouldn't knock Felony out had he not been a dog. Seated next to him, she could snatch Porky easier.

Joy and Patience looked at one another, never saying a word. Neither woman moved from their seats. An arrest by detectives they'd worked with wasn't an option. They'd already gotten into trouble, overzealously tossing around their missionary licenses like badges all over Pelzer.

However, Porky's dubious reputation, the only one he had, meant nothing to them; besides, he had Percy to rely upon.

Barely five minutes passed before they saw Porky stumbling out of the Playa's Cabin. He looked all wide-eyed and crazier than usual. He began zigzagging on the sidewalk, sidestepping three detectives running toward the Playa's Cabin. They had their shields in their hands.

Porky's wide hips almost sideswiped one detective as the man sped past, ignoring Porky completely.

Porky dashed inside the SUV, not caring that he almost sat on Felony, and screamed, "Let's move it!"

Patience had seen enough cop shows to know one shouldn't ask questions when a fool jumps into a car and says to put rubber to the road.

Even Felony was stunned. The dog didn't whimper when Porky slammed all his weight onto the stump of his tail.

Joy kept her mouth shut. She couldn't remember the last time, or if ever, she'd seen Porky act that dangerous.

"I said drive! Get the hell out of here!"

Whether Patience meant it or not didn't matter. She put all of her 115 pounds on the gas. It might as well have been just fifteen pounds on the pedal. The SUV's speedometer's needle barely touched twenty mph as she careened away.

They'd driven almost a mile before Porky finally fell back against the seat with a loud sigh, wiping his forehead with his sprained wrist.

And that's when it dawned on Joy that Porky had used that same supposedly sprained wrist to open the SUV's door. "Weren't you wearing your sling when you went inside that Playa's Cabin?"

As soon as Porky opened his mouth, he began stuttering.

The rat-a-tat sound of his oncoming lies was enough to get Patience's nerves and attention riled up. She peered into the rearview mirror for confirmation.

Porky jerked forward, quickly reaching over the back of Patience's headrest. He looked like a fish grasping for breath. His short arms kept elbowing against Patience's neck, wiggling as he grappled to take over the steering wheel.

"Fool!" Patience took her eyes off the rearview mirror and was about to scratch Porky's elbow off her neck when she heard him yell, "Look out, Patience—!"

The few seconds she'd used to glimpse away were broken by the blast of a car's horn and Porky's sudden warning. Patience never saw the other car until she'd hit it.

Unfortunately for Reign, blasting her horn wasn't enough. She'd seen the SUV too late.

★ ★ ★

One of the two police officers that arrived immediately recognized Joy and Patience. They both knew Reign. They could hardly recognize Reign's Navigator. The RAV had totaled it.

They left Felony alone inside the SUV, racing back and forth across the backseat, howling. It wasn't because Felony was a dog and couldn't speak. Everyone in Pelzer believed he was a crazy hound that a bullet would only make mad and liked pepper spray, so they'd heard.

The officers wanted to make a big deal of the accident, thinking since Reign Stepson, WPAK's darling news reporter, was involved, she'd give them free praise and a lot of press. However, she wasn't hurt and refused any medical attention.

Having failed to take advantage of the situation, one of the officers continued talking to Reign. The other officer separately questioned Joy. He'd already asked Patience, and an unwilling-to-answer Porky, to standby, but to not stand together.

Every question put to her Joy answered with uncommon sweetness and caution. She had a spotless driving record and saw no reason to change it. Although she loved Patience, she hadn't been the one driving.

On the other hand, the officer quickly found that Patience had quite a few fender benders on her record. He'd been amazed to learn her number of accidents almost matched the amount of typos found when she typed for the police department.

As soon as Patience saw the officer, she began a different dance than the one she'd shown during the years working at the Pelzer PD. She wasn't the nothing-but-business, nerdy, religious nut some labeled her behind her back. Patience, with her hair undone from the impact, secreted her reading glasses in her purse. Flashing and flirting with her honey-brown contact-lens girl power, she began her act.

Patience slurred her words, standing seductively with one

hand that kept sliding off her skinny hip. She kept tossing her hair to the side, so much it almost gave her whiplash.

Patience's unorthodox behavior didn't pass the smell test. All it did was make the officer give her a sobriety test.

She wasn't wearing her eyeglasses, mandatory according to her driver's license. It was nighttime, and the officer couldn't see those honey-brown contact lenses she kept flashing, anyway. And, of course, when she tried to walk a straight line and point to her pointy nose, her finger, accustomed to pushing up the now-absent glasses, kept missing. The only reason those crazy actions didn't end in handcuffs was because she did pass one final test—the Breathalyzer test.

Porky kept his answers to a minimum. With harsh but thorough words, he reminded the officers that his son was the famous Percy LaPierre. Porky also reminded them of his status on Ptomaine Avenue by handing them an unspecified amount of cash, placed under an official DEA card that Percy had given him.

Porky knew the cash worked better than the DEA card when the officers tore up the paper with his name on it. No sooner had he turned around to the others when he felt the heat of their glares. "What?" he barked. "Y'all know decorum. They knew de-cash."

Once the tow truck arrived and hauled away the remains of Reign's Navigator, she accepted the ride from Joy and the others back to their house, where she'd wait for Percy.

She'd earlier phoned the insurance adjuster, informing him of her accident. Because it was already late, he'd suggested they meet on Monday. Two days wouldn't make that much difference, he told her.

No one in the SUV said much, preferring to linger awhile in personal thoughts. It was certainly true for Joy and Patience. They still hadn't found out what happened to Porky's sling back at the Playa's Cabin. Moreover, he'd had the fastest healing they'd ever seen. He'd been up to something back at that den of iniquity, and they were determined to add what-ever it was to their list of other mysteries.

The trip back to Joy and Patience's home remained un-eventful. The only exception was Felony's actions. The mutt stood with one hind leg raised two inches away from Porky. It silently communicated that a dog fart was imminent if Porky did something stupid—again.

Chapter 26

It'd taken experience, gut feelings, and ingenuity but Percy finally traced Prophet to the Greenville-Spartanburg International Airport. On the cellphone, Prophet couldn't talk for long but managed to inform Percy that Deacon Whistle was bound for Manhattan, New York.

"I've already called my guy at One Police Plaza. They know I'm traveling armed, and they've already planned on having someone on me as soon as my plane lands." He hesitated a moment before continuing. "Wall Street is closed on the weekend, so I don't know why the deacon is going there a day early. The man normally takes day trips so he's not missed. He's also wearing a different disguise this time. I don't know why he's doing that; he's never done it before when I've tailed him."

Prophet went on to say that, because of the damage to Shaqueeda's apartment building, he doubted the deacon would return there. "Even if he came back just to see the place or to pick up something, he can't stay there, that's for certain. My gut tells me it was him that started those fires to cover up something. Don't know what that beauty salon had to do with anything, but I'm sure it being burned down to the ground was meant to send a message."

There wasn't anything Prophet said that Percy disagreed

with. He took his notes and, again, with a bad connection, the call ended.

When he'd reported in with his superior about an hour ago, to say he'd connected with Prophet, he learned about the accident. He was already upset his father and godmothers disobeyed his orders. He was even angrier when he heard it'd been Reign involved, yet glad to learn no one was hurt.

When he finished giving his report, he learned there was another matter to discuss. Someone then passed Percy on to an undercover detective. It was the same one who'd earlier busted the Playa's Cabin. Somehow learning that his father had been on the scene when the bust went down didn't surprise Percy at all.

The way events were rapidly changing and unfolding, by the time he'd hung up, he felt like a drunken juggler at his family circus.

Percy was officially on duty so there wasn't much he could do about any of the family drama. Yet he was certain it'd be there, with added craziness, waiting for him when he returned.

Pulling bits and pieces together in his head brought Percy to one conclusion. He'd played a dangerous game of I've Got a Secret with his godmothers, his father, and his fiancée. No magician alive could make all the secrets he'd kept, professionally and personally, disappear.

There also wasn't much time for reflection. He didn't know how this investigation would end. He never knew how any of them would, but God had had his back whether Percy thanked Him daily or not. "But for God's mercy," he murmured.

And because he didn't need nor want another terse conversation with Reign, he sent a coded text to her cell phone. The text was nonsensical to any other reader, and if he played his cards right, she'd not get most of it either. He just wanted to let her know he'd be out of reach for a couple of days, and she'd know why.

Luckily, he'd already picked up the airplane ticket Prophet left for him. A few minutes later, after properly registering his weapon with the TSA, he headed toward his gate where he'd wait to board a plane to New York City.

As soon as the announcement came over the airport loudspeaker, Percy knew the plan had changed. His flight had been cancelled due to bad weather. Strong winds and rainstorms had caused delays from Greenville all the way to Boston. After checking in with the reservation desk, he learned there was a possibility that the storm would let up and his flight would take off, hopefully by morning.

"After all," the reservation clerk informed Percy, "it is September. This is the hurricane season."

Percy translated it to mean that everything was up in the air except the airplanes.

Percy made the necessary phone call to his superior. He had the option of staying at one of the airport hotels for the night or returning home.

In the meantime, Prophet's plane had been one of the last to land at JFK airport in New York. With Percy still stuck in Pelzer, they'd need to get another man to cover Prophet immediately.

Percy started to call Reign. He wanted to make sure she was okay, as well as chastise his father and godmothers. He wasn't quite certain what he'd tell her since he hadn't told her everything earlier. He needed to sort it out. She'd already left a message saying she was at his godmothers'. He imagined she was there praying for him, the church, and her parents. He was almost certain she'd be a calming presence, keeping any trouble from happening between his father, Joy, and Patience.

And then suddenly, Percy thought about it again. This time he threw caution and rationale out the window. He began to speed, realizing that Reign wouldn't stand a chance with them without him there.

Chapter 27

By the time what had once been a trio but had become a quartet (and a dog) arrived back at the cousins' home, it was past ten o'clock.

They would've arrived sooner, but no one had eaten all day. Without taking a vote, Joy, who'd insisted on driving, had stopped at a fast food place along the way.

It shouldn't have taken long to get through the drive-thru, but Joy couldn't see clearly. The bumper kept getting caught whenever she tried to turn where the lane bended.

When they finally got their order, the bumper resembled one of the curly fries Patience had ordered.

Joy and the others sat around the table, ripping through the bag, looking for what they'd ordered. No one spoke. Each gave an Oscar-worthy performance, pretending to focus on the pile of ketchup, mustard, and other condiments lying in the middle of the kitchen table. Felony, busy licking and lapping at the buttered popcorn in his favorite bowl, also kept quiet.

"Reign, honey, I can't tell you enough how sorry I am to have hit your car," Patience finally said. "We have insurance, thank the Lord, and that's just metal. Baby girl, Lil P would've shot me had anything seriously happened to you." It was Patience's poor attempt to add a little humor to a serious situation. Again, no one responded, but she wouldn't give up.

"I noticed you kept checking your cellphone while we were coming here," Patience said to Reign while trying to gain control over a slippery and greasy hamburger. "Is everything okay?"

"Yes, ma'am," Reign answered. She quickly pushed the straw back between her lips, continuing to sip and avoid answering more questions.

"Did your mom get your dad settled in?" That time the question came from Joy. "I'd meant to ask sooner but—well, you know . . ." She pushed out her chin and nodded toward Patience and Porky who sat next to each other.

No sooner had Joy nodded than she elbowed a cup of soda, causing the liquid to spray across the table directly into Porky's face.

Porky raised his hand, the same one held captive in a sling earlier. "You did that on purpose!" Porky, using that same hand, grabbed one of the napkins and began rapidly wiping his face side to side.

"I knew it!" Joy pointed her finger at Patience. "How can you just sit next to him knowing that he caused us to have that accident that could've killed poor Reign?"

Porky's mouth clamped tight. He refused to say another word.

That didn't stop Joy. She turned to Reign, explaining how Porky supposedly sprained his wrist so bad that Percy had to take care of him. She went on to tell how Porky had gained her and Patience's sympathy, and they'd allowed him to stay at their home overnight.

Patience sat back in her seat, listening to Joy fabricate, stretch, and almost demolish the truth. *Have mercy, Father. We have wasted a perfectly good fast.* She shook her head as Joy continued to rail.

As soon as Joy finished hyperventilating, Reign quickly

turned to Porky. Unlike Joy, as a seasoned reporter and journalist she knew how to control a discussion. She'd already
gathered something was amiss by the way Porky reacted.
He'd suddenly shut up, which meant he was holding a lie inside his mouth.

Reign smiled as she pushed aside the fast food she'd ordered simply because the others had. She was more like Percy,
more into healthy eating whenever possible.

Joy looked toward Patience, who returned the look with
one of confusion. Rather than interrupt, they decided to see
if Reign could get the truth out of Porky. If she couldn't, they
were prepared to beat it out of him, or let Felony try.

Porky's shoulders slumped just enough to make him look
comfortable as he wiped the last of the liquid from his face.
He'd always loved Reign and secretly wanted Percy to marry
her before she got away. In fact, whenever she'd wanted to
know a little more than what Percy shared, all she needed was
to smile. Porky would give her the 411 in alphabetical order.

Reign decided she'd keep it simple and to the point. She
reached across the table for Porky's hands, which meant he
had to move forward. Once she had him in her grip, Reign
went to work.

"Papa Porky," Reign began.

"Yes." The beginning of a smile appeared on Porky's face.

"Don't worry about your cousins. You and I are family."

"So what are we?" Joy blurted. She quickly shut up when
Patience kicked her under the table.

Reign acted as though Joy hadn't spoken, preferring to
hold Porky prisoner with her smile and more questioning.

"Percy told me about how you'd hurt your wrist while
fishing. Did you hurt your wrist while fishing?"

"Yes." Porky could almost feel his body melting. Lord,
help him if she made him a grandpa. He could feel his wallet
shrinking, too.

"So, it's true. You did hurt your wrist while fishing, and it was put into a sling," Reign repeated. "And when you went into the Playa's Cabin you had the sling but when you came out, you didn't."

"That's right."

"What made you take it off?" Reign winked, her large almond-shaped eyes growing wider, signaling Porky that she'd believe whatever he cared to share.

"I had to take it off before I went inside."

"Say what?"

"I'd had Joy and Patience stop by there so I could ask a few of those thugs if they knew who'd hit my place a few nights ago. A couple of them told me a little sumpthin'— sumpthin', but not enough. They said they'd holla if they heard more."

"But wha—" Reign wanted clarification but the words wouldn't come.

"Just to make sure they'd still be around so I could get some answers, I tipped them off about the undercover bust about to go down, too. I also hit the number there a couple of times while I was away, and they owed me. So I stashed the cash in my sling. And, even if I hadn't put any money in that thing, I didn't want none of those hoodrats thinking just because I was using one hand, I couldn't handle myself."

"I see," Reign finally replied. She still held his hand, but she wasn't totally prepared to believe him. Future in-law or not, he was still Porky LaPierre, a born liar.

"So why didn't you put the sling back on once you came back to the car? I'm sure the doctor told you how long and why you should wear it. Didn't he?"

"Oh, it wasn't feeling too bad and having that money in it caused most of the pain to leave my mind. Besides, I didn't see no real doctor," Porky replied. "Percy put the sling on me just before we'd stopped in Anderson."

"Percy stopped in Anderson?"

"Yep, he sure did. And from there, we went back to your dad's old courthouse in Columbia."

Porky turned his hands so his covered Reign's. With a look only a proud father who'd never accomplished anything on his own, living vicariously through his son, would have, he began bragging. "Did you know Percy knows some folks who know the president of these here United States? My son walks in some high cotton!"

Reign jerked her hands away, causing Porky's hands and wrists to hit the table hard. Joy and Patience whistled, although neither knew they could do such a thing.

Porky was living proof that old dogs never learned new tricks. Again, his big mouth was set on blabbering and his off switch broken. By the time he finished telling Reign all she'd not asked, and not caring if Joy and Patience overheard it, too, Percy had a better chance of climbing Mount Everest butt-naked without getting frostbite than avoiding the chill he'd face when he came home.

Chapter 28

Prophet Long Jevity had his all-weather coat collar pulled up to his chin. With a baseball cap covering his head and large sunglasses, he no longer looked like an airline employee.

He'd been leaning against a wet pole outside Delta's Area B arrival terminal at the J.F.K. airport for almost thirty minutes. It'd rained hard when he'd first stepped outside, but now it drizzled.

He'd kept a safe distance from the time Campbell Whistle boarded the flight from the Greenville-Spartanburg airport. The airline's policy of keeping four seats available for last-minute law enforcement activity made it possible for him to take the same flight.

He'd dressed as an airline employee and boarded some moments before the others. He'd taken a seat in the back row, which made him look like an ordinary airline employee deadheading to NYC. From where he sat, he could observe the man.

Yet here he was in New York City, the sun hadn't quite come up yet, and he was bone tired. The flight had stayed on the tarmac back at Greenville-Spartanburg for almost an hour before takeoff. The pilot had announced there was bad

weather ahead going north. Yet even with the delay, he'd remained wide-awake, keeping an eye on Whistle.

Prophet scanned the sidewalk, glancing at two airport security guards. The men frantically waved the cars on, barely
allowing them to stop to drop off passengers.

Whistle hadn't moved from the bench he sat on. He kept
his head lowered as though unable to tear his attention away
from the book in his hands. He also hadn't picked up his luggage.

That hadn't escaped Prophet's attention. He knew Whistle had checked luggage—two regular size brown carry-ons
that he'd not carried onto the plane—before they'd departed.

He'd already begun taking notes, adding his observation
onto the pad. To cover what he did he began mouthing
words, as though he were talking through the Bluetooth device attached to his right ear and writing down what he
heard.

He'd just placed his ink pen back into his inside jacket
when he saw a luxury car turning into the pickup lane. Whistle had always taken an airport taxi the other times; because
the man had done nothing ordinary on this trip from the beginning, Prophet remained even more alert.

The luxury car suddenly began to slow down, allowing
two other cars to go around. The driver, with one hand extended through the car's window, held up a placard. It had the
name *Jason Lauder* written in huge bold black letters. Prophet
could read it plainly when he squinted, although he stood a
ways from the car.

The car came to a stop just a few feet away from Whistle.
It was nothing more than another gut check for Prophet that
told him he should commit the name on the placard to
memory. He'd write it down later.

He was right. Whistle started walking, his gait still awkward, toward the car just as the driver exited from its front.
No one rushed to the car and the driver seemed to accept

that Whistle was indeed *the* Jason Lauder. Prophet thought that perhaps Whistle saw an opportunity to get to where he was headed fast, and he didn't care how he did it.

Prophet quickly stepped away from the column, prepared to rush into the unmarked car of another waiting agent who'd stayed off to the right, unbothered by TSA security. They'd need to stay close to the luxury car, since Whistle had continued to go off script.

Before Prophet could get to the curb, he had to retreat. Although he'd nothing to put inside, for whatever reason, Whistle waited by the trunk of the car.

Once the driver popped the trunk, he handed Whistle two bags, a dark-colored carry-on suitcase and matching over-the-shoulder bag. The over-the-shoulder bag hung from his short arm looking like it hung on a hook. From what Prophet could see, the driver also handed him what looked like a large manila envelope.

The driver looked around, hopped back into the car, and sped away.

Whistle then began lumbering toward the departure level. It was a one-way entrance, and Prophet could neither walk fast enough to catch up nor could the other agent drive up the one-way ramp without drawing attention.

Prophet quickly phoned in the latest development, advising his superiors that he'd lost Whistle; the man had gotten one over on him.

He then immediately texted Percy's cellphone to let Percy know there was a problem, and it was a huge one.

Chapter 29

Campbell Whistle knew he had left Prophet befuddled. He was no fool. He hadn't been a fool for quite some time.

Setting the fire at Rev. Stepson's business office inside the church's outreach center was mandatory. It'd taken him some time to learn about some of Sister Boodrow's deathbed admissions. He couldn't take a chance that she'd thrown him under the bus on her ride to the afterlife. Besides, she'd accidentally learned a lot more than she should've, but he'd kept her under control with sex, exotic trips, and expensive gifts.

Setting his big-mouthed landlady Shaqueeda's salon on fire, along with his apartment in her building, was purely payback. It wasn't that she talked that much about his business alone, but she talked too much about everyone else's, too. He didn't like it, because folks that told everything so freely couldn't be trusted to know when to shut up. He'd also not had a chance to remove a little bit of anything that could come back to haunt him.

She'd caught his attention some time ago when she kept complaining about this Prophet Long Jevity fellow that Patience had brought to her as another tenant. "Every time I turned around, that man done took off. Then here comes Patience, asking me questions and looking for him. I ain't his keeper. I was halfway expecting her to ask about your comings and goings, too."

That'd been only one of a handful of times he'd bothered to respond to her. "Why would Sister Patience ask about my business?"

"I figure since every time you leave that Prophet fella does too, that perhaps y'all traveled in the same circles as Patience. I mean other than you handling the church's business," she'd told him.

He had to give it to her. He probably wouldn't have paid the man any attention if she hadn't kept throwing him up in his face, arousing his curiosity. Out of the six tenants in her building, he was the only one she complained about—at least to Whistle.

After a while she'd begun complaining so much, he completely didn't trust her. And she was also a longtime acquaintance, if not close friend, of Joy's. He had to take the blame for not knowing all about the blabbermouth when he first moved into her building. But he'd needed someplace to stay quickly, and someone at the church had mentioned her. But it wasn't good business, mixing apples and oranges, and those cousins were definitely fruits. Yet he'd still had to work alongside Patience and learned to use it to his advantage.

Pelzer's elite community should thank him. If he hadn't done something drastic, she'd have been digging up or burying her 411 bone in their private backyards. He couldn't have that.

For the first time since he'd left Pelzer, he began to smile. He got a chuckle when he remembered how he could also tell the times when Shaqueeda was fishing for something to spread about the neighborhood. All he'd had to say was "good morning," and she'd start talking about how much she'd disapproved of Sister Boodrow's extracurricular activities.

That relationship was something he hadn't been able to keep secret. Long before Joy had almost caught them, he'd learned Boodrow had started running her mouth.

"Please sir, may I see your boarding pass?"

The raspy voice of an overweight female TSA agent with dyed blonde hair and black roots, her huge chest covering half the small desk she sat behind, interrupted his thoughts.

He handed her the papers which he'd just moments before pulled from the envelope he carried. She quickly looked at the carry-on and said nothing as she scribbled something onto the boarding pass. "Have a great day, Mr. Lauder. Next!"

Having a small suitcase helped him to avoid requests from the skycaps wanting to make big tips. On his way to the gate, he stepped into the men's room. Moments later he exited, only this time walking a little stooped, like a man with a back problem or someone elderly.

He waved down an oncoming cart and gave the driver his gate number. Whistle hadn't realized how tired he was until he'd gone through security. Trying to walk up the ramp toward his gate, carrying the small suitcase, felt like a huge burden. The straps from the shoulder bag had begun to dig into his collarbone.

He did, however, take a look around him, scanning faces, particularly those of anyone wearing sunglasses inside the terminal. He might've left Prophet standing outside the arrival terminal, but it didn't mean Prophet hadn't done something to get inside departures. Hugging the suitcase to his chest, he almost dozed off.

Chapter 30

Loud noises from her living room woke Joy from a sound sleep. It'd taken time for her to get to that stage after hearing Porky's crazy confession. But he was such a liar, she didn't know what to make of it. Now there were strange sounds in her house.

At first, she thought she'd been dreaming, so she didn't react. Squinting at the LED clock on the wall over the dresser, which read two o'clock, she thought she heard Percy's voice, and she bolted from her bed. "What in the world is Lil P doing here?" He was welcome any time of day or night, but this just showing up without calling had her nervous.

Patience almost knocked Joy into a wall. Like Joy, she'd heard the noises. Rather than waste time apologizing, she and Joy grabbed their weapons of choice, a vase and an iron poker, and tiptoed into the living room. As soon as they entered with their weapons raised, they saw Felony. The dog was lying on the floor in the middle of Porky, Reign, and Percy. His big head swung back and forth as each one spoke.

When Joy and Patience had gone to bed, they'd left Porky in the spare bedroom and Reign lying on the sofa.

"Felony, come here!" Joy called out to the dog first because he hadn't barked or made a warning sound.

Felony didn't move. The dog half raised his head, letting one floppy ear droop even more, and gave Joy a look that said *This is your dumb family. I'm just lying here so they don't kill each other or knock over my popcorn bowl.*

The arguing stopped as soon as Percy and the others saw Joy and Patience standing in the doorway.

"I'm sorry, godmothers," Percy said. He'd begun adjusting his jacket collar so as not to let them know Reign had just snatched him by it.

Patience quickly noticed that Reign still had her fist balled and Porky looked like someone waiting for a hearse to arrive.

"It's praying time!" The call for prayer came from Patience. "Y'all about to make me sin up in my own home."

"I'm sorry, Sister Patience." Reign collapsed onto the sofa. Those eyes everyone called gorgeous were bloodshot, and the corners of her mouth appeared wrinkled.

Joy was about to say something when she saw Porky. Standing there at that moment he looked defeated and almost near death's door. If she had to describe a broken man, she'd pull out his picture.

Both Joy and Patience had been so knocked out earlier that they'd not heard the doorbell ring. Reign was asleep on the sofa. Rather than wake them up, she'd peeped out the window. Seeing it was Percy, she'd let him in.

The two had begun arguing almost as soon as he stepped over the threshold. It didn't take Reign but a couple of minutes to repeat everything Porky revealed earlier. She was beyond angry. She was ready to go to jail.

"We were supposed to do this together," she angrily reminded him. "If I can't trust you in a work situation, how can I trust you in a marriage?"

From that moment on, it worsened, and once Porky barged into the living room, it escalated to DEFCON infinity. The three began passing accusations between them like a game of hot potato, only it wasn't a game. People's lives depended upon truth.

Joy's spirit felt broken. Two of the people she loved dearly and one she tolerated had begun dismantling their relationships—father and son, and a soon-to-be husband and wife.

"I'm not gonna say it again," Patience blasted. She'd already begun twirling her glasses. It wasn't a good sign. "It's praying time!"

Felony finally rose. He raced to Patience's side and, with a low growl, lay at her feet.

"Don't y'all be like the Word says; if y'all don't praise the Lord, He'll have rocks cry out and use Felony, too."

It wasn't as poetic as she'd have liked, but everyone including Joy moved a little closer to each other.

Patience's smile was controlled. She liked what she'd done, but didn't want to appear too holy, especially since she'd hit and destroyed a Navigator yesterday.

Replacing her glasses on her face, Patience began reading. "Proverbs 18:21," she said slowly, looking around to make sure they were paying attention.

She really didn't need to read it from her Bible. She'd read that particular scripture so often she had a bookmark made of ribbon holding its place. "Death and life are in the power of the tongue, and those who love it will eat its fruit." Patience closed her Bible. Taking advantage of their silence she spoke again. "We're supposed to be a family and not just shared DNA but a spiritual family, too." She then pointed to Joy.

"Joy and I are ordained missionaries." Pointing to Percy and Reign, she added, "Lil P., you and Reign less than a year ago decided you wanted to be in each other's lives, both in marriage and in careers."

Patience didn't bother pointing at Porky, but they knew

she'd get around to him, too. "And you, cousin Porky. I know God's still working on you, so I can't come down too hard on you, but with or without the Lord, you know right from wrong. And I certainly won't leave me out. I've done so much craziness in the last few months, I'm sure Jesus had to look twice 'cause He didn't recognize me."

"Godmother, I didn't mean to come over here and get into an argument with Reign. I was annoyed because y'all hadn't listened to me. I thought I gave explicit instructions that you knew were meant for y'all to stop with the crazy idea about the president and other fruity plans."

"Oh, we listened to you," Joy interrupted. "We just didn't obey you."

"That's right!" Patience added. "Who are you to decide whether or not the president of these here United States of America won't help us?"

"That's right," Porky added. "These two gals marched with Martin Luther King to Thelma and Louise."

"Selma, Alabama." Reign shook her head. Perhaps she should rethink joining this circus.

"Hold up!" Joy and Patience chorused.

"We wanna know something. Just how did you know about our relationship with President Obama?" Joy asked.

"Yeah, how'd ya find out?" Patience asked before offering her own explanation. "The CIA!"

"I believe you're right. We need to write another letter and let the president know he's working with some blabbermouths." Joy sucked her teeth. "Looks like nothing can't get into Washington and nothing gets out."

"It doesn't matter," Patience snapped. "He don't need to tell us how he knew and he still can't tell us what to do or where to go. We changed his dirty diapers! We don't hafta take any more crap!"

Percy couldn't refute what she'd said. He'd tried to bully

them but for what he thought was their own good. Since neither of them knew their letters never made it out of Pelzer, he decided to drop it until there was a saner moment. Hopefully, that moment would come before Armageddon.

"All of us have said negative things over the last few weeks and months," Reign stressed. "In fact, Percy and I just said some things, moments ago, that I'm sure made us wilt and feel like we'd died inside."

"It wasn't always like that." Percy looked Reign up and down, his eyes coming to a stop at her heart, remembering why he loved her. "We used to be able to say beautiful words that made us blossom like flowers."

"Well, we're an ugly patch of weeds now." Porky had finally joined the conversation. In his usual Porky style, he'd said something positive in a negative way.

Patience thought with scriptures and prayer she'd bring her family together. The power of death and life was indeed in their tongues. By the time the truth rolled off each tongue, they were verbally wounded.

By the time the sun rose that morning, Joy and the others felt almost physically empty. A lot had been confessed, with each hopefully not holding back, taking turns adding their anger, concerns, hopes to the confession pyre.

When they'd finished moments ago, promising to forgive more often, lie less often, and pray for one another, Patience again took the lead. Borrowing several lines from a comedian friend who always ended her shows on a positive note, Patience ordered, "Since we're still sitting in a circle around this kitchen table, I want each of us to hold hands. Now we should say to one another, repeat after me: I love you, and there's nothing you can do about it."

Not willing to risk another impromptu Bible study or her wrath, they obeyed.

For the first few seconds, everything was fine. However, as soon as Porky turned to face Joy, the road to peace hit a bump. The two stubborn-as-a-mule cousins wouldn't so much as mumble the words. Instead, they looked at Felony, who lay between them, and repeated Patience's words of love to a dog.

The poor dog showed his confusion by raising that hind leg. That's all it took for Joy and Porky to quickly face each other, saying the words as Patience had instructed.

No one at the table bought Joy and Porky's act, but it was a start. At least they'd used the word *love* instead of *hate*.

Reign and Percy had pulled their chairs so close together they looked like Siamese twins. The thought of not being together had reignited what was meant to be.

However, Reign still wasn't satisfied with Percy's answer to her question about his stopover in Columbia, South Carolina, with his father.

"Ahem," Reign purred, using both hands to remove Percy's large hand from around her shoulder. "You ain't completely off the hook."

"Just give me a moment." Percy pushed back his chair from the table. He began mumbling under his breath, looking at his family, who he knew wondered why he let this little woman push him around.

Within a few minutes Percy had gone to his car and returned with a small box. It'd been partially wrapped.

Handing her the box, he tried to look stern, telling her, "Here you go, you little dictator."

The shocked look of suspicion on Reign's face when she slowly opened the box was priceless.

"Oh my God," she cried out, "Percy!" Reign began pulling out several pictures, one at a time, squealing at each, along with a few papers and a DVD. "Why didn't you say something?"

Joy and Patience raced around the side of the kitchen

table. They began jockeying for space to look over Reign's small shoulder.

Percy stood smiling. He winked at his father, who returned the look with his usual cluelessness.

Reign held in her hands four photos of a house; it was one of six that she and Percy had looked at several months ago, over in Anderson County.

"Oh Jesus! Look at it!" Reign began laughing, unable to control herself. "I'd told Percy that day that this eight-thousand-square-foot house was a dream." She began handing the pictures over her shoulder to Joy and Patience.

"Look at it," Reign gushed. "It has four bedrooms with huge two and a half baths."

"Oh my," Patience blurted, "this looks like a lot of money. God sure enough will bless y'all if it's meant to be."

"Sure does look mighty expensive," Joy added. "Didn't know anyone we knew could afford something like this."

Patience quickly elbowed Joy, letting her know she was letting out the air in the positive balloon.

Joy's words had an impact, and it showed immediately.

"I know, Sister Joy. I told Percy it might've been a bit too much out of our budget. Percy was so busy eyeballing that Olympic-size swimming pool I didn't think he'd paid any attention to me."

Percy simply replied, "You also said that it felt like a home."

"I did say that, didn't I?"

They'd wanted everything marriage-ready when they had their big day. Even with her father's health declining, she'd not wanted to push up their wedding day, but Percy did.

"Look at the paperwork," Percy reminded her. "Ask what you will in Jesus's name; believe it and it shall be done."

Everyone, including Felony, looked at Percy like he was brand-new. And he was smiling with a bit more confidence, which made the others a little uneasy.

Had he lost his mind, showing his fiancée the house of her dreams without handing her the key to the front door?

"I had to get them to correct the name," Percy said, pointing at the paper Reign had begun unfolding. "It's amazing how many people think the only way to spell *Reign* is *r-a-i-n.*"

Reign hopped off the chair, pushing Joy and Patience aside and knocking Percy into the counter behind him. "Oh Jesus—!"

This was just one more worry she wouldn't have. He'd taken care of purchasing their home.

"I have to tell you," Patience said laughing, "your mother looks mighty good standing in the corner by that huge refrigerator."

"What do you mean, my mama—?" Reign sprang from Percy's arms, snatching the picture from Patience's hands as she sat down. In her excitement, she'd missed it. How could she have not seen her own mother?

Again, Percy had to straighten things out before they escalated. Looking at Joy for backup, emotional or otherwise, Percy went to Reign, gently taking the photograph from her grip.

"Sweetheart," Percy began to explain, "as close as you and your mother are, there was no way I was going to go ahead and purchase this house without your mother looking and praying over it. I didn't want to just go back and buy it because we loved it. Your mother and her 'third eye' took almost two weeks of consulting God and fasting before she and I went back to Columbia to seal the deal."

"Yeah, Percy." Porky had finally come around to where Patience stood holding the other photos. He peered at one and told Reign, "This is one gorgeous house."

Porky then pivoted to Percy, scolding him as only a true hypocrite daddy would. "You should've told Reign about this mansion in the first place. We could've gone back to sleep hours ago. Learn to be honest, son, because Lord knows I've been telling you for years about keeping secrets."

Porky threw the pictures onto the table and backed away. "I'm tired. Y'all done wore me out with all this drama. I'm gonna take a leak and go to bed!"

Chapter 31

Although she hadn't slept but for an hour or so with all the excitement that'd happened in her kitchen earlier, Patience was up already, brewing a pot of strong coffee to start her day. It really didn't matter if she'd gotten enough sleep; it was Sunday. She knew she'd miss the first service, but if she hurried she could make the second one.

She was surprised to run into Joy coming out of the den. Joy had gone in there to check up on Reign and Percy, who they'd left reclining in separate recliners when everyone finally went back to bed. Now the couple was snuggled in each other's arms on the sofa.

Patience watched Joy tiptoe down the hallway, closing the door behind her as she entered her bedroom. Patience, being curious, wanted to see them; she peeped in and smiled. Percy had the mortgage papers in his hand. Reign still clutched the photos of their new home.

Patience had begun to slowly close the door when she heard Percy and Reign's cell phones go off. She backed completely out the door, not wanting them to wake and think she'd spied on them. However, with the door still cracked, her snooping habit overtook her. She remained outside the door but within earshot.

While Patience lurked outside the door, Percy and Reign began to stir.

Between the buzzes and the odd short melodic notes, new message alerts had completely taken over the couple's phones. Their cell phones as they lay on the coffee table then began vibrating as though possessed.

Percy was the first to hear his alert. Still somewhere between being asleep and awake, he bolted upright peering over at his cell phone. Reign by that time had completely awoken and done the same.

Patience stole a peek through the side of the door that had remained cracked. She saw them scanning their cell phones. It was obvious to her; they'd each received text messages.

Patience didn't know what the messages were or from whom. It didn't matter, because her conscience had begun pricking her like a pincushion. Giving in to her better judgment, she'd just begun to step away when she heard Percy speak up.

"Damn, Prophet's in trouble. Whistle got away."

As though she'd not understood the implication of what Percy had just said, Reign collapsed against the back of the sofa. "Oh no," she blurted, "don't tell me he's gone."

"Yeah, it looks that way." Percy rose. "I also got a text from the airline. Flights are delayed, but they will be flying. I've got to catch my flight." He stopped and pulled her gently from the sofa. "I know you understand. I love you for that."

"I know. This is serious business. But I got a no-show to cover over in Anderson. James Memorial A.M.E. is hosting the National Missionary Day Jubilee this afternoon. Some of the missionaries from Circle One are being honored. You do know that Missionary Joy is supposed to be on that dais; yet I haven't heard her say one word about it, not that she has to tell me anything. But I gotta cover it for a Religion Daily spot to air tonight."

James Memorial A.M.E. was the largest A.M.E. church in Anderson County, and whatever they did with whomever they did it always got coverage.

"I should be able to take my day off and go to something Mount Kneel Down is involved in without a camera," said Reign. "It's not right for none of the Stepsons' to be there, but this is part of my job."

Percy began gathering his belongings. He checked his gun, then slid the Glock into its holster before looking around for his log book. He found it nearby on the table.

Percy made the call to his superiors, knowing they probably knew or should've known Prophet's predicament. He received his update and specified his next move so he'd have backup should he need it. He'd already told Reign he'd drop her off at the television station where she had extra clothes. She'd be able to shower, change, and head to Anderson in the official WPAK van.

Reign didn't say much after Percy made his second phone call. She could tell by the conversation he was speaking directly to Prophet, getting all the particulars. As a journalist and reporter she had an uncanny ability to glean just as much from what she didn't read, see, or hear as from what she did. Percy was speaking in code. She was helping him with his investigation. It was her father's church—her church, to be exact. She knew who was suspected of embezzling the church's money.

Why was Percy speaking in code when it was just her and him in the room?

Chapter 32

Patience weakened. Her insides churned.

She didn't wait to hear the rest of Percy's conversation with Reign. Instead, she zipped down the hallway, her feet barely touching the carpet. She threw open Joy's bedroom door, collapsing onto the side of the bed, nearly falling on top of her.

Joy bolted straight up. Her eyes were wide and her wigless head with its speckled gray short braids sprayed out made her look like Medusa.

"Help me, oh my sweet Jesus!" It took her a moment to realize that no man or a broomstick had attacked her. Patience had dove onto her bed.

Patience calmed down enough to tell Joy what she'd just overheard. "I didn't wait around once I heard that my Prophet—I meant Prophet *Long Jevity* was in trouble. You see, Joy, that's why he hasn't called me. He's in trouble."

Patience's crazy reasoning shook Joy. Her cousin had truly lost her mind. "Patience," Joy said slowly as she pulled down her gown (when she'd hopped up in the bed it'd hopped, too; it'd risen above her knees and was about to show her unplowed field of lost dreams), "why would Prophet call Lil P instead of you?"

As soon as Joy asked the question she could've kicked her own behind. Because Patience hadn't put on her contact lenses but still wore her Coke-bottle glasses instead, to Joy she looked like Mrs. Magoo had visited that *Home Alone* movie.

Patience's surprised look almost took Joy's breath away. What had she done? She'd messed up for certain. Just that quick, she'd opened the door to Patience's common sense and curiosity. Nothing short of the truth would shut it.

Up to that second, she'd kept her promise to First Lady Deborah not to say anything to Percy and the others, and she hadn't. She wasn't certain how long she could keep her word.

Unfortunately, when Patience had barreled into Joy's room, she hadn't closed the door. Porky stuck his head inside. He'd been on his way to the bathroom when he heard them up.

"What's going on with you two?"

Joy and Patience glanced at the doorway. Porky stared back at them with both hands extended as though he expected a hug, or at least an invite to come inside.

When the women didn't invite Porky inside, he did what family was supposed to do. He barged inside. Taking a look at Patience, who'd calmed down somewhat, he turned and asked Joy why they were up so early.

"I know you two need your beauty sleep, but since y'all up, let me fix something for us to eat."

Porky had no intention of cooking. He knew once he mentioned or threatened he'd cook in Joy's spotless kitchen, she'd climb Mount Rushmore to keep him out.

"You put one of your nasty fingers near my pots, and I'm gonna forget we just had prayer a few hours ago."

The three cousins broke out in laughter. It felt suddenly natural and was the first time since their teens that they'd laughed together. Although death long ago stopped Grandmamma Truth from her constant pitting one against the other, they hadn't come together until that moment.

Down the hall, still fuming in the living room, Reign decided she wasn't leaving nor was Percy until she got answers. If he wanted to help Prophet out of whatever fix the man was in, then he'd better give her the short version of the truth; but it'd better be the truth. Reign called him out on the way he'd spoken in code with Prophet.

Not wanting to have a rematch, Percy leveled with her. He told her that he'd seen Patience's shadow earlier, when she'd stood hidden by the partially open door. Porky had already given him more information on what he thought was happening between Patience and Prophet than he'd wanted to know. What he'd learned from Shaqueeda hadn't calmed him at all. He just hadn't found a way to address it yet. Nevertheless, he couldn't take a chance on his zany godmother's interference, so he'd spoken in code to Prophet. He also reminded Reign that these were the same crazy godmothers who'd wanted President Barack Obama to help them be all they'd never be.

The last reminder sealed the deal. Reign had to laugh and, of course, they were back on the matrimonial racetrack again.

From inside the living room, Percy and Reign heard the chatter and laughter coming from Joy's bedroom. "We might as well let them know we're leaving," Percy told Reign.

A few minutes later, Percy and Reign knocked on Joy's bedroom door. Once they entered, they found clownish smiles and awkward winks on each cousin's face.

Reign looked at her watch. "Oh my goodness, it looks like y'all missed the morning service."

"We can still make the second service," Joy told her. "Me and Patience got to play catch up with the Lord. We've missed several Sundays since August and here it is September already."

"So that means you didn't go to church much at all last

month?" As soon as Porky opened his big mouth, he clamped a hand over it. The last thing he wanted was to remind his cousins what hypocrites they were becoming.

"Today is the third Sunday," Reign said. "There's no second service. Daddy would've sent someone over to the satellite church to preach if he'd been there today. Don't y'all remember the church schedule?"

Shame came and wiped the smiles from Joy's and Patience's faces. "Guess we didn't," Patience replied.

"You speak for yourself!" Joy glared at Patience and mumbled, "Don't admit to nothing."

Reign shook her head and smiled. "Well, there's the Jamestown Memorial A.M.E. Missionary Jubilee service tonight."

"Of course," Joy blurted. "I'm on the dais so why would I forget about that?" She *had* forgotten, and it angered her, but she was determined not to show it. She'd slipped and tripped over so many important things lately, she wasn't sure which end was up.

"So you can rest up a bit before tonight," Reign said quickly. She'd caught the exchange between the women. "I know you're tired. It's been a full weekend, and it's not over yet, to say the least."

Reign quickly mentioned the impact the fire at the church's business office next to the main building would have on future services. They'd probably be off schedule, but they could still use the small sanctuary whenever necessary.

She'd decided to play along, since she and Percy already knew Patience had overheard his conversation. "Also," Reign added, "please let Missionary Granville know that she should keep my father's name on the prayer list for the sick and the shut in."

"Of course, I will." Patience spoke directly to Reign. She didn't look at Percy or attempt to tease him like she'd normally do. "But aren't you off today?"

Reign explained one of the other reporters had laryngitis, and she'd need to cover the assignment. She didn't bother to mention it'd be their event. The women would find out soon enough. "I gonna catch a ride with Percy. On his way to the airport, he can drop me off at the studio."

"So Lil P, you off on another adventure?" Joy asked the question while noticing how often Percy kept looking at his watch. He'd also jerked quickly on the hem of Reign's jacket, surely a signal she should hurry. He'd done it as though he didn't want the others to see him. Joy had.

"Yes, ma'am. Like Reign said, I'll drop her off at the studio and head on out to the airport."

Patience glanced at Percy. He looked almost sad. Maybe he was just tired, but she couldn't feel concerned at that moment. She remembered what she'd overheard him say about Prophet. What she'd heard hurt her.

Porky, as usual, was oblivious to the change from last night. *My son done mortgaged his butt to buy his future wife a mansion. I can't wait to tell it!*

No sooner had Percy and Reign closed the door behind them than the three cousins went into action.

"Listen," Joy said. "I know y'all saw what I seen. Lil P looked too nervous, and it's probably because he's handling too many cases at one time."

"He hurt my feelings. I don't care how many cases he's handling."

"Patience, grow up. My son ain't hurt your feelings. He's just keeping everything professional. What we need to do is show some family support for him."

"Porky's right."

Porky and Patience looked at Joy, shaking their heads in disbelief.

"You are agreeing with me?"

"Yes, Porker, *err* Porky, I'm agreeing with you."

"Joy, you up to something, and you'd better tell it right now. What's scattering around in that brain of yours?"

"Yeah, scatterbrain, spill it." Porky started to place his good arm around Joy's shoulder but one murderous look and the sucking of air through her teeth stopped him cold.

"Porky," Joy began, "right now you look like a sucker, having your place robbed and burned, and you ain't did nothing about it."

"I ain't nobody's sucker!"

"She didn't say you were; she only said you look like one."

"Pay attention and stop interrupting, or me and Patience gonna solve this mess without you. Now if we can find out who robbed and burned the Shanty, we might also find out who set fire to the church business office, too."

"Yeah, that sounds like a plan, and it'll let folks know I'm still the doggone mayor of Ptomaine Avenue."

"And you can get out of our house!" Patience quickly covered her mouth, and added, "So that you can get back to serving folks in that community."

"And you can get back to chasing that Prophet to see what his prophesy can do for your loneliness!" Porky turned away quickly and looked at something invisible on the wall. He hadn't meant to respond like that. *She started it.*

Within minutes Porky and Patience apologized, promising to keep whatever nasty thoughts they had about each other to themselves.

Moments later Porky reentered the living room and sat down to wait for Joy and Patience. He'd finished getting dressed faster than them because he had only two outfits to choose from. Porky wore one of his less-than-clean sleeveless T-shirts and a baseball cap. The shirt was torn under one arm and the baseball cap had a missing lid and looked like a yarmulke. In his world, clothes fit in two categories: dirty and funky. So he'd worn dirty.

The women dressed quickly. Patience and Joy looked approvingly at one another's outfits. Both had worn their missionary two-piece white outfits with matching pillbox hats, carrying their Bibles.

"Now tell me we don't look important and as clean as the driven snow."

"Joy, you right about that. And we should look important; after all, ain't we snoops for God?"

"You got that right, and we're Barack's backup gals, too."

"What do you think, Porky? What word comes to mind?" Patience had asked the question believing they'd healed their momentary wounds moments ago.

"Delusional."

"You gotta lot of nerve. Just look at you! You stinking and you wearing flip-flops with your toenails looking like box cutters!"

"Joy, let it go. You know we ain't got the keys to Lil P's to get him some clean clothes."

They called a truce and grabbed Felony, thinking that with six hours to go before church that night, they'd get a lot done. They just needed to decide exactly where to start.

"How about hitting downtown near some strip clubs or the Messy Hussy Lounge near the airport?" Porky asked with a straight face. "Some of the same lowlifes that hang out around Ptomaine Avenue also takes they trifling arses over there, too."

This time the rebuke came from Patience. "When this is all over no matter what I said before, you gonna need to take a DNA test. All of us! May lightning strike us dead, if we ever try to sing, 'We Are Fam-ee-lee'!"

Chapter 33

Percy drove Reign to the studio. He decided to restart his gentlemanly duties by getting out and opening her door, taking her hand to help her exit. He gave her a quick peck on her forehead. "I promise you, I'll call and let you know what's up with Prophet."

"You'd better." Reign smiled, looked around to see if anyone was looking before she kissed him on his lips. "As soon as I'm done taping, I'll go back to your godmothers'. I hope you don't mind about that."

"Mind, oh heck no, I don't mind. I don't trust them to stay home until church service this evening. Just hearing my dad talk about church was enough to call it into question, so you'll get no argument here."

As he drove away, Percy allowed his mind to recapture Reign's quick kiss upon his lips. It was such a small thing, but whenever she kissed him like that it only made him want her more. His car suddenly swerved to avoid crossing into the adjacent lane. "Not now Percy," he reminded himself. "Keep your eyes on the other prize."

What would have normally been cool weather had suddenly turned warm for that September day. Only the large calendar numbers on his watch reminded Percy that it was the first day of the fall season. Yet there wasn't much time to admire the green to orange to brown color change in the leaves dotting alongside Highway 85. Moments after he'd dropped Reign off at the studio, he'd received a second text message. Prophet's plane had landed a bit early. He had no luggage; it hadn't made sense to wait around the airport.

Percy had texted a suggestion that they meet at a cheap, out of the way hotel. The Best Value Inn over in Clemson was someplace where the folks checked in and out, but whatever they did remained in the room.

On the way to Clemson, which was about another twenty minutes, Percy turned on the radio for company. As much as he liked silence, sometimes music or some noise helped him think.

He certainly didn't want to chance peeping at his logbook while driving, so he pulled from his inside coat pocket his digital recorder. It was such a tiny device he could've worn it as a ring and none would be the wiser.

Percy began recording his thoughts. Not in any particular order, more of an exercise, much like a psychiatrist gives. Toss out a word and say the first thing that comes to mind. He began the exercise, speaking words and following them with rapid answers. He wasn't certain how long he'd done it, needing to keep his eyes on the road while he ran his mouth. He hadn't time to check his car's clock or his watch.

Percy hit the playback button and listened. Some of his replies made no sense, but they were the first words entering his mind. Nothing clicked; no punch in the gut telling him that he was on to something. He was about to turn it off, thinking he needed to try something else, when the last word he'd spoken came through.

"Embezzle," he'd said into the recorder.

"Misappropriate," was the first thing that'd jumped into his head.

Why hadn't he replied with words like *steal, pilfer, skim, de-*

fraud or even *pocket*? *Misappropriate* was such a long word in comparison. It wasn't a word he'd use in either his personal or professional speech.

Percy didn't exceed the speed limit. His mind was racing fast. He'd been good at compartmentalizing issues. He'd learned years ago that if one situation had nothing to do with another, he could separate the two and still come out a winner.

Somehow it wasn't working today. He didn't like pieces that didn't fit a puzzle he was trying to solve. The word *misappropriation* was supposed to mean something to him. After all, wasn't it the first word to come to mind when he thought of *embezzle*?

Percy turned the volume up on his radio. Since he'd been deep in thought he'd forgotten it was on. Whatever program it was that he'd turned to, it had on a commercial. It was some travel agency pushing a vacation spot in Italy and how cheap it was to fly there.

The Civic jerked as Percy gave it what he called the heavy foot. He'd figured out why the term *misappropriation* bothered him. One hand kept sliding back and forth across the steering wheel while his other held the wheel steady. "I should've known!"

He'd been in a situation several years back where he was on loan from the NYPD task force to the Justice Department.

The assignment involved traveling to Europe, investigating an international bond scam between Wall Street executives, one of which was an up-and-coming television evangelist, and their Italian counterparts. It was a clique of eight men with computer knowledge, secret pass codes, and inside-trading acumen who did a little money laundering on the side, too.

Within weeks, he'd solved the case, had the guilty on both sides arrested, and returned to the States. He'd done his job, yet all the men were given a slap on the wrist—except the guy who claimed, every Sunday on two separate television channels, to know Jesus. He was sent to prison on money laundering and misappropriation of funds.

"Prophet's gonna love this. This isn't just a duo committing a crime; we didn't figure in the one that makes it a trio. Damn, I'm slipping!"

Just before Percy turned off the highway, he felt his small Civic shake. Another car had passed going so fast it'd created a small blast. He'd already begun to turn onto a small winding back road that would lead to Prophet's hotel and, aside from it being a dark SUV with rope on its back, he couldn't have identified the car if he tried. "Idiot's gonna get somebody killed!"

Despite his outburst, because another driver had obviously exceeded the speed limit he began doing the same. At that moment, he couldn't wait to get there. He needed access to a computer. He couldn't remember the evangelist's name, and that bothered him, too.

"I'm telling you, I saw Percy," Porky insisted. "I should know my own kid when I see him. Who else drives a rinky-dink customized Civic but Percy? You almost drove him off the road!"

"I powdered his butt," Joy barked, "so I'd know him, too! I ain't driven close, or fast enough, to clip anyone's car, so quit lying. Plus, I ain't the one that's accident-prone."

"I still don't know what you gonna do with this dog while we're trying to hunt down clues. Just because we've decided to save visiting them gangsters for last don't mean my say don't carry no weight."

"I already told you that Patience and I have decided we're gonna visit our beloved pastor without you and your demons clouding up the holy atmosphere. Hopefully, Rev. Stepson might be in his right mind today and say something that'll give us a clue about the church fire or who he thinks might've done it. Of course, if the first lady is there we'll just say hello and good-bye. During that time, Felony can stay in this van with you."

"What the hell? No that mutt won't!"

Felony immediately turned from his guard position, leaping over the back seat and barking and growling at Porky.

"That's dog-cussing for, 'Yes, the hell I will!'" Joy cackled.

With the Porky problem settled by a vote bark, for the umpteenth time the three discussed their plan.

It was a simple scheme according to the cousins. Their missionary licenses would secure their entry into the rehabilitation center. The center was located a couple of blocks from the Metro Center; it was a district where City Hall and the Governor's office, along with other municipal agencies, were located. The women had visited the rehabilitation center several times before for missionary purposes, and so there shouldn't be a problem.

"If the first lady ain't there, we gonna anoint the reverend with some holy oil, read scripture from the New and the Old Testaments." Patience reminded them, "That's Joy's assignment."

"And then Patience will begin to massage his scalp and say words that might trigger a memory or two. We know it will work 'cause we seen it on *Murder, She Wrote*. That Angela Lansbury got skills for certain. It worked for her. It'll work for us."

Porky sat there speechless, listening again in disbelief to their *Star Trek* meets *Alfred Hitchcock* plan. It didn't take him long to make a choice. If he was the only one at that moment with an ounce of good sense, then they couldn't pry him out of the RAV into that rehabilitation center with cold cash money and the return of Grandmamma Truth's Bible. Having been either a creator or victim of dimwitted, bimbo, and just plain stupid ideas, he knew how this would end.

Despite Felony's stump tail wagging dangerously close to his nose, Porky dug deep into his pants pocket. He prayed his cell phone's battery wasn't dead. All he had to do was find a way to get Percy on his cell phone, and not get caught doing it. *Things done got too far outta hand.*

Chapter 34

Campbell Whistle was in a good mood. He was dressed in his Sunday best scam-bait—an expensive, tailored navy blue suit and matching Stacy Adams shoes polished so bright they'd shine during a blackout. Pulling the carry-on suitcase by its specially customized long handle, which also had the shoulder bag strapped to it, the smile planted upon his face soon blossomed into a full laugh, which he quickly managed to stifle.

His smile began as a smirk back at JFK Airport. At the last moment, he'd wobbled away in an opposite direction on purpose, ditching the infamous Prophet Long Jevity. "He's probably scratching his head because I left him clueless. He's gonna be real mad with himself when he finally figures out, if he does, that I flew north."

While waiting for the clerk at the Boston, Massachusetts, Enterprise Rent-A-Car desk to pull up his reservation, Whistle dug through the envelope carrying his identification. Smiling a little too much almost caused him to give the clerk the wrong one. Had he not been alert, he'd have handed the young man a driver's license with the name Campbell Whistle instead of one with his birth name, Jason Lauder.

"Here you go, sir. You'll find the 2011 Cadillac DTS. It's the white four-door in space number twenty-three."

Whistle listened with disinterest while the clerk went on to give the prerequisite boring do's and don'ts. He wanted to snatch the keys from the clerk's hands, but he didn't. He'd learned from past mistakes to never do or say anything that would leave a memory footprint when scamming, unless it was a part of the scam.

It didn't take Whistle long to find the car, deposit his belongings in its trunk, and be on his way. He needed to be in New Hampshire before four o'clock that afternoon; so far he was making good time.

Using the Cadillac's hands-free feature, he called a cousin.

"Praise the Lord. Today is the day the Lord hath made. We shall rejoice and be glad. Please leave a message." When the three short beeps that followed the greeting ended, Whistle began to speak.

"I'm headed toward New Hampshire."

A long beep from the answering machine rang out, interrupting Whistle's message, quickly followed by a male voice. The man on the other end was his cousin, Stephon, a reverend of sorts.

"I see you made it in one piece."

"That's right." Whistle chuckled. "And I'm about to exchange one Prophet for another. I'm calling this one *p-r-o-f-i-t*," he said, spelling out the word.

They exchanged a short laugh before the other man spoke again. "Two and half years are a long time since I've worked with you, and you can be a bit overconfident; hell, sometimes I believe you get off on being your own worst enemy."

"But in the end . . . ?"

"But in the end, you always come through; it's what a Lauder does," Stephon admitted.

The two cousins-in-crime chatted a little while longer. They razzed one another about their shortcomings. They'd played the game since childhood, upping the teasing in adulthood when any of the Lauder family fraudulent money-making schemes succeeded.

Within seconds, their good-natured teasing turned almost silly for two grown men. It was mostly about Whistle's ability to do the unimaginable. Neither would've imagined he'd be in such sexual demand with his shortened arms. Everyone thought the out-of-proportion limbs would've been a disability when he was born.

It didn't take long before it turned around to Rev. Stephon Lauder's own delusion. Somehow he held the belief that he'd outwit God and get over on the church folks. For a long time he'd had a plan that'd worked well for him.

Most of the plan was based upon appearances. For a man in his fifties, he'd kept in good shape. He'd liked the attention his looks had gotten him in his younger days. These days, he continued dipping into the fountain of youth, maintaining his appearance with dyed blond hair, twinkling ice-blue eyes, and just a hint of an olive complexion. At five feet ten, without a sign of stooping shoulders, he was dressing in off-the-rack suits to appear as common as he could when it suited his purpose.

However, the most laughter came about when Prophet's name came up again. Whistle—someone who never told everything, not even to family—held back from the conversation the trick he'd pulled back at JFK Airport when he'd blindsided the man.

"His dumb azz should've stayed in retirement," Rev. Lauder snarled. "Since he's decided to butt in Chester's business again, with that know-it-all Percy LaPierre, I hope y'all kill two birds with that money stone."

"Payback this time is gonna be sweeter than when James Brown sang it." Whistle broke out into his supposedly soul rendition of the hit, which was as flat and tone-deaf as he. When he quickly finished mangling the song, he asked, "Have you heard from Chester lately?"

Chester, hardly able to do much more than crap out whatever he could hold down and use a telephone for short periods of time, was on the last leg of his earthly journey. The cousins had had no choice but to place him in a nursing home, approved by the parole board.

Except for Whistle, no one in the family visited much anymore. Whenever Cousin Chester needed his younger cousins for a dirty deed, he'd send a short message only to Whistle, saying, "I can't do it, but I know someone who can."

Whistle could hear Stephon's laughter fading, which meant the signal would soon be lost.

After chatting with Stephon, Whistle knew he'd made the right decision not to badger Stephon into helping him and Chester with the scam. Each time they'd spoken, it'd seemed Stephon had become more comfortable in ripping folks off the easy way, through the Internet. It didn't take skill to do that, in his opinion. All someone needed was typing skills and hopefully to know how to construct a sentence.

However, he was committed to Chester. Chester was there when other close family members shunned them, blasting them for ruining the good family name. He'd always wondered what was so good about farming corn in Iowa to where the others had returned and still lived.

He had already set up the meeting in New Hampshire for late afternoon, and the one tomorrow in New York City's Wall Street area. All he had to do in both instances was to show up with the deposits and bring back the receipts. As usual, he'd give the code, Chester's philosophy: "I can't do it, but I have someone who can."

Even when he promised Chester he'd take care of everything, he never shared just how personal he'd planned on making it; Rev. Lock Stepson, Percy LaPierre, and Prophet deserved special attention. Why just stop with killing a reputation or ruining a church?

However, before that bit of business took place, he needed to handle the present one. There was a ton of money lying around parts of New Hampshire. It was the type of money the Lauder cousins thrived upon, money no one wanted to share with their favorite uncle, Uncle Sam.

New Hampshire that Sunday enjoyed some of the same unusally warm weather as back in South Carolina. Whistle checked his GPS. He'd been to Lebanon, New Hampshire, only twice for a meeting and pickup; he didn't want to rely on memory and become lost. He also wanted to get the business over and find someplace where he could relax—hopefully, with a woman he'd met a time or two in nearby Claremont. If she behaved and did his bidding as she'd done before, he might keep her on his "get by" list.

Whistle heard the loud rumbling sounds of hunger from his stomach. New Hampshire, the live-free-or-die state was indeed beautiful, but there wasn't a soul food place in the entire Lebanon or Claremont area. He did the next best thing, stopped in the first McDonald's he came upon. He ordered a Filet-O-Fish meal and hoped they'd have hot sauce.

Chapter 35

Parking almost a block and a half away from the rehabilitation center was the last thing Joy and Patience expected. If there was an upside, at least they hadn't shown suspicion when Porky hadn't resisted when ordered, again, to stay inside the RAV until they returned.

"I guess Felony finally got old pork barrel trained." Joy, laughing and huffing, fought to remain conscious. She was out of breath racing to keep up with Patience.

"You need to walk faster," Patience ordered, looking behind her as several others heading that way cut in front of Joy.

Joy finally caught up to Patience once Patience stopped walking. Having raced down the sidewalk faster than they'd expected, they looked each other over, checking to make sure they still looked presentable.

Some of Patience's long hair had come undone, making her pillbox hat appear to unravel. Joy had a perspiration patch so big on her dress jacket, it looked like someone had drawn dark half-moons under her armpits. Her raspberry-red wig had wigged out almost a block ago.

"We look fine. Nothing to worry about, because we ain't gonna embarrass our pastor or us." *Father God, I sure could use a bit more of Your grace and mercy, please.*

Patience, although concerned about the perspiration stain on Joy's jacket, had already decided that if Joy lost every stitch of clothing trying to get to the rehab center's front door, so be it. They'd go inside arm-in-arm, standing on God's promises, naked as jaybirds singing the Lord's praises. *Lord, please don't let your servant Crazy Lock Stepson be too crazy today.*

Once inside, they discovered their pastor had been moved to another floor and room. After exiting the elevator, one of the attendants told them to follow the yellow arrow to the north side of the floor and look for the room number.

"Joy, doesn't this yellow arrow on the floor remind you of that movie where that Dorothy gal grabbed her puppy and danced down the yellow brick road towards Oz?"

"It sure does." Joy quickly began trying to untangle a piece of hair from her wig caught in the netting on her hat. "I'm with that, just so long as a house don't fall out the sky on top of us."

"Or some big, ugly, nappy-haired apes come along, grabbing us to take to the wicked witch," Patience joked.

They quickly began humming one of their favorite praise and worship songs. With as much conviction as they'd had when they concocted any of their schemes, they hummed under their breath Vickie Winans' "As Long as I Got King Jesus," making it their own by switching a word or two, like "As long as we got King Barack." They hadn't gotten to the second verse of the remix before they'd noticed several men dressed in orderly uniforms coming toward them.

"Well, suh," Joy said as she stopped humming, elbowing Patience to get her attention. "Whoever said that favor ain't fair wasn't joking. They look helpful."

Patience straightened her dress, checked her hat and began to smile. "And Porky mocked us and said that we wouldn't be able to pull this off. It looks like we got our special escorts to take us inside to see the pastor."

Chapter 36

Percy and Prophet were on their cell phones in the hotel room. Percy was barking orders into his cell while Prophet did the same into his.

Percy finished first. It made no sense trying to hide his exasperation; he was pissed. He'd known for some time Whistle would soon make his move. The fire at Shaqueeda's didn't fool him either. The man had used it to cover up whatever he thought would be found in his apartment next to it. "That fire was personal," he told Prophet. "Probably because she talked too much, and he didn't like it."

Percy rose and went to the laptop, still running a Google search. He'd already found more evidence that he'd overlooked when he'd logged onto the department's secured Web site. He leaned over the laptop, scanning the results, one hand in his pocket and the other held against the back wall. "Do you believe this?"

"Sure I do." Prophet snapped shut the cover to his cell phone, walking over to the hotel room window, and opened the Venetian blind. "If it'll make you feel any better, your future father-in-law's files were removed before the fire. They were discovered on a flashdrive among some of the latest personal items the first lady provided."

Percy hadn't realized he'd taken a few steps back until he bumped into the chair behind him. "Why hadn't we gone through those personal things before?"

"We just got them, along with some old sermon tapes, a few VHS recordings, and a crate of DVDs. There's supposedly some personal journals scribbled in his hand from when he sat on the bench in Columbia. He may have had an idea to one day write a book. Anyway, they came in two days ago, so I'm told."

"We need to get someone to start cataloguing those things. Do you think we should assign transcribing those journals or do it ourselves?" Percy's question hung in the air for another few seconds before he decided they would personally handle Rev. Stepson's journals. Percy wanted to make sure every part of their next move was covered and understood. There'd be plenty of egg on their faces to go around from the night before. "So, when do you head back to New York?"

"Just as soon as he does . . ." Prophet would have finished his answer, but a soft beeping sound came from the laptop. He and Percy went to it, their eyes scanning the screen before Percy hit the print command.

"It looks like you were right," Prophet said. He wasn't smiling; his emotions seemed more controlled than they needed to be, especially since it was just the two of them in the room. He handed a photo to Percy.

Percy walked back toward the window. "He looks different now, but there are still strong resemblances." He turned the photo around in his hands, using natural daylight; he looked at it from all angles. "I can't tell if it's the same nose or not. It looks a lot narrower and I don't remember what color his eyes were. He actually looks as sick as is stated on the report."

"That whole bunch is a sick lot," Prophet murmured with sarcasm.

"I was hoping you'd see something significant that would've made me miss it. I'm searching for a reason." He wouldn't admit it aloud, but the words *too much ego* echoed in his head. He flung the photo on the bed, biting his lip to keep from punching his own head.

"You need to stop beating up on yourself," Prophet warned. "How much of each case do you think I remember? Not much, I can tell you that. You'd lose your own sense of self if you did."

Percy wouldn't respond. He could tell by Prophet's tone that a sermon with a life-class lesson tied to its end was on the way out of Prophet's mouth. He just needed to take mental notes, as he'd done when they both were back in New York's Columbia Law School. "Different years, but same technique," he murmured.

"I can tell by that look on your face that you think I'm about to teach."

"Aren't you?"

"I most certainly am, and guess what else?"

"What?"

"I'm doing it from my own place of embarrassment. Don't forget, I did just get my butt handed to me earlier, when I lost Whistle at the airport."

A quiet laughter escaped their lips, but the laughter didn't last.

"Listen Percy, a few years ago you were on your way to the top. You hadn't been a detective that long before you'd proved me and the judge right about your natural criminal-solving insight. The brass saw the same thing we'd seen in you when we had you as a student."

Percy leaned against the wall, his arms folded and his eyes closed. He was beyond tired—his face itched from not shaving again, and he was certain his body could use deodorant—but willing to give control over to Prophet. Back in those days, he'd had his best interest in mind and nothing had changed.

Prophet reminded Percy what'd happened when he was a young detective. He'd been on loan to the United States Justice Department. They'd needed someone unknown yet who had the capability and gut instinct to bust a unique group of men who'd scammed several million people through a television religion scheme. The crime had its origins in Columbia, South Carolina. It'd been the type of crime that'd left a foul taste in a lot of folks' mouths.

Percy had tracked down the cartel's leader, Chester Lauder, out of New Hampshire, along with his other Wall Street companions and a very inept but popular black television evangelist from Harlem, New York. He'd tracked and found the men in Italy.

With his information and DOJ authority, he'd had the Italian police arrest the men and send them back to the States—all but Chester Lauder. Chester had escaped and avoided capture for nearly nine months.

Prophet took a break in his narrative and came and stood in front of Percy. He wasn't as tall as Percy, but he looked like the giant of a man Percy had always thought he was.

Prophet then spread open his arms.

Percy didn't know if the lecture was over and Prophet wanted a hug, or what. Then Prophet looked Percy in his eyes, removing all doubt, and began to speak again.

"I know you were pissed off back then because one got away. I'd have been and have felt that way, too," Prophet told Percy. "But if I've learned anything in these twenty-odd years of chasing the bad guys and teaching criminology, crime never pays. If the criminals don't pay it on its due date, they'll still pay it, but with a higher interest."

Percy finally spoke as he turned from facing his former mentor and professor. "You can say that because you came along and cleaned up my mess." His voice had sounded harsher than he'd meant. But he wouldn't apologize.

"Come off it!" Now it was Prophet's turn. He became agitated, almost as much as Percy appeared to be. "I was a Federal agent when you had that case. I hadn't been retired as a law professor that long either. I guess you've forgotten I was only vacationing in Italy because I'd lost my wife to leukemia. Joyce and I'd been married almost five years back then and were childless. I wasn't looking for Chester Lauder or nobody else. I wanted to be alone. I just happened upon him."

Percy turned around; he ducked under Prophet's outstretched arm and stood by the window. "That may be, but he might've remained a free man if you hadn't."

"Big deal, so he might've remained a free man for a time." Prophet dropped his arms, his voice dripped with frustration. "Didn't I just tell you that criminals pay, whether on a due date or later with high interest?"

Prophet walked over to where Percy stood motionless. He adjusted his sunglasses before he continued. "Percy, Chester Lauder would've served better time had he gone straight to hell instead of ending up in a South Carolina prison. Before the feds got him back on this side of the globe, he'd been kept locked up in a vermin-infested, feces-splattered Italian prison.

"From what I remember, he got roughed up every day by either the prison guards or other prisoners who didn't like criminals coming to their country and stirring the crime pot unless they were Italiano, too. It might've been an Italian man named Ponzi they named the Ponzi scheme after, but those Sicilian fellas weren't feeling Lauder at all.

"I remember how those Wall Street associates arrived at the Columbia, South Carolina, supreme court earlier that spring, armed with a herd of expensive attorneys. Those attorneys were well versed in South Carolina law."

"I remember, too, Prophet. According to the Wall Street gang, they'd tried to help a religious organization. They weren't aware of the fraud aspect."

"If I remember correctly, those Wall Street guys turned on him fast. They gave up information in alphabetical order on that evangelist, and later on, they did the same to Chester Lauder. That evangelist went to prison; for how long, I don't remember. Chester Lauder got convicted in absentia. Trust me; no one was happier than me seeing Chester Lauder finally extradited."

Prophet placed his hands in his pockets and began to pace the floor. "I gotta admit something, though."

"What?"

"Getting back in the saddle in Italy when I'd gone there to grieve and think things through helped me come to the decision to remain with the feds. I imagine I have Chester Lauder to thank for that."

"So are you saying that I didn't catch the man so he could help you make a life decision?" Again, Percy's voice became sarcastic. He just couldn't help himself.

Prophet decided he'd continue saying his piece. A lot of stress was in that room; they needed to show one another forgiveness and tolerance.

"You know, Percy," Prophet began, "when Lauder was finally extradited back to the States it didn't take that jury long before he was convicted again. That much I do remember. And I imagine you just saw the same thing I did when you read that report."

Percy's voice returned to its natural state of respect where Prophet was concerned. "Yeah, I saw it. Old Chester Lauder, sentenced to prison by the same judge who presided over the first trial of his partners."

"Except those Wall Street hustlers went free," Prophet reminded him.

"I don't know why he hadn't recused himself when he had a chance. He could've done it earlier before presiding over that televangelist. It had to be hard for one preacher to sentence another no matter if he was a charlatan. I find it ironic that when that preacher's turn came around, those others only spent money on their own defense. In the end, it didn't matter who'd sat on the bench. The jury had found him guilty, so case closed."

"Yeah, that was likely true," Prophet mused, but added, "Like I always say, don't mess with God's people."

"Besides . . ." A smile finally crept across Percy's unshaven face. It'd become his turn and time to remind Prophet of something. "When have you ever known old *Judge Crazy Lock Stepson*, pounding a gavel or waving his Bible around, to back away? The jury gave a verdict and the judge gave a sentence."

The hotel room class of sorts ended as quickly and as unorthodoxly as it began. They could only stand on regrets or remorse for so long. They had a case that'd just escalated. At least they saw some sort of connection. But old Rev. Stepson had sentenced and offended so many. It wouldn't be easy; but none of their cases ever were.

Prophet plugged in the hotel coffee pot. After the discussion they'd just shared, they both could use the caffeine. As soon as the light lit, indicating it was ready, Prophet poured cups for them both.

"You know, I was thinking." As soon as Percy spoke, his cup shook and some of the hot liquid spilled out. He shook it quickly off his hands, blowing the spot where the liquid landed.

Seeing as how Percy was busy trying to act like the hot coffee didn't hurt, Prophet looked at the paper again before he spoke. "I'm remembering a little more about the Italian case you were on. It's not so much about all the accused or even the particulars. I remember there'd been a glitch, and you didn't discuss it with me until you had to."

"I should've come to you sooner, but my ego wouldn't allow me. I'd hit a snag."

"It'd bothered me, Percy, that the Wall Street gang had expensive, experienced lawyers and had gotten those charges dwindled down to small misdemeanors without jail time.

They got a measly fine. Yet I knew from my investigations all of them were guilty of misusing those church funds, hiding them in the Caribbean. It wasn't right, bilking folks even if a greedy but dumb guy calling himself a preacher was involved, robbing Peter to pay Paul."

"That's true, but water under the bridge now, Prophet. From what I just read, that evangelist died some time ago. It's sad, but, again, Judge Stepson back then had to go by the jury's decision. The misappropriation of funds conviction fell on two men, that preacher and Chester Lauder. Remember, when those fellas got off, Lauder hadn't been brought back yet.

"Well, it's a different day but the same crap. My future father-in-law's all mixed up in this mess. Reign's gonna be hurt, and I've no one to blame but myself." Percy could feel anger rising again. *Why hadn't I figured out the misappropriation link long ago? I'd have never proposed. I could've waited; I might have to do that anyway before I marry her.*

Prophet Long Jevity placed one hand on his former student's, and now partner's, shoulder. "Listen, I have ties to the judge, too. You weren't the only one he taught at one time. I worked under him as well for a spell as a law clerk. When I didn't think I was good enough to go further in that field, he did. I went as far as I did, and was as successful as I was, off the shoulders of Judge Crazy Lock Stepson. Only for the two of you would I have delayed my retirement to help your church. Although, I can't lie; I didn't see this aspect coming either."

"It's a damn shame this is happening to the reverend." Percy bristled. "I remember why he got that nickname, Crazy. He used to close down that courtroom at the drop of a hat when things didn't go his way. Even a fly losing its wing was out of order. And now, his brilliant mind, spiritually elevated, helping so many, can't be relied upon to string a sentence together that amounts to any sense."

Prophet began unbuttoning his shirt, exposing and then

removing his bulletproof vest. "Well, for certain he can't help us since we never know when he's gonna be lucid for any length of time. It'd sure make things easier if he were. And it doesn't help that he was so tight-lipped before, he never shared a lot with his wife, either."

"Well, we've got two detectives from the Pelzer undercover squad at the center watching out for him. This is their first assignment, and they're posing as orderlies."

"They put a pair of newbies on a case this serious?"

"It's okay. They're from homicide and robbery. I've known them a while, and they know the Stepsons. They won't let anything happen. Hopefully, one of them will be in the room if and when the reverend does embrace some lucidity. They also know he's not to have visitors, except immediate family, and especially not anyone that can influence him."

"Won't the church members be a bit upset about that, Percy?"

"Yes, they will. However, the first lady is aware that this takes precedence."

"Hopefully, your godmothers won't take a notion to visit."

"They won't. They're too busy trying to stay out of trouble so they don't embarrass themselves in case they actually get to meet the president."

"You mean you haven't told them, Percy?"

"Nope."

"That's just plain mean. I feel sorry for you and Reign if they ever find out that you two knew the president was coming this close to Pelzer for an unscheduled meeting with the governor and didn't tell them."

"There's no reason for them to be in that area and, besides, I'm just trying to save a church and the president's piece of mind at the same time."

"Hope you're right."

Me too; Lord, Barack Obama has enough obstacles . . .

Prophet finished off his cup of coffee and then took a small bottle of water, already uncapped, and put it to his lips. He took his time, slowly drinking the room-temperature liquid until he'd emptied the bottle, before he spoke again. "I'm still waiting for the Google search to end. I've got another idea, but there's no sense in putting it out there until I find a reason to do so. It's time we begin gluing the facts, Percy. The fire at the church was no accident. Neither was the fire at Whistle's apartment or the one at that beauty salon either. We know some of those Lauders aren't anything but career criminals. Chester's supposedly clutching the knob on death's door, so who's helping him? I say we start with his family. If I'm wrong, then we've only wasted another hour or two."

Percy didn't press. It was one of the quirks most agents or investigators shared. Worrisome feelings in one's gut accounted for almost 75 percent of any success.

Again, a beep came from the laptop. Standing by the window each turned and saw the yellow-colored lines on the screen that indicated there'd been a hit within the search results.

They printed out the four pages. Each took two pages. The men raced to a table in the corner of the room where other papers lay.

"It's them!" Percy slapped a high five with Prophet and added, "It's not much of a family resemblance, but it's still them." He'd made the declaration aloud only because he felt the need to do so. It was confirmation he'd recovered some of his insightful detective mojo. He'd been fallible. *Pride goeth before a fall*, he thought, remembering the words Patience had tried to pound into his thick skull.

"Let's move," Prophet ordered, checking his cell phone with one hand while putting on his vest with his other. "As much as I'd love to let you wallow in more self-assurance, there's no time. Besides, there's a reason for all things; you'll have to grow a bit more to find that out. But right now, we need to see about waylaying another suspect. We got information from Fast Cat that he did the Internet hookup, for Stephon Lauder. We got the address on Fast Cat."

"I know who the dude is," Percy replied. "I had to use special persuasive methods to convince him not to hook up any more illegal cable or phony surveillance equipment in Porky's place again."

The scowl on Prophet's face told him that he shouldn't have made things personal with Fast Cat over something so trivial; he shouldn't boast about it, either.

Percy quickly changed the subject. "As smart as the Lauder cousins think they are, if they're involved why in the world did they think they'd not get caught again?"

"Do I need to pull a surprise quiz, Percy? Criminals don't think, they pay; whether on the due date or with high interest. They pay."

It was time to use some compartmentalizing and show Percy's ability to walk and chew gum. Percy was certain; he at least still had that going on.

Prophet and Percy gathered what they'd need. They searched the room, making certain they left nothing incriminating should things not go well once they left. The investigation always took precedence, and this one had way too many twists and turns.

"Are we both going silent?" Percy asked that question knowing they were about to go through an area where, despite signal scrambling and other defenses, anything they said on the direct connect walkie-talkie feature of their cells was compromised. Nothing was 100 percent.

"No," Prophet replied. By that time they were on their way to the parking lot, taking the back stairs to get there. "You're on silence."

"Not you?"

"Not me." Going ahead of Percy out the hotel's back door, he added, "Once we get into Anderson, we can stop by the base and pick up that new cell for you. With everything your father has shared, and I know for a fact he yaps, it's not in our best interest for you to use it now."

"You're right." Percy began to gnaw on his inside cheek, not bothering to hide his disappointment and anger with his father. Moreover, if he'd kept his mouth shut, too, then Porky wouldn't have had anything to boast about.

Picking up his new secured phone was just one more thing he hadn't taken care of. It'd been more than twelve hours since he'd gotten the message to turn in the current BlackBerry. A new phone, with enhanced security and a battery that would automatically extend its life twice before the need for recharging, was crucial. Once the investigation had headed in a new direction, the need for another work cell phone had become mandatory.

Percy, reluctantly, turned off his phone. Little by little, every piece of what he'd thought made him almost invincible and invaluable kept breaking away, causing him to doubt what'd always been second nature. There was no room for second-guessing. Now everything he'd done over the past few months had caught up to him, making him totally reliant on Prophet for communication with their base and for his own safety.

The Lauder family, especially Chester's cousins, were educated, connected, proven, and unpredictable. They weren't dealing with low-level street thugs. They needed to make a concrete connection between Chester Lauder and what was happening at Mount Kneel Down. They had the report, four pictures of some family members, but whether or how far the dying man's tentacles had spread, they still hadn't proved. Yet, somehow, believing a dying Chester would want to get even with the judge who'd sentenced him no matter if the judge was now as sick as him was very plausible.

They'd already decided that Prophet would stay on Whistle's trail, especially since he'd learned about a meeting on

Wall Street set for tomorrow. Percy would take another team member, head out to New Hampshire, and check out the re-formed ex-con Rev. Stephon Lauder.

Before today, neither Percy nor Prophet had believed Whistle would be that much of a problem. Then he'd pulled that stunt at the airport and proven otherwise.

Chapter 37

Porky twisted and turned around inside the small space of the RAV's backseat like an Oreo cookie crumbling fast in the Sunday heat.

Felony, trying to mock Porky, moved in circles, too, chasing his tail like any normal dog would.

Porky had tried to get a signal on his cell phone at every angle he knew. His crazy cousins had flown the cuckoo coop with an idea he couldn't have thought up, drunk or sober. If he was successful in getting a signal, once he reached his son, he didn't know how much time it would take for Percy to keep Joy and Patience from ambushing a sick and helpless old man.

Although he'd never admit he'd been hustled, the second-hand, ill-gotten phone he'd brought off a street hustler called Fast Cat apparently had limitations and came with a warning. "You know these things come with an unwritten street warranty; if it works it works. If it don't, well, you get what you pay for," Fast Cat had warned.

Leave it to Joy to park somewhere where nothing that's from the twenty-first century works. Joy had taken the car key when she and Patience left. He couldn't drive to another location if he'd wanted.

Every few seconds, someone witnessing Porky wiggling and acting confused knocked on one of the windows. The question was always, "Sir, do you need help?"

No sooner would Porky answer, "Yes," and that he needed to borrow a cell to make a phone call than Felony would begin to growl, acting crazier than normal. It was always enough to scare away any potential help.

All he could do was sit with a face looking disfigured from being squashed against the window as though he were on display, and wait.

Joy's and Patience's humming began fading from a murmured but enthusiastic remix of "As long as I got King Barack and the pastor's in room three eleven" to a hush, as they realized the approaching men already seemed focused upon them.

"Oh, I hope everything is all right." Patience kept her eyes glued to the men as they continued walking down the hallway.

Joy nodded her head toward the men. She could hardly contain herself. She planted a kiss on the ID pouch she'd hung around her neck, patting it as if to soothe her missionary license. She began practicing facial contortions, those she felt would make her look more professional and hide her real purpose of snooping.

"This is it," she told Patience. "I'm glad we brought our congregational membership cards and missionary licenses."

"I'm glad, too," Patience replied. "I'm not comfortable with the way these orderlies are eyeballing me. Especially that short yellow one; he looks like a throwback from a hunchback. He must be extra ugly. I can tell from this distance that he ain't a handsome fella."

"That other one looks like that character Lurch who played on that *Addams Family* series. Either way, I don't like the way those two negroes are now looking at us while they walk this way."

"Joy, they look too shifty."

"They do, don't they?" Joy confirmed, looking down her nose as the men's distance narrowed. She craned her neck and whispered to Patience, "We're unique and highly flavored." Remembering the predicament her pastor was in, Joy suddenly added, "You'd think they'd be professional enough to stick to the business of tending sick folks instead of lounging around the hallway looking to probably hassle innocent folks. These orderlies are out of order." *Give me strength, Father. I might have to kick some butt up in here if they ain't attending to my pastor like they oughta.*

"Miss Karry!" One of the men, the one she had thought looked like Lurch, approached her quickly. He then turned to Patience and took a second look, as did his partner.

The one Patience had described as a yellow Quasimoto began grinning before he blurted, "Wow, Miss Patience, is that you? I hardly recognized you without those huge binocu—"

The second man interrupted before his partner brought unnecessary attention, which was sure to happen if he continued running his mouth. "Without your regular glasses, he means."

"Yes, that's what I meant. Are those hazel or just plain light-brown contacts? You look fabulous."

"Thank you." Patience blushed shamelessly. "I guess I have changed just a teeny bit since I worked with y'all back in homicide and robbery. Last I heard, you two were being sent to undercover duty."

"Enough of this chitchat," Joy said. "Johnson, Blake— what are you two doing up here dressed up like orderlies?" Joy began switching her Bible from one hand to the other.

"Joy, stop being so rude, and what are you doing with that Bible? Are you planning on hitting them with the Word?"

"We're on assignment," Quasimodo Blake replied. "So just keep on pretending like you don't know us if anyone comes out into this hallway."

"Yeah," Lurch Johnson added, "and since it's Sunday, most folks would be in church. We're surprised to see you here at this time."

"We got a lot of time on our hands since we was dumped by y'all."

"Miss Joy, we didn't have anything to do with your layoff. You should know that," Detective Blake stated.

"That's right, Miss Joy. We didn't even report to human resources or to Percy what we were sure you were gonna do with that sharp scraper," Johnson added.

Johnson tapped Blake on the shoulder before suggesting, "And that bottle of whatever damaging liquid you had in your hand near that human resources car."

"That's all lovely," Patience said. She gave a quick wink to Joy before proceeding. "Joy, why don't you tell Blake all about Felony? I'm certain he'd like to know how the puppy is faring. After all, he did give it to you a couple of years ago, and he ain't been by to check up on it. In the meantime, I need to find a bathroom."

"Before I tell them anything about Felony, I wanna know why they up here dressed like this."

"Joy, since we know they were assigned to the undercover unit before we got kicked to the curb, it's obvious from their ill-fitting orderly costumes that they're working undercover."

"You were always a smart one," Blake said. His face twitched, signaling he was trying to bite his tongue. A smile appeared. "Can't tell y'all about the case, but Miss Patience, you can find a bathroom at the end of that hallway, by room three eleven."

Joy's and Patience's smiles suddenly lit up the hallway before Patience seemingly two-stepped down the hallway toward room 311.

Around the corner, about a half a block from where Joy and Patience had gone to visit Rev. Stepson at the rehabilitation center, a WPAK television camera crew's van had pulled up and parked. The van's doors swung open and several husky men poured out onto the street. They quickly threw pieces of equipment over their shoulders and dashed toward the building to set up for the shoot. Reign led the way while barking orders, showing her authority.

It wouldn't have surprised anyone who knew Reign that earlier she'd flipped the script when she learned the latest news on the president. The White House press secretary had issued a secure update that President Barack Obama had changed his schedule. The POTUS was having a brief meeting and photo op that very afternoon with the governor at the town hall in Metro Center along with several other officials before continuing on to New York for a fundraiser.

It hadn't taken her two minutes before she'd sailed into the assignment editor's office prepared to battle. However, with little effort she'd managed to convince the assignment desk to change her assignment from covering the James Memorial A.M.E. event. She reminded them of her status, saying that no one other than a seasoned reporter should cover the president's meeting. If the date of the James Memorial event hadn't changed, she'd have covered the president anyway.

From where Porky peered out the SUV's back window, he could see the WPAK van as it'd turned the corner. He'd thought about just leaving, with Felony standing guard, and going as far as the corner to check things out. He'd hoped Reign would be among the crew. Then he remembered that Reign was covering some church event, someplace he couldn't remember, and he slumped back onto the seat. "Reign or no Reign, I can't just sit here. I got to find out what's happening with those two nuts. I'm the man, and they need to respect me!"

As if Felony had read Porky's mind, the dog backed away from the door. When Felony lowered his big head, Porky muttered, "Are you finally realizing who's boss up in here? Or are you laughing at me?"

Meanwhile, as the WPAK camera crew bustled about, Reign walked over to one of the three cameras. She needed to make certain that each camera was set to capture the hot political atmosphere not only inside but out on the street as well. "It's always good to get the public's reaction to a visiting president," she told the crew.

Reign's cell phone chimed loudly. It meant she'd received an urgent message from the station. He's running late. We're gonna need to give the President about another forty-five minutes before he and the governor can meet.

Reign drew a finger across her throat, her signal to the inside crew to stop what they were doing. "Give me two minutes, then let's start again. I need to give an update. Looks like it's another one of these hurry-up-and-wait situations."

She'd just walked past the outside camera crew to tell them also of the delay when she saw Porky racing towards her, with Felony sprinting beside him. "Oh Lord." Reign didn't wait for the cameraman to zoom in so she could give an on-air update to the television audience; instead, she pulled out her cell phone, pressed the speed dial, and blurted, "What the hell?" And, of course, she forgot the outside crew was still live from the sound check.

Rev. Lock and First Lady Stepson's baby girl had uttered a profanity on live television.

Chapter 38

Reign pressed Porky as to why he was even in Anderson, much less in the same neighborhood as she until, she hoped, she had the truth.

"Why in the world would they go see Dad? All of you promised to stay put until the service tonight. Y'all gonna make me old and gray before I'm old and gray!"

With nothing but her press clearance in her hand, and Porky staggering and out of breath to keep up with her, they placed Felony back inside the RAV.

"Stay put, Felony," Reign hissed.

Felony immediately looked at Reign. The dog growled and lifted his hind leg. Porky immediately snatched Reign out of the way before he slammed the passenger door shut. "You don't want none of what that mutt's about to let out. One day that smell gonna bring out them environmentalist folks for sure."

Reign caught a whiff from the cracked car window before almost crumbling, but she and Porky recovered quickly and began racing the block and a half to the rehabilitation residence and up to her father's floor.

By the time they arrived, Porky was almost in stroke condition from being so out of shape, and Reign's WPAK dark blazer looked almost mildewed from sweat. Neither looked any better by the time they located Joy.

Joy had an orderly almost pinned against a wall while the other orderly stood by looking helpless. "Oh Lord. The insanity circus has already begun," Reign told Porky before returning her attention to the scene of a possible hallway crime.

"Miss Joy, what are you doing?" Reign hadn't realized she'd shouted in the near empty hallway until the other orderly rushed toward her.

"Reign, what are you doing here? Your dad's sleeping, knocked out from his meds. He's fine and about the same; besides, you're not scheduled to visit him until tomorrow. Didn't Detective Percy or your mother explain things to you?"

"Hi Johnson, didn't recognize you in that get up. Sorry, about this but—" Reign stopped and nodded toward Joy, who still had Blake pinned against the wall. "I thought there might've been a problem when I learned my future god-mothers-in-law were visiting."

"Visiting who?" Johnson asked.

"My father, of course; who do you think they're visiting?"

"We didn't get that far. We were going to ask, but Miss Patience needed to use the ladies room and Miss Joy is over there showing Blake how Felony corners the bad guys."

Porky stood a few feet away listening to Joy, who had Blake's total attention. He began to smile, muttering, "Gotta hand it to my cousins; Slick Wynona's the biggest con on the block, but she ain't got nothing on them gals. If these dummies can't see through what Joy and Patience pulling, then I ain't gonna help them."

"Hey Porky, you say something?" said Blake. "I didn't see you at first. I was over there chatting with Miss Joy about Felony. He's gotta lot of bust-a-criminal, according to her."

"Nope, I ain't said a word. I'm just here to observe."

"Blake," Johnson called out, "get over here quick!"

Porky's and Joy's heads swung in Johnson's direction. Neither said a word but looks exchanged between them read that they were on the same page of the plan.

Joy had already noticed Reign when she appeared with Porky but had decided to keep working on keeping Blake's attention, just in case Patience needed more time to do more than go to a bathroom.

Just as Reign and the undercover detectives turned the corner toward the reverend's room, they ran directly into Patience. She had a paper towel in her hand, which dripped water.

"What's wrong with y'all?" Patience quipped. "Y'all almost knocked me down. Was my going to the bathroom on a timer or something?"

"Sorry, Miss Patience," Blake said, "I'd meant to ask who you needed to visit on this floor, but we got to get back on our assignment. We don't wanna mess up our first one."

"Accept my apology, too, Miss Patience," said Johnson. "You, Miss Joy, and Porky have a nice day."

Within a second, all they saw were two flashes of white as the undercover detectives sprinted away toward the reverend's room.

"Speaking of which," Reign said, "I need to get back to mine." She quickly turned to Joy, Patience, and Porky. "It's getting late. You have a service tonight, and you probably need to be rested because I'm certain Percy will want to chat."

"How Percy gonna know what to chat about?" Joy asked slowly as she sucked her teeth.

"I'm gonna give him a subject or three." Reign nodded at each of them before she continued. "That's how he'll know. And I mean it, too." Reign's words were sharp.

Reign's cell phone chimed, indicating she had a text.

Porky quickly began speaking. "Reign, you know I can't

stand a snitch, and you'll probably think I'm just doing this to save face, but let me tell you what's really happening."

"Not now, Porky," Reign snapped. "I gotta go. I'm still on assignment, even if you three don't have anything to do but meddle."

They were dumbfounded. They knew she could be serious, but they'd never heard Reign come down on them that hard.

Joy turned and faced Porky. "If Reign messes things up between us and Lil P, your son gonna be missing a daddy, you dumb snitch."

"Always a threat!" Porky backed away. "Ain't nobody scared of you."

"You two need to take that show on the road." Patience peered around the empty hallway. "Reign will get over it," Patience said before she began whispering. "We need to get outta here before Blake and Johnson find out I was in the pastor's room."

"I thought that's what you were up to," Joy said proudly. "I did my part by not passing out from the bad breath of that Quasimodo Blake. I tell ya, his breath smelled worse than Felony's; which of course, I gave him an earful about."

Joy quickly turned to Porky. She circled him as she looked up and down the hallway. "Speaking of which, where's Felony! What did you do with my Felony?"

"Forget all that stuff. He's back inside the SUV, where me and Reign left him. And before you start going off again, it was you that took the keys so yes, it's unlocked—but whoever's dumb enough to get in won't get out."

"You'd better hope so. I'll turn him loose on you."

"Will you two ever stop? Please!" Patience pressed the elevator button.

Porky looked around the hallway, making sure they were still alone. "Are you gonna tell us what happened in that room or what?"

The elevator doors opened and the trio stepped inside. Just as it was about to close, they heard one of the undercover detectives' voices call out, "Miss Patience, wait. Hold on!"

Once outside the rehabilitation residence, the trio walked quickly back to the RAV. Neither could speak much during that time as their chests pounded from lack of oxygen and too much anxiety.

"Lord, that was a close call," Porky said as Joy entered the SUV and secured Felony.

"It's okay," Joy told them. "It's a bit of a stink in here, but I guess much of it has evaporated. Felony didn't mean no harm. He just didn't like being left alone because some-body"—she stopped and eyeballed Porky—"couldn't do what he was told to do and took matters into his unqualified hands."

"You two keep this up and I'm gonna keep it to myself what I found out!"

"Speak then." Joy placed the key in the ignition. "You can tell us while I drive. I gotta feeling that Blake and Johnson ain't too thrilled about us now."

Patience began by congratulating herself on being smart enough to get away from the detectives under the pretense of having to use the bathroom. "I was ready to start jiggling and everything if I had to do so to convince them."

"Can you please get to it?" Joy began pushing the pedal down to get away quickly.

"Anyways," Patience continued, "as I entered the pastor's room, he was mumbling in his sleep. None of it made much sense until he said Deacon Whistle's name. I figured he was just a bit upset or had forgotten that Whistle had been put in charge of things."

"And so what happened?" Porky tapped Patience on her

shoulder. "We don't need every detail; just give us the big detail."

"Today is Sunday, September twenty-first, right?"

"Patience, you are trying me."

"Oh Joy, just drive the car and let me tell this. I think I know what Whistle may be up to."

"And pray tell, Patience," Porky hissed. "What would that be?"

"When the pastor mumbled Whistle's name somehow I remembered that Whistle's supposed to take a plane ride tomorrow. I know because I picked up the tickets months ago for him and some other men named Jason and Chester something, to go out of town. I can't remember the men's last name, but I believe it began with an L or an I. Either way, I remember because I know just about everyone in our church, and I didn't recognize the names."

"What's the big deal?" Porky turned and looked through the passenger side window. "Everybody takes a trip sometimes. Maybe they're just old buddies or something. So unless it involves the Bible that turd stole from me, I don't care."

"Then why would he charge it to the church's account and have me pick up the plane tickets? We don't have any affiliate church in New York."

Joy swerved. She hadn't meant to drive in such a way as to attract attention, but Patience's news threw her. She couldn't reveal what she already knew about the man, but somehow she needed to do something. *The last thing I want is for Whistle to escape. I sure hope Lil P or Prophet has this same information.*

Thinking quickly, Joy told them, "I think we should just simply keep this to ourselves. After all, none of us was supposed to be up there with the pastor, and maybe we can beg Reign to keep her trap shut. Lord, I sure hope Blake and Johnson just wanted to say good-bye to you, Patience, when they called out your name back there."

"Joy, I don't think that's the case."

"Why not, Patience?" Joy asked slowly. It was taking all her strength to keep her hands on the wheel and not turn around and yank Patience out of the seat.

"Yeah," Porky chimed in, "why are you so sure?"

"I forgot my Bible and my congregation membership card is in it too."

"Maybe you left it in the bathroom," Porky suggested.

"No, you idiot. Patience never went to the bathroom!"

Chapter 39

It was almost seven-thirty that evening and despite the warm weather earlier that Sunday, nighttime carried a chill.

Percy and Prophet had chatted a while about the president slipping in and out of Anderson and learning Reign had the assignment to report on the visit with the governor. They'd also given their reports, received further instructions, and headed for separate reconnaissance meetings. The results from telephone and cellular records showed communication between Chester Lauder and Deacon Whistle. It hadn't been difficult to confirm the visits made by Whistle to the nursing home. His short stumpy arms were unforgettable to nursing home employees.

Now back inside a secret Anderson investigation base, three other members of their backup team entered, each with a file under his arm. They shook Prophet's hand and sat down. Each gave a brief oral report. When they earlier compared and added their information to the secret audit First Lady Deborah had ordered, they'd gathered enough evidence to prove they'd started on the right track.

Their reports, complete with phone records, area surveillance tapes, and the nursing home surveillances, showed that Chester Lauder would make a call or somehow get a message

to Deacon Whistle. In no time, the deacon would either return the call or visit the nursing home. After each episode, the
church's financial records showed unauthorized activity and a
discrepancy between actual monies coming in and those de-
posited into the church's bank accounts. A few days later, the
deacon always took trips, where Prophet followed him, to
New Hampshire or New York; sometimes he went to both,
yet he never connected with anyone named Jason. And just as
he'd done this day, he'd either fly or drive and then sometimes he'd do both.

The echo from Percy's youthful gait resounded as he
raced down the hallway toward the meeting room. He swung
open the door and, without greeting anyone by name, tossed
one sheet of paper onto the desk. "Bingo!"

"Whatcha got?" Prophet asked Percy. His eyes had already
begun tiring, and he wouldn't remove his shades. "Sum it up
so we can add to it if needed."

Percy fell onto one of the chairs with a thud. Sounding
almost idiotic and certainly unprofessional for such a serious
meeting, he blew a long hissing sound and then hummed the
O'Jays' "For the Love of Money."

"You've got to be kidding!" Whatever tiredness had beset
Prophet's eyes disappeared. He grabbed the paper, almost rip-
ping it in half. He hadn't read past the first few paragraphs
before he exclaimed, "Don't tell me prayers don't work!"

"You've been praying about this?" Percy asked the question with sincerity. He'd never thought about asking God for
help unless he thought his own life was in danger. How often
had that happened?

"I stay in a secret closet, but not the one y'all probably
thinking about," Prophet said blandly. His eyes continued
reading the report.

The other team members swapped confused looks. One
of them finally asked, "Either of you two wanna share? What

in the hell does the O'Jays have to do with this investigation?"

"Go ahead, Prophet," Percy said, leaning back with his
hands clasped behind his head. "You just read it. Tell 'em."

"Monee Coffers," Prophet said as he shook his head. "I
was right there. Months ago, the last time that guy came to
televise his latest freak show commercial, I was checking out
another lead. I'd forgotten he served time with Stephon back
in Seattle at one time."

"So where is he now?" The question sounded urgent, as if
the man asking wanted Prophet to stop dawdling.

"He's dead." Prophet's chin bobbed as he continued scanning the sheet. "Yep, he made his final deposit into Hell's
bank a few months after he'd set up that phony television
taping."

"Even while those thirty seconds of mess played a few
times on the air, the dude had already been put to rest," Percy
said, then added, "I guess that was the only shot my godmothers had of being seen on TV." He followed with a laugh.

The others didn't.

Prophet began laying out more surveillance reports and
other comments. He put other business aside and gave an
order. "Okay, let's take a break for a moment, fellas. Get your
heads together. Hit those computers. We meet back here in
twenty minutes."

Prophet remained in the room alone. Percy, as well as the
others, left to do what he'd ordered.

Thinking about Rev. Monee Coffers brought back
thoughts of Patience. It hadn't been easy, but once he was
certain she'd had no part in embezzling money from the
church, he'd backed off. He'd done it slowly at first, as if he'd
had to wean himself. Yet he'd be lying if it were that simple. It
wasn't.

Early on he'd begun to have feelings for the woman who

never would have appealed to him in his youth. She was too skinny, too religious. He'd had his close encounter with religion when his grandmother stood up at a prayer meeting when he was seven years old back in Birmingham, Alabama.

He could still see her. She'd been a tall, pecan-brown woman, sorta thin but, after having ten children, child bearing had taken its toll, too. She had bright eyes; yet now he couldn't remember their color. With her thick Bible in her hand, she'd announced that night long ago to her congregation, "My grandbaby, Longfellow Jevity, been called to see and tell Gawd's secrets," she'd said. "He gwine be a prophet. The Lawd Gawd hisself done showed me. His name won't ever be Longfellow agin. He's being called, from dis night on, Prophet, 'cause that's what he is."

And from that night on, he was. But that was then, and he'd grown obviously used to the single life since becoming a widower. Then Patience Kash came along.

He shook his head, almost violently, as if doing so would push thoughts of Patience aside. When she'd begun invading his thoughts before, he'd remember she was Percy's godmother, and it'd helped him to make the right decision. He wouldn't want to hurt either of them.

"Any more thoughts you'd care to share?" Percy asked. "You're not looking as happy as you were moments ago."

Prophet hadn't heard anyone enter the room. "I'm fine, but something in the ole gut tells me there's still something missing."

"Like what, sir?" The question came from one of the two backup team members who'd walked in after Percy but had remained quiet until then.

"Chester was as close to Jason as he is to Whistle, and Jason is family, so why haven't they communicated? As far as we've discovered, there's no family ties between Chester Lauder and Campbell Whistle, yet there isn't any record we've found where Whistle and Chester were past friends, up until about five years ago. Maybe they just considered each other as family. How'd they get together? Whistle never served time, so there's not the prison connection he'd have with Chester."

"Damn," Percy blew the word out his mouth, like it was smoke from a cigarette, before scratching his head. "I do remember one other cousin that was a preacher at one time that was supposed to be on the up and up. His name's Stephon. I'll look into his last known address and see if there's something we've missed. I don't wanna take a chance on resurrecting that tech-thug Fast Cat's involvement at this point."

"More missing family, I suppose?" Prophet said dryly before he added, "There are two close Lauder cousins who continued to shame the good family name over the years. I wanna know where's that cousin named Jason? I doubt it was a coincidence that I saw Whistle go to that town car with the name *Jason Lauder* written on a sign. It seems more like he was taunting. There's a connection somewhere. If there isn't a connection, why'd he hightail it in another direction?"

"Why would Chester not turn to family to do what they'd always done?" The question came from a backup team member.

"Exactly," Prophet replied. "When there are too many unanswered questions, it means too many holes for the con to escape through. None of this sits right with me."

All preparations to gloat had disappeared. Each man asked whatever questions remained in his mind. When they'd laid everything in the open, they decided to go with what they had. They'd keep their eyes and ears open, leaning on whatever street contacts they had.

Prophet shook his head again, as though he'd tried to untangle conflicting thoughts and feelings. The last thing he needed was another brain montage.

"Let's do this!" Prophet's thoughts returned to finalizing the plan to take down Chester Lauder and whoever worked with him. "Judge Stepson's church won't be destroyed because of some whimsical revenge. I don't think my gut is wrong about Chester Lauder being the mastermind."

Shortly after the meeting ended, Percy, Prophet, and their backup team met with several unit heads. Each of them had a lot of respect for Judge Lock Stepson and would push the envelope to see that the old man got justice for himself and his church.

Luckily, it hadn't taken much to convince the superiors that there was a definite connection between the embezzlement of monies from Rev. Stepson's church, his previous sentencing of Chester Lauder, and possibly three arson charges to lay at Chester's feet.

They'd almost ended the meeting when they learned what they'd just discussed was the tip of the iceberg. The announcement came from one of the team members as he pulled a paper off the fax machine. "Just when we think it can't get any weirder, it does. Your prayers worked, sir."

"What is it?" Prophet asked.

"It's confirmation from Quantico, sir. Campbell Whistle is the missing cousin Jason Lauder. He's been under our noses all the time."

"I knew it was more than a coincidence!"

"Just a moment, sir; we've got a doubleheader here."

"There's more?" Prophet asked to see the paper. After reading it slowly he handed it to Percy.

"God gives to those who ask in faith. That third cousin, Rev. Stephon Lauder, is doing pretty well for himself and is still living in New Hampshire."

"By the way," one of the other team members told Percy, "Blake and Johnson are waiting to meet with you. They're the ones on detail with the reverend at that rehabilitation place."

"Tell them to leave their report. We'll go over it later. I'm sure it's details about the reverend's snoring or something simple. If someone had gotten to the old man, they would've called it in earlier."

"Are you certain you don't wanna talk to them, Percy?" Prophet asked. "It's always good to commend your men whether they're on an easy or dangerous assignment."

"I will do it later. They know I appreciate them or I'd never have recommended them for this assignment. Right now, there's bigger fish to fry."

Since originally it'd been Percy's assignment that night to approach as well as investigate Coffers, the confirmation of the man's death made a visit to a cemetery unnecessary. Prophet then decided to order Percy to return home. "Rest up. Get a new perspective."

"I'll do it, but you know how I feel about it. We know that investigations are as unpredictable as the storms of life. Well-thought-out plans often change. I don't have much time for sleep."

"Then why are you trying to talk with one eye half open? Go home, Percy. That's an order."

Percy had driven only a few miles before he began to nod off. He'd wanted to crash on one of the lumpy cots back at the base. Prophet had quickly knocked down that idea. He'd told him, "I need you sleeping horizontally on a real bed for some real rest so you can wake up with some real ideas."

Percy looked around to pinpoint where he was. Nodding off had its disadvantages, aside from crashing. He saw the sign for Pelzer on Route 85 almost at the same time he happened upon men performing nighttime road work. He'd need to take a detour, one that'd take him past his godmothers' home. Since he hadn't heard of anything crazy enough to involve them, he decided he might as well stop there and close his eyes.

The truth was, he couldn't drive much longer without

falling asleep. They were the lesser of two evils. He reached over the seat for his jacket. He'd call them to tell them he was coming, since they had a snit-fit when he hadn't done so the last time. The jacket wasn't there. He remembered he'd placed it in the trunk of the Civic when the weather became too warm earlier to wear it.

"I sure hope they'll just open the door, let me in, cover me with a sheet, and leave me alone," he muttered.

He hadn't worried about Reign. He figured she'd been given another assignment since the one for James Memorial wasn't happening. Hopefully, she'd understand that he needed sleep more than conversation.

Chapter 40

The three cousins had continued sniping all the way back from Anderson to Pelzer.

"I can't believe it!" Patience began wringing her hands. "Lord Jesus, we was only a couple of blocks away."

Porky had taken over the driving with his one good hand since his other had begun to swell again. "Please shut up about missing the president's visit! I'm pissed off, too. I should've never asked for the radio to be turned on."

Twenty minutes ago, after they'd began the trip home after stopping to get a bite to eat, the news came over the radio about the president slipping in and out of Anderson. Joy and Patience nearly flipped their identical pillbox hats. And when they heard the radio announcer cut to Reign, who seemed overjoyed at having gotten a quick interview, they were beyond upset.

"You were with her, Porky; you knew she had that interview with our president. Admit it before I toss your black butt outta this moving car right in front of that nasty sty you call a restaurant."

"Joy, come off it," Porky told her. "Reign didn't tell me nothing about it either. And you won't even go through the

Ptomaine Avenue area with a police escort in the daylight. It's already turning dark."

"Well, I'm certain if Reign knew, then Lil P knew, too. Both of them what folks call Washington insiders!" Patience began pounding her seat. Her eyes became large with fury and her contacts popped out and onto the car floor. Unable to see, she nearly slapped Felony across his nose. He whimpered as though she had and trotted away to the rear of the car.

"Look at us! I'm so upset I done got stupid enough to let you drive my car!"

Finally reaching home, they saw two cars parked outside the house. Patience grabbed and adjusted her glasses, craning her neck to get a better look.

"That's my son's car." Porky panicked. The last thing he'd wanted was to be implicated in what went on inside that rehabilitation residence.

Porky wasn't the only one suddenly feeling remorse. Patience and Joy sat stiff in the front seats of the RAV. They hadn't yet thought up an excuse for everything that'd happened earlier that afternoon, but then they remembered they were upset with Percy and Reign.

"You know, those two got a lot of explaining to do," Joy protested.

"I'm reading the same page as you," Patience replied. She'd already begun opening the SUV's door. She had her pocketbook in one hand and swung her glasses with the other. She couldn't see that far but was so mad it didn't matter.

Once Porky saw his cousins' attitudes had changed from fear of rebuke to one of retribution, he relaxed. He decided to ride their retribution coattails inside, disappear into that guestroom, and hide out.

Reign and Percy had other issues, and at that moment dealing with Joy, Patience, and Porky wasn't among them.

Percy had arrived thirty minutes ahead of his godmothers and his father and only a few before Reign.

He'd seen only the kitchen light lit. When he'd checked the garage, the RAV was gone, too. Sister Betty stood on her porch as though waiting for someone and told him she'd seen his godmothers and father leave earlier that afternoon. She didn't know if they'd gone to a night service because she'd been at her own church.

That old gut kick hit him and his desire for sleep fled. He found the spare key they kept in Felony's doghouse. He'd hardly fallen onto the sofa when Reign showed up.

She'd been surprised to find him there and that his god-mothers and father hadn't arrived back yet. She sat him down and told him what had happened earlier when she interrupted Joy and the others. "They never admitted it, but I am sure they were trying to visit my father. And whether they were or not really doesn't matter. They were supposed to stay here until the service tonight. I'm sure when they sneaked out they didn't know the James Memorial Service was cancelled."

"Why, Lord, why?" Percy mumbled repeatedly.

Joy and Porky followed Patience through the side door. Felony instinctively stayed behind, rushing off to his dog-house without barking or snarling.

No sooner had they gotten all the way inside than they heard loud, mumbling voices. They raced toward the living room, where they found Reign and Percy.

Percy was seated on the sofa, head down with both hands bent upwards from the elbow. Reign was standing over him holding one of Patience's bottles of blessed oil. She began pouring a little in the palm of her hand, then massaged the oil into Percy's brow, then up into his scalp and through his hair.

"Give him strength, Lord." Reign repeated those words several times before changing to "Help us to hold out. Give us wisdom, Father."

She stopped, poured more oil into the palm of her hand, lifted it, and anointed her brow, saying, "Keep my thoughts Your thoughts, Lord. Remove any hostility . . ."

The three cousins stood dumbfounded in the doorway. They'd entered the house with their attitudes set to argue. All they'd found were Percy and Reign praying.

"What are we gonna do?" Patience whispered to Joy. "We can't wring their necks about the president while they're praying."

"You're right," Joy replied, whispering too. "If they're praying, then they can't be too mad at what we done earlier. I say for right now we just call it even until we can get back at them."

Joy and Patience smiled, thinking they'd join in. Porky, however, sulked and took a few steps back, afraid he wouldn't know how.

Joy and Patience flung their pocketbooks and hats aside in the foyer and rushed back into the living room, one after the other, falling to the floor like dominoes.

Joy's big hips were like buoys as she struggled to stand up. She wouldn't let that stand in her way; she began praying. "You said, Father, where two and more is gathered together, You'd come and stand in the middle!"

Patience, on the other hand, with nothing to prevent her from rising quickly, joined in. "Let Your people say so!"

The praying on Percy's and Reign's parts had ended as soon as Joy and Patience fell through the doorway. Neither had heard them come in. Their eyes fell upon Porky, who at that time had about completely backed out of the room.

Porky backed into Felony. They'd left the door cracked when they'd arrived, and apparently the dog had a change of mind and came inside. He growled, nipped Porky in the heel, and lifted one hind leg, whimpering. Felony's whimpering grew louder, causing the praying to cease and sending Porky sailing back into the living room. Felony then scampered off toward the kitchen, no doubt looking for something to eat.

And the circle of arguing began again.

Reign hadn't quite set Joy and Patience straight as she'd wanted earlier.

"Do y'all know how embarrassed I was when I almost didn't make it back to the town hall on time?" she asked. "Today I have cussed on live television and asked dumb questions of the president and first lady of the United States!"

She might've gotten them to at least apologize, until she mentioned President Obama's name and they got upset all over again.

"You finished?" Joy asked. She walked over to where Percy still sat with his head in his hands. He hadn't moved or spoken since they'd stopped praying.

Standing over him and pointing at his lowered head, she said, "You and Lil P knew how much Patience and I wanted to meet with the president. Your own mama prophesied that we should do it! All we wanted to do was to lay prostituted before the president of these here United States."

"The word is *prostrate* not *prostitute*!" Reign started to say more, but somehow the unchristianlike and murderous look on Joy's face didn't call for it.

Joy's warning came one word at a time, yet carried as much weight as she did. "You Might Not Wanna Try Correcting Me."

"Say that!" Patience chimed in. She'd begun hopping about the living room like a bunny on a mission, still swinging her glasses by its arm. "They knew it and didn't lift one finger to help us! Ain't no telling what else they hiding from us!"

Once Patience put out that declaration of everyone in the room being honest except Percy and Reign, a look of resignation came over her face. She looked at Reign and sighed.

Joy, forgetting that it was Percy's head that lay under her hand, let it drop.

Instead of Percy moaning from Joy's heavy fist falling on his head, the sound of a soft snore came through fluttering lips.

Even with Armageddon happening in the living room, sleep had finally arrived and saved him.

Chapter 41

It seemed the weather and the investigation plotted against Prophet's investigation. Yesterday, Sunday felt like spring; this Monday morning, the weather had turned cold and nippy. Just knowing how to dress was as arduous as looking under every rock for Whistle's other cousin, Rev. Stephon. When the team in New Hampshire went to his last known address, he'd already moved away.

Prophet hadn't called Percy last night. He'd hoped the young detective had slept soundly. Depriving a body of rest wouldn't help Percy at all, and he'd seen the evidence yesterday.

Prophet had seen Percy's signs of physical and emotional exhaustion. He knew the signs that'd lead to carelessness. He'd already lost sight in one eye as proof, and for several years, he'd kept the impairment a secret, hidden behind sunglasses.

All in all, Prophet hoped today would be different. At least now they'd proceed with better intelligence; that'd make things a bit easier than where they'd left it planned yesterday. He had his team to thank for it.

During last night, following Prophet's orders, his backup team had used strong-arm methods; they'd been told not to return without information leading to anyone connected to Chester Lauder, Campbell Whistle, and especially Rev. Stephon Lauder. "I don't care how you get it. I need it before Detective Percy returns to duty."

They'd hit the street, issuing threats that'd rousted every known informant, scattering them like roaches before snatching them up in the backseats of surveillance cars, darkened alleys where small envelopes were sometimes exchanged, everywhere including the Playa's Cabin. The Playa's Cabin yielded the best information. They'd busted the after-hours club last, knowing everyone they'd missed earlier in the night would gather there before dawn. Somehow before daybreak, they'd caught one of the known informants, a skinny fellow called Fast Cat. He'd been dark-skinned, but suffered from vitiligo; it'd left his complexion spotty like a leopard. He also had huge sunken eyes, needle-marked veins, and teeth the color of French's mustard; he was one of the best computer and anything-technology-related whizzes around.

They'd lucked out when he came by the Playa's Cabin. He'd been on the list to roust, because he'd hung around the Soul Food Shanty several times a week. He'd hawk his illegal geek squad capabilities and get a free meal from Porky, who everyone figured took a cut but was Detective Percy's dad and got a pass.

They leaned harder than necessary on Fast Cat, threatening to send Detective Percy LaPierre by to see him. "Everyone knows it was you that robbed the Soul Food Shanty. How you think that gonna sit with Detective Percy, you robbing his daddy's spot?"

"Man, quit with the bull. Y'all know I ain't robbed nobody," Fast Cat told them.

"We don't know nothing, 'cause you ain't said nothing yet."

"C'mon, y'all know I don't want that Percy dude coming down on me. Besides, me and Porky go way back, like dinosaurs and cavemen. He's one of my steady customers. I ain't got too many of them left since y'all decided to take a broom to Ptomaine Avenue. What kind of businessman gives up the 411 on his customers?"

Fast Cat watched one of the men yank out a cell phone and begin tapping its keys.

"Never mind," Fast Cat snapped, "get ya pads out. I'll tell ya what I know."

Of all the people that would hook up the computerized church service for the Reverend Stephon Lauder, like their report had shown earlier, it'd indeed been Fast Cat.

Meanwhile last night, while the other agents scoured criminal pits, Percy somehow managed to sleep soundly through one of the family battles. He got up and off this morning to an early start. He washed his face from a pool of water caught by his hands from the faucet, straightened his clothes. He didn't want to leave his godmothers' home without making sure all was well.

Percy looked out the kitchen window, saw Reign's car still parked outside, and knew she'd spent the night. Going from room to room, silently cracking doors, hearing the sounds of snores and grunts, he found her. She was balled up in her favorite position, like a kitten. Meanwhile Patience lay vertical, each sharing the bed yet giving the other space.

He rushed outside, grabbed the jacket he'd thrown into it the day before, then grabbed a bag of fresh clothes from the trunk of his car. He went back inside. The clothes were for Porky. Percy had forgotten they were there. He peeked in Patience's room once more. When neither woman stirred, he left through the side door, making certain to lock it behind him.

Daybreak hadn't fully broken, yet out of habit he looked around—but not for long. The weather had turned chilly, and he still wore a short-sleeved shirt.

He ran his hand over his face. There was no longer stubble on his lip; it'd grown into a mutton-like shape and felt like a beard. Laying his personal cell phone on the passenger seat, he quipped, "I wish I'd seen Barack yesterday. I owe him and he owes me, but I might as well give him the five dollars I lost during that pickup game and call it a day, especially since I've owed it to him since long before he became president."

Before Percy pulled off, he placed his Bluetooth headset on one ear so he could drive and listen to the other messages on his new secure phone. He hadn't heard beyond the first message before he heard the update from Prophet. His driving foot turned to lead.

He made it to the base in half the time it usually took. Within a short time, he'd showered, using one of the stalls set aside for those who worked overtime and wouldn't mix deodorant with funk. Before long, he was dressed in clean clothes and out the door with one of the backups following him in an unmarked car.

Thanks to Fast Cat's snitching, they had a good chance to get Stephon Lauder.

"Time to herd them in." The sudden call came through Percy's earpiece. He immediately recognized Prophet's voice. He was glad to hear him; cases like these sometimes made him anxious—but not in a bad way, more of an adrenaline rush. He could almost feel his heart beating a little faster; he exhaled then took in another breath and leaned back further in the driver's seat. He made himself comfortable, while using one hand to adjust the bottom of his bulletproof vest to check his Glock.

"Checkin' on more bulls in a Clemson pen—using two ropes," he confirmed to Prophet, as though the man wouldn't already know that he and his backup were in route to Clemson, South Carolina, to question Rev. Stephon Lauder. It appeared Lauder'd had two places of operation: New Hampshire and South Carolina. Once Percy brought in Stephon, he'd need to hurry to meet up with Prophet in New York.

Whistle had taken many trips before. He often drove and flew, zigzagging around the country. He'd done it while handling the sordid business for his ailing cousin, Chester, and whatever retribution made him and Chester happy. For the past several years, they'd left Stephon out of the picture. Stephon's data list and solid reputation within the evangelical community was very valuable to the scam.

However, this time he traveled under his real name, Jason Lauder. Moreover, he'd brought along Chester and his portable oxygen pack. Chester insisted on coming along to make the final delivery.

The Monday mid-morning Boston shuttle flight to New York was always crowded, so they'd booked an early flight.

Whistle wore a full-length, fifteen-hundred-dollar beige Prada coat with its sleeves tailored to fit his short arms. Under the coat he wore a chocolate brown Prada two-piece power suit and a shirt and tie that'd set Chester back almost two thousand dollars. Whistle's shoes were dark brown Dolce and Gabbana patent leather Derby, and had cost more than six hundred dollars.

Chester Lauder, stooped with a craggy face and waves of wrinkles running from his chin to his chest, plodded slowly beside Whistle, holding onto his arm. The elderly man, wearing a dark coat and a two-piece off-the-rack Walmart suit, stopped every few feet to breathe. He'd done so for the past few minutes after Whistle had helped him off the handicapped tram.

Both men clutched their coats, attempting to ward off the sudden cold air that'd replaced yesterday's warmth. As they'd hoped, there weren't many people around; the few hanging around ignored them as they walked the last few feet to the gate to board their flight into New York's LaGuardia Airport.

While aboard the US Air flight, they found and read a copy of that day's early edition of the *Wall Street Journal*. Because Chester's illness had robbed him of his eyesight seemingly almost as fast as it'd blackened his heart and soul, Whistle read some of the content aloud.

The men weren't surprised to discover that the paper carried details of a recent arrest of one of the former Goldman Sachs board members. The man was also under investigation by the Securities and Exchange Commission, which suspected that he'd passed along privileged financial information. Also according to the paper, the information helped to enrich a billionaire hedge-fund manager whose family hailed from India.

Whistle folded the paper and returned it to the seat pocket. Laughing, he had to ask. "Did you drop that dime to the powers that be to help this fella see the light?"

Chester nodded *yes*.

Whistle looked around the nearly empty small plane before leaning in closer, asking, "Did you happen to spread any more change around Wall Street? Say, perhaps, a few home addresses where the displeased can visit?"

Chester nodded once more; this time, his skinny chest began to heave. It wasn't because of any breathing difficulty. He laughed hard, inwardly knowing that he and his younger cousin were, so to speak, on the same page.

Off and on for the rest of the flight, until they landed, Whistle laughed. While Chester dozed off and on beside him, he kept his laughter inside, knowing he, too, had done something that old Rev. Lock Stepson and his sanctimonious church would soon pay for.

During the short flight on the plane, Chester Lauder woke up for a brief time. He refused an offer of something to drink; he'd already decided he wouldn't chance removing the hose from his portable breathing machine to laugh.

Whistle began laughing, unable to keep another secret.

He leaned in and shared that the day before he'd placed an urgent call to the Jamestown Memorial A.M.E. church.

"You'd been proud," he told Chester. "I told them Missionary Joy Karry was discovered in a drunken stupor. She couldn't stand up, let alone attend their event."

Whistle lightly tapped Chester on his arm, as much to check and see if the man still breathed as to see if he were still listening.

Chester moved slightly, raising a finger to prod Whistle on.

Whistle continued. "I'd kept my voice controlled, but I wanted to laugh so bad. I would've remained serious, but the church secretary had just answered the phone saying, 'Praise the Lord,' then out of that same sweet little mouth came a couple of cuss words. I had to slam down the phone, quick."

Suddenly, laughter overtook Chester. He almost ripped his air mask off as though he'd have a stroke on the spot. "And that's why the church cancelled!"

Chapter 42

Prophet and another agent had gotten to Water Street in the Manhattan Wall Street area ahead of Whistle and Chester. They'd flown by helicopter from the eastside, stopping by One Police Plaza, picking up the documents they'd need.

The New York team had already met with several Wall Street bankers from an investment group called Sal-Schiff Securities. The four of them had resembled an odd lot. All the men were well into their late sixties and early seventies. They'd hung on when the crash of 2008 had sent the weak-minded scrambling. They had a good thing going with a hodgepodge soup of hedge funds and municipal bonds, with some oil speculation thrown in for good measure. Things had changed from the times when they'd had their own personal pyramid-like schemes, which they'd dangled like carrots over greedy pharisees of every religious affiliation.

They'd thought they'd gotten away with it after hiding their deeds in Italy. Yet, it'd left collateral damage stateside. They'd decided to stick with their own kind, greedy bankers completely devoid of conscience. That atmosphere, they would survive in.

Out of the blue, it'd all started crumbling several months ago. The feds had come back around, armed with evidence they shouldn't have had. But they did have it, and it'd been the agent Prophet and the same detective, a bit more seasoned of late, who'd brought it. That'd been enough to convince them déjà vu and prison were not options.

They'd gotten away years before, hiring expensive lawyers and traveling ridiculously back and forth between New York and Columbia, South Carolina. They were too old to go through it again. The only truth they'd told when they were caught was that they'd no idea they'd dealt with churches again.

Once they'd begun cooperating with the SEC several months ago, these same greedy men had hoped to never be entangled with anything church-related again. Unbeknown to them, they'd supposedly been tricked into doing just that. Someone had turned on them, and the situation had escalated. Today, loose ends needed tying up.

Prophet had plenty to do, but a bustling New York environment would present a challenge. Whistle and Chester's meeting scheduled for two o'clock meant the end of the lunch-hour crowd and a mob of shift workers heading home early. Manhattan would be a beehive, but Prophet had brought plenty of green honey and enough spy equipment to see the pimples on their old brows.

Prophet oversaw the surveillance setup, reminding the Wall Street gang of the price they'd pay if things went wrong. There'd be no chance of having high-priced legal attorneys these days. What they'd pulled on Judge Lock Stepson back in Columbia, South Carolina, wouldn't fly this time.

The men were already aware that another one of their ilk had been arrested by the FEC just the day before. Of course, the last thing Prophet would do was tell them they'd actually been set up from the very beginning. He also now had a good idea as to why and how, but ideas were a dime a dozen. He needed more proof, and needed to get it while Whistle and his cousin Chester were here in New York. Once he finished on this end, he'd need to get back to One Police Plaza quickly. Percy should've arrived by then from Pelzer. Together, with the backup team, they hoped to wrap things up before dark.

It didn't appear that the weather would warm up anytime soon, and the chill had begun to get to them. It'd taken some doing just to get Chester into a cab so they could check into an hourly motel over on Eleventh Avenue. Whistle had stayed in the area before; he'd chosen the roach trap because of its proximity to several soul food places he liked. And, of course, at night, all he had to do was walk along the Hudson River docks in lower Manhattan and he could see the Intrepid Exhibit and find a female morsel or two interested in deep diving as well.

Not this time; he'd brought Chester. He'd have to make up for whoever he'd missed at another time.

It was already almost one-thirty. He wasn't certain how long a cab would take to maneuver through the traffic when it became time to leave. Chester had insisted they not be late.

Fortunately, the steroid medication Chester took an hour ago had taken. Whistle could already see a bit of light in the old man's eyes.

Whistle was about to go over the routine Chester had laid out some time ago, when the motel room phone rang. Whistle answered it and was surprised to hear Stephon's voice.

"What's wrong?" Whistle asked quickly. Stephon would've never called him on that motel phone if something weren't. He'd have called him on his cell phone like he always did.

"Fast Cat's out the bag and gone. I don't know what to do."

"Gone?"

"Yep."

Whistle heard the hesitancy in Stephon's voice. He'd need

to play it smart. Chester was sick, not stupid, so he'd need to get Stephon off the phone quickly.

What a time for this man to get a second wind, he thought, turning around and smiling at Chester.

Chester returned Whistle's look with a blank stare. However, Whistle had seen that look too many times. Chester could set someone on fire and be caught holding the match still giving that same blank stare, no emotion at all. Whistle learned years ago to never underestimate the minds of those with nothing to lose.

"Well, there's no Joyce Gone here," Whistle said, winking at Chester, attempting to reassure him if he'd become suspicious that it'd been a wrong number. He hoped Stephon realized he had to hang up.

"Okay, I see Chester's in your face. Don't worry about me. I'm sorry I bothered you."

Stephon spoke quickly, and Whistle appreciated that.

For quite some time, Stephon's hands-off approach when it came to Chester upset Whistle. He never could understand his cousin's approach to things that should've been simple because it involved family. So Stephon spent a little time in a cushy federal prison; who amongst the other cousins hadn't done time—hard and easy—in federal or state prisons?

Moreover, Stephon had played it safe the last few years; he'd done well, hiding out in his living room, facing a camera with his Internet church scam. "No Twitter or Facebook presence for me. Too much of a risk," he'd said.

But then again, Stephon had faced none of the risks like him and Chester. The law didn't have him in their sights, threatening to snatch away freedom at any moment—that had to be boring, Whistle thought.

Before they left the motel, Whistle dressed Chester in a thousand-dollar suit and five-hundred-dollar shoes identical to what he wore. Chester never attended a paper execution without appearing prosperous. He always wanted his victims to know he'd gotten over well. He then hooked Chester up to his portable oxygen pack.

On the street, an unwelcome cold wind kept them huddled for a few moments before they found a cab. With none of the traffic most New Yorkers had traveling from the west side of town, he and Chester made it over to Wall Street a little early.

The trip from the curb and through the doors of the smooth charcoal gray granite-stone Sal-Schiff building took longer than if he'd come alone. Yet Whistle gingerly led a fragile Chester through the lobby. He showed a prepared pass to the security guard and then they got onto the elevator. They rode slowly up to the twenty-sixth floor.

Exiting the elevator, Whistle held Chester's elbow in the palm of his hand. He did so gently yet firmly enough for the old man to lean upon Whistle's shortened arm with comfort.

Whistle opened the gold-plated frosted-glass doors that led inside the posh office. A young buxom woman, blonde hair swept to the side like a 1950s Marilyn Monroe, with thin lips and bright red rouge dabbed on each cheek, greeted them with a smile. As he'd done on previous visits, Whistle quickly admired her hourglass figure. He saw it as eye candy, something extra for any red-blooded visitor, straight or gay.

One by one, the four investment executives entered the reception area. They'd already begun turning into puppets, with the feds and the SEC pulling their strings. When the last man entered, after they'd greeted Whistle they feigned surprise at the sight of Chester.

One by one, they walked in a single line. Each man's diamond-crusted cufflinks sparkled in the light of the overhead hanging crystal chandeliers. Each chandelier hid surveillance cameras installed just hours ago by Prophet and his men.

Those men wore tailored suits with white-on-white

starched-collar shirts. They appeared stiff, like their day-to-day no-nonsense demeanors, in stark contrast to their inner cowardly souls that fed off the less fortunate.

The bankers continued to gush over the pair. Each pretended they'd expected to see Whistle come alone, as he'd done over the past several years.

"Chester Lauder, thank God you're able to make it and participate in this final act. After all," one man added softly, yet louder than necessary for a lobby conversation, "this is our homage to you. Without your vision, years ago, this wouldn't be . . ."

The fake greeting rolled off the lips of this short orange-tanned man who appeared about the same age as Chester—old, except the man looked more alive. The other men gently tapped Chester on his shoulder, showing deference to the old man, who two of them had thrown under the prison bus less than twenty years before.

Whistle watched Chester's reaction. He saw him snarl behind his oxygen mask, anxious to get the ball rolling.

It wouldn't take long before they stopped bowing and scraping. In the last few moments they'd spent sufficient time mentally bending over and grabbing their Gucci socks and shoes as Chester silently raped their supposed egos and intelligence with his presence; then it was time to go into the meeting room.

Surveillance just like that in the reception area lay hidden inside the meeting room. The room, the size of a small intimate home theatre room, was lavishly furnished. No less than several million dollars had been spent on the chairs, which nestled slick bottoms with handy massage buttons to soothe and finesse more millions from whoever sat there.

The meeting began with each man again, in as few words as necessary, apologizing to Chester before detailing the illegal gains they were prepared to turn over to him.

"We need Chester to speak," one of the agents, hidden in

another room, murmured to the surveillance camera. "Jason's doing all the talking for the old man. We only want Jason as collateral damage and for other crimes he's suspected of as Whistle back in Pelzer."

Unknown to him that they themselves were being watched, Whistle watched Chester's reaction to each man's movement, to each of their words, and to the way they said them.

He'd learned to pick up cues that way, since Chester's moments of speech had become less and less.

He'd already seen the fill mark on Chester's portable oxygen pack. *I believe old Chester has sensed something I've missed. He's hardly breathing with the pack at all.*

Chester finally slumped in his seat. His ice blue eyes narrowed, a signal to Whistle to hurry things along and get him out of there.

"Allow me to lay my cards on the table, so to speak," Whistle said slowly. He pulled from an attaché case several blue legal documents and at least twenty piles of cash that stood almost ten inches high. "The cash is just our little surprise gift to all of you."

Again, Whistle watched the men's reactions. These were men who came from several generations of crime families. Hidden among other Wall Street crooks, they pretended to operate under the guise of legitimacy. Each participated in organized crime, white-collar crimes; they were a clique of four men with uncanny computer knowledge who'd hacked into systems worldwide with secret pass codes and insider trading expertise. They'd also done a little money laundering on the side despite being caught years ago doing the same.

These same men suddenly looked as fragile as Chester. There weren't the greedy smiles and the high-fiving going on as they'd done before when gifted with such an extraordinary amount of cold cash.

"Just so you know, and as a full disclosure," one of the

bankers began, "we've decided to follow your lead and sell the rest of our portfolio. We see the signs, and the country is seeking retribution. Frankly, like Chester here, I'm tired and want to retire to a warm climate." The man lowered his head, taking a deep breath before he raised it again. That time he placed both hands on the table and asked, "Jason—I hope you don't mind me using your real name during our final meeting—I'm curious. Where will you and Chester go?"

The other men looked toward Whistle and Chester then nodded as though they waited for an answer, too. They'd done all their talking back in the lobby and saw no reason to step on whatever this man said. The feds had chosen him to speak on their behalf. They'd only speak up if he forgot the script.

When Whistle said nothing, sitting motionless and detached, the banker continued. Without thinking he wiped away beads of perspiration that'd broken out on his cheek. "Chester must be worn out," he observed. "Why don't we just go ahead with the Pelzer dealings first and get those out of the way."

"The Pelzer ones you want handled first?" Whistle finally spoke, asking the question as his weak eye that hadn't bothered him in quite some time twitched in Chester's direction. He didn't wait for an answer; instead he pulled from the bottom of the pile a thick document with the words *Mount Kneel Down Non-Denominational Church* typed on its front.

Suddenly Chester made a subtle movement with one shoulder. Whistle was certain no one saw it but him.

"That's the largest transaction," the banker replied. His voice became hoarse, as though his tongue didn't want to speak, but he continued. "We can do the others as well if you wish, and you can tell us what you want done with the cash. We weren't prepared for that. It will mean using digital signatures. That won't take but a few moments."

Chester began to twitch, and that time they all saw it.

It took a lot to shake Whistle. His ego would've never allowed him to show any discomfort in front of them. Yet, he looked around the room following the direction Chester's eyes scanned.

Something wasn't right, and now they both knew it.

Chapter 43

Percy hopped into the unmarked car that'd met him at the East Thirty-fourth Street Heliport in Manhattan. He knew it was cold in New York. The lightweight jacket he'd worn felt useless; he might as well have worn a thin sheet of paper.

He sat back, closing his eyes to avoid any idle chatter. The only thing he needed from the undercover cop escorting him was more heat.

Peeking through half-closed eyelids as the car sped in the direction of Chambers Street, he tried concentrating on his case. However, he suddenly glimpsed Manhattan's concrete world of boutiques, theaters, the rich, and the poor. His hands pulled at his unshaven chin as he turned his head and stared. He saw old couples adorned in mink coats and derby hats share sidewalk space with prostitutes and sidewalk hustlers. All those sights and smells reminded him of his time at Columbia Law School. How many times had he and his friends rushed onto a crowded subway car, giddy to experience all that was the Big Apple?

He looked at his watch. It was almost four o'clock and the last contact he'd had with Prophet, when he'd landed at LaGuardia, hadn't sounded hopeful.

"Chester Lauder hasn't said one word during the entire

time he's met with the Wall Street bankers. Whistle has done all the talking," Prophet had informed him.

He'd sounded beyond frustrated. Percy could tell he'd been in no mood for any screw-ups. Evidently, despite what they had gotten on tape, when they synched it by remote from the office at One Police Plaza, with the actual conversation, aside from Chester's name being mentioned and his presence at the meeting, it'd been useless on Prophet's end.

"We're here, detective." The driver had already gotten out and come around to Percy's side of the car. He didn't open the door, allowing Percy the time to gather his things and avoid unnecessary contact with the cold wind.

"Thank you," Percy told him, and quickly followed another waiting officer into the building.

Prophet had replayed what they had so far several times. Each recap gave the same inconclusive results. He'd been so busy telling Percy earlier on the phone what hadn't worked, he hadn't gotten Percy's report on what had.

Prophet heard the elevator chime as its doors opened. As soon as he saw the smile on Percy's face when he stepped off with a man wearing handcuffs, he felt his entire body relax.

The two men greeted each over with high fives and pats on the back. Prophet led Percy into a room filled with all sorts and levels of surveillance equipment.

No less than twelve men from different agencies, including the SEC, had gathered. Each man, with a shield and an ID hanging around his neck, belonged to a team armed with warrants for the bankers as well as for Jason Lauder, alias Campbell Whistle, and Chester Lauder.

The bankers had accepted their fate with an unusual plea deal. They now faced arrest with the punishment of banishment for life from any Wall Street dealings, along with the certainty of having to pay heavy fines into the millions, as well as be the subject of the twenty-four-hour news circle.

They'd balked earlier that morning at becoming perp-walked spectacles. They'd cited how protesters, who didn't know they'd already confessed, had somehow ended up marching around their private homes. In the end, they'd finally accepted they had no standing at all, and were lucky to get the heads-up about the investigation in the first place.

It hadn't taken long to get their dirty deeds done and by late afternoon Whistle and Chester concluded their business; both were uneasy yet ready to return to Pelzer. Whistle had hired two nurses—one black, as beautiful and sultry as Halle Berry, twenty-nine, and built for wear and tear. She was for him. The other nurse, a middle-aged no-nonsense woman favoring Bea Arthur with more degrees than most doctors, was for Chester.

He'd hired them to accompany him and Chester to the island of St. Maarten in the Netherlands Antilles; they'd meet up later. He'd already purchased a villa off the beach and nestled near friends who lived on St. Maarten's bustling Front Street.

Whistle and Chester stood together at the corner of Water Street. They resembled the letter *B*, with Chester now bending over almost in half, standing next to Whistle, who remained erect.

Whistle looked up at several skyscrapers with their windows lined up vertically, as though they marched skyward.

"Our plans are just like these skyscrapers," Whistle murmured. "The sky's the limit."

Chester wasn't paying attention. He hadn't stopped trying to look around since they'd left the twenty-sixth floor. The needle on his oxygen pack had moved down two notches; it meant he'd begun breathing heavier than before.

Whistle didn't press Chester to share his fake excitement. He, too, could feel his skin crawling, but he would not let his cousin down. He'd delivered to those bankers all they'd needed to bring down the man who'd destroyed Chester's life; the Reverend Crazy Lock Stepson, whether ailing or in just as bad a condition as Chester, would pay. Chester would be happy to see not only the judge's name splattered across the front pages, but his church's name, too. "They should've treated me better," he'd complained.

The fact that they would escape both Prophet and Detective Percy LaPierre brought a smile to his face. *They'll never be able to look in the mirror again. I'd pay money just to watch them try to pick up the pieces of their careers. How were they going to explain letting an old dying man who can hardly breathe—much less walk—get over on them?*

The thought of Chester dying was sobering. Like a needle pricking a hole in a balloon, his need to boast deflated.

What would he do without his older cousin? Chester had always been there for him, stepping in whenever his mother, with her self-esteem near zero from years of abuse from his drunken father, permitted any of her lovers to taunt him as a child at their pleasure.

Unlike Stephon, Chester had always stood up for him, never allowing anyone, family or strangers, to tease him about his short stumpy arms or his eye that often went its own way.

In his free arm, he carried documents representing the last haul from the money he and Chester had embezzled, defrauded, and outright stolen.

He'd especially love spending the money taken from embezzling Mount Kneel Down. That alone gave him enough money and power to make women treat him as though he looked like Brad Pitt. If he was lucky, in St. Maarten, he'd find his own freaky Angelina Jolie, but she'd need to know how to cook all his favorite soul food dishes.

Whistle looked at his watch again. If he was cold, he was certain Chester must feel like he was freezing. "Where is Stephon?"

Stephon was supposed to have flown in that afternoon.

Nothing in the phone call earlier indicated that the plan had changed. It'd sounded more like the kid Fast Cat, who had always done Stephon's computer setup, was in some sort of fix and unavailable. It had nothing to do with their plans. He'd needed Stephon to come along and take them to JFK Airport. He'd decided they didn't need to fly back the way they'd flown in. There wouldn't be time to drive to New Hampshire to say good-bye in person, and they couldn't do it back in Pelzer because Stephon had left the area.

He looked down at Chester. He could tell by the way the old man looked that he wanted to know what was going on. He'd not told Chester that Stephon was coming or that they'd return through JFK. He'd wanted their final good-bye to end well without Chester worrying. Stephon was still family.

Whistle finally saw Stephon driving a limo in their direction. He had his arm stretched out the window holding the placard with the name Jason Lauder.

Whistle secured his grip on the attaché case by its handle with one hand and took Chester's elbow with his other.

"Here's my surprise for you, Chester; it's headed this way. You don't need to look up, cousin. You can't see inside the limo because it's got tinted glass. I know you'll be happy when you see who's picking us up." Whistle began patting his foot as if that would make the limo come to them quicker. "I know I'll be happy." Whistle craned his neck, smiling with confidence, as another chill overtook him.

Chapter 44

Two cars moved almost side by side in the double lane stretch approaching Water Street. The street ran in one direction, offering no room or opportunity to turn around.

"They're standing on the north corner of Water," Percy said into his radio. "We're almost there."

"Good," Prophet replied, "I've got the surprise. . . . Give me another two minutes and block the lane."

Chester's weak pull on Whistle's coat went almost unnoticed. Whistle had focused on the approaching limo and not seen the traffic at the other intersection suddenly cordoned off. Foot patrol officers in uniform with orange vests had raced out, scurrying like ants from squad cars. Traffic lights meant nothing. The flow was now in their hands. By the time Whistle realized that it was Chester tugging at him and not a light gust of wind, it was too late.

A head appeared out of the limo's rear passenger window, the movement distracting Whistle just as Prophet hopped out of the driver's side door, tossing the placard; a gust of wind carried it farther and caused it to land almost at Whistle's feet.

Another plainclothes anti-crime detective bolted from the limo's front passenger side, one hand on her holster and cuffs in her other hand. She raced behind Prophet. Her long dark micro braids were pulled back, waving like a flag as a pair of dark sunglasses hid her emotions.

Percy's car careened to a stop several feet away on the other side of Whistle and Chester, blocking any chance of the pair trying to run; as if Chester could, or Whistle would.

A look that could only pass for hatred appeared upon Chester's and Whistle's faces; not because they'd been caught— but because they'd seen Stephon, his hands cuffed behind his back, his head hanging down, sitting next to Percy. At least as Lauders, they'd kept their heads up, Chester longer than before.

In the midst of a huge crowd that had suddenly gathered, surrounding a Channel 7 news crew—one among several— Prophet read Chester and Whistle their rights. At the same time, the female plainclothes detective yanked Whistle's short, stubby arms behind him, smirking and taunting him as she placed the cuffs about his wrists. "It's too bad I didn't bring any baby cuffs with me."

She looked at Chester, who by then had started shaking, and said, "This is for Judge Stepson."

She quickly turned him toward the cameras. She pinched his arm. "You don't mess with church folk," she whispered into his ear.

Chester, cuffed and unable to use his hands, yelped. As he jerked his head, his mask fell away from his face.

The rest of the country would see later that evening, and beyond, on every cable and broadcast channel, a frail, evil man, pasty and practically toothless, his face sunken and his ice-blue eyes swollen with red circles: the mighty Chester Lauder and his cousin T.rex.

Two weeks had passed since Prophet and Percy's Wall Street bust. They'd become celebrities within the federal and SEC agencies; Percy couldn't walk out his door in Pelzer for a newspaper without being heralded.

The mug shot of Deacon Campbell Whistle, aka Jason Lauder, was shown constantly on the news alongside the other Wall Street bankers. For a moment, it made the country believe that Wall Street would pay for its complicity in bringing about the crash of 2008.

"Hey, check this out," Percy called out to his team. "*The Daily Show* is making fun of Jason Lauder and his short dinosaur arms gripping that attaché case."

"Yeah, as if that was gonna protect him from getting arrested." The comment came from Detective Blake. He and his partner, Johnson, had only been reprimanded for allowing Joy and the others to pull a fast one on them.

Detective Blake lay a hand on Percy's shoulder, bending over as though he were showing him something. "Listen, Percy, me and Johnson still can't thank you enough for not filing a report against us. Trust me, we've learned."

Percy shook off the detective's hand. "Look," he said, "it wasn't cool what went down, but I certainly can feel ya pain. Those three have been in my life all my life. It takes a lot of getting used to, but just don't let it happen again."

"Thanks, man. I still don't see how they never get one over on you."

"I ain't in the grave yet. I'm sure they'll continue to try."

"Hey, Percy, look at this." Prophet raced over and turned up the volume on the precinct's television. "It's your fiancée, Reign. She's at the news desk instead of in the field. What's up with that?"

"Hush, Prophet; let's hear what my WPAK wonder woman is saying."

Her makeup was flawless and her short dark hair framed her beautiful face; Reign began, moving just slightly as she pronounced her words in a stoic fashion.

"Good day, this is Reign Stepson, sitting in for Clarence Monroe. Word has just come in that Chester Lauder, recently arrested for embezzlement and other crimes against the United States financial markets, has died in custody."

A picture of Chester appeared again, showing an aged and deteriorating body. "Who'd believe that old something, looking like death warmed over, would commit such things?" Percy shook his head and spoke to no one in particular when he continued. "To tell the truth, maybe it's good he's gone. The DA wasn't too happy that we didn't have him speaking on tape and had only Stephon's word against the dude."

"Too bad for old Whistle," Prophet added. "Now he's gotta take the heat for Chester."

"He won't have a chance to mess with churches, that's for sure. Besides," Percy continued with a smirk, "his arms are too short to defend himself in prison, and they're certainly too short to box with God."

"Those Lauders fell like dominoes," Blake interjected. "Stephon fell because Fast Cat turned on him. Stephon pulled the covers off his cousins so he'd never spend another day in federal prison again. And he had to give back all the money he'd scammed."

"Don't forget the feds did a little something extra to discourage him from reinventing his setup by plastering Stephon's face and details about him all over the Internet." Prophet laughed. "He'll be a lonely something. I hear the rest of his family still don't wanna have nothing to do with him."

"Don't count on him being too lonely," Percy said. "He's already on Mount Kneel Down's prayer list. I wouldn't put it past one of them to try looking him up for prayer. They're a stubborn bunch of folks who refuse to give up on a soul. Mount Kneel Down is still the same Christ-loving, forgiving church of worship that Reverend Stepson founded more than thirty years ago."

★   ★   ★

The repairs had already begun on Reverend Stepson's office inside Mount Kneel Down's outreach center, though no one could say when he'd ever use it again.

Shaqueeda began openly bragging about her comeback. "My Shaqueeda's Curl, Wrap, and Daycare Center gonna be reconstructed from the ground up. And anyone needing an apartment that's got some class and sense can rent that reprobate Deacon Whistle's old apartment. It's almost ready. It just needs a few coats of paint."

However, Porky hadn't fared as well as Shaqueeda. He went up and down Ptomaine Avenue complaining. "I can't believe this town wants me to pay all my back fines and taxes, as much as my only son has done for this ungrateful community. And they got the nerve to say they're cutting back on health inspections and that I can't reopen just yet anyway. What do them cutting back on health inspections got to do with me?"

For weeks Percy tried to keep a low profile. He continued traveling back and forth between Pelzer and New York. Often he flew with Prophet and other members of their backup team. Appearances before the grand jury hearing for Jason "Whistle" Lauder and the other Wall Street bankers sometimes came with short notice. He and the others stayed available for whatever the agency needed them for.

Over the time, Percy remained close to Prophet. Seeing the man alone, not getting close to anyone, not even Patience, bothered him. There'd been a lot of activity for almost the entire past year, and now without a new investigation, things slowed down dramatically. He'd begun to place several calls, along with the other team members, to check up on him.

"I'm doing what I need to do to put my adrenaline back into place," Prophet told each of them. "All of you can stop fishing in my private life now. It's working my nerves."

One day, on the way back from one of their New York trips, Percy had an idea. He'd told Reign he didn't want to continue paying the outrageous rent on his apartment and a mortgage on the new home, too. They'd both agreed he should stay in their new home until they moved in after their wedding. He could do whatever little fixes Reign wanted. They were so happy, he pushed the envelope. He asked if she'd mind if Prophet stayed there, too. "We could sorta detox together," he'd told her. "He'd be good company for me and when it's time, he's got other homes he can move back to."

Percy knew Reign probably saw through his flimsy excuse, but for whatever reason, he'd not wanted Prophet going back to his solitary existence. However, Percy didn't know what to do about it. The man was as stubborn as him, yet somehow, a few days later, he'd not put up much of a fight when he made the suggestion.

Waking to country sounds wasn't unfamiliar to Prophet as he sat on the bed facing the window; he loved those sounds. Since moving temporarily into Percy and Reign's home after they'd badgered him to keep Percy company, he'd welcomed the noise of every bird, cricket, or plane flying overhead.

Prophet began to familiarize himself with all the nuances of sounds. He was amazed to discover what he'd taken for granted, once he started. He pushed his shades farther up his nose; they'd begun to slip. Closing his eyes, he imagined his own face and how it once was. He'd had a strong jawbone, thinning hair, and dark eyebrows that grew too close together; they'd look like one long, wide eyebrow if he didn't pluck them often.

"Chirrup, chirrup."

It's a brown speckled wren, he guessed before opening his eyes to find he'd been right. Guessing bird sounds wouldn't be enough. He'd need to learn as much about sounds as possible until his ears became bionic. During the past year, according to the ophthalmologist treating him for macular degeneration, the loss of sight in his left eye had accelerated.

"Come on, Prophet," Percy said, knocking on the door to the guest bedroom. "You're off today, but I'm not. It's time to eat more of my unrecognizable breakfasts. It's too bad neither of us can cook."

"Give me another ten minutes. I'll be out. I keep telling you I don't need you to cook for me."

"Sure ya don't," Percy replied and walked away.

Prophet had been in a peculiar state of mind once he'd moved in with Percy, especially since the Wall Street bust. He found that he'd begun praying more, holding longer conversations with God. He'd even begun reading Percy's Great Grandmamma Truth's Bible; he'd found it one day when they'd begun painting. Percy had asked him not to say anything about having it to the rest of his family.

Then one day Percy took Reign to visit Rev. Stepson. No one really knew how much the old man knew or remembered; somehow he'd begun trying to quote scripture, showing slight signs of improvement. Percy also told Prophet the improvement began when First Lady Deborah began complaining some time ago about how the caliber of visiting preachers to Mount Kneel Down had slipped since the reverend had been unable to bring the Word.

That same day, Prophet read the New Testament in the Bible. He'd gotten to the part where Jesus was out and about healing when he received a surprise call from, of all people, Joy.

"Just calling to check up on you. I know Percy works some really long and crazy hours sometimes, but he's done gone to pick up Reign and they're off to the nursing home. And I'd also like to know if you would consider attending a welcome-back service for the Stepsons?" Joy said. "I'm just over the moon knowing that Rev. Stepson can make day visits. Aren't you?" She didn't wait for his answer. "I know things are pretty busy," Joy continued, "but we would really like to see you. I'm making last-minute preparations with the missionary board members and some other folks."

She continued, trying to make a joke and get him to laugh by adding, "You know, Porky's still staying with us until he can get the Soul Food Shanty back up and running, but he ain't enough man for me to cook for. He ain't as smart as you and, Lord knows, he don't smell as good as you do. And you oughta come by and get some decent food 'cause I know for certain that Lil P cooks as bad as his daddy."

He had laughed at her efforts, especially when she'd sucked her teeth, pretending she felt slighted. He also noticed that she'd not mentioned Patience's name; saying *we* was enough, he imagined.

However, in the end, he decided that when the day came he probably wouldn't attend. Perhaps he would send flowers and a huge donation for the church.

It'd be selfish on his part, but he didn't want to look his old mentor in the eye and not have the man remember him. And, of course, he had to admit that he didn't know how he'd react if he saw Patience.

"What is it about that woman?" As usual, when her name came to mind, he compared her to other women, especially his late wife, only to find that there was no comparison.

I can't wait to tie things up so I can get back to preparing for my retirement life. If I could ever get Patience off my mind.

Two days passed by and, whatever else that went on, sane or not, at that moment he needed something to quiet the rumbling in the pit of his stomach. He found a plate of leftovers from last night's takeout that'd only take a moment to reheat. Percy hadn't returned from a trip to the Columbia courthouse on some business for the Pelzer police and would probably eat before returning home.

It took a few seconds longer than he'd wanted to wait, but

soon the *drinnggg* sound from the microwave rang out, a signal that his plate of leftover Popeyes chicken and Cajun rice
was ready.

Prophet had to give it to Percy and Reign. They weren't
wasting time in prepping for their big day and the ones after.
The couple had made sure plenty of furniture waited for
them when they both finally lived in their new home.

However, what was perfect for them caused problems for
Prophet. Unlike Percy, who ate, sat, and slept all over the
house, Prophet didn't feel comfortable doing the same. He
didn't want to ruin any of the pieces, so he'd take an old
snack tray brought back from the base and use it as a table.

Prophet's fork had another inch to go before his tongue
would pull the meat completely off the bone in one chomp.
It was one of those crazy things he enjoyed doing when he
ate alone. He closed his eyes, preparing to enter Nirvana; then
the doorbell rang. The only one to come by since he'd moved
there was Reign, and Percy wasn't home. She wouldn't ring a
bell to her own house. *I don't want to see anyone.*

He figured if he didn't answer or make a sound, then
whoever it was would go away. Nevertheless, the bell's *rrinngg*
followed quickly with a *ding dong* sound that began gnawing
at his ears.

Prophet threw the fork down, shoved the tray aside, and
marched to the door. He picked up his Glock from where
he'd laid it on a shelf next to the door's hinge, palming it,
peeping through the peephole before he yanked open the
door.

Before Prophet could put two thoughts together, Felony
raced through the front door. The dog hopped onto Prophet's
chair, and with that oversized skull began lapping at Prophet's
untouched food.

"Whew! You sure took your time," Joy said, laughing as
she entered, out of breath and not taking her eyes off the
shocked Prophet.

She'd hardly walked in all the way before she began to strip. Joy quickly flipped a large orange pocketbook from her wrist onto a nearby table; she began tugging at the chin-sash of a yellow oversized bonnet, before flinging her coat toward the sofa and missing.

"Don't look so surprised," Joy remarked, picking her coat off the floor and placing it on the sofa. She chuckled again and nodded at her dog. "Don't worry any about Felony. He ain't gonna eat but a taste of it, unless you've got a chocolate chip cookie or some buttered popcorn in that bowl, too."

Joy stopped and winked at Prophet, whose mouth still gaped. "I brought you some food. The other day, I could tell you were pretending you wasn't hungry. Ain't no one who ever sniffed my pots turns down a meal when I offers it. I could hear your stomach growling even over the phone."

Like any good kitchen magician, she raised her other arm with a huge thermal-insulated bag dangling from it. "Oh yeah," she continued, pointing back toward the door, "brought some others with me, too."

Then Prophet quickly found his voice. "You did what?"

"We'd have called," Patience announced as she stepped from behind a tall pine tree that stood close to the front porch. "Frankly, I really didn't feel like it."

She wouldn't enter over the threshold; she stood on the front porch shivering from the cold. She had one hand on her hip; from the other hand, she swung her reading glasses by its arm. Whatever she'd worn underneath remained hidden by her long red coat with its black faux fur collar. The matching black beret sat atop a mass of long spiral curls. "Well," she said.

"Well, hell!" Porky appeared from nowhere.

Porky was dressed in a tight but very large brown wool coat, tied with a belt around his huge belly. He wore a dirty white baseball cap with the visor turned to the back and a pair of ugly brown Uggs. He raced up the front steps, dashing past Patience without waiting for an invite. "This is my son's house and y'all need to get inside and close this door before you freeze your stubborn arses off."

"Come in, Patience. Porky's right. You don't want to freeze your stubborn—"

"Excuse you!"

"Pay me no mind. I'm just a bit tired."

"*Harrumph!*" Patience marched right pass Prophet, nose in the air and still swinging her glasses.

Once everyone was inside, Prophet regained his composure and safely put away his gun in a locked chest in the hallway closet. "Joy, why don't you take Felony outside where I'm sure he'll be more comfortable?"

"Aw, he ain't gonna chew on nothing in this fancy house. I gotta fancy house, too, and he don't . . ." Joy stopped. "Well, I guess you might have something there." She then started to pull Felony out onto the back patio where she could be certain he wouldn't misbehave.

Felony quickly nixed that idea by raising his hind leg, growling, and staring Prophet down. "I think I know what that means," Prophet sighed. "We'll just trust that he'll behave. I don't think my stomach or this house could survive one of his dog farts."

Since Felony had won the argument, Prophet tried to save face by walking over to the fireplace. He started rekindling a fire that'd begun dying down.

"Well, I can't say that I'm totally surprised," Prophet said, stoking the fire. He'd yet to speak to Patience since misspeaking at the front door; however, he was certain her eyes were burrowing a hole through him. So instead, he turned and directed his words at Joy. "I guess we weren't clear from the other day."

"You'd be lying or crazy if you thought that." Joy laughed. "We must've had a bad connection, so I figured we could finish chatting in person." She hunched Patience, who sat next to her, hoping she'd been discreet when she'd done it.

Prophet saw the move, Porky saw the move, and Felony's tail stump wagged.

"Well, it's so nice that we're all together," Joy said with a wide grin. "Prophet and Patience"—she stopped to let her words sink in—"Felony and Porky; all of us in the same room."

No one said a word so Joy continued running her mouth. "Frankly, I was tired of Patience moping around the house—"

"She's not being truthful; I don't mope." Patience moved quickly away from Joy.

"You don't mop either, but that's not the subject." Joy turned from Patience and again set her eyes on Prophet.

"You know how much I respect you, Mr. Prophet; however, you haven't kept your word."

"What word?"

"We ain't met the president yet."

"You do know that they did come close though?" Porky blurted out. "Never mind. Say what's on your mind, Joy."

"You talked about going to a fund-raiser and that we may have a chance to meet our mentor—"

"Your mentor—Who is that?"

"President Barack Obama," Joy quipped. "Keep up."

"Oh, yes. Let's just say, I have something in the works and let's leave it at that."

Joy and Patience both leaned back on the sofa, swung their legs, and stared at Prophet. "We ain't giving you much longer," Joy replied. "We wait on the Lord and that's about enough waiting."

"Can we stop yapping and get to eating?" The question came from Porky, who'd already begun rubbing his belly.

"Quit rubbing that big gut," Joy shot back. "Ain't no three wishes in it."

As much as Prophet thought he'd not wanted company, he soon found himself laughing, mostly at Joy and Porky.

They need to take their argumentative show on the road, he thought.

For about the fourth time in the past twenty minutes, as they ate the food Joy had brought off paper plates, Prophet and Patience traded glances. Like two shy teenagers, they played a silent game of flirtatious stupidity, and either one of them could be the winner.

By the time they finished eating, Joy and Porky had talked themselves into a stupor and with the food settling in their systems, they'd already begun nodding off by the fireplace. Felony had long fell victim to the Popeyes chicken; he'd licked the bowl clean and fallen asleep.

That left Prophet and Patience. The two had too much to air not to get down to it. They gave sideway glances, each silently giving the signal that the other should go first.

Chapter 45

The weather cooperated with what Joy had planned for the celebration welcoming back Rev. Stepson. When she'd first begun planning it'd been cold, with winter on the horizon. Now, the celebration was finally going to happen and she dared snow, rain, sleet, or ice to interfere.

When ye ask, ask in My name and it shall be given unto you, she thought. She'd also fasted and, in her mind, that'd hold God to His promise. If she didn't remind God of His promise twenty times a day, then she didn't do it all.

Joy and the other missionary board members decorated the church and cooked mounds of food. Patience didn't want anything sent out for printing, so weeks ago she'd created and typed the announcements and mailed invitations. The response was overwhelming. Everybody that was somebody, and some who'd wrongly thought they were, accepted an invitation to come and rejoice.

Family and friends filled Joy and Patience's living room. The First Lady Deborah had invited Sister Betty, so Sister Betty stopped by to ride to the church with the others.

There was a lot of chatter going on, yet Patience hadn't joined in. She'd stayed planted in one spot by the living room window wearing a Cheshire grin and just a little makeup.

Joy couldn't get Patience to stop smiling. Laying a hand on her cousin's shoulder, Joy insisted, "Patience, you look foolish. Please stop it!"

Over the past month, Patience's silly grin had remained plastered on her face. She'd had a root canal done the week before and smiled so much the dentist didn't need wads of cotton to keep her mouth open.

Patience gently removed Joy's hand from her shoulder. "I'm fine. You know I only wear red when I'm feeling victorious. Hasn't God given us the victory over so much for our pitiful giving?"

"We give what we have, Patience," Joy replied, "and it's never pitiful."

"Oh Joy, you know what I mean."

"I know you've been sleeping, eating, and walking on a doggone cloud ever since that night we all went over to feed Prophet at Lil P's new house."

"That's right, I have. And guess what?"

"What?"

"I'll beat the hell outta Satan if he tries to come between me and what I'm praying for."

"And what are you praying for, Patience?"

Patience didn't answer. She winked and just kept on smiling, ignoring what anyone thought as she continued looking out the living room window, watching gusts of wind blow a yard full of brown and orange leaves around. In about thirty minutes, she should have her delivery.

While Joy was home trying to think of ways to peel the smile off Patience's face, Reign and Percy were on their way back from Columbia. One of their visits had been to see about Prophet.

"We're just checking up on you since you've been acting sorta different," Percy had told him. "You sure everything is okay?"

"Right as rain, copasetic, and anything else you wanna call it. I'm fine. Now can we go and visit with the reverend like you planned?"

Taking Prophet's advice, which he continued giving on a number of things from the back seat of the Civic, on their way back to Pelzer the couple had stopped and visited with Rev. Stepson. They'd brought him some new clothes the first lady had purchased for his great day. "Now you can arrive wearing your favorite colors, purple and gold," Reign had told him as she kissed him all about his forehead and face. "It doesn't matter about the wheelchair." She blushed. "Your nurse will be wheeling in a royal priest for the Lord."

Once they left the nursing home, Reign and Percy talked nonstop, rejoicing all the way to Joy and Patience's home.

"If I had a thousand tongues, I couldn't thank God enough for what He's doing with Dad," Reign said for the umpteenth time. "The last time I visited, I couldn't get over seeing him do something as simple as lift a spoon. Today, he's using a fork."

"He's come a long way, honey, a mighty long way. And it's only been a couple of months since he moved into that home."

"Thank you, Lord Jesus!"

Reign's happiness was infectious. Percy began humming one of Joy's favorite gospel songs: "I've Got Jesus and That's Enough."

While Percy and Reign sat in the front, praising God, singing hymns, booing and cooing, Prophet sat quietly in Percy's Civic. He had his head laid back against the backseat, looking out the window.

Like Percy and Reign, he'd been grateful for the reverend's signs of progress, too. Over the last several weeks, every time Reign and Percy came back from a visit, they'd gone on and on about things the reverend did that they couldn't believe happened. He'd felt they'd only seen what they'd wanted to. They'd had to convince him that the reverend was aware of his surroundings. He called each thing they'd pointed out by name each time they saw him.

Now he was a believer, too—for the reverend and, somehow, now for himself. He just didn't feel worthy, especially when his reasons for not visiting the reverend before were selfish. He'd also thought he wouldn't attend the welcome back ceremony that afternoon for vain reasons.

"You've got the next verse, Prophet. Come on, join me. I don't wanna sing off-key by myself." Percy looked in his rearview mirror, and noticed how Prophet had laid back against the car seat and was not moving. With those ever-present sunglasses covering his eyes, Percy didn't know if he was sleeping or not.

Prophet wasn't asleep. He'd heard the couple's nonstop chatter. As much as he wanted to join Percy in mangling the song, his mind kept visiting another place, a place that Patience occupied. He'd faced down many criminals, taught ideologue law students, and was probably a few months away from losing the sight in his left eye; none of that was as frightening to him as facing Patience.

The skinny woman with the thick glasses, long hair, and optimism to share had turned him to Silly Putty; at least that's what he felt folks whispered behind his back.

He'd lost his mojo, and he wanted it back. Since he'd met Patience, he'd slipped up and given her a prophecy, and had been outmaneuvered each time he felt he'd won. She even sniffed him for his cologne scent, like she was sizing him up for a wedding tuxedo; and there hadn't been a weekend for the past several weeks where her and Joy's cooking hadn't made him comatose. He wasn't certain what she'd told God, but he needed to talk to the Master, too. "Lord, help my unbelief."

"Hey Prophet, that's not the next verse. You need to bone up on your gospel tunes."

★ ★ ★

Joy brought Sister Betty a second cup of the old woman's favorite cayenne pepper tea. While she was at it, she thought she'd ask Porky, for the second time that day, "Porky, when are you moving out?"

"Stop mistreating me, Joy," Porky told her. "That's just why I ain't telling you what I found out."

"You've been threatening me with that nonsense for the past few days. I didn't buy it then, and I ain't buying it now. I just need a day and a time for your departure."

"Missionary Joy," Sister Betty said, "this is a day of restoration. Isn't that why you're having this special welcome-back celebration for Rev. Stepson?"

"What's that got to do with that thing standing over there?" She pointed at Porky, before adding, "We'd have to go back through generations, including silverback gorillas, to begin making him any different than he is now."

"Not true," Sister Betty replied. "You shouldn't say things like that. God don't like that sorta thing happening."

"She's a dam—" Porky caught himself. He didn't want to say anything sounding remotely like a cuss word in front of Sister Betty. Even on Ptomaine Avenue, her super-saint reputation trumped his. "You're so right, Sister Betty."

"Brother Porky," Sister Betty said sweetly, "don't you have something for Joy? Now is a good time to give it to her."

"Like what?" Porky said. He had both hands on his hips and that one liar-meter posing as an eyeball on his chubby face had already begun darting about.

Joy scowled at Porky, ignoring anything from that point on that Sister Betty did. She sucked her teeth, placing the tray she'd used to carry the tea onto a nearby coffee table and walking away. "He ain't got nothing I'd want!" she said over her shoulder.

As she watched Joy walk away toward the kitchen, Sister Betty pursed her lips. She began mumbling under her breath, fishing around in her pocketbook, hands moving like a worm on a hook, until she found what she searched for.

She yanked out her canister of blessed oil from her demon-fighting arsenal. It'd lain wedged between two small Bibles and a small gold cross, and had been covered with two packs of Handi Wipes towelettes. She lay the canister in her lap, one finger on the spray trigger, stopping long enough to nod at Joy's velvet-back picture of Jesus that hung on the wall. "In Your name, Father."

She'd also arrived carrying a large brown shopping bag. Pointing to the bag while she raised the canister of blessed oil, she warned Porky, "I plan on having a blessed day. I can make yours the same with prayer." She began moving the canister around in a circular motion. "Or I can get with this—your choice."

On her way to the kitchen, Joy heard the sound of a car coming into the driveway. She looked toward the hallway window and saw Patience peeping through the curtains. She could tell by the way Patience had started her skinny butt's backfield-in-motion routine, it was Prophet. "Lord, have mercy. That derriere's engine is like an alarm, and wags more than Felony's tail."

Joy, being playful, moved side to side and blocked Patience from making it to the side door first. "Y'all made it. Good, now c'mon inside."

Percy entered first, holding Reign's hand, with Prophet following close behind them.

Joy, still blocking Patience, greeted Percy and the others then quickly pushed Prophet down the hall toward the living room to join Sister Betty and Porky.

Prophet didn't know Joy's reasoning for pushing him like that, but when he looked over his shoulder and saw Patience swinging her eyeglasses by its arm, a questioning look came upon his face. "I'm safe as long as she stays out here and cools off," he murmured. "Can't think of nothing I've done recently, though."

Sister Betty held the shopping bag in the air. She was about to hand it to Porky when Percy entered the room. She saw Percy, sat back down, and lowered the bag into her lap. "You got here just in time," she told Percy. "Me and your daddy was about to dance."

Percy shook his head. Reign folded her arms, and Prophet landed on the couch after Joy shoved him gently.

"Now, this is me and Patience's home," Joy said. "We're gonna have some peace all up in here if I hafta beat the crap outta all of you, excepting for Sister Betty. I don't need her calling the Lord on that knee-phone, complaining."

Things calmed quickly after Joy spoke. Patience had finally entered the living room. Still pouting, she sat down next to Prophet as though anywhere he was, she should be, too.

Sister Betty, looking at Percy first and then nodding toward Reign, signaled for the two to come. As soon as they got within an arm's reach, she handed the bag to Percy.

"Now, I only came over here so I could ride with y'all to the pastor's welcome-back ceremony. But y'all have worked my last nerve. I'm going home and call for the church van. If I'd prayed first, I'd have done it already and could've kept my pressure down."

She then turned to Porky, saying, "Brother Porky. You need Jesus!"

Sister Betty didn't wait for anyone to walk her to the door. Before they could shut their gaping mouths, she'd gathered her belongings; wearing her all-white everything, she looked like a brown Casper the Ghost as she fled the house.

"Well," Percy said after hearing the front door close after Sister Betty had left, "I guess Sister Betty has left me literally holding the bag."

Percy took a few short steps until he stood in front of

Porky. "Here, Dad." Percy looked at Porky with a sheepish grin on his face. "I'm sorry. I only took this for your own good." Looking around the room, Percy added, "And for everyone else's good as well."

"What are you talking about, son?" Porky lifted the shopping bag from Percy's hand. "Wow, this bag is heavy. It didn't look so heavy when Sister Betty held it up like it was a bag of cotton balls."

"Will you stop with all the drama and open the doggone bag, Porky?" The command came from Patience. The others had to look twice at the couch. She'd moved close to Prophet.

"Patience ain't got a bit of shame," Joy muttered. "A flea with no wings couldn't get between her and Prophet."

Reign came and stood next to Percy. She didn't say anything but began mumbling words that sounded like praying.

In the meanwhile, Prophet looked toward the picture of Jesus on the living room wall. If he'd turned his head the other way, his lips would've touched Patience. She sat that close. He didn't move right away.

Porky still looked puzzled as he began pulling the heavy item from the bag.

Because Porky was speechless didn't mean Joy couldn't talk. "Heathen, you did have Grandmamma Truth's family Bible."

"Son, what does this mean?" Porky asked. "I don't understand."

Even as Percy tried to explain why he'd had to stage the robbery after Porky revealed details of his case, and that there was evidence hidden between the Bible's pages, Joy wouldn't shut up.

"Why didn't you just take the notes?" Joy asked as she dabbed at the tears that'd begun to fall. "You didn't have to take the Bible, too."

"I know," Percy replied. "I told you I was sorry. I thought

I was doing the right thing. I didn't want anyone to steal it after dad told where it was."

"Joy Karry," Porky jumped and shouted, "you have no right to lay into my son like that."

"I'll lay into Lil P anytime I want to," Joy growled. "What you gonna do about it?"

"I'm gonna shut yo' big mouth," Porky threatened. "You always got to have the last word. It's always gotta be about you! I'm sick of it."

Patience sat watching. As usual, it broke her heart to see her cousins going at it like that. She wanted to jump up and stop the fussing, but not if it meant she'd have to leave Prophet's side. She'd already pushed him to the end of the sofa and against the armrest. *They'll work it out,* she thought.

Joy and Porky kept at it for several more minutes. Each time Percy tried to intervene, they told him to butt out. Reign smartly stayed out of it and continued praying, harder this time.

"You only want that Bible to taunt me," Joy said. By now she was almost bawling. "You knew I'd always wanted that Bible."

"And you knew I wouldn't have taken it if Grandmamma Truth didn't want me to have it 'cause I was her only grandson. You keep acting like she never left you and Patience nothing!"

"Well, actually," Patience finally interrupted, "she didn't."

"Why not?" Porky had never asked the question before. He'd assumed they'd all gotten something and that what he had was what Joy wanted.

"We had Lil P," Patience explained. "I've never said anything to anyone; but over the years, I'd always thought she wanted you to have that Bible in case you ever went through anything as horrible as you did when we had to take over caring for him."

"Is that true," Porky asked, turning to Joy. "Do you believe that's the reason?"

"I don't know, Porky," Joy replied. Her tears had dried with Patience's revelation. "I'd thought she'd done it because she thought I didn't want it or had grown tired of reading from it."

"Why would she think that?" The question came from Percy. "What y'all are talking about I've never heard before."

Joy quietly told her family how Grandmamma Truth would rock in her living room while the rest of the house was quiet. There were Bibles surrounding her, much the way Patience liked to study. Neither Joy nor Patience were quite teenagers then and definitely not woman enough to hear what Grandmamma Truth read from the books of Deuteronomy and Leviticus. When she'd finished, they'd have to read the Psalms and Ecclesiastes as well.

"Those books had all kinds of sinning in them," Joy told them. "We were fascinated by them; although I believe it's certain Patience was more than she let on." She swung her head towards Patience just in time to see her move closer to Prophet, enough to share the same skin. She sucked her teeth at Patience to show her disapproval.

Patience had gone back to smiling. It didn't look like she cared what Joy said or thought.

"And then she'd tell me how David had done most of that kind of sinning," Joy continued. "But he'd learned to ask for forgiveness, then dance and praise his way out of a mess before he'd end up doing it all over again. She said God's people were pretty much the same way, but there was a 'way-out' clause."

By then, Prophet was mesmerized. It seemed he and Patience shared a lot more than he thought. His grandmother thought along those same lines. He'd thought she'd been a bit eccentric until, over the years, God would capture his tongue, causing him to give voice to the words God would whisper in his spirit to tell others.

Prophet reached for Patience's hand. He never said a word; when she didn't resist, he smiled, knowing there'd be lots of questions from the others as well as from her. At that moment, it didn't matter. He'd just keep his remaining good eye on her through his shades for as long as she'd let him.

"What was the 'way-out' clause?" Porky wanted Joy to get to it so he wouldn't have to read it but could begin the process. And he wanted to know just how much rope God would give him.

"The way-out clause," Joy explained, "is new mercy and forgiveness."

"How new," Porky asked. "Define new."

"Every day," Reign said, finally entering the conversation. "God gives it to us every day. All you need to do is repent and then ask."

That was all Porky had needed to hear. "Joy," he said, "Sister Betty said I had something to give to you, and you said you didn't want it. Do you still feel that way?"

Joy didn't say anything. She couldn't. There'd been a lot said using so few words, but they felt heavy on her spirit.

"Go ahead and do it, Dad. You know you want to, and you should." Percy winked at Porky. He caught Joy staring at him, and quickly added, "Do it now!"

Porky walked over to Joy and did something he'd never do even as soon as ten minutes ago. He began to speak softly with a kindness he'd not known he had. "Until a short while ago I'd thought I knew something that you'd like to hear. I was wrong. It looks like I have something instead that you'd like to have, and I want you to have it," he said. "Please forgive me for not doing this sooner." He hugged her and when she didn't punch him in the mouth, he picked up the Bible and placed it in her hand.

Joy scanned Porky's face. She was stunned that he'd given her Grandmamma Truth's family Bible and even more stunned that his eye hadn't twitched. "You've told the truth. Thank you."

Patience was overjoyed. Her two only cousins had hugged. She'd never seen them do that before. She leapt off the sofa, forgetting all about Prophet, and joined them. They kept kissing each other on the cheek and apologizing until they were hoarse.

Patience had just turned to ask Percy to join the family circle when she caught him winking at Prophet. She'd seen him do the same thing earlier when Reign had joined in the wink-fest. However, she'd been so caught up in being next to Prophet she'd dismissed it. She couldn't do that now.

They're up to something, she thought. There wasn't any amount of jovial conversations after that. Patience's taste for suspicion and drama had taken over again. She planned on satisfying it.

Chapter 46

The same balmy afternoon that Porky gave Joy the family Bible she carried it with her to the welcome-back celebration at Mount Kneel Down. She wanted to have it blessed, even if she had to place Rev. Stepson's shaking hands on the Bible herself while others prayed in his place.

There was standing room only at the celebration. Everyone came dressed to the nines, and Joy and Patience had specifically told the other missionaries to wear white while they'd planned on wearing those red two-piece outfits and ridiculous hats. Patience had even convinced Prophet he'd look better if he wore a red tie.

The ushers escorted Patience, Joy, and Prophet to the second pew before they sat Percy and Reign on the first pew. At Percy's insistence, Porky came along, but insisted on sitting on one of the back pews.

Sister Betty finally arrived. "I'm not led by the spirit to sit up front. I believe the Lord wants me in the back, riding Holy Ghost shotgun, if you will." She sat down next to Porky.

Also seated on the first pew were some of Rev. Stepson's closest friends, among them politicians, famous preachers, several supreme court judges, and a WPAK television announcer. Normally, First Lady Deborah would've sat on that same pew, but not this afternoon. She would enter with her husband.

Then came time to see what they'd all come for. And First Lady Deborah set it off almost as soon as she, the reverend, and his nurses entered the sanctuary. She looked fabulous wearing a purple two-piece suit with gold thunderbolt patterns on one side of the jacket. She also wore a purple two-layer hat trimmed in gold and matching shoes. The way she took her time going to her seat was the work of a true church diva.

At first, First Lady Deborah didn't speak. Instead, she blew short kisses to several former members who'd returned for the occasion. She recognized several young people christened by the reverend as babies who were now in college. Her eyes moistened beneath her veil. To many others she waved and nodded, patting a few shoulders as the ushers escorted her to join her family and friends. As soon as she sat, ushers rolled Rev. Stepson up to the pulpit.

Because the reverend needed constant professional care, despite his physical gains, the nursing home wanted two nurses with him. The RNs would remain by his side during the celebration.

"Look at him," Joy whispered to Patience. "He looks better than I'd thought."

Patience saw the improvement in the reverend, too. She wanted to jump up and run around the church. *Just look at God*, she thought. A wide grin broke out across her face. "Praise Him, Church. Give God glory!" Forgetting for the moment that she'd suspected Prophet and Percy of conspiring, she screamed with enthusiasm, evoking the Holy Spirit to touch each of them.

Meanwhile, Porky, seated on the back pew, began fidgeting. "What's happening to me?" He felt lost watching folks jumping and shouting. Ushers dressed in white starched uniforms were racing to and fro, covering with modesty cloths those who'd passed out with their legs gaped open, handing out fans to others who looked like they were on the verge of keeling over.

And then an emotion struck Porky again. "What in the world is going on up in this place?" He kept muttering and moving. He didn't want to wave his hands, but he had. He didn't want his feet to move, but they did. He hadn't wanted to say one word, but he had to. It was like a spiritual veil dropped upon him and took over.

Percy heard it first. His ears perked up and when he jerked around in his seat to confirm it, so did Reign and everyone else in the front of the church.

Prophet almost yanked his sunglasses from his face. He couldn't believe his one good eye saw what it did. There came Porky, accompanied by three bald headed male ushers in black suits.

The ushers didn't touch Porky, letting him do his thing for the Lord. Porky began slipping and sliding side to side. He'd turned into a chocolate James Brown and those ushers could've played his back-up dancers. By the time they'd made it to the front of the church, Porky began to collapse. The worn-out ushers managed to shove him onto the pew seat next to Joy.

Instead of Joy flicking Porky away as she would've done before, she waved her fan across his face—drenched in perspiration—to cool him, and took one of his hands into hers. "Porky," Joy whispered, "let go and let God."

Porky could barely speak above a whisper; he felt limp yet powerful at the same time. "Jesus does love me, don't He, Joy?"

Joy clasped his hand a little tighter before patting it. "Yes," she whispered, smiling, "and so do I."

Joy and Porky collapsed against each other.

Patience saw the exchange between Joy and Porky. She

didn't try to interfere, preferring they bask in the new start they had. *Somewhere and somehow I know Grandmamma Truth is smiling and saying, It's about time,* she thought. *All those years wasted, separated by miscommunication and fake favoritisms.*

One by one, testimonies flooded the sanctuary. There weren't many attending whose lives Mount Kneel Down and the Stepsons hadn't touched in some way. Then appeared a video montage of the reverend's preaching career, as well as of his time as a supreme court justice. Percy and Prophet had spent many hours putting together the video. They'd reached out to many unable to attend yet who wanted to share their well wishes.

As the video came to an end, the image of President Obama and First Lady Michelle filled the screen.

Percy leaned over the back of the pew. He and Prophet exchanged a high five and forced looks of innocence. Using a Skype session they'd arranged with the president's office, President Obama greeted the Mount Kneel Down congregation and thanked them for their community outreach, as well as their worldwide support of the less fortunate. He personally thanked Percy and Prophet for their recent Wall Street bust.

At the president's praise, all eyes in the sanctuary turned toward Percy and Prophet Long Jevity. Yet Prophet didn't flinch or acknowledge in any way such an honorable mention. It'd never been his style to showboat.

"We'll need to chat a bit later," Patience whispered through a wide smile meant for anyone else watching but him. Leaning in closer to him, she threatened, "You can believe that."

That got a reaction from Prophet. His foot began tapping to music that hadn't played while he thought, *Okay, Prez, if I don't survive this woman, you'll be one vote short come election.*

The president continued speaking. He thanked Rev. Stepson for his unselfish availability. He told how Rev. Stepson counseled him during his senatorial years, prayed with him when he'd felt lost and alone. He kept a picture on the nightstand in the White House bedroom, one of the reverend standing among thirty other preachers who lay hands upon his shoulders, praying, crying out to God to guide the young man who would become president. Since he'd studied under the reverend when he'd taught an undergraduate constitutional law class at Columbia, the president often called when he needed second opinions on constitutional law, too.

He also mentioned how the Reverend and Lady Stepson had never mentioned anything to the media and they could have, for their own prestige and glory. He invited them to come visit the White House after the 2012 election, joking that he wasn't taking reservations before that.

The congregation broke out in applause, repeatedly chanting, "Yes, we will."

First Lady Deborah hugged Reign while her eyes, swollen with pride and hidden under her veil, gave way to pouring tears.

She began remembering all that'd happened during the past year or so to bring down her church. Mount Kneel Down's demise sought by the Lauder cousins' deceitful need for revenge had failed. Like a phoenix, the church had risen, and she now saw the continuous hand of God upon Mount Kneel Down and her congregation and leaders.

All eyes then shifted to Rev. Stepson. He'd sat hunched in his wheelchair through most of the president's words, his eyes glued to the huge screen. The nurses didn't try to wipe his tears as he struggled to do more than he could, mouthing *thank you*, smiling while trying to lift his hand to wave at the president, as he'd learned to do with his fork to eat.

The congregation realized their pastor understood all that was happening around him. Their beloved pastor had recognized President Obama. Some exploded into praise again. Ushers sprinted through the aisles, trying to reseat those who'd forgotten the president hadn't finished talking.

"Give Him glory!" Then, as the clamor died down, the president said humbly, "Folks, hello, *err*, excuse me."

The congregation looked toward the screen, this time shocked but happy to see Michelle Obama begin to speak.

"I know you have more celebrating to do. If you'll give me another moment, please, this won't take long."

Michelle Obama picked up a piece of paper that lay in her lap, handing it to one of her daughters, who announced before she began reading, "Detective Percy, Mr. Prophet, I believe you have something for missionaries Joy Karry and Patience Kash."

Percy pulled a rolled parchment document from his inside pocket and placed it in Joy's hands. Joy's head swung around so fast and hard to face Percy, her big hat flew off, landing in one of the visitors' laps, and the visitor quickly tapped it to see if it was alive.

Patience couldn't speak or move. She just kept looking at Prophet, giving him a sideways glare, as he pressed a parchment paper tied with a ribbon into her hand.

Porky leaned over Joy and mouthed to Percy, "You see. I told you I could keep my big mouth shut."

When it came time to speak again, President Obama spoke first, telling them that he figured by that time they'd given out the White House citations and, hopefully, quicker than Percy's repayment of the five-dollar debt. He then went on to congratulate Percy and Reign, telling them that he was happy that Reign had let them know she and Percy had finally settled on a wedding date.

Again, he smiled. "Good day, and God bless America." The screen went dark as the Obama family waved good-bye.

Percy looked at Reign and shook his head. In his best

Ricky Ricardo voice, he whispered, "You've got some 'splaining to do, Lucy."

Percy then gently took Joy's parchment before taking hold of her hand. Both he and Prophet, who'd done the same with Patience, ascended into the pulpit. Percy then took the microphone. "I thank all of you for your kindness and your patience. I would like to read the cover letter that accompanied the White House citation about to be presented to my godmothers." He retrieved another paper from his jacket and began reading.

"Missionary Joy Karry and Missionary Patience Kash," Percy began. "On behalf of President Barack Obama and First Lady Michelle Obama, Malia and Sasha Obama, we'd like to present to you a very special citation from the Obama family. Percy and Prophet gave a very interesting story regarding your missionary installation service that occurred quite some time ago. First Lady Deborah also added her colorful details regarding a certain mission she believes our Lord has placed upon your shoulders. Given your determination, your drive, and your willingness to do whatever it takes to make sure this administration succeeds, let it be known that you will always remain in our prayers and thoughts, and that the Obama family's gratitude has no expiration date."

Mount Kneel Down traditionally ended their service with a corporate prayer. The prayer called on God to heal the sick and shut-in. The prayer particularly called on God to bless with wisdom and good health the leaders of the nation and especially the president. That would soon be followed by the benediction.

This time, the corporate prayer called by First Lady Deborah had a twist. She turned to her team of prophetesses. "Walk with me, Women of God."

They began walking through the congregation with First Lady Deborah, as the Spirit led her, selecting certain ones, including Prophet, for special prayer. Without pointing him out, she began a special prayer of healing him. She'd also asked during the prayer for God to flood Prophet's spirit with a calling he'd all but ignored.

As soon as Prophet heard First Lady Deborah say, "And, Father God, let the scales fall from his eye that he may see Your calling upon him; let it fall that he may see and know Your secrets. Let that veil fall from his eyes so that it becomes a third eye . . ." he knew exactly what she meant, as much as he then believed the prayer was for him.

Patience, struck with spiritual and mental paralysis since the Obamas appeared, didn't know Prophet had left her side. The prayer was over and he'd returned before she'd realized anything.

While the others on the first pew congratulated the couple, teasing them about the unusual way their wedding day was announced, Joy and Patience still hadn't moved. They sat looking on in disbelief.

Patience finally managed to speak, but she still couldn't move. "Joy, I swear. I couldn't say another word if I was a puppet sitting on a lap and someone was pulling strings and speaking for me."

Joy simply nodded.

Finally, a short time later, it took Sister Betty and several others to help Joy and Patience gather their belongings and head downstairs to the fellowship hall.

There was plenty of food, and Rev. Stepson could show how blessed it was to do something as simple as use a fork to feed oneself.

The WPAK cameras caught the entire event. Unlike before, when they'd had a heads-up that the president would slip into town for a meeting with the governor, they had been shocked when the president made his Skype appearance. The same camera crew that'd laughed a few months ago at Reign when she'd slipped and said a profanity on live television now smiled and congratulated her. "You know the station manager is gonna wanna know how you pulled this off and didn't give him notice," one cameraman teased.

Everyone sat at the tables inside the fellowship hall. Each table was decorated with harvest horns of plenty in their center and servings of delicious foods. Over constant chewing and loud talking, the festivities continued.

Reign gave a public apology to Percy, her parents, and other visitors for telling the president about the wedding date before her family. She'd hoped by doing so she wouldn't have to do it again later when she and Percy were alone.

Somehow Porky had again sat next to Sister Betty. They had their heads together chatting away like the old friends they were not. In between her reciting scriptures to Porky, she gave him advice on what detergent to use. "You're wearing something that's still not as sunshine-fresh as it should be," she told him. "And you doing all the shouting for the Lord didn't help. He only promised to cleanse your soul. He ain't said nothing about doing your laundry."

Joy joined Rev. Stepson and First Lady Deborah. She managed to squeeze in at his side, displacing several other special guests at their table with her wide hips.

The reverend struggled with each word; his dementia had robbed him of a lot but he still fought hard for what he had left. He also had to fight Joy tossing her special citation from President Obama in his face every time he raised a fork to eat. "I'm about to stab that hand with my fork," he stammered.

"Glad to see your mind is on the road back to full recovery," Joy replied before putting away the citation.

First Lady Deborah laughed at the two of them but hadn't touched her food. Instead, she thought, *What have Prophet and Patience slipped away to do?* He'd not said anything to her but she knew her prayers had power. She also knew the power of their common number, two. *They'll work it out*, she thought. *But not too soon, I hope.*

She sat back and looked toward the ceiling, smiling. "Help them, Lord. Prophet has ridden the marriage go-round before; Patience has never been near the ticket booth."

Patience's eyes were red, her suit jacket tearstained, as she cradled Prophet's head while they sat alone in the church's library.

"I sorta figured First Lady Deborah was talking about you when she was praying. I could feel her anointment sweep over the pew and especially when it landed on you. Don't ask me to explain it. I can't. It's something you'd have to experience yourself."

Prophet looked up as his head lay nestled in the crook of her arm. All he could do was give a half smile at the way she'd discerned what'd gone on earlier inside the church.

"And besides, I don't know why you felt you had to hide it. You have beautiful eyes and God's gonna make certain they stay that way."

Moments ago, Prophet had pulled away from Patience just at the very time she'd tried to remove his shades. He hadn't been quick enough, having been disarmed by the ease with which the two of them had held hands and walked into the library.

"But one of my eyes," Prophet whispered as he raised up to face her, "is blue with blindness."

"And God done promised through his prayer prophesy tonight that the other brown eye is able to take up the slack."

"Patience, I don't know what's happening, but my faith needs to grow stronger, and I'm tired in more ways than one."

"Why?"

"I'm tired of waiting to see if these new experimental

drops will work or if I'll lose sight in my remaining good eye. I'm tired of hiding behind these shades, afraid that my team members or criminals will think less of me or challenge my abilities. My life wouldn't be worth anything if that happens. Most of all, I'm tired of running from what I know God has purposed me for, and I'm certain I'm going through a heavenly reassignment."

"Are you tired of me yet?"

Her words, although said slowly, shot rapidly through his mind. "No, I'm not tired of you. I can't imagine you not being in my life in some shape, form, or fashion."

Patience smiled and the honey-colored contacts she'd worn became brighter as she fought to not over-analyze his words. "Would you like to come over this weekend and have supper with me?"

"I don't know."

"You don't?"

"I was actually thinking about breakfast."

"Well, I've never cooked breakfast for a man before."

"I'm a great cook with a particular knack for stirring things up."

"I know that's right."

"You do."

"Yep, I can picture you just stirring my pot right now."

"Say wha—"

Patience whispered a quick prayer of repentance and with her small hands she held Prophet's head in her palms and began kissing his face.

"I believe you may just have the gift of healing, Miss Patience."

"We two are about to find out."

Patience was about to allow her kisses to find their way to Prophet's lips when a loud noise sounded in the room. It'd come from the front.

"What are y'all doing in here? We've been looking all

over for you." Joy bounced through the church library doors, sucking her teeth; Porky hopped from one foot to the other behind her. "Were you two just kissing?"

"Now that's what I'm talking about." Porky continued hopping about like his feet were on fire. " 'Cause if there's kissing all up in the house of the Lord, then there must be a whole lot of interesting stuff happening since I stopped coming. You can believe I'm coming back to church starting with this Wednesday night's Bible study, and I hope they'll be studying the book of Solomon."

Epilogue

The Lauder cousins, Jason and Stephon, watched the news, along with the other inmates, in their two separate prison facilities. Although sent to out-of-state prisons, they refused to communicate. Stephon had cooperated with the feds and received a shorter sentence of four years. Jason, knowing Stephon didn't receive the same harsh prison sentence, hated Stephon for it as much as he'd hated him for never coming to Chester's aid.

Jason Lauder, aka Deacon Whistle, sat that Saturday evening at the table, marinating in hatred. Prayer didn't exist for him. In his mind, he'd pushed too far away from God. If he survived his twenty-five and fifteen-year sentences, running separately and not concurrently, it'd be a miracle.

Jason Lauder survived the only way he could while languishing in a self-inflicted prison cell—by watching the news as though he was on the outside. One evening, the news began by mentioning an event held at Mount Kneel Down in Pelzer, South Carolina, including remarks by the president of the United States regarding Rev. Stepson.

"Hell no!" Jason violently threw his chair against a far wall at the television, barely missing two other inmates.

Several prison guards rushed him. What they had waiting for him would've made Chester's previous prison experience a daycare romp. The prison guards hoped Jason Lauder read the Books of Deuteronomy and Leviticus . . . if he hadn't, they'd make sure he got to know verse and scripture.

HOLY MAYHEM

Pat G'Orge-Walker

ABOUT THIS GUIDE

The suggested questions that follow
are included to enhance your group's
reading of this book.

DISCUSSION QUESTIONS

1. Have you ever arrived at a crossroads of "big" change? What brought you to that crossroads—finances, health, or something else?

2. Have you ever received a prophecy? Did it come to pass?

3. Do you have any family members who are a little "left to center" in their Christian walk?

4. Should churches put money in the hands of investment bankers or in investments? If yes, why? If no, why not?

5. Do you believe the cousins knowingly or unknowingly judged each other out of jealousy? Discuss.

6. Do you have a family member who gossips? How has it affected you or your family?

7. Revenge is always a no-win action. Would you still actively consider revenge instead of leaving it to God?

8. The actions of the mongrel dog Felony were based upon the antics of the author's two-year-old half–St. Bernard, half–Great Dane dog, Titan, who'd fail any doggy sanity test. Have you ever owned a neurotic pet?

9. Do you believe Prophet should pursue a relationship with Patience despite his prognosis? How would you handle the possibility of entering a relationship knowing you were going blind? How do you think it would also affect him after years of a successful career in the CIA, where eyesight and insight are necessary?

10. Deacon Whistle was a mean character from the very be-
    ginning. Why wouldn't a spirit of discernment within the
    church pick up on his wickedness? Should the pastor
    have the final word over who is in charge of church fi-
    nances or should it be the church board?

11. Did you think the Lauder cousins (Chester, Jason, and
    Stephon) got what they deserved? Was Stephon's bogus
    Internet church as bad as the embezzling Jason and Chester
    did? Do you believe in the adage "Touch not my anointed
    and do my prophet no harm"?

Catch up with Sister Betty in

No Ordinary Noel

In stores now!

Chapter 1

For the past eight years, Reverend Leotis Tom pastored full time at Pelzer, South Carolina's Crossing Over Sanctuary church. From the moment he laid his right hand upon the Bible and promised to lead the church to holiness, he'd battled one church mess after another against the Devil and, quite often, against his congregation. The besieged reverend fasted so much for peace he hadn't gained an ounce since he accepted his position.

He'd been only thirty-three years old when installed, and so fresh out of divinity college that he'd actually believed all he needed was a few words of "thus saith the Lord" scriptures and folks would fall in line; and with a touch of his anointed hands, he expected them to fall out, too. With his youthful ignorance he'd taken the helm, but not without controversy.

When the reverend's name first came up there was concern from one of the few remaining founding members of the church. Mother Sasha Pray Onn was in her late sixties and a tad bit neurotic. Widowed by choice was the rumor, although never proven. She'd always been the go-to church mother, the keeper of the church gossip-laced politics and all things that made the church's sanctified bus ride hazardous.

On the day when the reverend's name was laid on the sacrificial altar for pastorate, Mother Pray Onn had issues. Fired up, she had left subtlety behind and was chained to her seat in the first pew.

"He ain't been seasoned enough with trials and tribulations and some hawt church mess!" she warned. "We need a Man of God who can take a punch from ole Satan and then knows how to pray that demon back to hell without getting the church scorched! I'm telling ya, that baby preacher y'all are considering, well he ain't that man!"

The Church Board never took into consideration that the old church mother might've known of which she spoke. After all, Sasha Pray Onn and her entire Hellraiser clan were Satan's first cousins, although they didn't brag about it a lot. Nevertheless, the Church Board took a risk and for the first time ignored Mother Sasha Pray Onn. It wasn't much of a risk. The old woman, by that time, had gone on a cruise.

Without the sanction of the other twenty-eleven boards, the Church Board invited the very handsome, six-foot-five Reverend Leotis Tom from nearby Anderson, South Carolina, with the ink still wet on his graduation parchment, to "bring the word." They'd also made sure it was for the fifth Sunday service. Back then and even now, folks set a limit on attending church more than four Sundays a month. Fifth Sunday remains the safest for church politics.

Even as naïve as Leotis Tom was then, he still knew that an invitation was really an audition.

When the day came, he'd arrived without a visiting preacher's usual church posse. There was no armor bearer to walk him up the three steps into the pulpit. He looked almost church-naked without some middle-aged nurse to wipe his brow or two or three Mothers to sit in the first pew and hype him and the congregation into a frenzy. Reverend Tom didn't even have a young minister-in-training to carry his Bible and his robe. Instead, he came prepared with faith and a vision from the Lord.

That Sunday morning, he'd stood at the pulpit, dressed in a black and purple, short-sleeved robe, with a modest gold cross stitched across the breastbone. His dark unruly hair was cut short. Whether on purpose or not his pecan brown muscles rippled, making his arms resemble the back of an alligator's tail splashing about.

Most folks probably couldn't remember what Reverend Tom preached that morning but the consensus was unanimous. The reverend was what the women folks and even some of the shameless men called, "hawt spiritual eye-candy who knew a little sumpthin' about the Word." The fact that the young man was single suddenly was in his favor, and most hoped that he'd never marry—unless it was to one of them.

That morning, the church's outgoing pastor, the Jheri curled and overweight Reverend Knott Enuff Money, could only marinate in envy. All the time he'd been single and pastoring, he'd had to fight off the gay and the bi rumors. Reverend Tom came to church with muscular arms and no mention of a wife or a girlfriend and the congregation appeared to lose its mind.

Soon after, the conversation got around again to the urgency of selecting a pastor to take the place of Reverend Knott Enuff Money.

"We can't keep putting off getting a new pastor," one board member pointed out after learning Reverend Tom had an open invitation to preach at another local church. "I suggest we hire him immediately."

The naysayers who attended only a few services and even less board meetings usually did what they were supposed to do when it came time to confirm anything, by saying, "No," and "Hell no!" But that time, even they went with the program, and voted on a few limitations to put into his contract should he accept their offer. They kept it simple. They'd wanted shorter sermons during football and baseball seasons, and no evening service on the night of the Stella Awards.

With agreement in place on how to regulate the pastor's preaching schedule, they hired Reverend Leotis Tom and hoped for the best. They also hoped Mother Pray Onn had a good time on her cruise because she would raise hell upon her return.

The installation service was a grand affair. Churches, big and small, bishops and pastors, the saved and the unsavory, were all invited. The Reverend Leotis Tom received many accolades, and large sums of cash; someone had warned him not to accept checks unless he was prepared to pay return check fees.

The food was first rate. Several overweight sisters hit that kitchen and anointed the oven. They cooked a feast big enough to feed a third world country. Of course, the auspicious event had local newspaper and television coverage. The video would be sold during a few upcoming conferences.

There was no doubt that Crossing Over Sanctuary had a new star. Everything was wonderful until later on that evening when the young preacher rose to say a few words.

The Reverend Leotis Tom gave the customary thank you and his vision for the church and community. Then he made a promise that set everyone on notice.

"There will be no politics inside the church or outside the church. Politicians are welcome to worship, but they will not receive special favors. We will not gamble on our salvation with unholy alliances and that includes gambling of any kind. God doesn't want nor will He accept tainted money or favors!"

But that was then.